A Fine Mess

By

Breanna Hughes

2016

A Fine Mess © 2016 Breanna Hughes
Triplicity Publishing, LLC

ISBN-13: 978-0997740530
ISBN-10: 0997740531

First Edition – 2016
Cover Design: Triplicity Publishing, LLC
Interior Design: Triplicity Publishing, LLC
Editor: Laura Brady - Triplicity Publishing, LLC

ACKNOWLEDGEMENTS

Thank you to Triplicity Publishing for helping to make this book a reality. To Allisa, who tirelessly gave me copious notes and advice, both on the book and in life. To Yvonne for giving me that final push and endless support. And to all the artists out there whose music continues to inspire me.

For Glenda

PROLOGUE

The road was particularly smooth this evening and the drive was nearly effortless. Paul Foley eased his foot off the gas as he rounded a curve in the road. He looked over at his wife, who was digging through her purse. "Trish, what are you doing? Your arm is being swallowed whole." He grinned, amused by how much stuff one bag could hold.

"I'm looking for my cell phone. I wanted to call the girls."

Paul smiled at his wife's worrisome nature. "I'm sure they're fine."

Unfazed by his comment, she kept searching. "Damn. I must have left it in the hotel room."

"Well, we'll be in town in a few minutes. I'm sure they'll have a pay phone somewhere."

"What's a pay phone?" asked his wife, playfully.

"Funny." He pressed his right foot down to accelerate a bit. "I'm sure Harper is probably at Finn's or with Kiley."

She zipped up her purse and leaned back against the passenger seat. "And Emily is probably out getting another tattoo while becoming impregnated by...I don't know—her math teacher."

Paul looked at her incredulously. "Don't be ridiculous, Trisha. She hates her math teacher. He failed her, remember? Plus, he's old."

1

Trisha rolled her eyes. "Very funny."

Paul laughed off his wife's concern. "Oh come on. It's a little funny. Honey, she's fine. She's just being a teenager."

Trisha opened her mouth to say something, but bit her lip to stifle whatever words she wanted to say. She watched a few cars pass by them, briefly shining a light into their car. "I just wish Emily had some friends. I mean, Kiley may be a bit on the wild side, but she's such a good friend to Harper. I think Emily could use something like that."

Paul took his wife's hand. "Let's forget about everything else and enjoy the weekend."

"I just worry," admitted Trisha.

"I know you do. That's what I love about you. But Harper is winding down from graduation and Emily is just blowing off steam." He squeezed her hand tighter. "Hey, can you believe it? Our daughter is a college graduate."

Trisha smiled to herself. "She did look really cute in that cap and gown, didn't she?"

Paul nodded and lamented for a moment. "And soon enough, it's going to be replaced by a wedding gown."

Trisha beamed, imagining her daughter in a long, white dress. "That's gonna cost us, isn't it?"

"Yep. But we'll work it out. Something tells me Harper's worth it."

Trisha adjusted her seatbelt and felt a bit relieved when she finally saw the lights of town approaching. The static on the radio was tuning into a clear station. "I'm starved. Why did we make such a late reservation?"

"Because I knew you would take forever to get ready so you could look your best. Nice job with that, by the

2

way. Is that a new dress?" He reached out and felt the fabric of her garb.

"Actually, I got it a few years ago and I finally fit into it."

"Well don't get too used to it. Because it's coming off later."

"Paul!" Trisha playfully elbowed him.

"What? What did I do?" He pulled up to the red light and stopped. "The restaurant is just up the street. Do you still want to stop and call the girls?"

Trisha thought about it for a moment. "No. You're probably right."

"What was that?"

Trisha shook her head and stated it more clearly. "I said you're right. Don't let it go to your head. Harper is fine. Emily is fine. We're all fine."

"I could get used to this 'being right' thing," said Paul with a self-satisfied smile. When the light turned green, he took his foot off the break and proceeded to the restaurant.

"Did you mail the electric bill?" asked Trisha.

He slapped the steering wheel, frustrated. "Damn, I forgot. I'll do it when we get—"

Paul's voice was drowned out by the sound of screeching tires as they were blinded by a glaring light. The smell of burned rubber wafted through the entire car. The screaming was followed by the deafening sound of metal smashing together. Then there was no sound at all. Then, blackness.

CHAPTER 1

On the surface, there was nothing particularly extraordinary about Harper Foley. And if you told her that, she wouldn't take any offense. In fact, she would agree one hundred percent. Sure, she had her own little quirks and idiosyncrasies that usually make a person unique from other individuals, but she refused to believe they were enough to make her anything but middle of the road. Her looks were above average with her honey blonde hair, and her body was above average due to her penchant for working out. She was smart enough, funny enough and pretty enough to warrant a second cursory glance from people. She knew she wasn't exactly invisible, but she was also, by no means, larger than life. And she was okay with that. At twenty-four, she was still trying to find her footing and exact place in this world.

Still, this rather ordinary, commonplace girl wasn't without her problems. One of which she was facing at this very moment. Harper hadn't been sleeping much these days. There have been several contributing factors to her insomnia, but she preferred to chock it up to the daylight savings time change. Though, that was a rather weak case seeing as how daylight savings was months ago and the insomnia started a couple years ago–at first intermittently, then on a more regular basis. She always did have a way with avoiding the problem at hand. She simply brushed it aside and always told herself she'd worry about it tomorrow. It was her Scarlet O'Hara complex.

Harper laid on her back and stared straight up counting the little bumps on the ceiling. When she got up to four hundred fifty-three bumps, she decided she'd had enough of impersonating her favorite Sesame Street character, threw off the covers and looked over at the clock, 2:50am.

Great. Why do I even bother? she thought.

She got up, turned on the light, put her shoes on and went out to the garage, which she liked to call her 'rec room.' She lingered in the doorway, shifting her focus between the punching bag hanging in front of her and the acoustic guitar sitting in the corner. Balking at the thought of attempting to create music right now, she sighed and grabbed her gloves and wraps off the nearby shelf. She was filled with way too much nervous energy to focus on music at the moment. As she sat down and started wrapping her hands, her cell phone rang from the living room. She ran to grab the phone while dragging the left hand wrap along behind her.

"Hello?"

"Damn. I was hoping you were sleeping."

Harper smiled hearing the voice on the other end. "Me too."

"Still no peaceful slumber?"

"Nope."

"Want me to come over? I'm just leaving Ryan's house."

"You mean Bryan?" asked Harper.

"Yeah, Bryan. Anyway, I'm exhausted. That guy wouldn't shut up all night. I didn't realize how much energy you can expend just trying to drown out the sound of someone's voice."

"Well, send him my way," suggested Harper. "Maybe it'll help me sleep."

"Mmm…I don't think sloppy seconds is your style."

Harper walked over to her couch and sat down. "You mean you slept with him anyway?"

"Why not? It was the only way I could get him to stop talking for a while. But then came the moaning and the screaming and— "

"Okay, okay. I really don't need to hear about that right now."

"Sorry."

Harper heard silence on the other end of the phone and really wished she hadn't sounded so prudish at that moment. There was something about Kiley that always made Harper overly cognizant of her own dorkiness. It's been that way pretty much since she's known her. Harper's best friend was always bolder and braver than she could ever be. They couldn't be more opposite, but somehow their dynamic worked. Ever since they met a few years ago, they became instant friends.

***

Standing in the near-empty parking lot in front of Tyson's Bar, Harper tried her best to not let nerves get the best of her, but was failing miserably. She gripped her black guitar case in one hand, while she removed her other gig bag from her shoulder and grasped the handle with her other hand. She didn't know why she was this nervous. It's not like it was the first time she'd been here. Tonight, however, was different. Tonight, she'd be putting her guitar to use. It never failed. Before any performance, there was always a wave of anxiety that washed over Harper. It usually subsided once she took the stage, but the moments leading up to it were the worst. Harper tried to shake off any fears she had creeping deep into her psyche and walked in, hoping that a drink would do the trick.

Her eyes shifted focus between the stage and the bar. She looked around for a familiar face–her parents, her boyfriend–but they weren't there yet. It was still fairly early and there were only about a dozen people there at the moment, so she traipsed over to the bar, figuring a drink should take precedence over setting up for her debut at this particular venue.

She maneuvered her way through the tables and chairs, stopping suddenly when she took notice of the girl behind the bar looking rather apathetic as she arbitrarily arranged some cocktail napkins and then wiped down the bar. She didn't think too much of Kiley when she first saw her, but when she finally spoke, it was enough to make a lasting impression.

"So…should I come over?" asked Kiley.

Harper could hear faint beeping in the background and knew Kiley was just sitting in her car with the door open and the key in the ignition waiting on her decision. She leaned back to rest her head on the couch, mulling over her friend's question. "No, that's okay. You should get some sleep."

"Are you sure?" Kiley started the ignition on her light blue Ford Focus.

Harper hesitated briefly. She could definitely use the company, but didn't want to inconvenience Kiley. "One of us should get some sleep and it may as well be you. I was about to hit the bag, anyway."

"Really? How can you exercise at this hour? You're a madwoman."

"Eye of the tiger, my friend. Eye of the tiger."

Kiley fastened her seatbelt and put the car in drive. "Okay. Call me tomorrow."

"Good night."

"'Night."

Harper hung up the phone and sat there for a moment. She really did want to say yes. She wanted, for once, to not feel so alone in the middle of the night in this empty house. She wanted to not be alone with her thoughts because they were starting to drive her a little crazy. Harper stood up quickly so as not to let herself get too deep in thought. She finished wrapping her left hand as she walked back out to the garage. Ready to put her Krav Maga skills to good use, she put on her gloves, hit play on her iPod and proceeded to deliver hits and roundhouse kicks to the punching bag with the sound of Paramore echoing through the garage.

CHAPTER 2

The following week, Harper pulled into the closest spot she could find in the parking lot, then made her way toward the entrance of "Between the Lines" bookstore. She walked through the automatic doors as she glanced at her watch, then headed towards the back of the store.

"Harper, can you shelve these in the children's section?"

Harper had just clocked in and stepped out of the break room when her manager decided to bombard her with her first task of the morning. "Sure," she replied as she tried to stifle a yawn and placed her nametag lanyard over her neck.

She dragged the overloaded shelf over to the children's section of the bookstore and prepared for another long day of fine literature and paper cuts. Working in such a tranquil environment, sometimes Harper's thoughts would wander and she would question how and why she ended up here. Graduating from college with an English degree, she thought an endless string of opportunities would come her way. But when interview after interview, turned into rejection after rejection, she began to lose sight of why she even majored in English in the first place. Or why she went to college at all. She came to the conclusion that it may have been for her parents. Harper's main passion in life is and always had been music. But what kind of future would she have with

4

that? While they were supportive of their daughter, her parents would often pose that question to her. Harper, never wanting to displease her parents, relented and chose a more "suitable" major. Now, not a day has gone by where she didn't regret it. If she had come to a better compromise, she could have studied music engineering. And would at least get paid more to work in a studio than slightly over minimum wage at a bookstore. But she learned to never complain about her life. It's something her parents taught her, and it was beginning to be more of a burden than a good quality.

She continued to shelve the children's books until one particular book caught her attention. She examined the blue and white cover.

"Many Moons," she mumbled under her breath. She opened the book and brought it up to her nose. She took in the aroma of the new-book smell, which was one of her favorite smells. She closed her eyes and, before she knew it, was in another place and time.

***

Harper adjusted her back against the pillow on her twin bed. The worn out Strawberry Shortcake blanket underneath her was beginning to make her legs itch. She was really starting to resent that blanket and felt that, at nine, she was way too old for it. Perhaps she would ask her parents for a new one for her birthday. As a woman of the fourth grade, it was beginning to bring down her coolness level. But she tried to stay as still as possible while turning the page of the book she was holding.

"The end," read Harper. At that, she quietly closed the book and placed it on her nightstand, hoping that had

done the trick. She knew she was not so lucky, however, when she felt someone tugging on her pajama shirt. She looked down to see a strawberry blonde moppet staring up at her with big blue eyes.

"Wead it again, Shishy."

Harper couldn't help but smile every time she heard the word 'Shishy.' Her four-year-old sister hadn't quite figured out how to say Harper, so she tried to say 'sister'. Due to her slight speech impediment, it came out "shishy." It's something Harper found interesting seeing as how it seemed much harder to say than her actual name. She'd been calling Harper that since she learned to talk and no one bothered to correct her. Their parents insisted it was too cute to correct her.

Harper rolled her eyes and grabbed the book from the nightstand. "Don't you ever sleep?" She adjusted her back one more time and opened her sister's favorite book once more. At this point, she could probably recite Many Moons *by heart. "Okay, but this is the last time, Emily. Then you're going to sleep in your own room, in your own bed."*

Emily nodded, repositioned herself and curled up on the bed next to her sister while Harper read her favorite story one more time.

***

Harper snapped out of her stupor when the smell of coffee permeated her olfactory senses. She opened eyes to see a cup of ice blended coffee hovering in front of her. She turned around and found that the cup was attached to Kiley's hand.

"I figured you could use this," said Kiley.

Harper grabbed the coffee and smiled. "Absolutely. Thanks so much." She practically downed half of the drink within ten seconds.

"What are you doing here?"

"I was just jonesing for some coffee. And I figured since you didn't sleep much last night...again...you might be crashing right about now."

"Well you're right."

"So I see. I think I came just in time. You were practically asleep."

Harper looked down at the book that was the culprit for her daydreaming and put it in its rightful place on the shelf. The dejected look on her face did not go unnoticed by Kiley.

"Something wrong?" asked Kiley, leaning on the cart full of books.

"Why would you ask that?"

"Because I'm not blind." Kiley took this opportunity to fix the loose strap on her black tank top which kept sliding down her shoulder.

Harper sighed. "I'm fine."

"Sure you are." Kiley put her coffee down and sat down in one of the mini chairs next to the mini table in the middle of the children's section. She looked like a giant from a fairy tale with her knees almost coming up to her chin due to her long legs. "You know that you're worth more than this, right? You could do so much better than this place. It's killing your mojo."

"My mojo?"

"Yeah. Do you have any idea how frustrating it is to see how talented you are and have you waste it by slaving away here?"

"It's peaceful here," replied Harper.

"Peaceful…another word for boring."

"It's not the job that's bothering me."

"So you admit something's bothering you."

"I don't know. I think it's just the weather."

"The weather?" asked Kiley as she took a sip of her coffee. "Sure…yeah. It could be the weather. Or it could be one of the multiple stress-inducing factors in your life. Do you think there's a slight chance that it might be about Emily?"

Harper looked at Kiley. She opened her mouth to say something, but no words were coming out. She continued shelving books.

"Or it could very well be your job. Working here while knowing there's so much more you could do."

"I'm doing it. I'm playing my music."

"Yeah, two nights a week. And when was the last time you were in a recording studio? You've written so many new songs. You need to get them recorded and get them out there for people to hear."

"I'm working on it," Harper replied half-heartedly. She knew it was pointless to argue with Kiley when it came to her music. Kiley was Harper's biggest fan and she'd made that known since the day they met. The overzealous reaction she got from the older girl after her first performance at Tyson's Bar said it all.

***

For Kiley, it started out as any other dull night at her place of employment. It was a warm Saturday night in July and she wasn't exactly thrilled to be working at her new job as a bartender/cocktail waitress at Tyson's Bar. But she had recently dropped out of community college, and this was the only job she could find that didn't involve stilettos and a pole. Being perpetually single, fairly personable and twenty-two, a bar seemed to be a good fit since she wanted tips, but abhorred any kind of food service. Luckily for her, this place only served appetizers. Appetizers, she could handle. Angry customers complaining that their meat wasn't cooked right with their kids screaming for more soda, she couldn't. Kiley had only been working here three weeks when Graham, the bar's owner, informed her they would start showcasing local musicians a few nights a week. After several nights of bad music by wannabe rock star bands, she was hoping for someone with at least a hint of talent. She figured tonight would be like any other night when in walked this petite, timid, unassuming girl, holding two guitar cases–one in each hand.

"Why the two guitars?" asked Kiley, as she wiped up some spilled beer from the bar.

Harper looked over at her, surprised that someone was actually speaking to her. She turned to see a tall, slender brunette looking at her quizzically.

"Oh, the spare is for my own peace of mind. I tend to break a string whenever I perform. Never when I rehearse, mind you. Just when I perform. So I've gotten in the habit of always bringing an extra guitar. I don't have time to change a string on stage."

"How...efficient," replied Kiley.

Harper gestured to one of her guitar cases. "Two capos, too...in case one breaks."

Kiley looked at Harper skeptically. "You've got a little bit of crazy in you, don't you?"

"No, I'm just kind of a klutz," replied Harper as she put one of her guitars down and leaned it up against the

14

bar. Unfortunately, it didn't stay that way for long when Harper pulled out a bar stool and accidentally knocked the guitar over. She cringed as it hit the floor with a loud bang, the sound echoing through the bar.

"Shit." Harper bent over right away to pick it up. "See?"

Kiley smirked. She could immediately tell there was much more to this girl than what was on the surface.

"Well, the stage is over there when you're ready to set up," she said, pointing behind Harper. "In the meantime, can I get you something? Wait...you are over twenty-one, right? You look kinda young."

"Turned twenty-one last month."

Kiley looked at her skeptically.

"You can ask Graham if you want. He knows me."

"No, that's okay. I believe you."

Harper reached out her hand. "I'm Harper, by the way."

"Kiley Young."

Once Harper gently placed both guitar bags on the ground, she sat down on the stool, reached into her pocket, pulled out two guitar picks and placed them on the bar.

Kiley looked at her suspiciously.

"Don't tell me you're one of those OCD people who have to do things in twos..."

"Me? No."

"Okay. Well, what can I get you?" asked Kiley.

"Two beers."

Kiley took a step back and felt her perpetual cynicism washing over her as she stared at Harper. She found this girl to be rather perplexing and couldn't decide if it fascinated or frustrated her. Kiley easily

15

towered over the younger girl by at least five inches, deducing that Harper couldn't have been more than five foot three.

Harper wasn't fazed. "Leffe, if you have it."

Kiley obliged and reached into the fridge to grab two bottles of Leffe. She opened up the bottles and gave them to Harper. Harper grabbed the beers and handed one to Kiley.

"This one's yours. Cheers." She clinked her bottle against Kiley's and took a swig of beer before she got up, picked up one of her guitars and headed over to the stage without giving Kiley another look.

Kiley stood there, impressed with this girl's gumption. She smiled as she took a drink of the Leffe and wondered if Harper was as talented as she was witty. She was hoping, for her ears' sake, that she'd at least be more talented than the other performers that had recently taken the stage at Tyson's Bar.

***

Kiley was silent for a moment. She looked away from Harper and kept her focus on the ground. "Okay, I'll let up on the music thing…for now." Kiley casually ran her finger over the bookshelf, absentmindedly checking it for dust. "It could also be your parents. Or the fact that you live alone in that house?"

Harper stopped what she was doing and looked at Kiley incredulously. "That house is all that's left of my family. I'm not getting rid of it."

"I know, I know. It's just…maybe you should get a roommate or something."

Harper smiled at Kiley. "Is this your way of telling me you've been evicted and need a place to crash?"

"Evicted? No. A place to crash…maybe."

"What happened?"

Kiley continued to look away from Harper and took another sip of her coffee. She hesitated for a moment. "I may or may not have slept with Jane's boyfriend."

Harper dropped the books she was holding and winced as they landed on her foot. Kiley knelt down and helped her pick up the books. "Kiley, you slept with your roommate's boyfriend?"

The disappointed tone in Harper's voice was enough to make Kiley jump to her own defense. "They were fighting! And I was drunk. And really stupid. And a complete asshole, I know."

"Poor Jane."

"She'll get over it. He was a dickhead. And what happened with us just proved it," said Kiley, defensively. "In the meantime, until she calms down, I may need to stay at your place for a few days."

Harper was silent for a moment. Kiley could tell she wasn't happy about what she had just heard.

"Are you mad?"

"I don't know."

Kiley stood up and took a spot leaning against a bookshelf. She absolutely hated when Harper was mad at her. Not enough money for rent, she could handle. Her car breaking down–no problem. Her parents telling she's wasting her life away, she couldn't care less. But if Harper cast even the slightest disconcerted glance in her direction, Kiley's heart would stop and an uneasy feeling would come over her and not leave until she knew her friend was no longer displeased with her.

"I don't know why I do these things. I really don't. I don't even *like* Jason."

"Justin," corrected Harper.

"Right. Justin," she paused for a moment. "Justin? Are you sure?"

"Yeah. I'm sure." Harper pulled off the last few books from the top level of the cart and shelved them in their rightful place.

Kiley knew it was best to change the subject if she knew what was good for her.

"Anyway, back to your dilemma."

Harper smiled and playfully rolled her eyes. "I'd much rather talk about your philandering."

"Really?"

"No. Not really." Harper turned around and started pushing the cart towards the next aisle. "I really should focus on finishing this."

"Because it's so very tricky?" Kiley followed her, refusing to drop the subject. "You know, we're leaving out one very key reason for your poor state of mind."

"I don't wanna hear it," warned Harper.

"Finn."

At the sound of Finn's name, Harper's breath caught in her throat. "Could you please leave him out of this? It's not the situation with Finn that's bothering me. It has nothing to do with him. I'm fine. And Finn is fine."

Kiley looked at Harper skeptically.

Harper reiterated. "He's fine."

CHAPTER 3

To say that the usually easy going and good-natured Finn Lewis had been a little down lately would be quite an understatement. Finn, along with anyone who's ever known him, always considered himself the quintessential "nice guy." He was temperate, tolerant and would always have your back in a fight. He was also a good man to have around whenever you needed a favor, though he was growing rather tired of that description of himself.

Today was a particularly hard day for Finn. The shrill sound of the alarm clock refused to let up until he reached his arm out and knocked it to the ground. He was adamant about not getting up today. He pushed himself up, picked up his pillow to flip it over and fell back down onto the bed, allowing his face to absorb the coolness of the other side. Yup, there was no way he was getting up today. He was just going to stay in bed until the sun went down, then get up to brush his teeth, and go back to bed to start the whole thing over tomorrow. Finn sighed as he rolled over onto his back. He slowly reached his arm over to the other side of the bed, not exactly sure what he was reaching for. He closed his eyes, hoping to fall back to sleep, repeating to himself "I'm not getting up today. I'm not getting up today."

He scoffed at his own empty attempt at stubbornness as he reluctantly removed the covers and pulled his six-foot, medium-build frame out of the bed. He yawned while running his fingers though his dark, wavy hair and braced for yet another day of his seemingly unending agony. He walked to the bathroom, turned on the faucet and splashed cold water on his face. Instead of drying off, he let the beads of water stream down his face as he walked into the living room wearing only his sweatpants and plopped down on his couch. He grabbed the remote and starting flipping through the different channels on the television. It wasn't even a minute before he clicked the power button and turned off the TV. He looked over at his cell phone, determined to win the battle this time. He was not going to call her. He was absolutely sure he was not going to call her. He was just picking up the phone to check the time. But as his hands started dialing numbers, panic started to set in. He closed his phone immediately and threw it next to him on the couch.

Finn stood up and walked to the kitchen to raid the fridge. He wasn't too hungry, but he knew he needed to eat if he wanted to start gaining some weight. In the past couple of months, he had lost seventeen pounds and had a few dizzy spells from lack of food. He took some orange juice out of the fridge and drank it straight from the carton. Then, he pulled some bread out of the bag on top of his microwave and put a couple pieces in the toaster. He pulled himself up onto the counter and waited. As he looked around, he noticed that everything was a mess. Half empty boxes were piled everywhere and clothes were scattered around his living room. There were several three-week-old pizza boxes and empty beer bottles on the table–relics from when his friend, Seth, came over and played video games with him all night.

Finn slowly began to realize that he'd never really stopped to take a look around at his apartment. Until now, he had just been going about his day, putting one foot in front of the other. Just trying to remember to breathe, not paying attention to the filth he was living in. He looked down at himself, then lifted his arm and hesitantly sniffed his armpit. He immediately pulled away and exhaled.

"Wow," he said to himself.

He hopped off the counter and popped up his toast. Instead of taking it, he left it in the toaster and headed to the bathroom to take the first shower he'd had in four days.

***

After another long and barely gratifying day at work, Harper sat in her garage strumming her guitar. With a pen by her side, she was concentrating hard on trying to create new lyrics to the melody she couldn't get out of her head. Unfortunately, her brain wasn't cooperating and the melody wasn't translating properly. For some reason, she was having more difficulty than normal. The music in her head refused to travel from her brain to her fingers and from her fingers to the guitar. She had absolutely no patience for writer's block, or music block for that matter.

Though she seemed like a natural when she performed, music didn't always come easily to Harper. As a kid, she always wanted to learn to play an instrument, so her father started paying for piano lessons when she was seven. She never had an actual piano and was only able to play at her teacher's house. Her parents did surprise her one Christmas with a big electronic keyboard, which she used to practice on. She got a lot of use out of that keyboard and practiced constantly for three years, but something just wasn't clicking. It always took her a while to learn a song and whenever she tried to create her own, it would just sound too rudimentary for her liking. She wasn't satisfied and after three years of struggling to master it, she wasn't happy with her progress and decided to retire from piano at the ripe old age of ten. But the music always stayed with her. Then, a few years later, she started coming up with lyrics and writing them down. Soon thereafter, she started putting a melody to the lyrics and suddenly, Harper decided she wanted to create music again. This time, she would pursue a different route. She thought about the drums and had fairly good rhythm, but she wouldn't have been able to put her lyrics to drum beats. Her dad, once again wanting to encourage her "hobby" as he would call it, took her to Music World where she picked up her first guitar. She loved the way it felt. It fit so naturally in her arms and though she didn't know how to play a note at that time, she knew right then and there that this was her future. Her dad, unable to say no to those pleading eyes, bought her that guitar. It was a decent guitar–rather inexpensive–but Harper loved and cherished it. And this time around, everything was different. After a few lessons, her guitar instructor said she must have been born with a guitar in her hands. Harper owned the instrument in every way possible. From the first strum of the first chord, it was easy to see she finally found what she was looking for.

That natural talent, unfortunately, wasn't doing her any good this evening. After hitting another flat note, she became increasingly annoyed and gave her guitar one dramatic, irritated strum, just to get the point across. The Gibson didn't like that gesture very much and as soon as her strum hit the strings, the d-string snapped and broke. This startled Harper as a slight adrenaline rush came over her. Once her heart stopped palpitating, she relinquished and put down her guitar. But refusing to be entirely defeated, she got up to look for her extra guitar strings, which she kept in a box on the shelf next to the rest of her musical equipment. She dug through the shelves to no avail and as her hunt continued, she realized several other boxes were missing, too. Not only had the box with her guitar strings disappeared, but also the boxes with her— microphones and cables. She stood there for a minute pondering where they might have been taken. Then, it hit her.

"Damn."

***

Despite doing pretty much nothing, Finn felt he had a fairly productive day. He just finished throwing out the last of seven full garbage bags. He managed to put most of his clothes away, and he had felt so refreshed after his first shower, he decided to follow it up with a second one. Today marked the first time in 63 days he didn't spend every minute thinking of her. Granted, there were only about 23 full minutes in the day where his thoughts weren't with her, but that's called progress. Finn sat comfortably in his recliner watching *Sports Center*. He was quite proud of the four bites he had already taken of his microwaved pasta and was enjoying a cold beer when his cell phone started ringing. A feeling of dread and despair washed over him when he glanced at the caller ID. He stared at the phone for a moment, contemplating what to do. Finally, he put down his beer, took a deep breath and answered.

"Hello?"

"Hey Finn." Harper tried to sound as casual as possible. When her voice cracked while saying his name, she knew she was failing miserably.

"Hey." He winced slightly at the sound of her voice.

Harper waited for him to say something else, but he didn't. "So, how are you?"

After a long pause, he finally answered. "I'm doing great. Just walked in the door, actually." It was the first time he'd ever lied to her.

"Oh. Good, good. Um…so the reason I called is…well…"

Finn braced himself for what was about to come. It could have been anything. Maybe she wanted to see him. Maybe she wanted to get back together. Maybe she was lonely and just wanted to make love to him one last time. All he knew was he was tired of doing favors for everyone. He was tired of being the good guy who always helped out. He was tired of being used as a proverbial punching bag. He knew if it was some sort of favor she was asking, he'd hang up on her on the spot. He refused to let people treat him like this anymore.

"What is it?" he asked.

"I think when you moved out you took some of my boxes. The ones with my music equipment in them. I'm in desperate need of guitar strings. Can you bring them over?"

Finn slumped his shoulders in disappointment. Her reason for calling was rather anti-climactic. He did have her boxes. He found them while he was cleaning up earlier. But what she was asking fell in the "favor" category. And he was done jumping through hoops for people. Absolutely finished.

Before he knew it, Finn was up and looking for his shoes. "Yeah, of course. I'll be right there."

He hung up the phone and shook his head in disappointment.

Damn, he thought. And he was just starting to make some progress…

CHAPTER 4

It was times like this that Kiley wished she smoked. It was a rather dull and empty Tuesday night at Tyson's Bar. She hated working the weekdays. The weekends were always packed with all sorts of interesting people who were drunk enough to tip very generously. Tonight, however, was a very different scene. She felt like she was about to go stir crazy due to boredom. If she smoked, at least there would be a reason to go outside for a little break and bring relief to the dullness that surrounded her. Kiley was concentrating on the piece of paper in front of her and making little notes with one hand while wiping down the same spot of the bar with the other hand, not even paying attention to the eleven patrons in the bar.

"You've been wiping that spot so long, I think it's gone from dirty, to clean and back to dirty again," remarked Graham as he placed a heavy crate of beer bottles on the edge of the bar.

Kiley looked up at her boss, then down at the towel she was using. "Oh. Yeah, I guess I should move this party elsewhere, huh?" She picked up the piece of paper, moved four feet to her left and continued with what she was doing.

Graham walked over and sat down on a barstool facing her. "Can I ask why you're so focused on that piece of paper when you should be working?"

Kiley looked around. "If someone needs me, I'll help them out. Don't worry." She went back to her paper.

Graham grabbed the piece of paper and started reading it. "Lay down five new recordings within the next six months. Perform at least two nights a month at a venue that ISN'T Tyson's Bar..." Graham looked at Kiley, suspiciously. "Kiley, do you have something against my bar?"

"No. I wouldn't dare bite the hand that barely feeds me. It's for Harper. It's a list of goals I'm making for her." She pointed at the bottom of the page. "And I started making a budget for her so maybe she can spend less time at work and more time working on her music."

Graham examined the paper, quite impressed with Kiley's organization skills. "So why aren't you making yourself one of these?"

"Because, sexy, my plan is foolproof. I plan on marrying you and inheriting half of the bar."

Graham handed the piece of paper back. "Didn't you know I'm already spoken for?" He gestured to the TV overhead, which was set to an entertainment news show discussing Angelina Jolie.

Kiley looked up at the TV. "Well I refuse to let you go without a fight."

Graham smiled. Of course he knew she was joking. Not only was Graham fifty-one with a beer belly, but he had also become somewhat of a father figure to Kiley over the last couple years. It started when Harper began to perform at his bar. Before that, he really couldn't stand Kiley and regretted hiring her in the first place. When she started hanging out with Harper, that all changed. Graham had known Harper since she was born. He was friends with her parents and had always adored her. He had promised to always watch out for her. Which is why she always had an open invitation to perform there whenever she wanted. Though, like Kiley, he firmly believed that she could do much better than this place. She just had to find her audience. Since Kiley was now a permanent fixture as Harper's best friend, he felt obligated to watch over her, as well.

"Why are you going through all this trouble for Harper?" asked Graham.

Kiley shrugged. "You've heard her. You've seen her play. She's incredible.

She's...transcendent. And she deserves to be happy."

Graham beamed with pride seeing how important Harper was to Kiley. "You're a good friend, sweetie. A damn good friend."

Kiley looked up at Graham. "I just really believe in her. Plus, the sooner she gets her music out there, the sooner she'll be rich and famous and I plan on riding those bra straps all the way to the top," she joked.

Graham's reply was merely a grunt as he walked off to finish what he was doing, before he got sucked into yet another one of Kiley's tangents.

A customer came strolling up to the bar. "Hey, can I get a Bud Light?"

Kiley didn't even look up from her paper. She reached behind her, grabbed a bottle, opened it and put it on the bar. "Here you go."

"Uh...this isn't Bud Light. This is Bass," the customer complained.

"Yeah, I don't believe in Bud Light. This is real beer. Trust me. You'll love it," replied Kiley.

The customer was starting to get irate until Kiley looked up at him, winked and flashed her signature smile. He was left searching for words. "Uh...I...okay. Thanks."

As he headed off back to his table, Kiley, once again, became engrossed in her project.

Kiley couldn't really explain the connection she had with Harper. It was just one of those things in life that you learn not to question. She figured part of it may have to do with the fact that Kiley's childhood wasn't the most stable. Harper, even with all her neuroses, accident-prone tendencies and random acts of silliness, was by far the most stable, reliable and unwavering person she's ever met. She's been the one constant in Kiley's life, even though they had only known each other a few years. Kiley came from somewhat of a "broken home." She often used that term loosely because her parents were actually still together. But they were living very different lives and had been since Kiley could remember. Her mother is a shell of the woman she once was. Her father was cold and unfeeling, and she had gotten over most of her painful childhood. She tried to separate herself from her parents as much as she could, but she still loved them. She cared about them despite how much they have potentially screwed her up. As much as she hated to admit it, she often found solace in the fact that she and Harper could relate to each other regarding parental issues, even though the issues were as different as night and day for them. Kiley was thankful she still had the option of seeing her parents, which was a rare occurrence. She often dreaded it, but about twice a year, she would make the trek out to Ojai to pay her parents a visit. She usually ended up leaving after about an hour.

A Fine Mess

Despite the less than stellar childhood Kiley endured, she managed to forge ahead and make a life of her own. She never really knew what she wanted to do with her life. She never felt there was a place she could call home. She was always afraid that she was destined to wander like some self-proclaimed nomad. She always had a tendency to care more about living for the minute than thinking about the future, so never gave much thought to it. But she wasn't vapid in any way, nor was she devoid of personality. In fact, she had it in spades. She had her likes: imported beer, game night featuring a rousing game of Boggle, "I Love Lucy," good music, good times, and good friends. She had her dislikes: bad grammar, the word "panties," new wave jazz, and doctors that tell you your appointment is at 9 a.m. and they don't end up actually seeing you until 10:30. She always figured she had plenty of time to figure out where her life was going. Right now, all she knew to do was get through the day alive.

Kiley had always been a looker; the kind of girl that always gets a second glance. The best part about her is that she doesn't even know it. And if she did know it, she didn't act like it. When she wasn't working, she usually let her long, light brown hair flow freely and rarely ever needed to style it. She was one of those girls with sterotypically perfect hair. Her skin seldom ever had a blemish and her thin, but toned body wasn't a result of long hours at the gym, but simply the product of good genes. Not only was Kiley beautiful, but also very real and loyal and grounded. She was also rather goofy at times and had a razor sharp tongue that would sometimes get her into trouble.

Her sense of style was fairly casual, but while at work she usually dressed a little less classy than she prefers, but she figured it was a good way to get tips. She hated degrading herself in that way, but she does what needs to be done. The rent doesn't pay itself.

Tonight was a slight exception to the "dressing like a slut rule" seeing as how it was relatively dead. She decided to take a break from her project for Harper, folded up the piece of paper and put it in her pocket. 'She'll probably hate it anyway,' thought Kiley.

"Smithwick's please."

Kiley looked up and observed a good looking young man with wire-rimmed glasses smiling at her. She noticed him earlier hanging out with a group of guys that left about fifteen minutes ago.

"Sure." She grabbed a glass from under the bar and started filling it up with the Irish brew. She put it on the bar. "Six dollars."

He pulled out a ten, threw it down on the bar and took a seat on the stool. "Rough night?"

"No." Kiley casually pulled the rubber band out of her hair and let her tresses fall naturally.

"Oh." He took a drink of his beer and looked around. "It's a nice night."

Kiley chuckled. "What's your name?"

"Sean." He reached his hand out to shake hers.

Kiley looked at his hand and looked back up at him. "Can I ask you something, Sean?"

Sean, feeling slightly rejected, pulled his hand back. "Sure."

Kiley leaned in toward him. "Are you trying to flirt with me? Because you're really bad at it."

"Oh…uh…well…"

Kiley smiled at him. "It's okay. I'm off in an hour, if you want to wait."

"Okay!" replied Sean, a little too enthusiastically. He straightened up and cleared his throat. "I mean, sure. I think I can wait around."

Kiley leaned in closer to Sean and whispered, "We'll have to go to your place. I'm having a…roommate issue."

Sean gulped, thrown off by how forward Kiley was. He wasn't used to women who were so up front and honest. "Uh…okay."

Kiley backed up and less-than-eagerly turned around to gather the credit cards of the patrons who opened tabs. The uninspired look on her face was quite the opposite of Sean's very noticeable smile.

CHAPTER 5

"You want some of my fries?" asked Finn.

Harper had just taken a gargantuan bite of her burger and tried to answer as tactfully as possible without showing too much of what she had been chewing. "Sure. Why not?"

Once she swallowed, she grabbed a couple of fries from his tray. After devouring them, she took a drink of her milkshake and started to look around, avoiding eye contact with Finn. She adjusted her position in the booth and felt the red cushioned vinyl stick to her legs.

Breaking the silence, a voice came over the speaker system. "Number 67, your order's ready!"

They were at their favorite fast food burger place that was conveniently open until 2am. It was a place they used to frequent a lot in the past, but given the current circumstances, it had been a while since they had eaten there together. Harper almost forgot how good this place was as she enjoyed another bite of her burger.

Finn's right foot was nervously tapping the ground and his hands were fidgeting with the straw wrapper on the table. He thought he'd seen the last of Harper after he dropped off her music equipment last week, so he was surprised to get a phone call from her at one in the morning asking him to meet her here. He finished ripping the straw wrapper to shreds and couldn't take the silence between them anymore.

"Are you okay?" he asked.

Harper brought her attention back to Finn and shrugged, "I don't know."

"What's wrong?"

Harper hesitated for a moment, then conceded, "I fell asleep around midnight…"

Finn perked up. "You did? That's great. It used to take you until three or four to fall asleep."

"…I woke up forty-five minutes later."

"Oh." Finn lowered his head.

Harper cautiously continued. "I had a dream that woke me up. About Emily."

Finn nodded in understanding. "What happened?"

"Nothing, really. She was just…there. Like thirty feet away from me. And I kept trying to get her attention, but she wasn't seeing or hearing me. When she finally made eye contact with me, I woke up. I tried to go back to sleep and finish the dream, but I ended up lying in bed only able to focus on the cricket chirping outside my window. It was really annoying."

Finn leaned back into his seat. "And you still haven't heard from her?"

"Nope."

Finn looked around, a little unsure of what to say. "Well, we can try to look for her again. Maybe we'll have more luck this time."

Harper laughed uncomfortably and shook her head. "No. I'm done. I'm not doing that again."

"Okay then. You want another burger?"

"No thanks." Harper finished the last bite of her burger and immediately regretted the meal she just consumed. Before she started to chastise herself for the thousand calories she just ate, her thoughts trailed off.

Her eyes fixated on the empty tray in front of her as her meandering thoughts turned into words. "I mean, it's not like she cared enough to even let me know she's okay. Why should I give a shit anymore?" She shook her head. "Screw it. I did everything I could."

***

The packed up duffle bag sitting by the front door said it all. There was no stopping her. Harper tried to fight back the tears materializing behind her eyes. She knew there was nothing she could do or say to change the situation, but she continued to plead, anyway.

"Emily, please. Don't do this."

Emily was unfazed by Harper's request. She frantically grabbed anything and everything that might be pertinent to her impending journey, even scouring the kitchen for food she could take with her. She went back into her bedroom to do one more sweep, just in case she missed anything. Harper followed her, her muscles tensing up with every step. Her eyes couldn't handle the number of tears welling up anymore, and they began to fall freely down her face. Emily chaotically opened and shut her drawers one by one, each slam getting louder and louder. Harper stood there watching her sister about to self-destruct.

"Emily, can we please talk about this. I think you're being a little irrational."

Emily scoffed at her sister's statement as she grabbed a wad of cash out of her top drawer. "Irrational? Are you fucking kidding me? You're trying to convince me to stay and you're doing so by insulting me?"

Harper relented. "Okay. I'm sorry. I just...I really need you to stay, okay? Please. I know...I know it's been difficult. And I know I've been hard to live with. I just worry about you. You're seventeen. I'm just trying to do the best I can for you."

Emily stopped for a moment and turned to face her sister. "I can't stay here anymore. Don't you get it? I can't do this. I can't be here anymore. I can't keep being reminded of everything. And the fact that you're constantly breathing down my neck just makes it worse."

"Well what do you want me to do? Just not give a shit?"

"You do what you want. Let me do what I want," replied Emily as she headed out the bedroom door.

"Fine. Do what you want. Just do it here. Please." Harper tried blocking her from leaving the room, but Emily managed to evade her.

Emily shook her head as she walked past her sister. "I have to go."

Harper followed her once again. "You don't even have a car. How are going to get anywhere."

"It's called public transportation."

"Can you at least tell me where you're going?" pleaded Harper.

"I really couldn't tell you. I won't know until I get there."

"Can you please spare me the typical clichés of a runaway?"

Emily got to the front door and threw her duffle bag over her shoulder. Harper grabbed Emily by the arm and pulled her in for a hug. It was her last-ditch effort to keep her sister here. Maybe in this one embrace, she could prove to her sister how much she needed her to stay.

Harper's arms began shaking as she pulled her sister in closer to her, crying into her shoulder.

Emily allowed her sister this one last hug. She even mildly returned the embrace for a moment before she pulled herself away and opened the door.

Harper stood there searching for anything else to say. Emily gave her one last look before she walked out the door. She was halfway down the driveway when Harper yelled after her.

"Emily! I can't get through this without you!"

Emily heard her, but kept walking.

***

An irksome scraping sound filled Harper's ears. She realized she was moving her straw up and down inside the lid of her cup and the grating sound of plastic on plastic was enough to make her pull her hand away. She thought for a moment, then looked up at Finn.

"Have you ever just woken up one day and realize you have no idea who you are? Like the person you were five or ten years ago is the person you always thought you'd be?" She wasn't expecting an answer. She was just sort of throwing her words out there to see if any of them made sense when they were spoken. "Because when I try to think about it, I can barely catch a glimmer of that girl."

Finn cocked his head. "You've had a lot of stuff happen to you in the past couple years. That changes a person." He looked down at their empty burger wrappers and empty tray of fries and mumbled quietly, "Maybe it made you do things you might regret."

A Fine Mess

Harper heard every word of that last sentence and knew exactly what he was trying to hint at. Finn had once again tried to break down the wall she had built for herself. But the fortress surrounding her had always been difficult to penetrate, even when she was younger.

Harper had always been somewhat of an enigma, even to herself at times. Her popularity in high school was of absolutely no help in curing the irreparable damage her grade school years had inflicted. Tomboyish, shy, and a little on the chubby side, her nine-year-old self often found its way back into her psyche no matter how many years had passed. And no matter how much positive reinforcement and validation had been thrown her way, the feelings persisted. In the simplest of terms, Harper was now a pretty girl–thin, athletic and toned. But those three years of relentless teasing between ages nine and twelve never quite disappeared, and would occasionally rear its ugly head. Though she started developing rather young at the age of ten, it took some time for the rest of her body to catch up before she could confidently flaunt her assets. Once the weight fell off and her clothes got cuter, her awkward self was all but forgotten by everyone except her. Though physically she had changed, her shyness still ruled her, making it hard for her to believe she deserved anything better than what she already had. It also made it fairly difficult for anyone to be let in. Kiley was pretty much the only one who was able to break down that barrier, and occasionally Emily to some extent. Not even her parents knew what was really inside of her, which Harper thought was probably for their own good. That's not to say she wasn't a joy to be around. She was guarded, yet personable. Private, yet friendly. Shy, but an absolute riot once you got to know her. She was even voted "funniest" in her senior class, most likely due to her biting wit and constant sarcasm. Despite all that, Harper had always been a tough one to figure out. She knew a lot of that had to do with the fact that she was truly afraid of what she really wanted. This was the case in all aspects of her life, but particularly in her career and her love life. Harper never let the fact that she was afraid to go after what she wanted bring her down, but that's why she kept so active and often took her frustration out in physical activity. She spent her entire life doing what everyone else wanted her to do — a notion she got used to, so it was a daily routine for her.

Her stereotypical life and experiences growing up were simply a mask hiding the real Harper, and she was terrified of revealing too much. Lately, she had been feeling more and more restless about the fact that throughout her life she had never done anything for herself. Though she missed them every day, the farther removed she became from the memory of her parents and living under their rules and trying to meet their expectations, the freer she felt to make changes. Granted, she didn't dare venture out into anything on her own accord just yet, but she was getting to the breaking point. The fact that it seemed more and more likely that Emily was never coming back somehow lit a fire under her to start over and start living her life on her own terms.

Harper looked across at the remnants of her old and "safe" life. She didn't have the patience to get into whatever Finn was trying to bring up, so she grabbed her purse and slid out of the booth.

"Thanks for meeting me. I know it's late…or early. But thanks." She paused briefly next to his side of the booth and started to lean in, but then she immediately pulled back. "I should go. I'll talk to you later."

Finn was left sitting in the booth, knowing he'd spend the next few days over-analyzing the conversation they just had. He pulled his cell phone out of his pocket and started dialing.

"Hello?"

"Seth? Hey! I can barely hear you!" yelled Finn.

"Finn! What's up man? Yeah, I'm at this party at Monica's. You should come over! It's still going on."

"I don't know, man. I'm exhausted. I just met up with Harper." Finn got up out of the booth, covered his free ear with his hand and walked outside.

"Are you serious? What did I tell you about that? Stay away!"

"I know, but she really wanted to talk."

"Who cares, man? You need to seriously stop pining over her."

"I don't know. I think she might —"

"She won't! It's not gonna happen! Dude, why do you have to be such a *woman* about this?! You're probably going over every single word she said to you and trying to figure out what it all means, aren't you?"

Finn was silent.

"Dude! Stop being such a wuss! You know I like Harper, but come on. She's over it. You should be, too! Now come over! I'll text you the address."

"Okay. I'll think about it."

"Liar," replied Seth. "Whatever. Call me later."

Finn hung up the phone and walked to his car, knowing full well he was going to get an angry phone call from Seth the next day asking him why he didn't go. But he figured he'd deal with that tomorrow.

***

A few days later, Finn made his way through the long corridor on the fifth floor of the office building, looking for the right suite number. He tried to control his nerves as he was getting closer to approaching his destination. He tried to forget about the fact that he hadn't heard from Harper since that night at In 'n' Out. He had bigger things to focus on and more important things to ponder; the first being: what the hell was he doing here? He found the correct number and reluctantly opened the door and stepped into the waiting room. His heart began to pound as he was greeted by an overly cheerful woman behind a desk.

"Come on in, honey. Sign in here and then have a seat. Dr. Harris will be with you in a moment."

Finn smiled uncomfortably and tentatively walked up to the desk to sign in, then took a seat next to the magazine rack. There weren't many magazines to choose from. He was hoping for Sports Illustrated, but since there weren't any, he settled on last month's issue of Glamour. He flipped through the pages and perused the contents, hoping he'd find something that would hold his interest. Unfortunately, all he got was a dizzy sensation from the aroma of the nine different perfume samples inserted inside the pages of the magazine. When his eyes began to water from the combined scents, he closed the magazine and plopped it down on the side table next to his chair. Before he could recover from Calvin Klein and Hilfiger overload, the office door opened up and a brunette woman in her early forties stood in the doorway. She adjusted the collar on her white blouse and then proceeded to wipe some crumbs away from her gray pencil skirt.

"Finn Lewis?"

Finn was caught in somewhat of a trance. He hadn't met her before and he only had a name to go on, but he definitely didn't expect her to look like this. He wasn't really sure what he expected.

"Yeah. That's me."

She smiled sweetly and gestured. "Come on in."

Finn got up and followed her into her office. She closed the door behind them and gestured for him to sit down on the couch across from her oversized beige chair. He took a seat in the middle of the couch and brought his left foot up to rest over his right thigh. He carefully examined the woman in front of him, who was making notes on her clipboard. To anyone else, she would likely be considered rather nondescript looking. Her hair was pulled back in a clip, her reading glasses were resting on the edge of her nose, and her white Keds didn't exactly match the rest of her outfit. She looked up and noticed Finn gawking at her shoes.

"My heel broke going up the stairs this morning. I always keep an extra pair of shoes in the office, just in case. Besides, they're ten times more comfortable."

Finn nodded. "Oh."

"…just in case you were wondering." She took a moment to study her new patient, then reached her hand out to him. "I'm Dr. Susan Harris, by the way. It's nice to meet you."

Finn shook her hand. "It's nice to meet you, too."

Dr. Harris leaned back into her seat and placed the clipboard on her lap. "So, let's talk."

Finn swallowed hard. "Okay."

Silence enveloped them. Finn was debating on what to say and Dr. Harris was simply waiting for a response.

"Should I just…say something?" asked Finn.

"If you want. It's your hour."

Finn nodded. He looked down and noticed a piece of lint suck to his jeans. The only sound that filled the room at that moment was the sound of his fingernail scraping against the material of his pants, trying to remove the lint. Once it was gone, he wiped the rest of that area of the denim, then folded his arms across his chest.

Dr. Harris gave him a little push. "Why don't you start with the reason you made this appointment?"

Finn took a deep breath. He was unable to bring himself to look directly at her, so he focused on the silver doorknob attached to the door. "Well…I've been kinda down for the past couple months."

"And why's that?"

He shrugged. "I guess it stems from a breakup I had. Two months ago."

"So it's still pretty fresh."

"Yeah."

"How long were you two together?"

"Four years."

Dr. Harris nodded. "Well that can't be easy."

Finn subtly rolled his eyes. He was afraid of this. He had a feeling if he saw a psychiatrist, this is all they would do—just state the obvious. Now he was just waiting for the cliché question of 'how does that make you feel.'

"No, it's not easy," replied Finn.

"And does this person know how much you're hurting?"

This person, thought Finn. *So she thinks I'm gay. That's just great.* "I'm pretty sure she does," said Finn, slightly emphasizing the "she."

"And how does that make you feel?" asked Dr. Harris.

Finn shot her a look.

"I'm kidding," laughed Dr. Harris. "I was just getting it out of the way." She leaned forward. "You can relax, you know. I know it's going to take some time getting used to talking about your issues with a complete stranger, but the defensiveness will eventually fade away if you allow it to. I'm just here to provide an unbiased outlook and help you to answer the questions that need to be answered."

"Like why she left me?" asked Finn.

Dr. Harris shook her head. "Like why you're asking questions like 'Why did she leave me?' instead of focusing on yourself and helping to uncover ways for you to never feel like this again."

Finn opened his mouth to say something, but nothing came out.

"So why don't you tell me what happened."

Finn took a deep breath. "That might take a while."

Dr. Harris looked at her watch. "You still have forty-three minutes."

***

Finn awoke in the middle of the night and took a moment to remember exactly where he was. It was 4:00 am and the gas-fueled fireplace against the wall was still roaring, allowing just enough light for his eyes to easily adjust to the darkness. The only sound he could hear was the crackling of the fire. He tried to get a sense of a presence next to him, but knew it was no use. He was getting used to waking up alone. It's been a more frequent happening since the insomnia started.

He brought Harper to this cabin in Big Bear in order to cheer her up. It had been a year and a half since her life had completely fallen apart and he just wanted to take her somewhere to get away from it all–just the two of them. With Christmas coming up, he didn't want her to be sad thinking about everything that's gone wrong. Things had been somewhat lacking between them lately. Finn figured now was a good time to try and rekindle the remaining embers of their once-flourishing relationship. It wasn't easy. Harper had never been one to fully open up to anyone, so he was used to prying information out of her. But recently, she hadn't been offering anything other than "I'm fine. I promise" and "Everything's great. I'm just out of it from being so tired." Finn wasn't buying it, but he decided to let her sell it for the time being.

The ride up here was excruciatingly silent. The radio was their one saving grace. Every now and then when a song came on that they both loved, they'd turn it into a duet with Harper providing the harmonies. It was a glimpse of how things used to be.

Once his eyes fully adjusted to the dim light of the fireplace, he spotted Harper's silhouette out on the balcony. When he got out of bed and slid the glass door open, he was met with an icy wind, chilling him to the bone. He folded his arms and immediately started shivering.

"What are you doing out here?"

Harper whirled around, startled. "Just getting some fresh air."

45

"*It's fifteen degrees out.*"

"*Go put on a shirt. You must be freezing.*"

"*Well, I WAS in a warm bed. Come join me. Now that I'm wide awake too, we can keep each other company,*" suggested Finn.

Harper looked back out into the vastness of the early morning. "*It's peaceful out here.*"

"*It's warm in here.*" He stood in the doorway and watched as the moonlight reflected off the diamond on her left hand. He put it there nearly two years ago and couldn't help but notice its brilliance slowly fading every day.

Finn braved the cold and stepped out onto the balcony in his bare feet. He wrapped his arms around Harper and gazed out at the sky with her, hoping to find exactly what was so intriguing to her. He gave up and turned his focus on what was most intriguing to HIM at the moment. He tugged at the collar of her robe to reveal the soft, porcelain skin underneath which was immediately covered in goose bumps the moment it came into contact with the cold air. Finn gently kissed her neck and then rested his chin on her shoulder.

"*Come to bed with me,*" he pleaded.

Harper didn't answer.

Finn turned her around to face him, then leaned in to kiss her.

"*Please,*" he whispered almost inaudibly.

More silence.

"*Harper, what's wrong?*"

"*Nothing.*" Harper smiled, but Finn could see the vacancy in her eyes. "*You're right. It's freezing out here. Let's go in.*"

***

"So…you two were engaged," stated Dr. Harris.

Finn nodded.

"And she called off your wedding?"

Finn nodded again. "A week before we were supposed to get married."

"Wow. Well I can understand why this has been so difficult for you."

Finn glanced at Dr. Harris. "So, how do I get over this?"

"Time," replied Dr. Harris. "And money."

"Money?"

"Unless your insurance covers this," joked Dr. Harris.

Finn laughed. It was the first genuine laughter he's had in the past two months. "Yeah, I'm covered."

"Good, so then I'll see you next week?"

"Is that your way of sucking in patients?"

"Of course. How can you say no to that?"

"I can't. You got me. I'm beat."

<u>CHAPTER 6</u>

Harper tried to keep her breathing even as her legs were working overtime trying to make it up the hill. Her sprint had slowly turned into a light jog as the hill became steeper. Though she was enjoying the scenery of the nature in front of her and the million dollar houses below, she was in the zone and completely focused on her goal of reaching the top. Her focus was broken when she heard an out-of-breath straggler trying to catch up with her. Harper turned around and started jogging backwards.

"You're breathing like a Wookie," remarked Harper.

Kiley, out of breath, didn't have the energy for a clever comeback. "Oh God, can you please not use your nerdy 'Star Wars' references right now?" She struggled to catch her breath.

Harper continued jogging backwards, relishing in her friend's lack of energy. "Uh…you understood the reference, so obviously you've got a little bit of force within you."

"Please stop with the 'Star Wars' puns," begged Kiley. She could swear she was about to cough up a lung.

"And I believe when I first showed you the movies, you were the one who was pleading with me to show you 'Return of the Jedi' right after 'Empire Strikes Back,'" reminded Harper.

Kiley took a swig of water from her bottle and spit it out, trying to control her coughing fit. "Is it my fault they left me wanting to know what happened to Han? Besides, I wanted to see more of Lando. He was just uber cool."

Harper turned around and continued jogging up the hill.

"Okay, I'm gonna need a break," pleaded Kiley.

"We're almost at the top. Come on!" Harper felt her feet start to move quicker as she picked up her speed. Kiley, who's breathing was now resembling that of a smoking asthmatic, felt her legs starting to give out from under her and she started coughing uncontrollably.

"Just to let you know, I am literally eating your dust right now. If you were anything of a friend, you would show at least a tiny bit of concern."

Harper stopped and turned around to find her friend bent over with her hands on her knees, spitting her excess phlegm out onto the dirt.

"Wow. You truly have never been sexier," remarked Harper.

Kiley smiled, too tired to think of a worthy comeback. "Um…suck it?"

"No thanks. I'm good."

Kiley was slowly beginning to recover. She stood up and started walking. "Are you now? Is that what Finn would tell me if I asked him?"

Harper relented and slowed her pace so she could walk next to the taller girl. "Please don't talk to Finn. Or about him."

"I wouldn't dream of such a thing," informed Kiley. "But…if I *were* to ask him, what would he say?"

"He'd say mind your own damn business. And you have stupid hair."

Kiley lightheartedly pushed Harper. "He would never say that about my hair."

Harper smiled. "Seriously, though. I told you before, I've never had any complaints. From him or anybody else."

"I know, I know. You should get more practice though. I mean before Finn it was just those three other guys, right?"

"Yeah."

"Well, maybe it's time you start getting back out there. I mean, how long has it been?"

"A few months."

"That's tragic," replied Kiley.

"Uh…that's normal. Just because your libido is off the charts doesn't mean it's the same for me."

"Sure it does. We all have that instinct inside us. Some are just more in tune with it than others. I'm sure you and Finn went at it like crazy when you first got together."

Harper started picking up her speed, not knowing whether it was due to the nature of their conversation or the fact that she just wanted to reach the top already. "I guess. Maybe."

"You guess? You told me—"

"I may have exaggerated. I mean, it was a lot. Just maybe not as often as I let on."

Kiley turned her focus to the trail in front of her trying to control her breathing. "Oh. Why?"

"I don't know. I just felt like I had to keep up, or something."

"So you lied like a guy in a high school locker room?" Each word bore a sharp staccato sound with every breath she took.

"I embellished," replied Harper as she turned her power walk into a light jog.

"Why?" Kiley kept up with Harper's pace, determined to get an answer.

Harper kept silent as her jog turned into a sprint in the final stretch of their excursion. Kiley understood Harper's need to finish strong. There was no distracting her friend when she got that 'go big or go home' mentality. The girls pushed their legs up the hill as hard as they could, working up a sweat and kicking dust behind them. Finally, they reached the top and their panting soon subsided once they took in the view of the city below them. Twilight was setting in as the last glimpse of the sun disappeared behind the hills. Harper stood there, looking out on Los Angeles, feeling relieved to be away from the city lights for a while, but enjoying seeing them light up from afar like stars. She thought about Kiley's question and had no idea how she would explain her answer. Harper could feel her face getting warmer and turning red, and it wasn't from all the exercise. Once the redness reached her ears, she tried to hide it by turning away and looking down at the trail they've just completed.

Kiley couldn't be fooled. She immediately took notice of Harper's now-fuchsia face. "Oh, my God. Are you blushing?"

Harper continued to look away. "I don't know."

"You totally are. Come on, Harper. It's not that big a deal."

"I know it's not! You know me. I turn red if someone compliments the shirt I'm wearing. And turn to full-fledged purple if I hit a wrong note when I'm performing."

"Well you don't have to be embarrassed about this. It's just sex."

"To you, maybe."

Kiley took Harper's comment to heart. She knew how different they were and how sensitive Harper was. Kiley had been on her own for a while now. Much longer than Harper had been. They were raised differently with diverse values and views on certain aspects of life. Kiley sometimes envied Harper for her naivety.

Harper took a seat on a nearby rock and gazed out at the glowing lights scene below them. Kiley sat down next to her and waited for her friend so speak, knowing she obviously had something on her mind. They were silent for a few moments until Harper was ready.

"I used to cry every night...after Finn and I had sex."

Kiley looked at her friend, concerned. "What?"

"Not at first. But in the last few months of our relationship, I would just cry." Harper started kicking the dirt at her feet. "He never saw me. I never let him see me. I knew it would upset him. But I'd go into the bathroom and I would cry. And I had no idea why. I still don't, really. I just knew something obviously wasn't right."

"Is that why you called off the wedding?" Kiley wasn't exactly sure how to react to this revelation. She had always known something wasn't quite right between Harper and Finn, but always chalked it up to her own lack of relationship experience or perhaps even a little bit of jealousy. Who was she to say what was normal in a relationship?

"I don't know. Maybe. I mean, there were other contributing factors. But I just knew that wasn't a good sign."

Kiley nodded, not really knowing what to say. There had been times she cried after sex, too, but for very different reasons and not with someone she really cared about. It was more due to self-loathing than anything. "I wish you would have told me."

"Why? So you'd know what a freak I am?"

"Oh please. You know you're not a freak. Don't even say that."

"Well then what's wrong with me?"

"Nothing. Nothing at all. Things change, people change. You grow up, you grow apart."

"I really hurt him."

"He'll get over it. He's a guy. You'd be surprised at how emotionally disconnected they can become."

Harper rested her hands behind her on the rock, leaned back, and stretched out her legs. "Apparently I have that same ability."

"What do you mean?" asked Kiley.

Harper looked up and spotted the first star appearing in the night sky above her, watching as it flickered, fading and turning bright again. For a moment, she felt at peace. It was the simple things in life that satisfied Harper. Sitting at the top of this hill, taking in a breathtaking view, sharing her innermost thoughts with the person she trusted the most, sitting in silence when words weren't necessary…these factors were all adding up to be one of her most treasured moments in life. She couldn't help but think that there was a beautiful song somewhere in this moment.

Harper sighed as she relinquished the inhibitions of her thoughts. "I didn't feel anything."

"What?" Kiley patiently asked, knowing there were no shortages of cryptic non-sequiturs in conversations with her best friend.

"I didn't really feel anything. When Finn proposed. I didn't cry when it happened. Everyone I know who's ever been proposed to has cried. I didn't. I just sorta said yes. And that was it."

Kiley noticed how dirty her shins were from the run and started wiping the dirt off with her hands. "Did you want to say yes?"

"I don't know. I think so."

"So you felt nothing at all?"

"Shocked...sorta blindsided, I guess."

"Well, he did it in kind of a cheesy way. Christmas morning? With your family there? I mean, your parents knew about it before you did!"

"I know. But it was sweet."

"Yeah, sweet. But not the way you would have wanted it, right?"

"Yeah. How did you know?" asked Harper.

Kiley finished wiping off the rest of the dust from her legs. "Because I know you. When you told me he proposed and how he did it, I oohed and awed because that's what a best friend does. But I had a feeling you wanted to be excited but were just..."

"...going through the motions."

"Yeah," agreed Kiley. She looked at her friend and gave her a friendly nudge in the arm with her elbow. "There's nothing wrong with not crying, you know. Some people just aren't built that way." Kiley leaned her head on Harper's shoulder, taking this moment to catch her breath. She had no idea if what she was saying was any help to Harper. Advice wasn't her forte, but she was hoping at least some of what she said would bring a smile to her face and maybe bring her just a bit of comfort.

Harper nodded. "Yeah, I guess you're right."

"Besides, you're better off without him. You don't want to spend the rest of your life crying yourself to sleep." Kiley detached herself from the comfort of Harper's shoulder and looked at her watch. "We should probably go." She got up and started stretching her legs. "It's pretty dark and it's a long way down. And I'm tired and hungry. And my feet hurt. Carry me?" Kiley surprised Harper by jumping on her back. "Okay, I'm ready. Let's go."

Harper lurched forward, not expecting Kiley's sudden outburst. "I don't think so. Find your own way down."

Kiley got down and started running. "See you at the bottom."

Harper tried catching up with her. "Wait! Where the hell did all this energy come from?"

"I told you, I'm hungry. When I have food on my mind, there's no stopping me!" yelled Kiley as she made her way back down the path. "Besides, downhill is easier."

<u>CHAPTER 7</u>

Kiley could feel her mild headache getting worse as she approached the table right under the red and yellow Stella Artois neon sign. She started clearing away the glasses left by the group of guys who were treating a friend that had just lost his job. She grabbed the last couple of near-empty glasses containing melted ice and diluted gin and tonic and brought them over to the bar.

"He was kinda cute. You should have gone for it," remarked Kiley.

"Oh sure. That's exactly what I need. Another mouth to feed," replied Erin, the bar's other server.

"At least without a job, he'd be home all the time. Free babysitting."

"Nah. I've pretty much resigned myself to the fact that not only will I never have another boyfriend, I'm probably never gonna get laid again. At least not for the next fourteen years. And by then, I'll be too old to enjoy it." Erin was behind the bar, filling up five glasses of draught beer.

"Don't be so negative. It lowers your hotness factor."

"Can't go much lower than zero."

Kiley picked up an empty crate, put it on the bar and started loading it up with empty bottles. "Confidence. Try it sometime. It helps."

Erin placed the beer-filled glasses onto a tray and carried them to a table near the back. "That sounds like too much work," she stated while walking past Kiley. After delivering the drinks, Erin walked back to the bar and watched as Kiley finished filling up the crate with empty bottles. Kiley picked up the crate and headed towards the back door leading into the alley.

Erin grabbed her purse from under the bar and followed her. "I think it's time for a break. I need a cigarette and you need someone to open the door for you." She swung the door open and allowed Kiley to go in front of her to deliver the crate on the floor near their recycle bin.

"You're way too hard on yourself," informed Kiley. "Hell, you're three years younger than me. You've got youth on your side."

Erin pulled a pack of cigarettes out of her purse. "Yeah, but I look thirty-two, not twenty-two. You at least look like you're still eighteen." She fumbled around with her lighter, placed the cigarette in her mouth and brought the lighter up to the cigarette, igniting a flicker in the dark alley.

"That's because I don't smoke," retorted Kiley, who was almost tempted to pull the cigarette out of Erin's mouth and throw it on the ground.

Erin inhaled the smoke, causing the end of her cigarette to light up even more, then exhaled dramatically. "No. It's because you don't have a four-year-old kid at home depriving you of sleep."

Kiley nodded in understanding. "Touché. But the smoking probably doesn't help."

"It's my one vice. Let me have it." Erin sat down on the dilapidated folding chair right outside the back door and flicked the end of her 'vice' to get rid of the excess ashes.

Kiley stood in front of Erin and folded her arms. "It's getting cold."

Erin nodded. "You can go back in if you want. I just need a few more minutes."

"That's okay. I'll wait." Kiley ran her left hand up and down her right arm, trying to prevent herself from getting goose bumps from the chilly air setting in. She watched as Erin drew in more smoke from her Marlboro Red and gawked intently as the smoke escaped from Erin's nostrils. Kiley simply could not understand the appeal of smoking. She had done her fair share of rebellious smoking as a teenager, but it was mainly for show. In reality, she hated the ashy taste in her mouth and the musky aroma that clung to her clothes afterwards. It didn't take her long to realize it wasn't worth it, but far be it from her to preach about it to Erin. "You know; I really do think you should put yourself out there more. I think it would be good for you."

Erin scoffed at Kiley's suggestion. "Thanks, but I don't think so. I'm damaged goods. And eventually, I'll just be an old barmaid."

"Look, just because some asshole knocked you up at seventeen and then left right after you gave birth doesn't mean you're damaged. It means HE is. You don't have to shut yourself off to guys. And you don't have to work here for the rest of your life. This is just a temporary fix."

Kiley didn't know why, but she felt a sort of sisterly bond with Erin. There was this inherent need to protect her, like an older sister would. Perhaps it was because Kiley never had a sister and always admired how protective Harper was over Emily. All she knew for sure was, like Harper, Erin wasn't living up to her full potential.

Erin threw the rest of her cigarette on the ground and stomped it out with her shoe. "I don't have a choice. I do this because I have to. And right now, I have nowhere else to go. I've got a kid to take care of."

"I know."

Erin stayed seated and adjusted her form-fitting t-shirt, pulling the hem down over the back of her jeans to block the draft. "What about you?"

"What about me?" asked Kiley, wanting to go back inside. She hated when people turned things around on her.

"You don't need to be here. You could be doing so many other things with your life."

Kiley walked over to the door and leaned up against it. "Like what?"

"Anything. You can travel. You can go back to school. You can model."

Kiley started to laugh. "Doubtful on the modeling thing. You need coordination for that."

"My point is, you have the freedom to do anything. Why are you still here? This town can so easily break people. Why do you stay?"

Kiley leaned her head against the door with her arms still crossed. "I don't know. It just doesn't feel right to leave. I've got responsibilities. And friends."

"You have a car payment and Harper."

"A car payment is a very big responsibility. And I do have other friends besides Harper."

"You do?"

"Yeah! I'm not a loser with just one friend. I happen to be very popular. Always have been. I have…well, there's you. And Graham is like a brother to me. A really old brother, but a brother nonetheless. And…well, the point is, I have friends. And I'm not ready to leave them."

Erin stood up and faced Kiley. "Well just out of curiosity, if you didn't have all these friends, what would you want to do with your life?"

Kiley contemplated Erin's question for a moment. She couldn't remember the last time anyone asked her that question. She had never really thought about it, even when she was younger. The lack of stability in her home life reflected her current situation. Coming from someone who was deprived of any real consistency as a child, what with her father's temper and her mother's emotional detachment. Kiley found it difficult to choose any sort of career path. She couldn't see herself doing the same thing day in and day out. With bartending, she felt some control over having the ability to leave whenever she wanted and do something else. Even though she hadn't done so yet. This was the longest job she'd ever held, though there have been days when she had come close to quitting.

The only thing Kiley ever really wanted to do was travel. She wanted to see the world. Or at least the rest of the country, but she had no idea how she would make a living doing that. She could write a travel book or work as a correspondent for a travel show. But she felt such undertakings would require too much time, money, and talent. Kiley refused to believe she had any sort of skill. The only skill she thought she had was finding the talent and aptitude in others, yet she always failed to use her skill on herself.

Kiley still had no clue where her life was going, but there was one job that she always saw herself doing. It was far from fancy, didn't pay well and required some manual labor. Yet the thought of it excited Kiley for reasons she couldn't explain. It was an idea she came up with when she met Harper and watched her perform for the first time.

She smiled and looked at Erin. "I wanna be a roadie."

"A roadie?" Erin wasn't quite expecting that answer.

"Yeah. Wake up in a new place every day. Hang out with talented musicians. Doesn't sound like a bad gig to me."

Erin held the door open to go back inside.

"Hmm…well, do you know any bands that you could be a roadie for?"

Kiley walked past her, back into the bar. "Why do you think I get on Harper's ass about performing and recording more? I'll be HER roadie."

Erin shook her head and grinned while closing the door behind them. "Whatever makes you happy. Sounds like fun."

***

Harper watched the lights on her tuner switch back and forth from red to green as she adjusted the machine head on her acoustic Alvarez guitar. When the final string was in tune, she switched off the tuner and strummed the ¾ size guitar, releasing a perfectly tuned G chord radiating off the Elixir guitar strings. She got up and placed the Alvarez on the guitar stand next to her electric Fender Stratocaster. She then grabbed her Gibson J45 by its neck and sat back down, putting the guitar pick on the arm of the chair she was sitting in. She lightly ran her fingers over the strings, picking out the melody of one of the first songs she wrote. As quietly as she was hitting the strings, the music still echoed fairly loud through the garage. Harper loved the acoustics in this place. She always thought it would be the perfect space for her own studio because of the stellar sound quality. Unfortunately, a studio and all the equipment that comes with it, costs money.

The mortgage for the house was low enough for her to be able to pay it every month. And she was making enough at the bookstore to get by, but there was no way she could afford the luxury of a studio. So she recorded her songs in other people's studios for about a hundred dollars an hour. It wasn't the most ideal situation, but it was enough to make her happy knowing her songs were at least recorded, regardless of the quality. Lately though, seeing as how the bookstore didn't pay her much and she was only getting about fifty dollars in tips when she performed, Harper hadn't had enough money to record anything. Still, she considered herself lucky. She had food to eat, a roof over her head, and clothes on her back. And if things ever got really bad, though she hated thinking about it or even admitting it, she could always sell the house. That would be the last thing Harper would ever want to do, but she always kept it in the back of her mind as an option if her money issues were ever out of control.

Harper took her capo and fastened it to the third fret on her Gibson and started arbitrarily plucking the strings, enjoying the sound each note was making. She loved this guitar. It was her pride and joy, and the most recent addition to her collection, if you can consider three guitars a collection. She worked tirelessly, saving up little by little for four years. Until finally, a year ago, she was just two hundred dollars shy of having enough money to get it. Finn and Kiley ended up pitching in a hundred each, with a fair amount of protest from Harper. They insisted on giving her the money, especially after the terrible year she had just endured, and she finally brought home her coveted four-thousand-dollar guitar. For Harper, it was worth every penny.

In the past year, she had written some of her best songs with that guitar and knew there would be a lot more to come. Harper rarely ever spoiled herself. The only thing she owned that was more expensive than her Gibson was her car. Other than that, she pretty much tried to live within her means, all the while trying to refrain from thinking about Oscar Wilde's famous words: "Anyone who lives within their means suffers from a lack of imagination." Obviously Oscar Wilde never lived in LA, where if you took one step outside your monetary comfort zone, you could easily be bankrupt within a year. All because you wanted that big screen TV or a new BMW. Harper never saw the point of spending big when all it did was cause stress and buyer's remorse.

The Gibson would have been the fourth guitar in Harper's collection. Not a day went by where Harper didn't wish she still had her first guitar with her: the acoustic Takamine her father bought her. It was the one she used to write her first song. She may have used that guitar a little less when she bought her Alvarez, but it was still important to her and one of the best memories she had of her father. But Harper tried her best not to dwell on it. The Takamine was gone and there was nothing she could do about it. She closed her eyes, positioned her left fingers on the strings of her Gibson and began to strum. After the short intro, her voice began to fill the garage as she sang the words she had written two years ago, right after her sister ran away. She could feel herself letting the words affect her. Everything she had ever felt, all the fights they had, every problem she had with Emily, how much she missed her and had been hurt by her, came pouring out of her voice and into the air, with no one there to hear it. At that moment, Harper found herself wishing Emily was there to hear her words. Maybe then her little sister would finally understand how destructive she'd been to herself and everyone around her.

***

The closet that once held all of Harper's clothes and other personal belongings was now nearly empty as she threw the last article of clothing over her head, landing behind her in a pile of other clothes. Once the closet was completely empty, she got up and looked around her room. The horrified look on her face was not the reaction to the disarray her room was in and the fact that all of her belongings were strewn everywhere to the point that you could no longer see the carpet anymore, but was more the result of the fact that she still hadn't located what she'd been searching for. She hopped, skipped and jumped her way out of her room in order to avoid stepping on anything valuable along the way and proceeded to scour the rest of the house for the third time. Her footsteps covered all areas of the living room, kitchen, garage, and even the bathroom. She peeked her head into her parents' room, but knew it wouldn't be there. She went back to her bedroom, stood in the doorway, and leaned over as far as she could to grab the keys off her dresser. With the keys in her hand, she went outside, unlocked the car door and frantically began searching the back seat, without any luck. She then popped the trunk and examined its contents very slowly, making sure nothing was missed. All that lay in the trunk were jumper cables, a gym bag, and a half empty jug of coolant. Dejected, Harper slammed the trunk down and went back inside.

She decided to search her room one more time, got down on her hands and knees and sifted through all the items on the floor. The feeling of panic that had set in an hour ago was now turning into full-fledged terror. Harper didn't dream of calling her parents to ask if they've seen it. She didn't want to interrupt their much-needed weekend vacation in Las Vegas, but she also wasn't in the mood to hear any lectures of how important it is to keep track of your stuff and how irresponsible it is to lose something like that. Harper got into a pushup position and stuck her face under her bed, hoping she had missed it. She collapsed in defeat when it was nowhere to be found.

"Em! Have you seen my guitar?" yelled Harper, not bothering to get up from her vanquished position. She buried her face in a pile of her clothes while waiting for a response.

Emily stood in the doorway of Harper's room, eating a bowl of cereal. "You lost it?"

"I didn't lose it. It's just not where I left it."

Emily nodded and took another bite of her cereal. "Drag."

Harper brought her head up to look at her sister's disheveled appearance. Her normally healthy, shiny hair was stringy and looked like it hadn't been washed in days. Her black and white camo pants were wrinkled and her black spaghetti string tank top didn't even cover the fresh tattoo on Emily's shoulder; the one she had been so desperate to hide from her parents.

"I just played it last night. Can you help me look for it?" asked Harper.

"I would, but I don't want to." Emily turned around and started to walk away.

Harper, still on the floor, called after her. "You look like shit, you know that? When was the last time you showered?"

Emily turned around. "When was the last time you minded your own fucking business?"

Harper started to get up. "You keep dressing like that, and mom and dad are gonna notice that tattoo."

"Well, they're in Vegas right now, aren't they?" Emily put the cereal bowl down on the coffee table in the living room.

Harper stood there, observing her sister and realized just how much her appearance had altered. It broke her heart to see her little sister turning out the way she was, but deep down Harper was hoping it was all a phase. Still, it wasn't just her appearance that had changed. Her personality and mood had altered as well. Harper never touched on the subject, but she pretty much knew what her sister had been doing in the last six months and knew it was the reason for how much she had changed.

Harper cocked her head to one side. "You mind if I take a look in your room?"

Emily folded her arms. "It's not in there."

Harper started walking towards Emily's room. "I'm sure it's not, but I just want to check for myself."

Emily followed her older sister. "What, you don't trust me?"

Harper turned to face her sister. "Of course I trust you. I trust you more than I trust anyone. You're my sister. I just think I'm gonna go crazy if I don't search everywhere. Hell, I looked under the couch cushions. I'm desperate." She turned around and headed into Emily's room.

Emily charged after her. "Wait! Harper, it's not in there, I promise!"

Harper stopped once she was in her sister's room. She realized she hadn't been in here in a while and noticed that it had changed just as much as Emily had. Where there were once posters of Disney characters and dolphins, were now blank walls, with the exception of a few disturbing drawings hung up on the bulletin board. The floor was much filthier than Harper's, and Harper at least had the excuse of having the entire contents of her closet currently on her floor. She looked over at Emily's dresser and noticed a bag of marijuana sitting there in plain sight. Emily knew her sister had spotted it, and closed her eyes, bracing for the worst. Harper walked over to the dresser and examined the bag. Then, she opened the top drawer and dug around to find another bag, this one almost empty containing with a white, powdery substance.

Harper scrutinized the bags for a minute. "Shit," she mumbled to herself and turned around to face her sister. "Emily...what are you..."

Emily's eyes were still closed, anticipating Harper's words.

Instead of giving her sister a verbal lashing, Harper stood there, stunned, as a sickening feeling penetrated her stomach. She felt her face go flush as a sad epiphany slowly entered her mind. Harper was no longer concerned with the drugs she just found in her sister's dresser, and more concerned about what else she would find. She dropped the bags on the dresser and started digging further into the top drawer.

Emily opened her eyes and hurtled toward Harper. "There's nothing else in there."

"I'm inclined not to believe you."

"Harper, please. I promise, there's nothing else." She grabbed her sister's arm just as Harper had pulled out a wad of cash.

Harper stared at the money for a moment, then slowly started counting it. Her nausea began to increase with every twenty-dollar bill she tallied up. "Three hundred dollars."

Emily could feel a lump rise up in her throat.

"Harper..."

"Three hundred dollars," repeated Harper. "Three hundred. Which is about how much my guitar would go for." Once all the pieces were added up, Harper grew dizzy knowing exactly what the outcome was. She violently threw the money at Emily. "You sold my guitar!!?? You fucking sold my guitar!!??" Unable to control her rage, she lunged at Emily, grabbing her arms and forcefully shaking her. "Where is it? Where is it!?"

Emily was speechless. All she could do was shake her head.

"Where's my guitar!?"

Emily couldn't stave off the piercing pain in her arms anymore. She broke away from her sister's grip and took a step back, rubbing her right arm with her left hand. "I'm sorry. I'm so sorry."

Harper took a deep breath. "Where is it?"

Emily shook her head again. "It's gone. I'm sorry. It's gone. I don't know where. I don't even know who I sold it to. Just some guy."

Harper started to rub her head with her hands, trying to keep any tears from pouring out. "You sold my guitar for drug money?"

Emily was silent.

"How long has this been going on, Em? How long have you been..." Harper paused. "Wait. You know what? I don't care. I don't care because you and I are done. So I don't give a shit." She shoved her little sister as she stormed out of the room, leaving Emily standing alone with three hundred dollars cash at her feet.

***

The flatness of the A string on her guitar infiltrated Harper's ears, causing her to grimace at the out of tune sound. She turned the tuning peg slightly to the left to bring the string back in tune. Instead of continuing to practice, she put the guitar down and tried her best not to dwell on the fact that she longed just one more time to play the Takamine her father bought her. Instead of reflecting on the past and gearing her anger toward Emily, she decided it was time to take out her frustration yet again. She fastened her wraps, secured her gloves, hit play on the cd player, and proceeded to practice her jabs on the punching bag, listening to the wise words of Freddie Mercury repeating the words "don't stop me now."

CHAPTER 8

It didn't seem to matter to Finn that his shoelace was untied. He didn't even notice it until he brought his leg up to rest on his other thigh. He allowed the loose shoelace to dangle, rubbing up against his leg as he restlessly bounced his ankle up and down. The silence in the air was filled with the cracking of each of his individual fingers, one by one as he unwittingly crushed each knuckle with his thumb. When there were no more knuckles to crack, he discovered there were still plenty of fingernails to gnaw on, transferring his nervous energy to every part of his body he possibly could. Anything to avoid actually speaking, not knowing exactly what to say. Eight minutes had passed by the time he got to the middle finger on his left hand. He had no idea where to go from there.

"You know, I've heard that cracking your knuckles can lead to arthritis when you're older."

Finn momentarily stopped nibbling on his nails. "Oh yeah? And what about biting fingernails?"

Dr. Harris leaned back into her chair and cocked her head to one side, "Just a really gross habit."

Finn brought his hand down and rested it on his lap. "Okay. So what's on the agenda for today?"

"You tell me."

Finn shrugged. "I haven't heard from her in a couple days."

"Well, you're broken up. That's natural."

"Yeah, maybe. It's just, she's been through a lot. And I want to be there for her. I just don't know how I can without it seeming like I want to get back together with her."

"Do you want to get back together?"

Finn paused for a moment. "Yeah, of course. I love her."

"Does she still love you?"

Finn looked over toward the window, not wanting to answer the question. He knew the answer; he just didn't want to say it out loud. Thinking about the whole situation and finally opening up about it was starting to wear on Finn's emotions. He continued to stare at the window as he felt his eyes welling up with tears, afraid to blink in fear of letting one escape. His attempt to prevent such a thing from happening, was an epic failure. Once one tear started rolling down his face, it was soon joined by two more, then five more until he finally had to wipe them away with his shirt sleeve.

***

"I need another trash bag! This one's full."

"I'll get one for you, Mom." Harper got up from her comfortable spot on the couch and ran to the kitchen to get more trash bags. When she returned, Finn was sitting in her seat.

"Out," Harper gestured with her thumb. "Come on. Up you get. That's my spot."

Finn looked around. "Is your name on it?"

Harper scoffed. "Generic, much? Come on." She bent over and picked up a piece of wrapping paper covered with snowmen, wadded it up and playfully threw it at Finn.

Harper's mom chimed in. "Finn, you might want to do what she says. That's been her spot every Christmas morning since she was six years old."

"Well, she can sit on my lap. I can be her new spot," explained Finn as he grabbed his girlfriend and pulled her down onto his lap. Harper smiled as he gently kissed her neck. "I love you," he whispered just loud enough for only Harper to hear.

"I love you, too," she whispered back. "But I still want my spot back."

"Get a room, kids…Wait! No…don't." Harper's dad was in the middle of unwrapping a present when he paused, looking at who it was from. "Harp, where's your sister?"

Harper shrugged. "Probably still in bed. I knocked on her door twice already."

"Unbelievable. She can't even drag her ass out of bed on Christmas morning? I want her here when I'm opening her present," complained Harper's dad, Paul. "EMILY! GET YOUR BUTT OUT HERE NOW!!!!"

"Shhh…Honey, you're gonna wake the whole neighborhood," Harper's mother warned.

"It's Christmas morning, Trish. The whole neighborhoods already awake."

"I'm here. You can stop yelling now," said Emily, rubbing her head and sullenly taking a seat on the recliner. Her bloodshot eyes didn't go unnoticed by Harper, who's disapproving look made Emily keep her focus on the ground.

"Merry Christmas, sweetie." Mrs. Foley kissed Emily on the forehead and handed her a present.

"Thanks, Mom." She looked over at her dad, who just opened her present. "So, what do you think, Dad?"

He held up a black, stylish button-down shirt. "I think you're trying to make me cooler than I actually am."

"Well, with that shirt, now you can fool the world."

Mr. Foley smiled at his younger daughter. "Thanks for thinking I can pull this off."

"Well, mom helped me pay for it." Emily started unwrapping her present from Harper, still avoiding eye contact. She pulled the last of the Santa Claus wrapping paper away to find four different cd's that she had been dying to have. She grinned thinking about how scary it was knowing her sister knew her so well. The grin soon faded when she thought about Harper's reaction if she ever found out she already had those cd's hiding underneath her bed so no one would suspect she had stolen them. "Thanks, Harper. These are great."

"No problem. It's good to know you at least have some good taste in music," replied Harper.

Emily looked over at her sister's boyfriend. "So Finn, what did you get my sister? The $4,000 Gibson guitar she's been drooling over for the last two years?"

Harper shot Emily a look. "If he did, I wouldn't let YOU anywhere near it."

Emily retreated and went back to lackadaisically thumbing through the cd's Harper got her.

Finn chuckled nervously, obviously too focused on his own agenda to notice the tension between the two girls. "No, not exactly."

Harper, still sitting on her boyfriend's lap, looked back at him and wrapped her arms around his neck. "Good. You know I'd have a fit if you ever spent that much money on me." She leaned in and whispered, "But you did get me something, right?"

Finn smiled. "Yeah. Yeah, I did." He looked over at Harper's parents, who smiled and nodded, anxiously awaiting Finn's next move. He took a deep breath, started to get up and sat Harper down back in her spot. "Um...well, Harper...I...I talked to your mom and dad and...um...," Finn took a moment to compose himself. He walked over past the Christmas tree and reached behind to pick up his present to his girlfriend he had hidden earlier that morning. He walked back over to her, took in one more deep breath, and got down on one knee in front of her. "Harper, I love you more than I ever thought I could be capable of loving someone. I met you and everything in my life started making sense. And I knew why I was here and why you were brought into my life." Finn paused a moment to regain his composure. He was trying extremely hard not to let his voice crack. "I know we're young and I know you still have another semester left of school. But I'm willing to wait. I'll wait for you as long as you want me to. As long as you do me the honor of one day becoming your husband." He brought the ring box up to her and opened it revealing a half-carat diamond ring. "Will you marry me?"

Harper sat there, her mouth half open, almost in shock over what just happened. "I...uh..." She was completely taken aback. Guitar strings and a tuner, she was expecting, but this...this was definitely a surprise.

Finn had a smile plastered on his face. Harper simply couldn't resist that beaming look on his face and she smiled right along with him.

She nodded. "Yes. Of course."

Finn jumped up and pulled Harper up to hug her. He held her tighter than he'd ever held her before, not wanting to let go. It was by far the best moment of his life.

***

"So what's wrong with me? Am I depressed, or something?" asked Finn.

"Do you feel depressed?"

"I don't know," he sniffled. "I guess I just feel shut off. Like I can't allow myself to feel anything, otherwise it'll hurt too much. I just feel so stupid for proposing. And for not seeing that maybe her heart wasn't in it." Finn cleared his throat, which was cracking from the little sobs he was giving off. "I'm sorry."

Dr. Harris reached for the box of Kleenex on her desk and handed it to Finn. "For what? Crying?"

Finn nodded in embarrassment and tried to stifle the sound when he blew his nose.

"Have you cried since the breakup?"

Finn wadded up the used tissue in his hand. "The night it happened. I was blindsided. It seemed to have come out of nowhere. So I cried because I didn't know what else to do. But this is the first time since then."

"Well that's good," encouraged Dr. Harris. "That's progress. You're getting in tune with your emotions instead of avoiding them. It's a step in the right direction."

Finn let out a cynical chuckle. "It feels like I'm regressing."

Finn's tears started to let up. He wasn't used to this. He wasn't the type of guy who expended a lot of emotion over things. A lot of it had to do with his upbringing. He grew up the son of a typical middle class family in Ohio. His father taught him early on to suppress any pain or sadness. It started when Finn was in first grade and a bully had been threatening him. One day, Finn had enough of the bullying and pushed his aggressor back into the swing set on the playground. It was a brave move, but unfortunately, not a wise one because his tormentor rallied back with a punch to Finn's nose. He ran home crying, mortified over what had happened. His father sat him down and told him that crying was for weak men and that he was proud of his son for standing up to the bully, but not happy knowing he cried all the way home. After that, Finn did everything in his power to keep from crying during stressful or upsetting situations. He was unsuccessful at times because he was only human. However, he couldn't help feeling guilty over what his father might say if he ever witnessed him shedding a tear.

Finn managed to survive his grade school years, despite that pesky bully and grew up into a fine young man that would make any parent proud. He moved to California to study business and graduated Cum Laude with an MBA from USC, and now worked as the head sales manager for one of the top case manufacturing companies in the country. He sold cases of every kind: guitar cases, drum kit cases, p.a. system cases, sports equipment cases, shipping cases. He took the job because it was sort of a common ground for him and Harper. Though they got along great and loved each other very much, they didn't have a lot of the same interests. He figured this would be minor way of having some sort of common bond since she loved music and he sold music equipment. He had even supplied her with a few free guitar cases over the years. After starting the job right out of college and quickly moving his way up, he now felt stagnate with where he was professionally. His boss loved him and he couldn't complain about the pay, but nothing seemed as good as it was when he had Harper to come home to every day. His professional career didn't seem to matter as much to him as long as he had her. He felt everything else in life was inconsequential. It was a mistake he had grown to regret. He never should have allowed his entire life to revolve around another person and he was determined to not let it happen again. And if that meant crying in front of a woman he'd only met a few times, then so be it.

"I just don't like it when she's in pain," remarked Finn.

Dr. Harris crossed her left leg over her right and leaned forward. "Well, does she care about you when *you're* in pain?"

"Yes. Well, obviously not right now, but she did. She really is a good person. She's just had a lot on her mind lately. It's not her fault."

"I understand that, Finn. I do. And I'm not trying to vilify anyone in any way. I'm just trying to help you gain some perspective on a post-breakup relationship." She put down her clipboard. "Tell me, why would she be in pain? What's going on with her?"

"Well, a lot has changed for her over the past couple years. And recently, she's been having issues with her sister."

"Her sister? What's going on between them?"

"Well, nothing. That's just it. Her sister took off almost two years ago and hasn't been heard from since.

Harper tried looking for her. We all tried, but I guess she just didn't want to be found. And Harper's been thinking about her lately. A lot, from what I understand. I think a lot of it has to do with the fact that two years ago—"

"Dr. Harris, sorry to interrupt you." The door flung open so quickly, a gust of wind blew through the office.

Dr. Harris turned around and responded curtly. "I'm with a patient. What is it?"

Sarah, Dr. Harris' receptionist, hesitated for a moment. "I'm sorry, it's just...he's on the phone. You told me to tell you if he called..."

"Okay, okay. Thank you. I'll get it."

Sarah backed up out the door. "Okay. Line two." The door closed behind her and Dr. Harris turned back around to face Finn.

"I'm so sorry. I have to take this. It'll just be a minute." She walked over to her desk, picked up the phone and smiled at Finn. "Don't worry. I won't charge you."

Finn gave her a half smile and sat patiently, trying not to listen in on her phone call.

"Hi...I'm surprised you even called...Yes, I know...I know, but that's no excuse to...Steven, I'm not going to argue with you about this." She turned away, put the phone receiver closer to her mouth and began to whisper. "Because it's *your* responsibility, too...Well, I'm having a hard time believing you..."

All the way from the couch, Finn could hear the muffled voice on the other end of the phone. Whoever it was did not sound happy.

"You're five months behind...I'm doing what I can, but I need...No. No, that's not acceptable...No, you promised me you'd...Steven, don't hang up. Don't hang up…can you at least give me a number where I can…Hello? Hello?" Dr. Harris sighed and hung up the phone. She came back around to sit in her chair. "I'm so sorry about that. You shouldn't have had to witness that. Anyway, you were saying?"

"What was that?"

"Nothing. It was nothing. Just some unfinished business."

"Sounded pretty intense."

"Yeah. Well I like intensity. It spices things up." She nervously grabbed her clipboard and pen and began tapping her foot on the floor.

Finn took this moment to fully take in Dr. Harris' wardrobe. He hadn't really noticed before because he was too busy focusing on himself and his problems, but now that he really looked at her, he realized she brought casual Friday to a whole new level. Her yoga pants and ribbed tank top were accessorized with her gray sneakers. It was a rather odd way for a professional woman to dress, whether it was Friday or not.

She noticed he was gawking at her garb and she looked down at what she was wearing. "Oh, I have a yoga class after this. I hope you don't mind me being so informal."

"You take yoga?"

Dr. Harris grinned. "No," she replied sheepishly. "I mean, I have…twice. But that was about all I could handle. I just told you that because it seems like a more legitimate reason. But I'm actually going paintballing after this. I try not to schedule anything past noon on Fridays, but I made an exception for you."

"Paintballing?" Finn was stunned. That was not the explanation he was expecting at all.

"Yeah. I'm in a paintball league in Pasadena. We meet up every Friday."

Finn was taken aback by her response. This wasn't the type of woman he figured would go paintballing on a regular basis. It was then he realized he really didn't know that much about the woman who was listening to his problems every week. For all he knew, she could be a raging alcoholic or an ex-con posing as a psychiatrist in an attempt to extort people. Finn talked himself out of those thoughts when he regarded the diplomas and certificates all over her wall. He also remembered she came highly recommended by one of his co-workers. So he decided to give her the benefit of the doubt, despite the fact that she seemed to be somewhat of an oddball. He actually found that rather comforting.

"I can't say I've ever been paintballing," remarked Finn.

"Really? Oh, you should try it. It's so much fun and a great way to relieve stress."

Finn found it charming that Dr. Harris' eyes lit up when talking about her extracurricular pastime. "I prefer playing videogames."

"Well, maybe there's a paintballing video game. Then we could go head-to-head."

Finn laughed, "I'd school you."

"We'll have to see about that. You should come paintballing with me."

Finn froze for a moment. He definitely wasn't expecting that. "Really?"

He sensed that Dr. Harris immediately regretted suggesting such a thing, likely reminding herself that she was the doctor, and he was a patient. She sat up straight and began to tap the pen on her clipboard.

"Uh...well, on second thought, that probably wouldn't be appropriate. I apologize for that. But, you should maybe think about taking up another hobby. Something besides video games to get your mind off of the breakup. And to keep yourself sane."

Finn could tell Dr. Harris was slightly mortified, but he didn't see the big deal about it.

"I'll think about it. I used to be an excellent badminton player."

Dr. Harris was avoiding eye contact at all costs. "Really?"

Finn shook his head. "No. Never played badminton. But I used to have some good bowling skills." He noticed Dr. Harris was still a little uncomfortable about what she said and decided to cut the tension by keeping up the conversation; a first for them since she's usually the one who has to twist his arm to talk. "So how did you get into paintballing?"

Dr. Harris discontinued the tapping on her clipboard. "I know. It's odd. A forty-three-year-old gun-toting woman running around in a field picking off unsuspecting paintballers one by one. And yes, in case you were wondering, I'm awesome at it."

"Impressive."

"I know. You should be thankful I'm your psychiatrist. You'd be hard pressed to find anyone cooler. In all seriousness, though, a friend of mine took me for my fortieth birthday, just as a joke. She said it was either that or skydiving and skydiving was way too expensive for her and this way, we could keep our feet on the ground. Little did she know, I actually had a knack for it. Impeccable aim. It was the most fun I'd had in a long time."

Finn leaned in, very interested in Dr. Harris' story. "And how does that make you feel?"

"Very funny," she scoffed. "It makes me feel just fine, thank you. But enough about me. Let's get back to you. What happened to Harper and her sister two years ago?"

Finn was hoping she wouldn't come back to this. It was a long story and there was no way he could tell it within the next eighteen minutes of his remaining time. "Believe it or not, I kind of don't feel like talking about Harper right now."

Dr. Harris began writing on her clipboard.

"What are you writing?" asked Finn.

"I'm marking the date and time. I'm thinking this is a first for you."

Finn shook his head and heaved a sigh. Of course he managed to find the most frustrating head doctor in all of Los Angeles.

***

After his appointment, Finn headed straight home feeling vulnerable and a little more exposed than he was comfortable with. He knew it was a positive thing that he was being more open and forthcoming with Dr. Harris, but it scared him knowing that someone besides Harper was beginning to see past his exterior. The whole way home, he was debating on whether or not he would go back to therapy. Still, in the back of his mind he couldn't stop thinking about the quasi-invitation he got from Dr. Harris, and began to regret not going paintballing. Though it was rather crisp outside due to the impending fall weather, the sun was still shining with hardly a cloud in the sky. It would have been a nice day to spend outside getting some much-needed exercise. That was one thing he missed about Harper. She always stayed in the best shape she could, which made him want to do the same. Lately however, that's all gone out the window. Depression can take a serious toll on one's body, and it was nearly impossible for Finn to get motivated to do much of anything anymore.

Finn got out of his car, and walked toward his apartment complex, absentmindedly twirling his key ring around his finger. He was so immersed in his thoughts, he paid no attention to his surroundings and before he knew it, he was on the third floor of his apartment building. He had no recollection of walking up the stairs, but he came back to reality just in time before he nearly stumbled over someone sitting on the floor, leaning against his doorway. He came to an abrupt stop and studied what exactly it was that was preventing him from entering his apartment. It didn't take long to realize it was a young woman who was sleeping at his door with a jacket draped over her. He had no idea who she was waiting for and wondered if she had the wrong place.

While looking her over, for a split second, his heart jumped when he briefly thought that maybe it was Harper sitting out in the cold, waiting for him to come home so they could talk. That was short-lived, however when he knelt down and discovered it wasn't her. He gently brushed his hand against her arm. The girl began to stir, finally opening her eyes and squinting at the man hovering over her. She pulled the jacket off of her and sat up straight without taking her eyes off of him.

"Finn?"

Instead of jumping, Finn could swear his heart stopped beating altogether when he became eerily aware of why he thought the young woman was Harper. She sounded just like her and had the same piercing blue eyes. Finn cocked his head to one side and examined the girl in front of him. Her clothes were slightly worn and tattered. A mini skirt, tights with holes in them and tennis shoes weren't the best choice for the chilly weather. Her hair was dark, almost black, but Finn could tell it was dyed because of the obvious blonde roots that were growing in. She was wearing layer upon layer of makeup, including dark lipstick and thick mascara that was smudged from her eyes tearing up because of the cold. This girl looked like she'd been to hell and back. After perusing the girl a little longer, Finn could see through the makeup, the clothes, and the hair and realized who this young girl was.

"Oh, my God. Emily?"

CHAPTER 9

Finn took a couple steps back trying to comprehend exactly what was happening. After two years of futile searching, making endless phone calls, and putting up missing person fliers, he refused to believe Emily could be back in their lives just like that. It just seemed too easy and felt somewhat anticlimactic after all the effort they put in trying to find her. He stood there, his mouth half gaping open, his heart racing with a thousand questions running through his mind. Emily got up, tucked her jacket under her arm, and picked up her bag.

"So, are you gonna let me in? I've been out here for a while."

Finn nodded while struggling to find his apartment key. He tried to keep his hands from visibly shaking, but his nerves were making it difficult. Once he got the door open, he allowed Emily to go in first. He closed the door behind him as Emily dropped her bag on the floor and looked around Finn's modest abode.

"Hmm…"

"What?" asked Finn.

"Nothing. Nothing at all."

Finn stood in the middle of his living room as Emily gave herself a tour of his one-bedroom apartment. There were too many questions swirling around in his head. It was only a matter of time before he had to vocalize them.

"Where have you been?"

4

Emily peeked her head inside the bathroom. "Lots of places."

"When did you get back to L.A.?"

"Just today."

"Well…what have you been doing this whole time?"

"Finn, please. I've been up for seventy-two hours straight. My head is wrecked. I'm filthy and I'm starving. I need a minute to just chill before you start with the interrogation." She headed into the kitchen and started rummaging around. "Do you have anything to eat?"

Finn was confounded by how presumptuous Emily's behavior was. "Please. Help yourself," he remarked sardonically.

Emily turned an empty bag of potato chips upside down, hoping to catch a few residual crumbs. "Finn, are you really gonna let me starve?"

Finn's eyes rolled up, exasperated. "No. I have cereal. No milk. Boxed mac and cheese, but again, no milk and no butter. And I have bread. But I think it's moldy."

Emily's eyes spotted the cereal boxes on top of the refrigerator and she quickly grabbed the half full box of Lucky Charms and began greedily consuming it by the handful right out of the box. On her third handful, she leaned her head back and brought her hand to her mouth, making sure not to drop a single piece. With her mouth still half full, she leaned back against the kitchen counter and glanced around to observe Finn's living situation.

Deciding to turn the questioning around on him to take the heat off herself for a while, she swallowed her mouthful of dry cereal and moved in for the kill. "So, Harper ended it, huh?"

"What? How did you…"

"You're living here. Alone. In a place much dumpier than your old apartment. You were practically living with us before I left."

"Well, Harper needed someone to be there. You weren't exactly around much, and when you were, you'd come crawling through the door at 5 a.m."

Emily wasn't expecting Finn to retaliate so quickly, but she refused to cease fire just yet. "So what happened? I know you didn't cheat on her because...well...we both know you're not that kind of guy. So what did you do?"

Finn tossed his keys on the coffee table and sat down on the couch, leaning forward with his elbows resting on his thighs. "What makes you so sure it was her that ended it?"

Emily shrugged. "Just a hunch."

She decided not to elaborate too much on her "hunch" in order to spare Finn his feelings. After all, he was being awfully nice for letting her into his apartment and eating what was left of his cereal. She took another handful of cereal out of the box and swallowed it before she could even finish chewing it.

"Whatever," replied Finn. "But yeah, we're not together anymore. So it's probably best if you go see Harper and leave me out of this, okay?"

"Mmm....I'd love to do that for you, Finn. Really, but I can't. I came to you for a reason. I thought you could hook me up with a place to stay with one of your friends, or something. But since you're living here now and you have this big couch, I was thinking maybe I could stay here for a little while."

Finn balked at Emily's suggestion. He was still trying to wrap his head around the fact that she was even here. "Emily, I…I don't think…Wait, how did you even know where I live?"

"My bus let me off a few blocks from where you work. They told me you left for a doctor's appointment. I told them I was Harper's sister and one of your co-workers told me where you were living now. Which led me to believe you two split."

"Well, what lovely, obliging people my co-workers are."

"Finn, please. Can't I stay here? Just for a couple days. I'll stay on the couch and you won't even know I'm here. I can't spend another night in a bus station. Please."

"You were sleeping in a bus station?"

Emily shrugged. "Sometimes."

"Emily, where the hell have you been? Seriously, where were you? What did you do? How did you get money?"

Emily put the cereal box on the counter and began to massage her temples with her fingers. "Can I please answer questions later? I really cannot deal right now, okay? If I can't stay here, then I need to go so I can find someone who'll let me crash with them."

"Okay, okay. You can stay. Of course you can stay. But I have to call Harper." He reached into his pocket and pulled out his cell phone.

"Why?"

"Because she has to know you're here and that you're okay."

"Please don't do that."

Finn started dialing Harper's number. "I have to. It's only fair for her to know."

Emily charged at Finn and knocked the cell phone out of his hand. "Don't!"

Finn pulled back, startled by Emily's sudden outburst. "What the hell!"

Emily knelt in front of Finn, immediately regretting what she did. "I'm sorry. I'm really sorry. I shouldn't have done that, I know. But please don't call her."

"Why not?"

Emily had a million different reasons why she didn't want her sister to know she was back in LA. The main reasons being that Emily knew how badly she behaved and wasn't ready to face her sister yet, and she wasn't prepared to face Harper's imminent interrogation and line of questioning.

Emily got up and sat down next to Finn on the couch. "I'm just not ready to see her. Please, Finn. I know you're probably dying for a reason to call her, but please don't let me be the reason."

Finn scoffed at the thought. "I'm not trying to find—"

"Okay, fine. But the thing is, I don't even know if I'm gonna stay. I just needed a place. And some food."

Finn stood up, angered by Emily's audacity. "You can't do that. You can't just come back here and not see Harper. Do you have any idea what you put her through?"

Emily instantly felt guilty, but refused to show it. She decided to turn to her old friend, apathy. "I'm sure it's not that dramatic."

"How could you know that? You weren't here. She was worried sick about you. And you didn't even bother to call or let her know you were okay. She cried over you. A lot. Every time her phone rang, she'd be wracked with anticipation, hoping it was you and scared to death that it might be someone calling to tell her you were dead."

Finn's words affected Emily more than she expected them too. She tried to fight off that nagging sense of guilt that had been creeping up on her over the last few months, but she couldn't hinder it any longer. She leaned back on the couch and sighed. "I know. Believe me, I've thought about it a lot. You have to understand, I was in a really fucked up place for a while. And I just wanted to evade everything that had to do with what I left behind here. And that included Harper." She leaned forward and searched through her bag, pulling out a cigarette. "Look, I do plan on seeing her. I mean, I want to. I think. I just don't want her to see me like this, okay? I need a little time. A few days to…clean up, or whatever." She pulled a lighter out of her bag and lit the cigarette.

Finn reached over, pulled the cigarette out of her mouth and dropped it in the half empty beer bottle on the coffee table. The cigarette hissed and fizzled when it came into contact with the stale brew.

"Don't smoke in here."

Emily nodded. "Sorry. I wasn't thinking."

It was at this moment, Finn took notice of Emily's eyes. It was the first time he allowed himself to really scrutinize her since she stepped into his apartment. It was in her eyes he could see she was struggling; fighting to stay as obstinate as she so badly wants to appear. But it was easy to see that feelings of remorse were rushing over her, drowning out any power she previously had over her emotions. Finn observed her tired eyes as they looked to the floor. Emily put her head in her hands as her shoulders slumped over. Finn strained his ears to listen for any sign that she may be crying. So far, he heard nothing, which was somewhat of a relief. He didn't think he could handle any tears from her at this moment.

Finn brought his hand up and gently placed it on Emily's lower back, slowly rubbing the material on her shirt, trying to comfort her the best way he could.

"Can I use your shower?"

Emily's words were muffled, but Finn could just barely make out what she was asking him.

"Of course."

"Thank you." Emily got up, walked over to the kitchen counter and grabbed the box of Lucky Charms. She finished off what was left of its contents and looked at Finn in a rather pitiful way. "I don't suppose you have anything else?"

Finn shook his head. "I'll order take out. You like Chinese?"

"Chinese is perfect."

"Kung Pao House is the best around here, but they don't deliver. Are you gonna be okay if I go pick it up? I'll be like fifteen minutes."

Emily nodded. "Yeah, no problem."

Finn stood up and grabbed his keys. "Okay, well the bathroom is down the hall on the right. Towels are in the closet right outside the bathroom door. Do you want anything in particular?"

"Cashew shrimp. And anything with noodles."

Finn watched Emily as she walked across the living room to the hall. He hadn't realized how gaunt and weakened she appeared, which was quite a departure from the last time he saw her. She'd always been thin, but her huge personality more than made up for it. But now, there seemed to be a definite change in her demeanor. It made him wonder what else had changed about her.

"You know…" he started, but immediately clammed up.

Emily turned around. "What?"

"I…uh…I don't have any money lying around, or anything. So please don't make a mess looking for any. You won't find it."

Emily grew tense and defensive, but she reminded herself of her track record and tried to respond as calmly as possible. "I don't want your money, Finn. I wouldn't do that to you."

"But you would do it to Harper."

"No! God, that was one time and I swear I felt really bad about it. I still do. I don't do that stuff anymore. I stopped. I mean, I'm trying to stop. I haven't done anything like that in over four months. Okay?"

Finn felt a tinge of remorse over what he had said. He nodded in understanding. "Okay, I'll be back in a few."

Emily opened the hall closet, pulled out a towel and stepped into the bathroom as she heard the front door close. She peeled off her clothes as the bathroom mirror started steaming up from the hot water. Once she stepped inside the shower, immediate relief fell upon her with every drop that rolled down her body. While she began to rub the fresh-smelling shampoo in her hair, she couldn't help but think of Harper and what she would say to her.

Emily knew that, no matter what her excuse was, she'd always be seen as an asshole. It was a label she believed was fully deserved. She had a decent life, had decent parents that were still married–a rarity amongst her friends. She never quite understood her need to destroy everything that was good in her life. She knew it would be so much easier to blame someone. Her sister for being born first and being labeled as the "good one," her parents, her friends, the school system…but she was smart enough to know that the blame lies solely with her. She rested her hand against the shower wall and lowered her head, allowing the drops of hot water to bead down her neck. From the moment she stepped off the bus in Santa Monica, all she could think about was how badly she wanted a shower. She was hungry, exhausted, and an emotional wreck, and she firmly believed that a shower would make everything better. And for one fleeting moment, she was right. For that brief moment, she felt all her sins and all the shame she had been carrying with her for the past two years wash away. But just as soon as they were gone, her burdens came right back, weighing her down once again the moment she thought of Harper and how she was going to have to explain everything to her sister. She lifted her head and began to rinse off her hair, suds sliding down her body, creating a pathway to the drain. She couldn't shake the haunting questions swirling around her head. What if Harper rejected her? What if she never forgave her? What if Harper refused to allow her back into their home?

***

"Okay, I want you to tuck that blanket behind the dresser. Make sure it's secure so it doesn't fall off," directed Harper.

"Okay," replied Emily, her short arms reaching as far as they could behind her dresser drawers. *"I got it."*

"All right. Now duck back under and come help me tie this sheet to the bed post," said Harper.

Emily crawled her way back over to where her sister was and held onto the sheet for her. Once the sheet was securely tied to the bed post, Harper grabbed a pillow from Emily's bed and pulled off the case. She draped it over the blanket that was hanging between the dresser and the side of the bed.

"This will be your doorway," explained Harper, as she lifted it up for Emily to go under.

Emily's eyes widened with delight. "Cool!" She quickly got on her knees and crawled through the pillowcase inside her own little sanctuary with blankets and sheets as her ceiling. There wasn't much room for kneeling, but she could easily sit up without her head touching the blankets above her. It was rather dark in there, but that's just how she wanted it. She grabbed the flashlight from under her bed, turned it on, and poked her head out from the pillowcase.

"Aren't you going to come in?"

Harper smirked at the wonderment in her sister's eyes. "Am I invited?"

Emily giggled with delight. "Yeah! Come down here!" Without any delay, Emily's head disappeared back inside her little fort.

Harper got on her hands and knees and crawled into the fortress she had built for her sister. She scooted her legs all the way in and reached over to bring the pillowcase back down. The dull beam from the flashlight was the only light they had. Emily pointed the flashlight up, dimly illuminating their faces.

"Can I sleep in here?"

Harper hunched over, tucking her legs behind her. "Only if mom and dad say it's okay."

Emily laid her head back on the pillows they used as her makeshift bed. "Will it really work?"

Harper smiled, envying her sister's innocence. "Of course it'll work. It worked for me when I was your age. I know it'll work for you."

Emily reached over and grabbed her stuffed Tigger doll, pressing him tightly to her body. "Maybe I can stay in here tomorrow, instead of going to school."

"I don't think that'll happen. But once you get home, it'll be here waiting for you."

After a long pause, Emily pleaded with Harper. "Do I have to go school?"

"Yes, you have to go. Mom and dad will only let you stay home if you're sick and you don't want to waste your fake sick days on grade school. Trust me."

Harper felt her sister's pain; she really did. She knew exactly why her sister didn't want to go to school. A couple of girls were making fun of Emily, for no reason whatsoever; just to do it. But they were the girls that the entire second grade class looked up to, so of course no one came to Emily's defense. Not even her friends, who were too scared they'd get teased as well. Harper couldn't understand why anyone would tease her sister. Sure, she was the smallest seven-year-old in her class, but she was incredibly smart and very sweet. But everyone had their issues at school—whether it was being teased, like Emily, or having embarrassing rumors spread about you, like Harper did. School was never the best place to be to build your self-esteem, and sometimes the teasing was too relentless to bear. Harper knew that all too well, so when Emily came home crying, she wanted to help assuage her sister. So she built her a fort in the area between Emily's bed and dresser, just as Harper had done for herself a few years ago. When school proved to be too much for her, she came home and found sanctuary amongst the blankets and sheets she used to cover herself from the outside world. Now, it was Emily's turn. With Harper in junior high now, they didn't go to the same school anymore, so she wasn't around to defend her little sister if needed.

"What if they're mean to me again? I don't want to cry in front of anyone" said Emily.

"Then you come home and cry in here. And no one will know. No one will see you and no one will laugh at you. And then, when your tears are dry, you come out and tell me who was mean to you and I'll go talk to them."

"No. Don't do that. I'll be fine. I'll just stay in here and it'll be okay."

Harper switched positions, lying down on her stomach with her head resting on a pillow. "All right. But you know I'll always be here if you need me."

"I know."

***

Emily shut off the water and stepped out of the shower, wrapping the towel around her body. She still felt a little shaken and nervous thinking about her potential reunion with Harper. She'd been through a lot in the last couple years, but didn't think Harper would understand exactly what it took to get her to this point. The misadventures Emily had been through, the places she slept, the less than pleasurable things she had done and seen, she knew none of it would be enough for Harper to take pity on her. Emily had always been a wild one. Her mercurial personality made it easy for her to do as she pleased without taking anyone else's feelings into consideration. It was those capricious ways that led her to develop a sense of apathy that no one else could understand, which eventually led to her alienating those she loved the most.

Her head began to ache thinking about the consequences she was about to face. After tentatively going through Finn's drawers with the sole purpose of looking for something to sleep in, she settled on a pair of sweats and an old high school varsity soccer t-shirt. She never thought a couch could look so inviting. But once she stepped into the living room and lay down on the sofa, she was passed out within five minutes and proceeded to sleep for seventeen hours straight. When Finn came home to find her asleep, he put the Chinese food in the fridge, along with some milk and a new box of cereal he picked up. He then grabbed an extra blanket from his bedroom closet and draped it over Emily, doing his best not to wake her.

CHAPTER 10

Kiley knew she was supposed to be working, but Graham had left early and since it was last call, the place was starting to clear out. They were a little short-staffed since Erin called in sick, but Kiley was confident she could run the place smoothly enough. If she made it through the night without burning the place down, she knew she would have succeeded. She took a seat on one of the bar stools and started clapping along with everyone else when Harper finished her song.

"Woooooooo!! Yeah!" Kiley's hands were starting to hurt from clapping so much, but she didn't care. She loved the nights when Harper would play. It put her in a remarkably good mood and it made her shifts go by so much quicker.

Harper smiled when she heard Kiley's voice cheering for her. The other claps were a definite boost to her ego, but they significantly paled in comparison to the cheers of her self-proclaimed "biggest fan." Harper grabbed her capo and secured it to the second fret on her guitar.

"Thank you. Um…so I'm just gonna do one more song and then you'll all be put out of your misery."

Harper's little self-deprecating joke garnered a few chuckles.

"If you like what you've heard tonight, I've got cd's for sale, so just come see me afterwards. Thanks a lot."

4

Harper closed out her set with a song called "Been There, Done That," which she wrote about a guy in high school who made it his personal goal to sleep with every girl in their class. He didn't reach his goal, but unfortunately, Harper was one of the many girls who fell for his smooth lines her senior year. It took a while for her to get over him. But it was perfect fodder for a song and once she wrote it, she was over it. With her eyes closed and her fingers wrapped around the neck of her guitar, Harper belted out the song secretly hoping she'd get at least a few more tips in the tip jar from a few obliging patrons.

In the meantime, Kiley continued to watch her friend in complete awe. Unbeknownst to her, a wide smile sprawled across her face every time she watched Harper perform. She simply couldn't understand why this girl wasn't famous yet.

"You must really like this song."

Kiley tore her eyes away from the stage to see who dared approach her during Harper's last song. "Huh? Yeah. I like all her songs."

"Is she a friend of yours?"

"Yeah." Kiley went back to watching Harper.

The young man wasn't deterred. "So, can I get a Jack and Coke?"

"Huh?"

"Jack and Coke. Can I get one? It's last call."

Kiley looked over at the young man, who was standing a little too close to her. "Can you give me a couple minutes? Just until the song's over."

"Is this any way to run a business? Denying a customer a drink?"

Kiley looked back at Harper. "I'm not running a business. I just work here."

"What about customer service?"

Kiley was starting to get annoyed with this guy. She knew by the tone of his voice he wasn't serious, but he was being a little too smarmy for her taste. "Fine. Jack and Coke, it is." He didn't hear her mumble the word "jackass" under her breath. She walked back over behind the bar and began to make his drink. Making sure to add much more Coca Cola than she normally would, just to help lower this guy's obvious ego. She handed him the drink. "Anything else?"

He smirked at Kiley. "What are you offering?"

Kiley rolled her eyes. "How original. That'll be seven dollars."

He handed her a ten. "Keep the change." He picked up his drink and spilled a little bit on his white Affliction shirt and jeans. "Damn it."

Without giving it a second thought, Kiley poured some club soda into a glass and handed it to him with a clean towel. "Here. Before it stains."

He started toweling off where he spilled and it seemed to be working. "Thanks. Next time I gotta remind myself that acting like an ass means instant bad karma."

"Well, admitting it is the first step."

"I'm Matt, by the way." He put down the club soda-soaked towel and stuck out his hand.

"Kiley." She grabbed the towel and tossed it in the empty crate to her left.

"Well, thanks." Matt took his drink and started walking back to his group of friends.

"No problem," replied Kiley, who looked back up at the stage just in time to see Harper sing her last note as the audience began applauding once more. A few customers took her last song as a sign that the bar was officially closing, even though they were open for another twenty minutes. So after they cleared out, there were only a few people left.

Harper unplugged her guitar and knelt down to put it back into her case. She fastened the locks on the case, then started rolling up the cables that she unplugged from the sound system.

"You know you're a badass, right?"

Harper turned around and automatically grabbed the traditional beer that Kiley always handed her after every show. "Shut up."

"I'm serious! You're so good and you don't even know it. Do you have any idea how frustrating that is?"

Harper took a sip of her Duvel and proceeded to put her speakers back in the case. "I'm well aware of your frustration. You make it known constantly."

"Well get with it, already! I can't keep working in this dump much longer."

Harper zipped up her speaker case and laughed. "You know, I love how you just assume I'm gonna take care of you if I ever make any money."

"Well, of course. The symbiosis in our relationship is what keeps me going."

"Symbiosis? What exactly do you bring to this friendship?"

Kiley turned around and started walking back over to the bar. "Sex appeal. And spunk."

Harper watched Kiley walk away. "You exhaust me."

"You love it." Kiley grabbed a trash bag and started filling it up with empty bottles from the various tables she was clearing.

After Harper finished packing up all her equipment, she grabbed her tip jar, sat down at the bar and started counting out the bills.

Kiley came back around with a full trash bag. "What's the word?"

"Sixty-two…and some change. Not bad for an hour of playing. Even if the first twenty came from Graham."

"That was nice of him."

"He's a generous soul. I think he's just looking out for me."

"A generous soul. Yeah, toward *you*. If he were really generous, he'd give me more money and less hours."

Harper folded up the money and put it in her pocket. "Stop complaining. It's not like you work that hard, anyway."

Kiley opened her mouth to say something, but no words came out. It was no use…she'd been beat. She stuck her tongue out at Harper, not caring about how juvenile it made her appear. "I'm gonna throw some of this trash out. I'll be back." She looked over at the group of guys still finishing off their drinks at a nearby table and called out to them as she headed towards the back door. "Guys, we're closing up! Time to clear out.

The group of guys finished off their drinks and started gathering their belongings as Harper pulled the money out of her pocket to recount it again. She had noticed one of the guys in the group talking to Kiley earlier and something told her she wouldn't be seeing the last of him. She really wasn't in the mood for one of Kiley's many suitors coming up to "the friend" to try to set something up, which happened more often than she liked. So she kept her focus on counting the bills in her hands as she spotted him out of the corner of her eye. He was putting on his jacket and reaching into his pocket for something. Harper had reached the number sixty-two four times by now, hoping they would leave and she could stop looking like an idiot repeatedly counting an easy sum of money. As a few of them started filing out the door, she thought she was in the clear. But once she turned around, she was met with an unfamiliar face.

"Hi."

Harper was taken aback. This wasn't the guy she was expecting. "Uh…hi."

"I really liked your set." The young man smiled shyly.

"Thanks." Harper cocked her head to the side, trying to get a read on this guy.

"I really liked your third song. The part about spending thousands of dollars on an education you'll never use."

"You're sober enough to remember that?"

"I only had one beer. I got voted designated driver tonight."

Harper tried her best to stifle her emerging smile. This was the first time since the engagement ring came off her finger that a young, good-looking guy talked to her without looking eight inches below her eyes. "Well, I guess your friends are probably waiting for you."

He looked over at the door. "Yeah, I guess. Well, maybe we can hang out sometime. Or tell me the next time you're performing. I'd like to hear you play again."

Harper could feel her face getting warm as embarrassment was slowly setting in. She found his invitation flattering, even though she wasn't at all interested. "Um…I play here a lot. Usually on Saturdays."

He nodded and smiled. "Okay. Good to know. Well, maybe I'll see you around." He backed away and headed toward the door. But before he could take another step, Matt came charging up, putting his arm around his friend, leading him back over to Harper.

"Hey. My friend thinks you're hot," announced Matt, slurring his speech a little.

"Neat," replied Harper. "I'm sure he appreciates you embarrassing him."

Matt laughed, unaware of the jab Harper just took at him. He reached into his pocket, pulled out a piece of paper and handed it to her. "Hey, so tell your friend to call me. She's really hot."

Harper took the piece of paper, unimpressed with his approach. "I'll relay the message."

Matt continued to drape his arm around his friend, whose name Harper never caught. "I'm serious. Tell her to call me. And you should call Greg here. Because he's a nice guy. And he loves music and chicks that play guitar. He's like a guy groupie."

"Dude, would you shut up?" Greg was obviously not amused.

"What? I'm just trying to get you laid."

"Dude, let's go. We're done here." Greg looked over at Harper. "I'm sorry about that." He guided Matt towards the door. "You throw up in my car and I'll kill you."

Harper lifted her beer. "Here's hoping he's drunk to the point that he'll pass out tonight and wake up with a new personality."

Greg laughed. "If only the world were that lucky…"

They disappeared out the door and Harper was left alone, waiting patiently for Kiley to finish closing up. She looked at her watch and once she realized it was two o'clock in the morning, her body immediately began to feel exhausted. She reached her arms up and stretched out her back. She finished what was left of her Duvel and lifted herself up to throw the empty bottle away in the nearby trashcan. Embracing the rare silence in this place, she rested her hands on the bar, which was made out of rich, dark mahogany. After swiveling the stool around, she leaned back against the bar and glanced at the empty stage ahead of her. She found herself wondering what it was like to be in the audience watching her perform. Did people enjoy it? Did they applaud only to be nice? Did they wish there was a jukebox here instead of some girl screeching out songs she's written? Did anyone really care about the words that came out of her mouth or the notes she was playing on her guitar? She often wondered why she even bothered with all this. But she always came to one solid conclusion that she often repeated to herself as a mantra: I want to make music. I can't imagine my life without it, so that must be what I love the most.

Harper loved being in Tyson's Bar at closing time. There was something eternally comforting about this place. The setting itself was kept rather dim with a few neon signs scattered throughout the walls. It could be considered a dive, but it had a much more relaxed feel. Its charming appeal often attracted a younger crowd, and Harper never really felt cause for concern among the clientele. They all seemed relatively normal, with the obvious exception of a few overly drunk people. It didn't have the "smoky air" that's usually characterized with other bars. After all, this was LA. Smoking indoors was practically unheard of in this town. There was nothing particularly extraordinary about this place. There were no kitschy gimmicks, no crazy posters on the wall or funky uniforms for the staff. There weren't any clever sayings or signs in the restrooms or over-priced drinks. It was simply a bar and that's why it was so popular. There were so many other choices for bars and clubs on Ventura Boulevard but Harper, along with many others considered this the best bar in the valley.

"Almost done," informed Kiley as she came in from the back.

Harper was startled by her friend's sudden, stealthy entrance, and slightly jumped.

"Wow…why are you so jumpy?"

"My breath was taken away by your boyfriend."

"My boyfriend?"

"Yeah. You better be careful. He's a smart one." She reached into her pocket, pulled out Matt's number, wadded it up and threw it to Kiley.

Kiley opened up the piece of paper and read it. "Ohhhhh…THAT boyfriend. Yeah, kind of a tool, but he seems harmless enough."

"True. I think brain cells would be required for inflicting any intentional harm."

Kiley laughed as she tossed the phone number into the trash. "You ready?"

"Yeah." She walked back over to the stage and grabbed her two guitars.

Kiley flipped the light switches on the wall until the entire place was dark. Once they were outside, she set the alarm and locked the doors. Harper paused for a moment and watched Kiley head toward her car. It only took the leggy brunette a split second to realize she was walking alone. So she turned around to see Harper still standing by the door.

"Do you plan on walking home? Because I can't condone that at this time of night."

Harper grinned. "No. Sorry…I just…"

Kiley took a few steps back over to her. "You just what?"

Harper could feel her pulse quickening as she took a deep breath.

Kiley could tell there was obviously something on her mind. Harper wasn't exactly the best at hiding her emotions. She searched her face to see if there was any clue as to what she wanted to say would be revealed.

"I just nothing. I completely lost my train of thought. My brain is sticking tonight for some reason." Gripping her guitar cases, she started walking. "Let's go."

Kiley wasn't satisfied with that answer, but knew it was pointless to even try to get something resembling the truth. "You need some sleep."

Harper nodded without saying a word.

They were just getting into Kiley's car when a voice called out to them.

"Hey! You're not gonna leave without saying goodbye, are you?"

They turned around to see Matt walking toward them, with Greg awkwardly following a few steps behind.

"Did you get my number?" asked Matt when he approached Kiley, standing a little too close for her comfort.

"Yeah, I did."

"Well, I figured I'd save you the trouble and just wait for you." He leaned up against Kiley's car, leaving fingerprints in the dust on the roof.

"My hands and fingers work just fine. I know how to dial a number," informed Kiley.

"I didn't want to wait too long to hear from you."

Harper stood with the passenger door open, unsure of whether or not to get in. She glanced over at Greg, who was standing with his hands in his pockets, kicking the ground in front of him.

Matt refused to let up on his advances. "It's too early for me to go home. You wanna go get some coffee, or something?"

"Coffee?"

"Or tea…whatever. Come on. You gotta admit, I'm kinda cute."

He was moving in closer and closer until Kiley could smell the stale beer, whiskey and cigarettes on his breath. She looked over at Harper, her eyes questioning her friend on what she should do.

Harper shrugged. "Hey, do what you gotta do."

Kiley skeptically looked at her friend. "Really? Are you sure?"

That was a tricky answer. Far be it from Harper to keep her friend from having any fun, but she also wasn't a fan of being ditched in the middle of the night.

"You don't have a car?" asked Matt.

"I do. But I got a ride from her tonight," replied Harper.

Greg took this moment to finally speak up. "I can give you a ride."

Kiley looked over at Greg, then back at Harper, who at this point, closed the passenger door and stepped away from the car. Kiley was beginning to feel the same as Harper, not wanting to be ditched in a parking lot in the middle of the night. But she knew her friend needed this. Greg was cute and seemed fairly respectful, so who was she to deny Harper the chance to finally be with someone who wasn't Finn?

Kiley smirked playfully. "Oh, I'm sure Harper would love for you to give her a ride." Leave it to Kiley to leave no double cheesy double entendre unturned.

Greg walked over, took Harper's guitars from her and went to go put them in his car. Harper was still a little unsure of what exactly was going on. There were times she wished her best friend was a little more abstemious and a little less promiscuous. This was one of those times. "So…okay. You'll take Matt home and I…I guess I'll go home with Greg?"

"Is that okay with you?" Kiley had difficulty getting those words out seeing as how Matt, somewhat lacking in discretion, immediately started kissing her neck and ever so smoothly trying to shove his tongue down her throat.

Harper shook her head and impatiently started to walk over to Greg's car. "Yeah, I'll be fine." She stopped and turned around. "Just be careful, okay?"

Kiley started giggling as Matt started biting her ear. "I will. Call me tomorrow okay?"

Harper continued walking over to Greg, who was already standing with the passenger door open for her. "My car's kind of messy. Sorry."

"That's fine. Thanks." Though she didn't look up, she could hear Kiley in the distance.

"All right, stud. Calm yourself. Get in the car."

Greg came around to the driver side and closed the door. "You cold? I can turn on the heater."

"Sure." She couldn't bring herself to look at him. She actually had no idea what was going on. Who was this guy? Why was she all of a sudden in his car? What was he expecting from her? She tried to stay calm and felt that looking straight ahead out the windshield was her best option. Her mind was racing. Why did Kiley think it was okay to abandon her? Why does she even care? She can take care of herself, so why was she so upset?

"He's actually a decent guy."

Harper snapped out of her trance and looked over at Greg. "Huh?"

"Matt. He's actually an okay guy, so you don't have to worry. Your friend will be safe with him. He just likes to talk a big game." Greg turned the ignition and started the car.

"Oh."

"I actually feel kind of bad for your friend. Matt tends to pass out if he's really drunk. And he's practically immobile. But he's not too drunk tonight, so it might be okay."

"How do you know each other?"

"We're roommates. We met in college. I let him cheat off me once and since then, I can't seem to get rid of him."

Harper nodded. She appreciated the fact that he was at least trying to fill the awkward silence with something.

"So…where do you live?"

"Me?"

"Yeah. Did you want me to take you home?"

"Oh, yeah. Um, turn left at the signal. Then right on Laurel Canyon."

"Okay." The methodical clicking of the blinker was the only sound interrupting the silence between them until Greg spoke up. "I really tried to get him to go home. He just kept insisting to wait around. I think your friend impressed him."

"She impresses a lot of people."

"How so?"

"Just her personality. You think he's the first guy that's ever tried to hook up with her?"

"I guess I didn't really think about it."

"She'll probably forget his name by next week."

Greg shifted uncomfortably in his seat. Harper could tell she was making him somewhat ill at ease.

"Sorry. New subject. What do you do for a living?"

"I work for a PR firm in Culver City. It's a fairly small company, but we're starting to build a good clientele. The hours are a little hectic."

"Keep going straight. So do you commute from the Valley?"

"Yeah. It's not too horrible. I've actually mapped out a pretty decent route avoiding all freeways and it gets me there a lot faster."

"Does Matt work with you?"

'That's right, Foley. Just keep asking questions and you'll be home before you know it,' Harper thought to herself.

"No, he works out here. In retail. In his free time, he likes to perfect the art of being an asshole."

Harper snickered at his candor. "Well, it's nice to know he's motivated. And pretty successful at it."

The rest of the ride home, they started to feel a little more at ease with each other and bantered back and forth about adequately conventional subjects. He expressed his disdain for reality television. She discussed the reasons why the Beatles were better than the Rolling Stones.

They continued their polite badinage until they reached Harper's street. Neither of them even realized they had already reached their destination.

"Wow, that was fast," he stated.

"Yeah. That's me…fifth house on the right."

He pulled up to the curb and left his engine running idle. "So, if it's okay with you, I think I might just chill out here for a bit. I don't think I can go home quite yet."

Harper knew exactly what he meant. "You really think they're…"

"Oh yeah. Definitely."

Harper opened the door to get out, but paused for a moment. This wasn't her, but maybe she was tired of being herself. Maybe it was time to do something different, something reckless. Maybe she was just feeling angry and guilty and unsure of everything that was happening tonight. Whatever it was, she decided that she didn't care. She looked over at Greg, no longer hesitant. "Do you want to come in?"

CHAPTER 11

The shrill sound of her cell phone echoing in her ear stirred Harper from her slumber. This did not help the massive headache throbbing through her cranium and travelling through her entire body. She groggily reached over and switched her phone to silent, wondering who would have the audacity to call her this early in the morning. Lying outstretched on her bed, Harper opened her eyes and began to squint, trying to adjust to the sunshine creeping in through the bedroom window. She definitely was not ready to greet the day at this moment and wish she had arms long enough to pull the curtains completely closed. She turned over on her side and closed her eyes to go back to sleep. Her eyes were only shut for a moment when they abruptly opened again and she bolted up.

Wait a minute, she thought as she looked over at the clock. It was 8:30a.m., which by her calculations meant that she had been asleep for at least four hours; a record for Harper in the last few years. She smiled to herself, very proud of her accomplishment. Her smile began to fade, however, when flashes of what happened last night immediately filled her psyche. *Oh God*. She slowly turned over to see and sleeping next to her was a guy she had a vague recollection of.

Oh my God. It didn't take long for her to realize what she feared most. She slowly peeked underneath the

4

blanket and sure enough she was, in fact, naked. As was the young gentleman lying next to her. She pulled the blanket back down onto them and looked around the room. A half empty vodka bottle and a few shot glasses on the floor caught her attention and then it all came back to her.

After she had invited Greg in, they sat in a rather awkward and uncomfortable silence, so she suggested a drink in order to lighten the mood. All she had was an unopened bottle of vodka and since she hadn't been shopping in a while, there was nothing to mix it with. So straight vodka shots it was! After one shot, they continued to sit in silent stillness. After two shots, they began the obligatory small talk. After three shots, they had each other cracking up for no apparent reason. After four shots, Harper's normally rational judgment became somewhat obfuscated. It was the first time in quite some time that she had finally managed to go five minutes without thinking about what's been bothering her. It's true that it a took rather large amount of alcohol to drink away said pain. But at that point, she was feeling pretty good and pretty much lost all sense of reality once that fifth shot set in. They were in the middle of an intense game of "Go Fish" when Greg got that pair of kings he was looking for and cracked a smile. Harper was immediately charmed by that genuine, sweet smile. She had no idea what came over her, but she leaned forward and kissed him. She didn't remember much about the kiss. All she remembered was that he kissed her back and the next thing she knew, they were half naked in her bed. And now, in the light of day, it appears they completed that arduous task of drunkenly undressing in the dark and having inebriated and most likely clumsy sex.

Harper plopped her head down on the pillow, feeling completely helpless and beginning to regret how last night's events played out. Greg began shifting on the other side of the bed. He awoke abruptly, realizing he wasn't in his own bed and that he, like Harper, was fully unclothed. He turned over to face Harper, unsure of exactly what to say.

"Uh…good morning."

Harper continued to stare at the ceiling. "Morning."

Greg looked around, trying to get a grip on what was going on. "So…did we…?"

Harper nodded. "Yeah."

"Okay. I mean, it's not that I didn't remember. I know we did, I just wanted to make sure you know we did. Because…I mean, look at you. You're gorgeous. How could I not remember?"

Harper chuckled nervously. "We had a lot of liquor. It's really okay."

"Yeah, I guess we did. Last night was fun. From what I do remember." Greg rested his head on his elbow and used his other hand to gently stroke Harper's arm.

All Harper wanted at that moment was to be alone. She didn't want this guy in her house. She didn't want him in her bed. And she definitely did not want him touching her at this moment. In fact, she began to cringe as he leaned over and kissed her shoulder. *Oh Christ*, she thought. *When am I supposed to ask him to leave?*

Greg was obviously unable to read her thoughts, seeing as how he began to nuzzle her shoulder, which was grating on Harper's nerves with each passing moment. She began to feel claustrophobic and panicky.

Greg continued his sickeningly sweet snuggle fest. "So what are you doing today?"

'What am I doing today?' thought Harper. 'Seriously? He still wants to hang out? We have nothing to talk about unless we're drunk. Wait…what AM I doing today?' Suddenly, she just shouted out the first thing that came to her mind.

Harper bolted straight up and shouted. "CrossFit! I have to get to my CrossFit class! It's in about a half hour, so I should really get going."

CrossFit? What the hell am I saying? thought Harper. *I've never done CrossFit a day in my life.*

Poor Greg never saw it coming. His head landed on the bed with a thud as the previously seemingly normal girl he had met last night got up and frantically searched her room for something to cover her naked form. He reluctantly got out of the comfortable bed and reached for his clothes, slowly dressing himself and trying to calculate his next attempt at some form of communication. It was becoming increasingly obvious to him that she was blowing him off. What he didn't comprehend was why. Once his pants were on, he sat at the edge of the bed anxiously moving his toes around in his socks.

"Did you wanna do something tonight? Or tomorrow? Dinner, or something?" It was his lame attempt to try and salvage the last of was what evidently their brief, ten-hour relationship.

Harper, only half listening, began to frenetically hop up and down trying get her shoe on. "Oh, uh…I don't know. I'll have to see how I feel. I might just call it an early night tonight."

"And tomorrow?"

Once her shoe was on, Harper scoured her closet for a sweater. "Um…probably tomorrow night, too. I haven't been sleeping much lately."

"You slept just fine last night."

"It was alcohol induced…and maybe a little sex induced. Who knows?"

Still sitting on the side of the bed, Greg nodded and slipped his feet into his brown shoes and apprehensively tried to smooth down his mussed up hair. He wanted to leave the whole thing alone. He wanted to get his stuff and get out of here as fast as he could. There was only so much rejection he could handle. But Harper's spastic rushing was beginning to make him nervous.

"You know, you don't have to do that."

"Do what?" asked Harper.

"Rush to get me out of here. I'll leave. Don't worry. But you need to calm down. All this stress isn't good for you."

"Thanks for the advice, Zen-boy."

That was enough for Greg. "Fine. I'm outta here."

The second those words came out of Harper's mouth she immediately regretted them. Who was she to be so cruel to the guy? He was just some innocent bystander who happened to cross paths with a rather messed up individual with issues to spare.

"Wait. I'm sorry. Please, you don't have to go. I shouldn't have said that. I don't know why I did."

Greg was at the bedroom door when he stopped and turned around to find the distressed looking blonde sitting on her bed.

"Did I do something wrong?" he asked, earnestly.

Harper shook her head. "No. You didn't do anything wrong. You've been incredibly sweet."

"My downfall."

"No, it's good. It really is. Girls like that in a guy. My ex was the same way."

"Well, seeing as how you're trying to get rid of me, I can only deduce that you're into bad boys who treat you like shit?"

"No. Of course not. It's just…right now isn't a good time. For anything, or anyone. And I guess that includes really cute, sensitive guys that I meet at a bar."

Greg walked over and sat next to her on the bed. "Okay, I get that. I totally respect that. You've got your shit going on in your complicated life. That's fine. But we all have that. Something tells me there's a bigger picture. Is there something more to your story?"

Harper was feeling increasingly vulnerable, so she could barely choke out one word. "Maybe."

Greg put his hand on her thigh in a comforting manner. "Well, I won't pry, but whatever it is, I hope you figure it out. You'll save the next poor unsuspecting sap the trouble," he said teasingly.

"Oh, making jokes at my expense, are we?"

"Hey, my pride's been trampled on. I have to save face somehow."

Harper sat there for a moment, finally allowing herself to enjoy Greg's touch. "Well, if it's any consolation, it really was nice meeting you."

Greg smirked. "Really no consolation at all. More like salt in the wounds. Please spare me the phrase 'we can be friends' because I don't think I can handle hearing that."

Harper smiled. "Fair enough."

Following another moment of awkward silence, Greg stood up. "Okay, well I guess I'll see you around. I really do like your music, by the way. You should play more often."

"So I've been told."

Greg paused at the doorway. "Can I ask you something?"

"Sure."

"I know you're, like, sad and all, but take that out of the equation…was I any good?"

Harper couldn't help but burst out laughing. "Yes. You were *very* good."

"Okay. Just checking." He turned to walk out the door. "See ya."

Harper gave him a half wave, fell back onto her bed and thought to herself, *Man, I'm gonna kill Kiley.*

***

"So basically, any biography you're looking for will be found in this section. Is there a particular book I can help you find?"

'Please say no, please say no, please say no,' thought Harper, who was not in the mood for any kind of human interaction at the moment.

"Actually, yes. I'm looking for a book on Marilyn Monroe," replied thirty-something woman with a two-year-old boy sound asleep in a stroller.

Harper tried to stifle her sigh and put on her best fake smile and headed towards the "M" section. "Sure. We've got quite a few."

"Are you a fan?" asked the customer.

"I guess. I mean, who isn't? It's Marilyn! But her story is pretty well known." She grabbed a book on Marilyn, then headed for the "W" section and pulled out another book. "But if you want a really good read on an actress, let me suggest this one." She handed the customer a book on Natalie Wood. "It really doesn't get much better than Natalie."

The woman looked at Harper hesitantly.

"I'm serious," Harper continued. "She was so talented and her life was just as tragic as Marilyn's. Plus, she also died young under mysterious circumstances." Harper waved the book in front of her, trying to tempt the woman to take the bait.

"Hmm…maybe I'll get both."

"Even better. It keeps us in business."

"Thanks for your help."

"No problem." Harper took notice of the woman's child. "Cute kid, by the way."

"Thanks."

As the woman walked away pushing her stroller and carrying her books, Harper turned around and was abruptly startled by Kiley, who was dangling a bag in front of her.

"Hey!"

Harper jumped and grabbed her chest after feeling her heart nearly jump into her throat. "Jesus! Don't do that."

"Sorry." Kiley handed her the bag. "Two donuts from that shop down the street that you love."

Harper took the bag. "Just what I need. More carbs."

"Eat them and enjoy them. Or I'll be personally offended."

"I will on my break." Harper started walking over to the next aisle where the history books were located. Kiley followed her.

"So…am I to assume you're mad at me seeing as how you haven't returned my calls?"

Harper tried to make herself look busy by arbitrarily arranging some history books.

"I've been busy."

Kiley placed the bag of donuts on the shelf next to her and languidly ran her finger along the cold, metal surface of the bookshelf.

"Too busy to answer your phone for the past three days?"

Harper used her hand to push a few books back in order to straighten them out, purposefully avoiding eye contact with the taller girl.

"I guess."

Kiley could feel her heart sink and stomach tie up in knots upon hearing that response. She knew this was coming. Ever since they went their separate ways from the bar that night, Kiley knew she had done a pretty terrible thing.

"I'm sorry."

"For what?"

"Well, you're obviously pissed about the other night. And you have every right to be. I shouldn't have bailed on you like that."

"Hey, who am I to care? It didn't surprise me. You followed your unwavering libido…again. I'm used to it."

"Then why do I get the feeling you're ashamed of me?"

Harper turned around and grabbed the bag from off the shelf. "I'm not supposed to have food near the books."

Kiley took the bag. "Sorry. I'll hold onto it."

The two stood there, incapable of really speaking, neither knowing exactly what to say. Kiley grabbed a book on ancient Rome and began scanning through it, not really caring about the historical facts that were in front of her. All she cared about right now was making sure Harper wasn't mad at her so that everything would be right in the world.

"If it makes you feel any better, it was probably one of the worst nights of my life."

Harper relented for a moment. "Explain."

"Well, it was…sloppy. And afterwards…oh God."

"What?"

Kiley closed the hardcover book and put it back in its rightful place. "He spent the rest of the night throwing up in my bathroom."

Harper tried to suppress her laughter, but was failing miserably.

"That's fine. Go ahead and laugh. I had it coming."

"Maybe." Harper managed to regain her composure and continue her unnecessary task of making sure the books lined up properly. It was the only thing she could think of doing right now that would make her look somewhat busy.

"So what happened to you that night? Obviously you got home safe."

"Nice of you to worry."

"Hey, you're the one with the killer right hook. Any guy would be a fool to try something with you if you said no."

Harper could feel her stomach drop thinking about having to tell Kiley what happened, mainly because she didn't feel like an interrogation. But she knew somehow

Kiley would figure it out, even if she didn't say anything. There was no point in stalling the inevitable.

"I slept with him."

Kiley took a step back. She didn't know for a fact, but she was pretty sure her jaw had significantly dropped and her mouth was now open and was easily giving away the sense of shock she wanted to try so desperately to hide. She examined Harper's demeanor, her face, the way she was standing, the position of her arms and how her fingernails on her left hand were nervously scratching the top of her right. The silence was becoming increasingly more palpable, but Kiley literally felt like someone had come out of nowhere and punched her in the face. No warning, no apologies, and no mercy. She wanted to speak, but had no idea what to say.

Harper couldn't handle it anymore.

"Is your delayed response due to the immense amount of judging going on in your head?"

Kiley flinched. She knew she was being spoken to. Something about judging. "I...uh..."

"Seriously, say something."

"You...you slept with him? Are you fucking serious?"

Obviously hurt, Harper retreated back to the books she was organizing. "Okay, I'd rather you had said nothing."

"I'm sorry. I didn't mean that. I just...I really wasn't expecting that."

"So now *I'm* being reprimanded?"

"No. I was just caught off guard."

"So you're allowed to sleep with whoever you want, but God forbid I –"

"I'm sorry! It's not like that, really. I'm happy for you. I mean, I think I am. It was good right? I mean, how was it?"

Harper shrugged. "I think I may have scared him off. We were really drunk."

"How did you scare him off?"

"I may or may not have had a mini-meltdown the next morning."

"Oh." Once again, Kiley was rendered nearly speechless. "I really shouldn't have left you like that. I'm so sorry."

Harper shrugged it off.

"So, how did it happen?"

Harper didn't really feel like rehashing the gritty, and sometimes embarrassing details of that ordeal. "Look, I should really get back to work."

If it was even possible, Kiley felt worse than she did before. She tried one last time to lighten the situation. "Hey, I shared my 'vomiting in the bathroom' story. You could at least tell me about your night of drunken debauchery."

Before Harper could answer, her boss suddenly appeared from around the corner and interrupted them.

"Harper, there you are. There's a backup at the register. I need you to help ring people up."

"Okay, I'll be right there." Harper turned to look back at Kiley.

"Okay. Well, we'll talk later then," said Kiley, as she handed the bag of donuts to Harper. "Enjoy."

Harper watched as a defeated Kiley walked way. She opened the bag and inhaled the sweet scent of her favorite indulgence and instantly felt guilty about treating Kiley so badly. The problem was, Harper really didn't know what to say to her friend. Yes, she was disappointed in Kiley's decision to ditch her, but she also understood that that's just who she was. She was someone who always lived in the moment and never really gave much thought to the future or the potential consequences of her actions. Harper, on the other hand, was the polar opposite. And that was her cross to bear. She didn't expect Kiley to understand her way of thinking and her need to make sure that everyone around her was happy and taken care of, even if it meant sacrificing her own happiness. Though seemingly selfless, Harper was not without her faults. She was racked with self-doubt with an ultra-low confidence level. Needing some form of comfort, Harper reached into the bag and pulled out one of the donuts, wanting nothing more than to consume it right now.

"Harper! Are you coming?"

Hearing her boss's urgency, Harper reluctantly dropped the donut back in the bag and headed over to the registers. Only two more hours until her break. She was counting the minutes.

CHAPTER 12

Emily's body looked as though it was being swallowed whole as she dug around the bottom cupboard in Finn's kitchen looking for a colander. Once she found what she was looking for, she crawled out of the cupboard, managing to inadvertently take a few pots and pans with her.

"Sssshhhhhh."

She immediately felt stupid and had no idea why she was shushing the pots and pans for making noise as they fell to the floor. No one else was home. Finn was still at work. Emily thought it would be a nice gesture to make dinner for him since he was being so understanding about letting her stay with him. She used the money he left for food and went to the store to buy stuff for the only thing she knew how to make. Or, at least she thought she did. Spaghetti was supposed to be an easy meal. She thought there'd be nothing to it. So why was it taking her so long? And why was the kitchen suddenly much messier than it was before? Perhaps she didn't think this through, but Emily was confident and decided to forge on.

While she waited for the noodles to cook, she started chopping up the lettuce for salad, but stopped when she heard something bubbling.

"Oh crap."

The heat for the sauce was up too high and an explosion of sauce was bubbling all over the stove, covering it in a crimson hue. She turned off the heat and began wiping down that area of the stove with a paper towel. As she was cleaning the stovetop, the fire underneath the pot carrying the spaghetti started flashing and flickering. The water was boiling over, creating a hissing sound. Emily went to turn down the heat when some of the water splashed onto her hand.

"Ouch! Son of a bitch! Ow!"

She began hopping around the kitchen almost in tears, covering her hand with a dishrag. She was able to calm herself down and finish making the dinner she was preparing for Finn. She managed to strain the noodles without incident and tried her best to stay away from the possessed stove for the rest of the evening.

Emily scooped the spaghetti onto two plates and covered it with the sauce she heated up all by herself with her own two hands. After setting the table and mixing the salad into a bowl, all she wanted was a nap. She couldn't fathom how her mother managed to make dinner for them almost every night. She proudly observed her work of art and realized she was missing the most important ingredient. What kind of spaghetti would this be without parmesan? Emily scoured the refrigerator, which didn't take long with the five full items lurking in there. Unable to reach the top pantry, she grabbed a chair, stood up on it and rummaged through it.

Obviously frazzled by making this stressful meal, Emily's inner klutz once again reared its ugly head and she tipped over a ketchup bottle and knocked some canned soup to the ground. The sound of the cans falling drowned out the sound of Finn's keys jingling in the door, the door opening and then subsequently closing.

Finn stood there watching Emily for a moment, trying to figure out exactly what it was she was trying to do.

"Shit." Emily climbed down off the chair and began gathering up the rogue soup cans and put them on the counter, not wanting to climb the chair again.

Unfortunately, she forgot the salad was still on the counter and bumped into the bowl while turning around. Her breath stopped as she watched the leaves of lettuce fall to the ground in what seemed like slow motion.

"You've got to be KIDDING me!"

Finn decided it was time to finally make his presence known. "Yes, the lettuce wants nothing more than to kid with you. That's its sole purpose in life. Silly, tricky lettuce."

Emily jumped at Finn's voice, unaware that she had gained an audience.

"How long have you been there?"

"Long enough to see you destroy my kitchen."

Emily looked at him sheepishly. "I made dinner."

"I see. Well, I hope you don't expect me to eat the salad."

"I can wash it."

"That's really okay."

Emily gathered up the lettuce and put it back into the bowl. "Clumsiness runs in my family."

"Oh, I know…Harper had it in spades."

"New toys never stood a chance with us when we were kids," replied Emily as she threw the lettuce into the trashcan.

Finn took off his jacket and dropped the keys onto the counter. "Well, this is really nice of you. You didn't drop the spaghetti on the floor did you?"

"Oh come on. Be nice. This entire ordeal had me give a whole new meaning to 'slaving over a hot stove.'"

Finn sat down at the table, which he'd never actually used for eating before and began inhaling the pasta. He was halfway done by the time Emily sat down and started eating.

"Hungry much?"

"I'm meeting Seth in an hour."

"Call of Duty?"

"Actually, basketball. I decided to start playing again. Besides, I hear fresh air is good for you."

"It's overrated," replied Emily as she picked at her food.

Finn was making some serious headway on cleaning his plate. He wasn't overly hungry, but found eating as an easy excuse for stalling. He knew it was time to have a serious talk with Emily, but had no idea how to start it. She had already been staying with him for three weeks and nothing about the situation has changed. Emily had made no mention of Harper or shown any interest in seeing or speaking to her. She was nice enough to do her part by keeping the place clean, but hadn't shown any initiative in finding a job or even finding another place to stay. Finn was beginning to feel like she was taking advantage of his hospitality and he didn't feel like packing his bags when she would inevitably take him on another guilt trip. He looked down and saw that the food on his plate had been depleted which meant that there was no more stalling. It was time.

"So…"

"I know," Emily interrupted.

"You know what?"

"I know what you're about to ask me."

"What was I going to ask you?"

"Do I have any intention of evacuating your apartment anytime soon? Have I even been trying to get a job? Is there the slightest chance I'm going to let Harper know I'm back in town?"

Finn nodded. "That pretty much sums it up. So…"

Emily sighed. "Eventually, yes, and I'm still not ready."

Finn started tapping his fork onto the paper plate. "Emily, I don't know how much longer you expect to carry on like this. Sleeping on a couch? Staying home all day? Being thirteen miles away from your sister who's been searching for you for years and not even letting her know you're here and that you're okay?"

Ever since Emily returned to Los Angeles, a faint lump began to form inside her throat. With each passing day, that lump had grown bigger and bigger. And now, with the mere mention of how much she was hurting her sister, she didn't think she could hold that lump back any longer. Before she allowed a single tear to fall, Emily swallowed hard and looked at her watch.

"You're going to be late. You don't want to keep Seth waiting."

Finn heard the crack in Emily's voice and decided not to press the subject any further. He was able to scratch the surface at least, and was slowly making progress with her.

"I'm always waiting on him. He can wait for once." He got up and threw his plate away. "Thanks for dinner. It was really good."

"No problem." Emily tried to choke down another bite.

"I'm gonna jump in the shower." Finn paused before he reached the hallway, and looked back at Emily. "Just think about what I said, okay?"

Emily nodded. "I have been."

Finn disappeared down the hallway to take his shower. Emily was left alone at the table picking at her food. Her formerly gargantuan sized appetite had now dwindled down to nothing after Finn brought up the subject of her sister. She put her fork down and pushed away her half-eaten plate.

***

"What is Denpasar?"

Harper smiled to herself when she heard the same response repeated on her television. As she relished in her victory of her knowledge of Bali, Alex Trebek read the next answer in a new category: Films of 1964.

"What is 'A Hard Day's Night'?" answered Harper. As she heard one of the contestants give the same answer and Alex say 'correct', Harper felt like patting herself on the back. Her mini-celebration was short-lived, however, when she came to a sad realization. Knowing the answers on Jeopardy wasn't as fun when there was no one there to high five about her vast intelligence. She quickly lost interest in the game show and dejectedly turned off the TV. She sat on her couch, sulking for a while. The sun had set and her living room was growing darker by the minute, but she wasn't in the mood to get up and turn any lights on. Loneliness was beginning to sink in. Since she'd been avoiding Kiley's phone calls and Finn was no longer around, Harper found it difficult to fill her days when she wasn't at work. The days seemed to drag even more for her since she couldn't even sleep away her boredom. It's not that Harper was unpopular. Quite the contrary, actually. She used to have a lot of friends, but somehow or another, she began losing touch with them one by one. Finn happened, college graduation happened, life happened, reality happened. And now Harper found herself alone on her couch. Three years ago, she never thought she'd find herself in this situation.

There's gotta be something I can do, she thought. The poor girl was going stir crazy thinking of who she could call or what she could do to pass the time. Kiley was the first person she thought of, but that obviously wasn't going to happen. And she really didn't have any reason to see Finn right now. Staring ahead at the blank wall above the TV set, Harper felt lost and a little helpless. Then, the blank wall gave her an idea. Pictures! She could finally hang the pictures that have been stored in Emily's old room for the last year. Hanging pictures required nails, which she had. However, it also required a hammer, which Finn seemed to have conveniently taken with him when he moved into his new apartment. Well, that's it, then. It left Harper no choice. She needed that hammer. She needed to hang those pictures. She needed it for her own sanity. And she was completely full of crap. She knew her brain was just trying to come up with an excuse to see him in order to quell her extreme solitude. But she didn't care. At this point, she was desperate enough to call up Greg, but figured Finn would be a safer, less awkward choice…if that was possible.

Harper got up, ran to her desk in her bedroom and grabbed the spare key Finn gave her just in case she ever needed anything from his new place. Finn's initial hope was that she would use it to surprise him in the middle of the night if she ever felt lonely or was away from him long enough to realize she wanted to get back together with him. Sadly, that never happened and at this point, Finn had pretty much forgotten he had given it to her. Harper thought about calling him to see if he could bring the hammer over, but she felt guilty about always relying on him to do everything. So she put on a sweater, grabbed her keys and walked out the door, anxiously wondering if he would even be home right now.

***

Finn paced back and forth on the grass as Harper sat on the steps leading to her back yard. Finn's incessant pacing was becoming unnerving for her. She glanced over at the rundown playhouse she and Emily shared as kids. Tucked away in the back corner, it was practically dilapidated at this point, but Harper couldn't bear to get rid of it. Too many memories rested inside the walls of that playhouse. Memories she didn't want to lose in case she never saw her sister again. She pulled her focus back to Finn, who had finally come to a standstill.

"You can't be serious."

"I am."

"Baby, please. Please don't do this. You're just freaking out."

"Yeah, I am. Shouldn't that be a sign?"

"It happens to everybody. Hell, I've freaked out from time to time. It's normal."

"I know it's normal."

"Then why are you doing this?"

Harper started massaging her head with her hands. "Because I have to."

Finn wasn't happy with that answer. His legs began to tense up and his body started oscillating back and forth once again. "What do you want me to do? I'll do anything. Just tell me what I need to do to fix this."

"Nothing. There's nothing to fix...except for me."

Finn paused and looked over at his potentially soon-to-be ex-fiancée. "You think you're broken?"

Harper shrugged. "Something's just not right. I mean, look at you. You're perfect. You're sweet and loving and..."

"Stop. I don't wanna hear it."

"Well, how can I NOT be broken? You're pretty much perfect!"

"No I'm not! You think I'm this flawless guy who just adores you and would do anything for you. Well, you're about to see me get really pissed off! The wedding is in a week. ONE WEEK! And you're telling me this now? How fucked up are you?"

Finn sighed, knelt down in front of Harper and gently grasped her shoulders. "You're not broken. You're just afraid. And you have every right to be. I know you've had a hard time these last couple years, but don't let that stop you from being happy. I know you feel immense guilt. You want your family here with you to see you get married. I get that. But baby, I'm here. Let ME be your family. I can do it. Don't sabotage your happiness."

Harper took Finn's hands and held them in hers. At this point, she wasn't even bothering to fight back her tears. They were free-flowing down her face as her hands were shaking while holding his. She had never felt so horrible in all her life and after what she was about to say, she knew she'd always be viewed as the cruelest person Finn would ever come across. But she had no choice. He wasn't giving up.

"I think if I marry you, I would be."

Harper could see Finn's face drop. His eyes, which used to be full of hope and promise, were now empty and apathetic. He pulled his hands away from her and stood up, unable to speak.

"Please don't hate me, Finn. I don't think I can handle it if you hate me."

Finn's eyes remained fixated on Harper, searching her face for any sign that she might take back what she had said. But her decision remained resolute.

"It's really over, isn't it?" asked a bewildered Finn.

Harper slowly nodded, trying to wipe the tears from her face.

Finn indignantly walked up the back porch steps past Harper. "You call everybody. Tell them it's off. I'm outta here."

He slammed the back door behind him and Harper flinched when she heard the front door slam as well. As the engine started on his car and Finn pulled away, Harper sat there, enveloped in silence for a few moments and wished more than anything that she didn't have to break Finn's heart.

***

Harper held her stance in front of Finn's door. Suddenly, dropping by unexpectedly didn't seem like such a good idea. What right did she have showing up out of the blue just a few months after calling off their wedding? Meeting for a burger in the middle of the night is one thing, but making a surprise appearance at his place felt like crossing a line for Harper. The key was already in her hand and heading slowly for the keyhole. Once the key was securely inside, there was nothing for her to do but turn it. She opened the door slowly, peeking her head inside once it was cracked open. The TV was on, but the sound was down. She opened the door further to reveal the sound of someone in the kitchen washing dishes. Assuming it was her ex-fiancé, she cautiously stepped into his apartment and turned to close the door.

"Hey Finn. I hope you don't mind, but I came by to borrow the ha—"

Harper's words ended there. Even if she tried, she couldn't continue her sentence. Something rendered her voice, and her entire body, useless. When Emily heard the front door close, she turned around to unwittingly reveal herself to her sister.

"Oh, my God. Harper." Emily stood motionless—a statue holding a mixing spoon.

Harper stared in disbelief. At first, she was inclined to think that she was in the middle of a dream. She's had this dream several times before and every time, she wakes up disappointed. But she wasn't waking up this time. She could hear her breathing grow sharper and quicker. She batted her eyelids, scrunching and squinting her eyes to examine what she thought was an apparition in front of her. Harper refused to get her hopes up. Could this really be happening? Could this actually be Emily standing in front of her? She stayed completely still, examining her sister. Emily had easily grown a couple inches since her disappearance, and her once blonde hair was trying to find its way out of a badly done dye job. No longer radiating with brilliance, she was frighteningly skinny and almost sickly looking. And her formerly vibrant pallor was now pale and almost gray. Standing before her was a girl who has obviously seen hard times, been beaten down and dragged through the mud. A girl who was lost and hopefully now found. A girl who at one time was her little sister. Someone she would do anything for and wanted to protect at all costs. Finding those undeniable blue eyes on the face of that girl in the kitchen, Harper knew instantly that she had found her sister. And though her natural instinct was to run to her and hold her, her body wouldn't move. She was still in a state of shock.

"I…I should have told you," said Emily.

Before Harper could respond, Finn came out from the bathroom donning only a towel wrapped around his waist.

"Hey Em, have you seen my gray USC shirt? I saw you wearing it the other day. I wanted to wear…shit." Finn's legs halted and he stood there dripping onto the living room floor as Harper stared back at him incredulously. "Harper. Hi. Wha…what are you doing here?"

Harper, finding the strength to move her arm, held up the spare key Finn had given her.

"Oh. Right. Shit."

Harper looked back and forth from Emily to Finn. Upon the third glance, she noticed Emily wearing a shirt she had given Finn one year for his birthday. That combined with Finn in nothing but a towel led her to come a horrifying conclusion. A conclusion that finally helped her vocal cords work again.

"My sister, Finn? My sister?! Jesus, she's only nineteen! What, is this some sort of sick revenge for breaking up with you?"

Finn took a step forward. "What? What are you…" He looked down at himself in the towel and realized how this must have looked to Harper. "No! No, no, no! That's not it. I swear. I know how this looks, but I swear. Nothing happened."

Harper looked back at Emily, who came to Finn's defense. "He's telling the truth. I swear."

The rush of adrenaline inside Harper was slowly beginning to fade. Still unable to move, she kept her eyes fixed on Emily, still wondering if she was merely a specter who was going to disappear. "Emily? Is it really you?"

CHAPTER 13

Harper could feel the struggle in her arms, but refused to loosen her grip. Emily's breathing was becoming more and more faint until she finally gasped for air. Her attempt to get air into her lungs wasn't very successful as Harper tightened her hold. Emily tapped on her sister's back, gesturing to her mouth.

"Harp, I can't breathe," she barely got out in a whisper.

Harper shook her head and held her stance, keeping her firm embrace around her sister. "I'm not letting go."

"Okay, that's fine. Just loosen it up a bit. Please." The words barely escaped Emily's mouth, but were audible enough for her sister to hear. Harper obliged and gave a little slack on her hug, still holding on enough just to be sure her little sister didn't somehow magically disappear.

The tears welling in Harper's eyes were now freely flowing down her cheek. "I'm sorry," she sniffled. "I just...I never thought I'd see you again."

Emily's back was starting to hurt. She hadn't been able to reposition herself since Harper practically tackled her ten minutes ago and refused to let go. She didn't exactly envision her reunion with Harper to be in the middle of a poorly lit kitchen in a rundown apartment. But here they were, together at last. And any fear Emily had of her sister hating her suddenly vanished the moment she felt her arms around her.

Harper slowly pulled away from Emily. Part of her was expecting her sister to run away again as soon as she let go, but her fears were quelled when she saw Emily was staying right where she was.

Harper couldn't stop her hands from shaking. Every ounce of terror and dread that had built up inside of her for the past two years was finally coming to the surface. Two long years of waiting and wondering and hoping had all added up to this moment. Harper was beginning to feel queasy and had to sit down. Emily quickly helped her over to the couch and sat down next to her.

Finn, who had emerged from the bedroom after changing into something a little more decent than the towel he was wearing before, took this moment as his cue to leave. He grabbed his keys and headed for the door.

"Um…I'm gonna go meet Seth. I know you two have a lot of catching up to do, so take your time." He looked over at Harper. "I'm sorry. I should have told you."

Harper nodded. "Yeah."

"We'll talk later?" asked Finn in a hopeful manner.

Harper could barely see him through the tears in her eyes. "Yeah. Fine."

As Finn walked out the door, Emily turned to her sister. "I promise you, nothing happened with me and Finn."

"I know."

The two sat there in silence for a while, neither one wanting to be the first to break the silence. Harper stared at the ground while Emily stared straight ahead. The silence was completely deafening to Emily. Several more minutes passed by and neither of them had said a word. Emily nervously began tapping her fingernails on her lap, waiting for her big sister to lay into her about what a horrible human being she was. The silence was growing more prominent by the minute and Emily could only see this as the calm before the storm. She finally looked over at Harper, who still refused to look at Emily or put an end to the excruciating silence.

"I missed you."

There. The first move had been made. The sound barrier had been broken. The white flag had been waved. The ball was now in Harper's court. But after a moment of silence, it was clear that she wasn't ready to play.

"I thought about you all the time," offered Emily, her voice quivering.

More silence.

"I even called you a couple times. But, I didn't know what I would say to you, so I hung up."

Harper still said nothing.

"I was really messed up." Emily offered. "I'm STILL really messed up. But not as much as I–"

"Did I answer?"

Emily wasn't expecting her sister to speak so suddenly. "What?"

"Did I answer the phone when you called?"

Ashamed, Emily conceded. "Twice."

"So you heard my voice and you just hung up."

"I have no excuse. I know."

"I'm just trying to get a grasp on everything here. You missed me, you thought about me all the time, and you even called me, but didn't bother to tell me you were okay? A letter would have done it if you didn't want to talk to me. A postcard. Anything."

"I know."

"But you were really messed up, right?"

"Don't do that. I know I have no right to give you any excuses. I'm just telling you what I know," said Emily.

"Okay." Harper was silent again.

"I couldn't handle it, okay?" said Emily, not wanting to start up the 'who can stay quiet the longest' game again. "It was a difficult time for me."

"So you did what you do best. Just escape. Run away. You think I had it easy? You think I could deal with what was happening? I was a freaking wreck. And I needed you!" Harper stood up, realizing that her anger was slowly taking over. "You were all I had left and you just walked away like I didn't matter. Like I could handle all this on my own."

Emily put her head in her hands, hoping for some sort of break from being berated.

"You were the strong one, Harper."

"I was the strong one?" Harper couldn't believe what she was hearing. "Jesus, Em. You have no idea how weak I am. I just wanted everything to be okay for you. You were my only concern. I figured I'd be brave, I'd put up as much of a front as I could just to make things okay for you. And I'd break down at some later date."

Emily wanted to crawl into a hole at that moment. She had fought and lost against some pretty major demons in her life, but the worst thing she's ever done was now staring her in the face and asking 'why?' And she had no answer.

***

"Everyone is staring. I'm sick of people staring." Emily folded her arms as if trying to cloak herself from everyone else.

"Me too. We just have to suck it up for a couple more hours," replied Harper as the two of them watched their house become inundated with close family friends, acquaintances and people they had never seen before in their lives. Neither of them were in the mood for this, but they really didn't have much of a choice. Over the sound of strange voices rumbling and people talking amongst themselves, a familiar voice was heard above the rest.

"Oh, yeah! I'll bring out a fresh plate of sandwiches right now. Just give me two minutes."

Emily looked over to see Kiley running around like a madwoman making sure everything was in order. She was refilling food and making sure the guests had drinks. She had been a Godsend to the girls through this entire ordeal. Kiley, dressed in a stylish black skirt and dark blue blouse, rolled up the sleeves on her black cardigan sweater before carrying out the fresh plate of fruit and sandwiches. Through all the madness, she glanced over at Harper while placing the food on the table, sharing a knowing look with her, doing her best to let Harper know that everything was going to be all right.

"Well, I think I'm gonna go hang out in my room." Emily turned to leave.

"Em, don't. Just stay out here a little longer please."

Before Emily could make her escape, she was headed off by one of her mother's co-workers.

"Hi sweetie."

Emily was a bit thrown off guard. *"Oh. Hi, Mrs. Monroe."*

"How are you holding up, honey?"

A Fine Mess

Emily cringed. She hated when adults patronized her by labeling her with any kind of term of endearment. It was insulting.

"Oh, I'm okay. Just...you know..." Lying was all she could do at this point.

Harper watched as an unsuspecting Emily was unable to dodge Mrs. Monroe's advances as she pulled her into a hug.

"Oomph." Emily let out a gasp as her face was pressed against the woman's shoulder. She was actually grateful for the force of the hug. With her face pressed into Mrs. Monroe, it was a little easier to drown out the smell of the woman's potent, overpowering perfume.

"I'm so sorry dear."

"Mmmssokay," mumbled Emily. Her muffled mouth made it difficult to enunciate her words.

Her throat was starting to close up and just when Emily felt she couldn't take anymore, Kiley appeared out of nowhere seemingly coming to her rescue.

"Emily, can I get your help with something in the kitchen?"

Mrs. Monroe finally let go of her and started straightening out Emily's shirt.

"You go on ahead, sweetie. We'll talk later."

As Mrs. Monroe walked away, Emily followed Kiley into the kitchen. This was one of those rare moments when she actually appreciated Kiley.

"Thank you so much."

"No problem. If you see her coming toward you again, just burst out into tears and run into the bathroom. She won't follow you. And if she does, I'll spill something on her."

"That's very...sweet of you."

"I do what I can."

Emily opened the fridge, grabbed a bottle of water and took a drink before choking on the words she was about to say next.

"Seriously, though. I really do appreciate everything you've done in the last couple days. Calling everyone, planning everything, taking care of the catering and stuff. You've really helped out a lot."

Kiley put her hand on Emily's shoulder.

"Hey, Harper's my best friend. I'd do anything on this planet for her. And you, too. I just wish there was more I could do. Is there?"

"You've done more than enough. Really. Harper's lucky to have a friend like you."

"I'm here for you, too, Emily. I hope you know that."

Emily decided to trade her bottled water for a bottle of tequila and headed towards the back door.

"Yeah, sure."

Kiley put away the bowl she was cleaning. *"Emily, wait. Don't you think you should..."*

"Just let me have this, okay? And don't tell Harper."

"Emily, please. Just hand me the bottle."

Emily opened the back door.

"My parents just fucking died, Kiley. Leave me alone." She closed the door behind her, leaving Kiley wondering what to do next. She thought it was best to let it go. Being seventeen is never easy, especially after you've just lost both your parents.

***

A Fine Mess

Emily sat uncomfortably in the passenger seat of Harper's car. They agreed it was best to hash everything out at home instead of having Finn come home to two emotionally drained females. They sat staring straight ahead out the windshield. The only sound that filled their ears was the whirring and buzzing of the wheels on the pavement and the occasional bump or pothole along the way. Emily didn't know what was going to happen when she walked into the door of her former home. She didn't know if Harper would let her go straight to bed or if they would be up all night fighting and crying and trying to blame each other for everything that happened. She tried to clear her mind when the one thing she wanted to forget kept creeping back into her thoughts. One of the main reasons she left was something she never wanted Harper to know. She definitely didn't want to ever think about it again, but she knew it would come out eventually. Plus, maybe it was a good way to get Harper talking again since she hadn't said one word since they got the car.

"Harper, I'm sorry. I really am. I know you don't want to hear any excuses, but can I just say one thing?"

"Fine."

"Mom found out."

"Found out about what?"

"She found my stash. She confronted me about it and I just didn't care enough at the point to try to deny it. So I told her I'd been doing drugs since I was fifteen."

"You told her?"

"I didn't feel like lying. Besides, I had a feeling she sort of knew anyway. Finding it just confirmed it for her."

"So what happened?"

Emily could feel her legs shaking with nerves and tears began to fill her eyes. "She basically told me I was a complete disappointment in her eyes. She said she could never look at me the same. She said she was gonna tell dad, but…I don't know if she ever did. Maybe she never got the chance. It happened just a couple days before the accident." Emily's legs were now visibly trembling and her voice was choking up. "The thing is, I think she may have told him. Because when they said goodbye to me the night before the trip, there was something about the way he looked at me and the way he hugged me and…I felt like he knew. But since they were going away for the weekend, he didn't want to deal with it at the moment. And mom…she didn't even look at me. She just said 'I'll see you when we get back on Monday' and that was it."

At this point, Emily's face was buried in her hands. She was afraid of this. Once she opened the floodgates, there would be no turning back.

"That's how they remember me. Their last memory of me is of some ungrateful, drugged out, spoiled brat loser. They died thinking they had failed raising me." That was all she could get out. The tears and sobs had now completely taken over her body.

Seeing how distressed her sister was, Harper pulled the car over and put it in park. So much for trying to make Emily feel guilty.

"Jesus, Emily. I had no idea."

She heard her sister mumble something, but couldn't quite figure out what it was. It didn't matter. She reached out and tried to soothe her sister by rubbing her back. The idle car engine sputtered softly as Emily continued to bawl, hoping one-day forgiveness would find her.

CHAPTER 14

Harper paced up and down the hall, hoping each creak and crack of her feet on the hallway floor didn't disturb Emily's slumber. After breaking down in tears, Emily decided she wanted to go straight to bed and passed out as soon as her head hit the pillow. Harper thought this would have been a great opportunity to try and get some sleep, but it turned out that having Emily home made her even more apprehensive and it was nearly impossible for her to even close her eyes. What if Emily decided to wake up in the middle of the night and take off again? Harper couldn't bear the thought of having to lose her sister once again.

She took a break from her pacing and stood in the doorway watching Emily breathing deeply in and out. The darkness of 2 a.m. made it difficult to make out her silhouette, just hearing the sound of Emily's breathing brought a bit of comfort to Harper. After a half hour of hanging out in the doorway waiting for any kind of change in Emily's sleeping pattern, Harper began to feel a bit creepy and stalkerish. So she gently closed the bedroom door and backed away into the hall once more. She stood there for a few minutes completely paralyzed and unsure of what exactly to do. She decided it was safe enough to at least go into the living room for a while. If Emily was going to leave, she definitely wouldn't go out the window. That thing hasn't opened since Emily's little experiment with the super glue when she was eight.

Harper, dressed in her faded old Donald Duck pajama pants and pink tank top, plopped down on the couch and sat contemplating on whether or not to pick up the phone and dial the number her fingers knew by heart.

***

Harper's head was beginning to ache. Part of her just wanted to follow Emily's example and head straight to her room to shut everyone out, but that wouldn't be the proper thing to do, would it? She looked around, hoping to find at least one ally who wouldn't look at her with infinite concern and pity.

Finn walked into the front door with his black blazer hanging over his arm. He loosened his tie and hung up the blazer in the front closet. When he spotted Harper, he made his way over, put his arm around her and kissed her on the cheek.

"How are you holding up?"

"Do you want the truth or the answer I've been giving everybody else?"

"Sorry. It was a stupid question." He lightly massaged her shoulder. "Sorry I'm late. I had to give people directions here from the cemetery."

"I figured you got held up."

"Do you need me to get you anything? Something to drink?"

"I'm okay. Thanks, though. You should get some food."

He kissed her on the cheek one more time. "Okay. I'll be back."

As the day progressed and afternoon turned into the evening, people slowly started trickling out of the house after offering their condolences to Harper and — once she emerged from drowning her sorrows in the back yard — Emily.

With alcohol fresh on her breath, the younger sister sat at the counter dividing the kitchen from the dining room and picked up a photo frame that held a picture of the four of them at Disneyland eight years ago. Harper walked over to join her.

"I think that's my favorite picture of us."

Emily continued to study the photo. "So what do we do with it?"

"What do you mean?"

"Well, what do we do with all their stuff? And the house? Do we sell it? Do we rent it out?"

"Whoa, Emily, slow down. Let's just take it one day at a time. We'll figure all that out at a later date."

"I don't think I can do this one day at a time. I kinda just want to go to sleep and wake up in a year."

Harper could smell the liquor on her sister's breath.

"Well, drinking the pain away isn't gonna help you at all."

With that, Emily threw the photo down back on the counter, shot Harper a disconcerted look, then hopped off the chair and ran straight to her room. Harper started to go after her, but decided to leave her alone for now.

Kiley finally took a break from her post in the kitchen and came to talk to Harper with two freshly opened beers in tow.

"Have you eaten?" asked Kiley, handing a beer to her friend.

"A little. I'll have something later. Right now, I just want everyone to leave. Emily's really not up for this."

"And you?"

"I just want to take a nap. I feel like I haven't slept in forever." She took a drink of the beer.

"That's because you haven't." Kiley looked around. "Well, they're almost all gone. We're pretty much out of food, so that should help them to leave a little quicker."

Harper nodded indifferently. She could feel her wall starting to crumble. In the past few days, she had managed to remain stoic and brave, but the mask was slowly deteriorating. There was only so much longer she could keep this up without entirely falling apart, but she refused to do it in front of strangers. Feeling as though she couldn't stay standing for much longer, she leaned her head on Kiley's shoulder hoping her friend could lift some of the weight she had been carrying with her for the past ninety-six hours. After crying for seventeen hours straight, she managed to pull herself together long enough to start making some arrangements. Her brain and body were stuck on auto pilot and now it was time for the real Harper Foley to return to herself. The human Harper who was in mourning and allowed to feel sad and fall to pieces when everything around her was becoming unraveled.

"Kiley, I need to not be here right now."

Kiley put her beer down and grabbed Harper by the hand and led her to her bedroom.

"All right, come on. Follow me."

"No, I can't. There are still people here."

"Let me and Finn deal with that. You should rest."

She opened the door to Harper's bedroom and pulled the covers off the bed, then led the exhausted, almost delirious girl to the bed and sat her down. She knelt down to take off Harper's heels, then opened the middle drawer of the dresser to pull out a t-shirt.

"Okay, arms up."

Harper obliged and put her arms up. "But what about..."

"Shhhh...don't worry. Whatever it is, I'll take care of it." She pulled Harper's black dress off and replaced it with the old Def Leppard t-shirt she found in the drawer. She grabbed a pair of sweats from off the floor.

"Are these clean?"

Harper's eyelids were beginning to win out over her stubbornness. "They should be, I only wore them once."

The more she spoke, the more delirious she began to sound.

"Okay, left leg in first. And now the right." Once both Harper's legs were in, Kiley pulled the sweats up to her waist and laid her down onto the bed, sat on the side and adjusted the pillow.

Harper gazed up at Kiley, thankful she was here at this moment. "Thank you."

"Of course."

"Emily's upset. Like, really upset. I should go talk—"

"Don't worry about it. I'll keep an eye on her. She probably just needs sleep, like you," assured Kiley. "I'll check on her in a bit."

A small, appreciative grin crept across Harper's face. For the first time since her world turned upside down, she actually felt safe for a brief moment. It was a welcomed change and part of her wished that this moment could last forever because she was tired of feeling so unsure and afraid of what the future held.

***

Sinking lower into the couch, Harper hesitated briefly before she picked up the phone and called the one person she had been avoiding. It only rang once before a voice answered on the other end.

"Oh, so NOW you wanna talk. I've called, left you messages, been waiting by the phone…but when it's convenient for YOU, 'Miss 2:30 in the morning', then you suddenly wanna talk." Kiley was still slightly hurt at Harper's reluctance to speak to her, but she was trying to lighten the situation by gloating a bit.

Harper knew she was joking, but wasn't exactly in the mood to play along.

"Kiley…"

"No, no. It's fine," Kiley dramatically interrupted. "It's not like I have a life, or anything. I don't need to spend my time thinking about how you're mad at me and…"

"Emily's home."

There was nothing but silence on Kiley's end until she could muster up one word. "What?"

"Emily. She came back." Harper waited while the news sunk in for Kiley, then heard the words that pretty much could have gone without saying.

"I'll be there in ten minutes."

They hung up and Harper sat there in the dark, contemplating everything she had experienced tonight. She hadn't even realized over twenty minutes had passed until Kiley lightly tapped on the door.

"Hey," she whispered as she held up a six-pack of Spaten. "Sorry I'm late, but I figured you'd need a couple of beers. God knows I do."

Harper smiled at the gesture. "How do you always know what I'm craving?"

"It's simple. It's almost always beer, donuts, or Italian food. I have a one in three shot of getting it right. And I'm really good at playing the odds." Kiley grinned as she walked past Harper. She put the six-pack down on the kitchen counter and pulled out a bottle opener from the drawer. First a fizz, then a pop as the metal from the bottle cap clanged onto the counter.

"Here ya go," said Kiley as she handed the beer to her friend.

"Don't you ever get tired of serving drinks?"

"I guess I hadn't really thought about it until you brought it up. Thanks." Kiley grabbed a beer and made herself at home on the couch. "So she's sleeping right now?"

"Yeah," Harper replied, still standing in front of the coffee table. "She's been passed out for a while. Must be nice."

"Well, she's probably been through a lot. Besides, maybe you can sleep easier now that she's home."

Harper scoffed at that statement. "Doubtful. At least not for a while."

"Well, maybe the paranoia will fade." Kiley leaned back and savored the beer from her now half-empty bottle. Upon noticing that Harper was still standing uncomfortably, she implored her. "Sit down. Chill for a minute."

"Right." Harper joined her on the couch. They sat there for a moment, in a comfortable stillness. Kiley had a million questions, but waited for Harper to show she was ready to talk about it.

"She was at Finn's, you know? That's where I found her."

"Seriously?"

"Yeah. She'd rather go to my ex's place than come home."

"Well, she probably didn't know he was your ex at first. And she probably just needed some time to think about her next move. At least she's here."

Harper nodded.'

"Why didn't Finn call you? I would think he'd jump at the chance to bring you such incredible news."

"I don't know. I guess some sort of pact between them prevented him from doing so." Harper took a swig of her beer.

Kiley contemplated for a moment. "So…where do you think she was all this time? I mean, what could she have been doing? How did she make money?"

Harper shook her head emphatically. "I don't know. I don't wanna know. I don't wanna think about it."

"I can't even imagine what she's been through. When you're young, you never really have that goal of 'I want to be a runaway and live life day to day not knowing when or if I'm going to eat again.'"

"Yeah, I guess that's not really one of the options when people ask you what you want to be when you grow up."

"What did *you* want to be?"

"Me?" Harper chuckled to herself. "Oh man, I don't think I wanna share that with you."

"Why not," asked Kiley.

"Because you make fun of me enough as it is."

"Okay, now you *have* to tell me."

"I know I do. I was just hoping to prolong it. Ugh, fine. There was a time when I was eight years old, for about three weeks, when I wanted to be a hooker."

Kiley looked over at Harper. "Okay, are you taking notice of my blank stare? Details please, before I start laughing so hard, I can't hear your explanation."

"Hey, it was before I knew what it actually entailed. My parents had rented 'Pretty Woman' and I just so happened to watch it while they were away and my babysitter cared more about talking to her boyfriend on the phone than actually watching Emily and me. So I watched it and I just loved how glamorous Julia Roberts was and wanted Richard Gere to pay me to hang out with him and…I really had no idea. My friend Amy was much more mature than me, and her older sister told her everything. So she set me straight on what exactly a hooker was. I really had no clue. So after that, I just decided I wanted to be an astronaut. I knew what that meant."

Kiley sat staring at Harper, awestruck.

"Shut up," said Harper.

"I didn't say anything."

"Well, you were going to, so just don't. There's a reason eight-year-olds shouldn't watch R-rated movies."

"That's for damn sure."

A sudden flash of fear washed over Harper. It had been in the back of her mind ever since Emily left, but she never brought herself to actually consider the option. "You don't think Emily ever…I mean. I know she needed money but she would never have…you know…"

Kiley knew Harper wasn't ready to go there just yet, so she steered clear of that conversation. "Anyway, I wanted to be a flower delivery person when I was younger."

Harper welcomed Kiley's thoughtful avoidance of where she was going with that little speech.

"Really?"

"Yeah. I've just always liked the idea bringing flowers to people who need to be cheered up. Plus…flowers are pretty." "It's the simple things for you, isn't it?"

"Yup. Although, I also wouldn't have minded being a Hollywood tour guide. 'Now on your left, you can see the bungalow where Marilyn Monroe was found dead. And coming up, you'll soon find the house Tom Cruise once lived in.'"

"Sounds like fun."

"I feel special when I know things other people don't know. It makes me feel powerful."

"You're a dork."

Kiley flashed her infamous million-dollar smile. "Well aware." She finished off her beer and got up to get another one. "But at least I knew what a hooker was when I was eight."

"I was sheltered. Jackass."

Kiley opened another bottle. "You want another beer?"

"Always."

Kiley popped the cap off another bottle looked over at Harper. "I'm really glad you called, by the way. I really thought that this might be it. I finally pissed you off to the point of hating me."

"Not possible. You're a pain in my ass Young, but I wouldn't have it any other way," assured Harper.

"Well, for what it's worth, I'm really sorry. I shouldn't have left you like that."

"No. You shouldn't have, but I should have spoken up. I'm such a pushover sometimes."

Kiley brought the beers over to the couch. "Well now that your *other* pain in the ass is back, what happens now?"

"What do you mean?"

"I don't know. Do you think things will go back to normal?"

Harper sighed. "Were things ever really normal in the first place? Em and I never had a chance to go back to normal after mom and dad died. Everything's been in such a state of flux for the last two years. You'd think her coming home would be the answer to everything, but the truth is, I'm absolutely terrified. I'm afraid to even close my eyes in case I wake up and she's not there anymore. It'll probably be another two years before I can even think about getting any sleep."

"Well, I don't have anywhere to be. And I've pulled my share of all-nighters before so if you want to try to get some sleep tonight, I can stay up and keep an eye on things."

Harper put the bottle to her lips and thought about Kiley's offer for a moment. "That's okay. You have a life you need to get back to. Besides, I'm pretty wound up. I'm not even really that tired and I'd be too paranoid and stressed out to fall asleep."

***

Three hours later, Kiley was starting to feel the weight of Harper leaning against her with her head heavily resting on Kiley's shoulder. For an insomniac who claimed she wasn't that tired, Harper sure had been sleeping like a champion for the past two and a half hours. All was quiet in the Foley household. The only cause for concern Kiley had was about an hour ago when she heard Emily get up to use the bathroom, then go straight back to her room. Kiley had hoped Emily would make at least a brief appearance in the living room seeing as how she hadn't seen her face in so long. The only thing that was Kiley's saving grace throughout the night and early morning was Nick at Nite. Though she wondered why they no longer showed classics like *I Love Lucy*, *Green Acres*, and *Gilligan's Island*. She sure could have gone for at least an episode of Three's Company. Instead, they replaced those iconic shows with questionable "modern classics." *Malcolm in the Middle*? Really?

When the channel went from *The Fresh Prince of Bel Air* to a cartoon she had never heard of, Kiley changed the channel to an infomercial for the hits of the '70s. With the sounds of Supertramp, David Cassidy, Bread and Boston filling her ears, it was tempting to call and order the super collection. But she had to remind herself of the gardening claw she ordered that's sitting in her hall closet because her apartment doesn't have a garden. The same goes for the Slap Chop that was used only once when she attempted to make a homemade stew. And she didn't even want to think about the Snuggie she used to sop up the water from a leak in her apartment ceiling. She really had to stop the splurging on items she would never use and start saving. Yes, the sounds of the '70s would have to be heard in thirty-second increments in the iTunes store.

Kiley could feel her 'restless leg syndrome' kicking in as fatigue swept over her body. Two yawns and a couple of eye-widenings later, she finally gave in and began to doze off. Before she could enter a full REM cycle, she was awakened by the sound of a spoon clanging against a glass bowl. She opened her eyes and looked over to see a young woman who looked vaguely familiar sitting on the floor in her t-shirt and underwear watching MTV.

Emily took a bite of her Golden Grahams cereal and felt someone's eyes on her. She turned around to see Kiley sleepily staring at her.

"I was wondering when you'd show up. Didn't take you long, did it?" whispered Emily.

"I came as soon as she called me."

Emily glanced over at the front door. "I wasn't gonna take off, or anything."

"I know," replied Kiley. She gestured toward Harper, whose weight was now causing Kiley's entire right side to go numb. "I just don't think she knew for sure."

Emily looked at her sister, who was peacefully sleeping, then turned back to the TV. "I hope you don't mind, I changed the channel."

"It's fine," yawned Kiley, who tried to stifle her stretch. "What time is it?"

"About six. My hunger was outweighing my fatigue. Thank God there's plenty of cereal."

"Harper always kept it stocked…just in case." At this point, Kiley was beginning to get annoyed. She began to wonder if Emily ever even thought about Harper at all while she was gone. It seemed like a pretty messed up situation seeing as how Harper agonized over Emily every single day.

Before Kiley could say anything more, Harper's head popped up from Kiley's shoulder. She looked around dazed, trying to take in where she was and what was happening. She looked at Kiley imploringly.

"Did I drool, snore, or do anything embarrassing?"

"You mumbled something at some point and then said 'ah shit.' Then, not another peep."

Harper's eyes were slowly coming back into focus in the dim room. "How long was I out?"

"About three hours."

"Nice. This is good. I'm progressing."

Kiley waited until Harper was fully off her shoulder and sitting up on her own accord before she got up from the couch and excused herself.

"Well, my bladder is about to give out, so if you'll excuse me…"

"You could have just woke me up to go."

"No, I couldn't. But I'll be right back. And then I think I'm gonna take off."

Emily took another bite of her cereal. "Aww, so soon?" she asked, mockingly.

"I know. You're devastated." Kiley shook her head as she headed toward the bathroom. It was fascinating to her how sometimes things change, and sometimes things are exactly the same. She couldn't believe how different and more grown up Emily looked, but really wasn't surprised at the reception Emily gave her. Theirs was a rather tattered, love/hate-but-mostly-hate relationship and Kiley never really understood why. Emily just seemed to take an instant disliking to her from the start.

She walked out of the bathroom and back out to the living room to find Harper lying down on the couch and Emily still focused on the TV set. "I'm gonna go home and get some sleep. You two probably want to catch up, but call me if you need anything, okay?"

Harper nodded. "Thank you for coming."

"Thank you for not hating me." She looked over at Emily as she walked out the door. "Emily…always a pleasure. Welcome back."

Emily held up her hand and made a slight waving movement without turning around. Once Kiley was gone, Harper continued to lie out on the couch as her sister's back still faced her. After a few moments of what someone considered music ringing in her ears and a few awkward 'booty' videos infiltrated her eyes, Harper finally had enough.

"Emily?"

"Yeah?"

"Could you turn that off for a minute?"

Emily grabbed the remote and hit the power button. "Sure. Why?"

"I just…I think we should talk. Last night, we were both just an emotional wreck and I think maybe we should just…be normal for a minute. Have a nice, normal conversation."

Emily scooted herself around to face the couch. "Okay."

Harper sat up, crossed her legs and gave her sister a nervous smile. "Well…uh…"

She couldn't believe it. Harper had rehearsed this a million times in her head. She knew what she would say, how she would say it and even imagined every possible setting, scenario, and response her sister might give. She would be tough, yet understanding. She would ask questions, but not be overbearing. She would bring up past memories that would make them laugh if there was

162

an awkward silence. Now, after years of waiting, dreaming, hoping she'd come back and planning out their first real conversation after the reunion, she couldn't even get a word out. After all, what was there really to talk about? How did one begin a conversation that would no doubt turn into an epic story neither of them was ready to discuss?

Emily decided to cut the awkwardness short. "Uh…I'm gonna go back to bed. I'm exhausted."

"Oh, okay," replied Harper. "Have fun." Immediately she felt stupid for saying that. *Have fun? Really, Harper? Smooth.*

Once Emily disappeared into her room, Harper sank back into the couch, lying down flat and pulling the quilt resting above the couch over her head. Why was she so awkward? Why couldn't she just say exactly what she's thinking? She pulled the blanket off her head and used it as a pillow, spending the next couple hours rethinking the events that had played out in the last twenty-four hours. What more could she do? She didn't work that day and was far from being able to fall asleep again.

She hated herself for not being able to muster up the words she wanted to say to Emily just because she felt it was important to walk on eggshells for the time being. Well, not anymore. Since when did she have such difficulty relating to her sister? Sure, they were different as night and day, but the sisterly bond was always there...at least it was until they were separated by years of distance and isolation. Harper lay there wondering if she could ever truly restore her fragile relationship with Emily.

<u>CHAPTER 15</u>

Dr. Harris tossed back her long, dark brown hair. She wasn't used to wearing her hair down, but today was different. Her hair clip had broken earlier, so her typical bun was non-existent today. As always her ever-present clipboard was being used as her favorite go-to prop. She quietly tapped the eraser-end of her pencil against it as Finn sat there with a rather obvious smirk on his face.

Dressed in board shorts and flip flops, Finn was much more casual today than he had been in the past. Usually, he came to his sessions straight from work, but today he decided to take the day off and go to the beach after his appointment.

"You seem more chipper than normal," observed Dr. Harris.

"Chipper?"

"Would you prefer a more masculine term? How about less broody?"

"Do I?"

"Yes."

"Well…Emily's back."

Dr. Harris nodded. "Emily is your ex-fiancée's sister?"

"Yeah. She just showed up on my doorstep a couple weeks ago. Right after our last session, actually."

"Wow. How is your ex handling it?"

"Harper's fine. I mean, she's ecstatic. I haven't really gotten a chance to talk to her much since it happened, but I'm sure she's happy."

"Well good. That's good for her. And what about you?" Dr. Harris felt some loose strands of her hair fall into her face. She quickly brushed them out of the way.

"With Emily back, everything is as it should be in Harper's life, except for her parents of course."

"Right. Her parents. Do you mind me asking about that? How did they die?"

"Car accident. They were on a weekend trip up north. They liked to take their little weekend getaways to keep their romance alive, I guess. Harper always said that grossed her out. But I think deep down she thought it was pretty cool that her parents were still in love and constantly making efforts to stay that way."

"That's always endearing."

"Yeah. Anyway, this one night as they were leaving the hotel to go to dinner, some asshole in a Yukon decided to run a red light and plowed right into their car." Finn paused for a moment, remembering the exact second he got that phone call from Harper telling him what happened. Even after all this time, it was still painful to think about it. "And then everything changed in that one instant."

"And Harper hasn't really been the same since?"

Finn shook his head. "No. I mean, how could she be? She lost both her parents at once and then just weeks after their funeral, her sister takes off leaving her in an empty house."

"A house that used to be full and vibrant," added Dr. Harris, who was finally beginning to realize the full magnitude of everything Finn had been through with Harper.

Finn nodded.

"I can't even imagine living through a tragedy like that," offered Dr. Harris. For a moment, she began to feel silly and even a little guilty dwelling on her own petty problems. After all, she was nearly twenty years older than Harper and couldn't even imagine losing her parents now.

"It was six months after I proposed. The wedding plans sort of fell by the wayside for a while after that. Anyway," continued Finn, "Emily's back and Harper's happy. Which means there might be a really good chance of us getting back together."

Dr. Harris was slightly taken aback by this statement. "Why do you say that?"

"Well, I think her life was just in complete turmoil. And now it's a little less complicated than it was."

"Oh, I'm sure it's still plenty complicated," retorted Dr. Harris.

"Maybe so. But I just have this feeling something good is gonna happen."

"Something good *did* happen. Harper is reunited with her sister. You should be happy for both of them. But Finn, as much as I'd like to see you content with everything you think has gone wrong in your life, please don't get your hopes up about Harper coming back. You've made so much headway. Do you really want to return to that sad, beaten down guy you were when you first started coming here?"

Finn was appalled. He wasn't quite sure how to react to that. "Wow. You really know how to deliver a low blow, don't you?"

Dr. Harris shrugged, trying to remain as impartial and apathetic as possible. She had always tried her hardest to distance herself from her patients. Though her heart would break over certain patients and stories–molestation, abuse, death, and even the occasional coming out story would tug at her heartstrings-she still managed to remain unbiased and indifferent to most of them. However, Finn Lewis made it quite difficult for her. She couldn't comprehend how a young, good looking, well-educated man could think so little of himself by insisting that the only way he can be happy is if he's with a girl who rejected him. From what Dr. Harris could tell, she never really seemed all that interested in him in the first place. She really couldn't figure out why Finn frustrated her so much, but the fact that her professionalism seemed to be wavering was really starting to piss her off. She tried to compose herself when Finn looked at her quizzically.

"You don't think we'll get back together?"

Before she could respond, she was silenced by a scuffle coming from her office lobby.

"You can't go in there! She's in the middle of…"

"Shut up!"

The door suddenly opened and then slammed shut. Finn looked over to see a man in his early forties, dressed like he was in his early twenties wearing a fitted Pink Floyd shirt and tight jeans and carrying a motorcycle helmet. Once he removed his sunglasses, Finn could tell this guy was obviously way too good looking for his own good. Finn started to think that maybe his appointment had run late and this guy was just impatiently waiting. Though, it soon became clear that he and Dr. Harris didn't quite share a doctor/patient rapport.

167

"Man, that assistant of yours is a real bitch," asserted the intruder.

Dr. Harris remained calm in her seat. "No, she's just a good employee and knows who NOT to let in."

"Well, I'm in."

"What do you want, Steven?"

For some reason, that name sounded familiar to Finn.

"What do you think I want? You were supposed to drop Andrew off last night."

Dr. Harris stood up and put her clipboard down on her desk. "The last two times I went to drop him off with you, you were nowhere to be found. You won't return my calls. What was I supposed to do? Disappoint him again?"

"The custody agreement states that I get him the first and third weekend of every month," challenged Steven.

"It also states that you are required to pay child support every month. You're five months behind."

Finn suddenly realized why Steven's name sounded familiar. He was the one Dr. Harris was arguing with on the phone a few weeks ago.

"You can't hold my son hostage just because I'm a little behind on payments."

"And you can't blow him off one weekend and expect to see him whenever you want. It doesn't work like that."

"Susan, I want him at my place by six o'clock tonight, or I'm calling my lawyer," threatened Steven.

"So you can afford a lawyer, but you can't afford to give your son money for new shoes?"

"Shut up!" Steven was now dangerously close to Susan. He angrily began to lunge at her, but before he did anything drastic, Finn jumped up and stood between them.

"Hey! That's enough. It's time for you to leave. Now. Or I'll call the police." Finn could feel his heartbeat accelerate as an adrenaline jolt shot through his entire body.

Steven retreated as his heavy, frustrated breathing quickly dissipated. "Six o'clock tonight."

"And what if you're not there?"

"I'll be there."

"He's at school and I arranged for the babysitter to watch him until 5:30."

"Good. Then six shouldn't be a problem." Steven slammed the door on his way out.

Dr. Harris turned to face Finn. "I don't even know what to say. I am so sorry. I profusely apologize. That should not have happened in front of you."

Finn's heart rate was beginning to slow down. "It shouldn't have happened at all. Does he always treat you like that?"

"Not always. I rarely even see or speak to him anymore except when it comes to our son." She sat down in her chair, still slightly shocked over what had just transpired. "I'm so embarrassed."

"Don't be. We all have our baggage."

"Yeah, but this was beyond unprofessional."

"It's fine. Really." Finn leaned against the desk. "So, I'm assuming he's your ex."

"Ex-husband. We were married five years. Five very tumultuous years. And that unholiest of unions produced a pretty incredible kid." She stood up and grabbed the picture on her desk to show Finn. "Andrew's eight."

"He's cute."

"Yeah. I'd like to say he gets it from me, but…well…you saw his father."

"Don't sell yourself short." Finn handed the photo back to Dr. Harris.

Dr. Harris took a deep breath. "I'm sorry. I'm just so frazzled right now. Look, I won't charge you for today's session and we'll just reschedule for next week."

"Okay. Whatever works for you." Finn instantly took notice of how tense she was. He really wasn't expecting such an action-packed session, but he was thankful he was at least there to help diffuse the situation. "Dr. Harris…do you want to come to the beach with me?"

"Are you serious?"

"Yeah. You look like you could use a break. Take the rest of the day off and come with me."

"Oh…no, thank you. I appreciate the invite, but I can't."

"Why not?"

"I have another patient coming in an hour."

"Is that your last one?"

"Yes, but…"

"Then reschedule it. Come on, it's the first really warm day we've had in a while."

"I really can't. It would be extremely inappropriate."

"Why? Because I'm your patient?"

"Well, yeah."

"Fine. I quit. I'm cured. So I no longer need your services."

Dr. Harris laughed. "I'm afraid there's a lot more to it than that. You can't just quit. You still have a lot of work ahead of you. Besides it's Friday and I have paintball later today."

"Blow it off. Just this once."

"I can't do that."

Finn started walking towards the door, then turned around. "Look, it's just a friendly invite. You don't have to go, but if you change your mind you can meet me there. Santa Monica beach near the pier. I'll be the one looking nice and relaxed lying in the sun. If you can't find me, you have my number. I'd really like you to meet me there. I could use a friend right now."

Dr. Harris shook her head. "I'm not your friend, Finn."

"Okay then. I'll be here next Thursday, 4pm. I'll let your receptionist know." As he walked out the door, Finn left Dr. Harris with some parting words. "Just don't let some immature asshole ruin the rest of your day. No matter how sickeningly handsome he is."

***

Finn sat on his beach chair with his toes digging into the soft, warm sand. The tiny grains were massaging his feet as he kept digging them further into the ground. With his eyes closed, he felt more and more at ease each time he heard the ocean waves crash along the shore. The seagulls were out in full force with their high-pitched squawking lingering in the air as they flew around above him. Finn breathed in the fresh ocean air, enjoying the fact that the beach was fairly empty since most people were still at work. He was loving the fact that while he was here soaking up all this beauty under a perfect California sun, his colleagues were no doubt stuck in their cubicles working the day away. The burdens that had been weighing so heavily on his mind suddenly took a back seat to the tranquility he was experiencing at this moment. It had been a couple weeks since he had seen or spoken to Harper and he honestly thought she would have called him by now, but he remained patient. These things take time. Besides, he couldn't be bothered with that right now. Not on a day like this. And definitely not with a neurotic and adorably paranoid sidekick sitting next to him, who ultimately decided to join Finn.

"You know, I really shouldn't be here."

Finn chuckled and looked over at Dr. Harris through his Ray-Bans. "Yeah, I know. You've been saying that for the past hour."

"Well, it's true."

"Nothing you can do about it now. You're already here. Just enjoy it. How often do you get to the beach?"

"I haven't been in a few years."

"But you're so close to it."

"I know. I've been busy."

"Well, take this time to just breathe. You don't have to pick up your son for another three hours. You've got no patients to see. Enjoy it."

Dr. Harris took in several deep breaths. "Okay. I'm enjoying, I'm enjoying." She was repeating those words like a mantra, but neither of them were truly convinced that she was fully enjoying herself. She started brushing away some stray sand from her towel. "Thanks for letting me use your towel, by the way."

"No problem. I always have an extra in my trunk. My friend Seth and I used to go surfing a lot."

"Well, I'm glad I had a pair of shorts in my car. But my legs haven't seen the sun in a long time. Sorry if they blind you."

"Why do you think I'm wearing my sunglasses?" joked Finn.

"Very funny." Dr. Harris straightened out the towel underneath her, moved the sunglasses that were resting on her head down to her eyes, and laid down on her back, letting the sun shine down on her SPFf 30-covered face. She couldn't remember the last time she actually took a moment to herself to just stop and let go. She found it to be a rather insurmountable task. She began to envy Finn for his ability to remain so quiescent at such a difficult time in his life and was beginning to wonder what she was even doing here. This was not at all what she expected. She imagined some sort of special "outdoor" therapy session, but Finn was being surprisingly taciturn for someone who usually talks up a storm in her office. His aloofness wasn't as bothersome as her own inability to shut everything out for a moment and allow herself to listen to her surroundings. Her sad attempt to unwind as her body searched for the slightest bit of inertia was immediately truncated when she glanced over at the pier and spotted an ice cream stand.

"They have ice cream at the pier?" she asked, suddenly craving her biggest vice but also trying to hide her excitement.

"Yeah. You've never been to the pier?"

"No. But I may have to excuse myself. I'm gonna get some ice cream."

"I'll come with you. I haven't been over there in a while."

***

The two leisurely strolled down the pier. Dr. Harris licked the melting chocolate chip ice cream from the cone as Finn, who opted for a less messy frozen treat, enjoyed

173

a cup of vanilla frozen yogurt. Neither had said a word since paying for the ice cream, but a lot of that was because Dr. Harris was intently focused on eating hers before it melted. The pier was starting to get a little busier as more and more people were gathering on the beach. The seagulls were still lingering with the hopes that someone would drop part of a pretzel or some cotton candy along the way. Finn felt surprisingly at ease. He really didn't know what to expect when he invited Dr. Harris to the beach. He originally had no intention of asking her, but after seeing the look on her face and how upset she appeared after their encounter with her ex, he felt it was the right thing to do. He honestly didn't think she'd end up coming, but he was glad she did.

"So, Dr. Harris…"

"You know, we're not in my office. I'm not your doctor at the moment. Call me Susan."

"Okay, Susan. Does anyone ever call you Susie?"

"Not if they want to live to see another day."

"Good to know. So, you haven't been to the beach in years and you rarely take time for yourself except for your paintball league. How do you keep sane?"

Susan started making her way to the cone, having eaten most of the ice cream in record time. "My son keeps me sane when he's not driving me crazy. He's my life. And in ten years, when he goes off to college, maybe I'll have some semblance of a normal life. But by then, I'll be an old spinster."

"I highly doubt that."

"Well, we'll see."

"You know, for a psychiatrist, you really are self-deprecating a lot of the time."

"I know. I've been working on it. It's scary when I think about it. I mean, look at the mess I've made of my life. Who am I to be the arbiter in other people's lives? But I'm good at it, you know? I like knowing that I'm helping people, or at least trying."

"That's admirable." Finn walked over to the trashcan to throw out his cup. "So if you don't mind me asking, what happened with your ex? How did you two split up?"

Susan took a bite of her ice cream cone and thought about whether or not she really wanted to delve into this with her patient. 'Oh, what the hell,' she thought. 'He trusts me enough to tell me the truth. Why shouldn't it work both ways?'

"Well, his views on monogamy were a little different than mine."

"Meaning?"

"Meaning, I believed in it and he didn't."

"Oh. Sorry."

"Yeah, but the sad thing is, I knew it was happening. And I knew it was with multiple women. We fought about it a lot and I threatened to leave, but I always ended up going back to him."

"Why?"

"Oh, I don't know. Probably that age-old theory of women thinking they can fix a broken man. It never works, especially in this case. The last straw came when I found out he introduced Andrew to one of the women he was seeing. I never really understood the expression 'seeing red' until that day. Apparently that's a real thing. So, I took Andrew and left. The sad part is, I actually thought he would care more than he did. He only tried once to get me back and it was sort of a half-assed attempt. And then, during the divorce proceedings, I began to find out a lot of other things about him that I didn't know. Including his occasional drug use."

"Seriously?"

"Yeah. That's how I ended up with primary custody."

"Wow. So how long have you been divorced?"

"Three years. It was hard at first, but gradually it got easier. And now I'm at the point where I'm finally grateful to have him out of my life for the most part. At least in the relationship sense."

"I'm sorry you had to go through all that."

"I'm not. It was a learning experience. If we don't royally screw up every once in a while, how will we ever be able to appreciate the things we get right in life?"

Finn pondered those words of wisdom as he kept walking, feeling the wooden floorboards move beneath his feet. The squeals from the people on the rollercoaster behind them resonated in his ears and the rumbling of the coaster as it sped across the tracks made the floorboards vibrate. It was a familiar feeling, almost like déjà vu.

"I used to come here with Harper all the time. Sometimes we would just sit and watch everyone walk by."

"It seems like a nice place to people watch."

"It is." Finn was terrified to ask the question that had been weighing on his mind for the past half hour. He braced himself for the answer he was about to get. "So, do you really think Harper and I won't get back together?"

Susan wasn't expecting such a candid question at this moment. She wished she hadn't shoved the rest of her ice cream cone in her mouth just a second ago. She chewed quickly and tried to swallow without choking.

Finn laughed. "Take your time. I don't know the Heimlich."

"I can't really give you an honest answer. I don't know Harper. I don't know her mindset. I don't know the entire story or your entire past with her, so I really couldn't say. All I ask is that you seriously ask yourself if you really want to get back together with her. And then ask yourself why. You might be surprised at the answers you find. Just allow yourself to be honest. No one will be judging you."

When they reached the end of the pier, Susan turned to face Finn. His wind-blown hair was messy and significantly longer than it was when he first walked into her office a few months ago. She noticed he was smirking at her.

"What?"

"You really enjoyed that ice cream, didn't you?" He gestured at her cheek.

Susan rubbed her cheek and found some excess ice cream had somehow avoided her mouth and strayed over.

"I was saving it for later." Susan, trying not to show her embarrassment, wiped it off and smiled to herself. It was then when Finn noticed the youthfulness her face. She really didn't look like she was forty-three and he often forgot about that fact. With the exception of a few smile lines, Susan could have easily passed for someone ten years younger.

"So what do you say? One more trip up and down the pier?"

"Actually, I really should get going. I have to pick up Andrew."

"Okay."

"But thank you. I really did have a lot of fun. And I needed this."

"You're welcome. I'm glad you came."

They both stood there for a moment, each one wondering what the other one was going to do. Do they hug? Do they high five? Or do they just walk away from each other while backing up awkwardly at first? They went with option three and each took a few steps back– Finn actually creating some sort of back-up shuffle.

"Okay, so I'll see you next Thursday."

"Yup. Sounds good."

Finn watched as Susan walked across the sand toward her car, then he sat down on a nearby bench and commenced his favorite pier pastime: watching it come to life with an array of different people—families, people on their first date, and teenagers celebrating the impending weekend.

CHAPTER 16

Emily sipped the last of her lukewarm coffee while staring out the window, watching the people on the street walk by. She smiled at the sight of a man jogging with his puggle. Once her vanilla latte was gone, she brought her attention back over to Harper, who was sitting across from her reading the newspaper that someone had left on the table. Harper looked up briefly, just long enough to see Emily glance out the window again, obviously avoiding eye contact.

Emily began to regret coming along, but she wanted to get out of the house, so she took Harper up on her offer to go get coffee. Things had been a little tense between them at home. They spoke to each other, but it was usually nothing more than the obligatory 'Good morning. How are you?' jargon. Emily had hoped this outing to Starbucks might force them to actually talk to each other, seeing as how they were sitting at the same table. That wasn't the case, unfortunately. Emily's attempts to avoid eye contact were rather moot seeing as how Harper's focus was on the paper in front of her.

The silence between them was starting to grate on Emily. She searched for something to say…anything.

"Good coffee."

"Yeah. I really need to switch to decaf."

Emily tried for more. "You still read the comics section?"

"Always. It's the most uplifting thing in the paper."

More silence soon followed. Emily shook her empty cup and made one more attempt at verbal communication. "I think I'm gonna get another one."

Harper pulled five dollars out of her pocket and gave it to her sister. "Knock yourself out."

Emily, thankful for a few moments away from the excruciating awkwardness, went up and ordered another vanilla latte. Upon returning to her seat, Harper was in the same position on the same page of the newspaper, leaving Emily to question whether or not she was actually reading it or just trying to look occupied. Emily braced herself for more silence as boredom soon set in and she began tearing the cardboard sleeve off the coffee cup and asking herself why she bothered to come along.

When Emily was halfway through her second latte, Harper closed the newspaper and glanced at the time. "I should get you home. I have an open mic to get to."

Emily perked up. "Really?"

"Yeah."

"Where is it?"

"It's in Silver Lake."

Emily nervously took a breath. "Can I come?"

Harper cocked her head to one side. She wasn't expecting that response. "You really want to?"

Emily nodded. "I've never seen any of your gigs."

"Well, it's not really a gig. It's just an open mic. I'm only allowed one song."

Emily shrugged. "Still…I'd like to see you perform. If that's cool with you."

"I didn't think you really cared."

"Well, I do," informed Emily.

Harper grinned, thankful that there was finally some sort of breakthrough between them, small as it was. "Yeah, sure. You can come."

Harper hadn't planned on losing her nerve. She intentionally invited Emily to Starbucks so they could finally open up and talk to one another, ending the discomfited silence between them. However, after the quiet car ride on the way over, Harper began to lose her courage. She finally came to the decision that it might be best to let Emily open up about what happened on her own accord and in her own time. In Emily's absence, Harper had plenty of time to think about all the things she may have done wrong and should have done differently. Perhaps she had been too controlling and overbearing. Those were instincts that couldn't be helped. Her protective nature toward Emily began the day her sister was brought home from the hospital. At merely five years old, Harper would sneak into her sister's room every night to make sure she was okay, especially if she heard the slightest cough or sneeze. Her mother caught her a few times and didn't know whether to praise her daughter or scold her for being up so late at night. And so it continued–Emily would be in need of something and Harper would move the earth to give it to her. Whether it was a bottle as a baby, a trip to the zoo when she was obsessed with animals, a cute shirt when she started junior high, or Harper's favorite necklace that Emily wanted to borrow when she went on her first date. Harper made it a point to make her sister happy and grant her anything she wished. Even when someone picked on Emily, her older sister was there to make sure that never happened again. Looking back, hindsight being what it is, perhaps that need to safeguard Emily came off as being overbearing and smothering. It did taper off, though, when Emily hit her teens and began her phase of solemn solitude and experimental substances. As much as it hurt, Harper began to pull away after that. She couldn't bear to watch her sister's decline, but was powerless to stop it. She often asked herself why things turned out the way they did and what exactly happened to make her sister change so dramatically. Sometimes things just happen and there's no way of knowing why. Harper knew that it would be easy to drive herself crazy trying to figure out what went wrong when there really was no clear cut answer. After it was discovered that Emily had purloined Harper's guitar, it was pretty much the end of their relationship. According to Harper, they were sisters bonded by blood only and nothing more.

That detachment and resentment all changed for Harper, however, after the death of their mother and father. She felt it was only natural to attach herself to the only immediate family she had left and maybe did so a little too much. Emily wanted nothing more than to be left alone during that time, which was a concept her sibling simply couldn't understand. Granted, when it first happened, they came together as sisters should, but it was a rather fleeting occurrence. Now that they were reunited after Emily's hasty exit two years ago, it was apparent to both girls that neither of them had anything in common anymore and it was going to take a lot to salvage what was left of their rocky relationship.

***

Emily's face was buried in the pillow with no plans of moving an inch no matter how muffled her breathing was. She vaguely heard the phone ring just moments ago and Harper was in the living room talking to whoever it was that called, but Emily tried to drown out the sound. She'd had a long, rough night with her friends and had just fallen into bed about an hour ago. Being seventeen, she usually had a curfew she was supposed to adhere to. But since her parents were out of town on one of their "rekindling the romance" weekend getaways, she figured her curfew didn't matter all that much. Especially since she pretty much broke it every night anyway. Harper's voice had faded and had finally gone quiet. Emily reveled in this for a moment, hoping she could finally fall back to sleep. Her hopes were dashed when Harper knocked on the bedroom door and walked in.

"Em?"

In that one syllable, Emily could tell something was off. The inflection, the nuanced quivering, the tentativeness in Harper's voice caused Emily's stomach to drop. She suddenly felt her face go flush.

"I'm sleeping." She was hoping to brush it off. If it was something important, surely it would wait until later that morning.

"Em, wake up," implored Harper.

This time, the sound of Harper's voice stirred more of a reaction from Emily. The younger girl slowly sat up, rubbing her eyes and not seeming to care that she was smearing last night's makeup all over her face.

"What is it?"

Harper turned the light on which only aggravated Emily's alcohol-induced headache. She sat stoically on the edge of Emily's bed, not really sure how to begin.

"I just got off the phone with Cottage Hospital in Santa Barbara."

183

A Fine Mess

Emily moved her legs underneath the blanket and sat up further. "Are mom and dad okay?"

Harper looked at her sister, tears stinging her eyes. She slowly shook her head as one of those tears fell.

Emily's breath started to quicken. "What is it? Is one of them in the hospital? Were they in an accident or something?"

Harper nodded.

Suddenly, Emily was wide awake as her heart began to pound uncontrollably. "What happened?"

Never in a million years did Harper ever think she would have to deliver this kind of news to her sister. This was the first time she truly felt helpless when it came to protecting Emily.

She cleared her throat and tried to keep herself calm. "I guess they left the hotel to go to dinner. Another car ran a red light and..."

She couldn't bring herself to finish that sentence. If she said it out loud, that would make it true and she just needed it to be untrue for a little while longer.

"Well, are they okay? Is it mom?" Emily pleaded with Harper to form at least a full sentence so she could know the severity of the situation. Harper seemed lost in her own world, staring intently at the floor.

"Harper!"

Harper took Emily's cue and snapped out of her daze. She looked into her sister's pleading eyes and couldn't hold back any longer. She began to sob as she pulled her sister in for a hug. She only managed to choke out two words: "They're gone."

***

Breanna Hughes

It seemed rather redundant to Emily to go from Starbucks straight to a different coffeehouse, but she opted to not vocalize her observation. She sat quietly, squirming in an uncomfortable seat inside this hole-in-the-wall café. The smell of stale coffee permeated her nose along with the cigarette smoke courtesy of the smokers just outside the back door. Judging by how dumpy the place seemed, she was surprised at how crowded it actually was. At least seventy-five people were crammed into the small space, half of them with guitars. She looked over at Harper, who was busy tuning her guitar, and leaned in toward her.

"I didn't realize how many wannabe musicians there are around here."

"Are you kidding? This is LA. And this is a slow night," whispered Harper.

Emily watched her sister manipulate the tuning pegs on her guitar and suddenly found a new appreciation for her determination in chasing her dream. The whole thing seemed so tedious to Emily. You wait through several bad singers singing even worse songs only to hear a worthy voice every once in a while. Then, you go up on stage, sing one or two songs, and that's it. It's over. She couldn't believe how patient Harper was in sitting through everyone's sad and sometimes excruciatingly bad songs, showing her support by clapping for them whenever they finished. Emily couldn't bring herself to be so obliging. She was getting anxious for them to call Harper's name, not necessarily because she was bored (although she was), but she wanted to watch her sister sing. She had always known Harper had talent having listened to her incessantly playing through the bedroom wall. She even found herself humming along to her songs

185

from time to time. But when Harper started performing it was usually in a bar, so even if Emily wanted to go, she couldn't. Though at the time, the chances of her actually *wanting* to go were probably pretty slim. She was too stupidly concerned with other things.

Emily leaned back in her chair, stretching out while contemplating getting another coffee. A fleeting thought entered her mind and she tried to shake off the boredom as quickly as she could. It was times like this she wished she had something to help her get through it. She couldn't help but think how just one line of cocaine could make this night go a little faster and be a little less uncomfortable. Before she could even entertain the idea, the organizer of the open mic finally got up on stage after a gray-haired gentleman finished up his Hank Williams-type song.

"Okay, up next we have Harper Foley."

Harper sheepishly grinned as her face turned from a dull pallor to a rather rosy color. She walked to the stage and plugged the cable into her Gibson. She adjusted the microphone, made herself comfortable on the lone stool sitting on stage and cleared her throat. Her right hand started shaking as she tried to catch her breath. After grabbing the pick out of her pocket, she fastened the capo to the second fret of the guitar. While grabbing the microphone with her left hand, she could feel the nerves piling up inside of her.

"Hi. My name is Harper Foley. If you like what you hear, I play at Tyson's bar on Ventura Saturday nights." She cleared her throat one more time, then looked over at Emily, who was looking right back at her. She placed her fingers on the strings and began to strum. After the intro built up, she began to sing.

"I guess I'm not surprised looking back on everything
Running away is all you ever knew
I did the best I could to make it all okay,
But even my best wasn't good enough for you.
Maybe I stopped trying, gave up on you too soon
And I let you walk away without a sound,
And I guess you believed I didn't matter anyway,
So maybe we just let each other down."

Harper closed her eyes as she delved into the chorus, knowing full well that Emily was listening. Perhaps it was a little too obvious, but she figured this was the best way to communicate for now without having to actually talk. Her soulful, rich voice took flight as the lyrics and music swelled.

"Sometimes we stay and try to hold our own
Sometimes we choose to simply walk away
And then there are the times our fear outweighs our pride
And I know now that I can't make you stay
But I was hoping for at least another day."

Her guitar strumming continued as she geared up for the second verse absolutely terrified to open her eyes to see her sister's reaction. She would just have to deal with it once the song was over, but not now.

"I could feel it coming, the beginning of the end,
You couldn't hide the sadness in your eyes,

Now I think it's time we finally stop blaming one another

What's done is done, let's let our hatred die."

Emily scrutinized her sister's entire performance, hanging on to every word, knowing full well who and what this song was about. She should be upset. She should be furious at Harper for even thinking it was okay to bring their relationship to light amongst all these strangers. She should want to get up and leave just to prove a point, but she couldn't. She simply couldn't bring herself to feel anything but remorse and understanding. It was too tiring to feel angry anymore. Maybe Harper's words were right. It's time to stop the blame. It's time to own up. Emily sat there as her sister's voice filled the entire room and noticed that everyone in the crowd was completely captivated by what they were hearing. She wanted to smile. She wanted to cry. She wanted to beam with pride, but all she could do was stare. Showing any kind of emotion would evidently lead to another meltdown and she wasn't ready for that.

"And I don't see the point in trying to explain,
They're just words and you won't hear them anyway.
Sometimes we stay and try to hold our own
Sometimes we choose to simply walk away
And then there are the times our fear outweighs our pride
And I know now that I can't make you stay
But I was hoping for at least another day."

Once the song was over, the audience erupted in applause. She opened her eyes and saw Emily clapping

188

with a sense of both pride and anguish in her eyes. Harper's heart was pounding as she said her 'thank you' to the crowd, unplugged her guitar, and walked off the stage back to her seat.

Emily was still clapping as Harper sat down, then reached out to put her hand on her shoulder.

"That was beautiful," whispered Emily.

Harper, relieved that Emily had at least some sort of positive reaction, nodded. "Thanks."

That was their last exchange of the night. They drove home in silence and went to bed without so much as a 'good night' from each other. Somehow though, it was okay. The unspoken words between them would eventually find a voice and Harper's song was undoubtedly a good start.

CHAPTER 17

There had been no shortage of pleasantries exchanged between the sisters throughout the next couple of weeks. There was the usual "Good morning", "The trash is full", and "Did you want to finish that?" Neither one had really said much about Harper's performance at the open mic night. Harper even made it a point to wait until Emily was asleep before she started playing her guitar in the middle of the night. On this night however, she was unaware that Emily was still awake and could hear her practicing very clearly.

Harper was trying to piece together some chords to go along with the lyrics she had jotted down at work a few days ago. The fingers on her left hand formed a B minor chord as the fingers on her right hand gripped the pick and continued strumming. The strumming was short-lived, however, when the pick slipped out of her fingers and fell into the sound hole of the guitar.

"Damn." Harper turned the guitar over and started shaking it violently before the pick was forever lost in the abyss of the sound hole. She often referred to it as 'the place where picks go to die' because for some unknown reason, it was damn near impossible to get them out once they had fallen in. The grooves of the wood inside the guitar made it too difficult. Every time she changed her strings, she'd reach inside the guitar and find a goldmine of picks.

She continued shaking until the pick miraculously fell to the floor. When she bent down to pick it up, she realized it wasn't the same one that just fell in. *Oh well, at least it's something*, she thought, as she continued to play. The song was coming together nicely. She was proud of the melody that flowed with the lyrics. Once she strummed the final chord and made some last minute notes in her notebook, she slightly tuned her D string, then put the whole song together and played it in its entirety. After the final note was sung and the last chord was strummed, Harper was startled by the sound of clapping coming from Emily's room. Obviously Emily had stumbled upon her secret rehearsing time. Harper smiled to herself, knowing that Emily seemed to approve of what she had just created.

"Thank you! I'll be here all night," yelled Harper.

"Encore!" responded Emily; her voice muffled behind the wall.

Before Harper could play it again, her phone rang.

"Hello?"

"I'm gonna go out on a limb here and assume that I didn't wake you."

Harper's stomach roiled deep inside her, but she couldn't help but grin at the sound of Finn's voice.

"How right you are."

"I hope you don't mind me calling."

"No, actually, I'm surprised you didn't call sooner. I would have called you, but with everything that's been going on…"

"I know. I figured I'd give you some time to adjust to everything." He was silent for a moment. "How's it going?"

Harper put her guitar down and lay back on her bed. "I don't know."

"You don't know?"

"It's different. But I guess it's also kind of the same." Harper suddenly felt herself getting warm, so she used her feet to kick off her socks. She still felt somewhat awkward talking to Finn after the way she broke it off with him. Even though he repeatedly made it clear that he wanted to work things out, she still felt that there was an underlying hatred he felt toward her, and with good reason. She was awful to him, but never really got to explain why she ended it. How could she? He would never understand. No one would. "We have good days and bad. It's off and on with us. Usually off. We're trying, though."

"Has she shown any kind of sign of wanting to leave again?"

"Not really. At least none that I can see. I think she's still just trying to recover from everything. She sleeps a lot."

"Are you jealous?"

Harper chuckled. "Kind of."

"So, are you okay with all of this? How are you holding up?"

"I'm okay. I'm much better than I was when she was gone, so that's a plus. Honestly, I still think it's too soon to tell." Harper didn't really want to be bombarded with questions about Emily at the moment, so she searched for a subject change. "How have you been?"

"Uh…good, actually. Really good."

"Is that so?"

"Yeah. I mean, as good as I can be, you know, considering…"

"Yeah, I know." Harper didn't know what to say. An apology seemed to be too little too late. But seeing as how Finn was finally talking about it, it was becoming increasingly clear that maybe he was starting to hate her less and less.

Finn cleared his throat. "It's getting better. I've been seeing someone."

"Oh." It felt like a blow to Harper's gut. "Really? That's great."

"Yeah, she's really been helping me. Apparently I'm not the lost cause everyone thought I was."

"Wow. That's so great." Harper wondered if she could pull off fake sincerity in her voice. "Good for you. What's her name?"

"Uh…Susan." Finn sounded perplexed.

"How long have you been seeing each other?"

Finn started laughing. "Okay, maybe I should clarify. I'm seeing someone. Meaning I'm seeing a therapist. Not dating. Just…therapizing."

"Oh." Harper did her best to not show her relief. It's not that she wouldn't have been happy for him, but as selfish as it sounds, she was still in the fresh break-up mentality of 'I don't want him, but I don't want anyone else to want him either.' It seemed to make perfect sense, even after all this time. Being a woman is funny that way.

"I didn't realize you needed to see someone."

"Yeah well, it turns out getting over you is a little harder than you might think."

Harper could feel a slight pang in her chest. The day she called off the wedding, she knew she had deeply hurt him. This was the first time she actually allowed herself to fully realize the effect it had on him. In the past, any time she had even come close to thinking about their breakup, Harper forced those thoughts away. There was too much guilt weighing on her to feel bad about yet another thing gone wrong in her life. But now here was Finn, forcing her to come to terms with her emotions about their past relationship. She wanted to apologize. She wanted to ask his forgiveness. She wanted to explain her reasoning behind everything, but she couldn't. Not yet. What good would it do anyway? Finn was already well on his way to fully recovering from their breakup, so why rehash it? She wasn't ready just yet to take responsibility for Finn's emotions.

"Well, I'm glad you're doing well. I should get going. I'm in creation mode."

"New song?"

"Yeah."

"What's it about?"

Harper sat up and looked over her lyrics. "That's a good question. I'll have to get back to you on that."

"Fair enough."

"So, I'll talk to you later, then?"

"Okay."

"And Finn? Thanks for calling."

"No problem. I'm just glad Emily's back home. Good night."

Harper lay back down on her bed and began to contemplate her role in Finn's heartbreak. Obviously, she had her reasons. Obviously, it simply wouldn't have been fair to either of them had she gone through with it. Obviously, she couldn't marry someone when she was in love with someone else. But was it fair of her to deprive him of so many answers? Sometimes we just do things because we have to, even though the people around you may not understand. Some things are just too difficult to explain…and much too painful to face. Harper squinted while staring at the ceiling as the light began to slowly flicker. It was in this moment she suddenly had an urge to talk to her sister. She jumped out of her bed and headed down the hall to Emily's room hoping to find that she was still awake. The door was cracked open and Harper could hear Emily's steady breath. It was evident that her sister had fallen asleep, but Harper wasn't deterred. She would simply talk to her when the moment presented itself. For now, she wanted to attempt getting at least ninety minutes of sleep.

***

Harper felt her feet tingling beneath her as the whirring in her ear grew louder. She glided seamlessly along the pavement trying to build up enough momentum with her rollerblades to reach the top of the hill along the final stretch back to her house. She was thankful there wasn't much further to go since an undeniable sense of thirst was overpowering her and she had run out of water a few miles back.

The uneven strides of the dawdler behind her were becoming increasingly audible. Harper turned around to see Kiley, who was bringing a whole new meaning to the term "second place."

"Come on! Only another half mile!"

"Shut up, Harper."

"Seriously. This is the last hill. Then we're done. You want to get enough momentum for the hill."

"Shut up, Harper." Kiley's legs were burning. Three miles ago she wanted to ask

Harper to head back, get her car and come back to pick her up while she rested on the curb, but she opted to suck it up instead.

Harper continued skating backwards. "Wow. Either you like feeling inferior to me and all of my awesomeness, or you just really love staring at my ass."

Kiley tried to stop herself from grinning and concentrated on her footing.

"Shut up, Harper."

Harper smiled and turned back around to make her way up the hill. She was actually surprised that Kiley hadn't given up a while ago and was genuinely impressed with her determination.

Kiley struggled up the hill as each stride stoked the flames that were growing in the fire that was once her legs. What the hell was she thinking when she agreed to do this? Rollerblading definitely wasn't her sport. She was okay at it and was good enough not to fall, but it didn't come easy or naturally to her. Every time she worked out with Harper, she'd get inspired to get in shape after seeing the stamina that Harper has built for herself. But by the end of every workout Kiley just wanted to curl up and die, thinking it was best to just be thankful for being naturally thin and fit looking. But Harper inexplicably had this way of talking her into doing anything. Kiley found it difficult to resist.

Harper was now on the descent of the hill and turned the corner, resisting the urge to cheer on her friend because it would undoubtedly sound patronizing in some way. She slowed her pace as she turned left onto her street and waited for Kiley to catch up with her. She knew Kiley hated their exercise outings together and never really knew why she always agreed to go along.

But it was certainly charming and somewhat endearing listening to Kiley's rants about how much she hates it and how her body should never be subjected to this sort of hell.

An out-of-breath Kiley finally caught up with Harper.

"I swear, the only thing that should require this much panting and sweating is sex."

Harper turned around and began to skate backwards again. "You know, I often wonder how I ended up with such a classy friend."

"Well…we DID meet in a bar, so…"

Harper turned back around, skated up her driveway and came to a stop using the break on her right blade. Kiley then rolled up the driveway, put her hands out and used Harper's car as a stopping device.

"You know, one of these days, you should actually learn how to stop," informed Harper as she sat down on the porch.

"What's wrong with my way? It works every time." Kiley joined her friend on the porch as they began to take off their rollerblades. "Can I ask you something?"

"Sure."

"How do you live with being so good at everything you do?"

Harper couldn't help but laugh. "Are you kidding me? I'm really not that good at much. I mean, have you seen me dance?"

"Yes, I have. There's a spastic charm to it."

Harper massaged her foot as her left rollerblade came off. "It's overrated. Being good at things. Because it becomes a frustrating burden when you can't figure out how to use those things to generate income." She

197

struggled to yank off the other rollerblade. "Besides, there are several things I'm not good at. Look at me. I'm a klutz. And I've never been good at math. And apparently I'm really bad at sparing people's feelings."

Kiley looked at her quizzically.

"Finn."

"Oh."

Harper continued. "I also suck at having honest conversations with the ones I love."

"You mean Emily?"

"Emily is among them, yes."

"Well, how can you say you can't have an honest conversation? You're having one with me right now. You do all the time."

Harper grew quiet, unsure of how to respond to that statement. If only Kiley really knew. While she did divulge more to her than she has anyone else, Harper could still write a Bible-length book about all her secrets Kiley didn't know about.

"Let's go in. I'm thirsty," suggested Harper.

They walked inside to get some water and Kiley took this opportunity to sprawl out on the couch in order to relieve her aching legs.

Harper threw her a bottle of water. "By all means, make yourself at home."

"I may have to. Since Jane moved out, I've had to handle the rent on my own for the past few months. I'm meeting with a potential roommate tomorrow. If it doesn't work out, I may have to call this couch home for a while."

"Oh great. Another mouth to feed."

"I think I can safely say that I am NEVER sleeping with my roommate's boyfriend again. It's just too much drama."

"Yeah, not to mention the fact that it's just common courtesy."

"That too."

As Harper finished her bottle of water, Emily walked through the front door.

"Hey. I thought you were still asleep," said Harper.

"No, I woke up about an hour ago. I felt like getting out, so I went for a walk."

"You look nice." Harper examined her sister's wardrobe further. "Is that my sweater?"

"Yeah, I hope you don't mind me borrowing it. I wanted to look somewhat presentable."

"That's fine. It looks good on you."

"Thanks." Emily looked over at the couch and finally acknowledged Kiley. "Rollerblading too much for you?"

"Eight miles of it is, yes." Kiley sat up and took notice of Emily's appearance. Her blonde hair was now more prominent as the black dye was nearly faded. It also looked like she had put on some weight, which was a good thing. She appeared to be almost fully recovered.

Kiley took a drink of her water. "Actually, I hate to break it to you guys, but I think that's MY sweater."

"Hey," protested Harper. "It's been in my closet for over a year. The one-year rule makes it officially mine."

Emily took off the sweater and curtly tossed it to Kiley. "Here. I'm done with it."

"Hey, I was kidding. I don't even wear it anymore."

"Whatever," replied Emily. "I just borrowed it to apply for a job."

"You applied for a job?" asked Harper.

"Yeah. Actually, they were looking for someone right away, so they hired me on the spot. I start Saturday."

"Where?"

"Gulcher's down the street. I just got tired of sitting around the house doing nothing."

"That's great! Congratulations! We should celebrate, or something," said Harper.

Kiley took that as her cue to leave. She wasn't in the mood for any more of Emily's jabs. "You guys go right ahead. I'm gonna go home and shower. I've gotta get ready for my date."

"Date?" This was news to Harper.

"Yeah, just this guy I ran into at the store. It's nothing, really."

"Oh. Okay. Well, have fun, I guess."

"I'll let you know how it goes."

"Great," replied Harper, half-heartedly.

"What are you guys gonna do?" asked Kiley.

"I don't know. We'll think of something. Maybe we'll go crazy and order some Chinese and play a board game."

Emily laughed. "Do we still even have any board games?"

"Oh yeah, I've kept them all."

Regardless of how Emily treated her, Kiley suddenly felt the need to warn her about something. "Uh, Emily, you probably don't want to play a game with Harper."

"Why not?" asked Emily.

"Just trust me."

"Why? What happened?"

Harper started to get nervous. "Kiley, don't!"

Kiley couldn't resist. "I'm sorry. I have to." She turned to Emily and started to recall the infamous story.

Harper's eyes grew wide as she realized that Kiley was actually going through with it.

"Kiley, please don't."

Kiley stood up, preparing to act out the story. "So this one night—"

Harper jumped up from the couch and grabbed Kiley by the arm, twisting it behind her back. "Don't even think about it!"

Kiley started giggling and tried to ignore the discomfort of her arm while she continued the story. "Your sister and I were bored and we decided to play a board game. Well, we were at my place and it turned out Monopoly was the only game I owned at the time."

Harper took her hand and attempted to cover Kiley's mouth while her other hand was still holding firm to the taller girl's arm. "I'm begging you not to do this," pleaded Harper, while forcing herself to hide her smile.

Instead of conceding, Kiley playfully tried to bite Harper's hand, while trying to finish her story. "So we opened some wine and ordered a pizza and started playing what turned out to be a pretty intense game of Monopoly..."

At that point, Harper jumped on Kiley's back using both her hands to cover Kiley's mouth. Emily, meanwhile, was enjoying this odd series of events being played out in front of her. Part of her kept telling herself to be annoyed with the petty childishness they were portraying. But another part was somewhat jealous of their relationship, since she never really had anyone she could mess around with like that. And she pretty much screwed up any chance she may have had at a normal, easy going relationship with her sister. Emily flinched as Kiley started charging towards the couch. She turned around and threw Harper off of her, making sure she landed safely on the cushions. Harper hid her face in embarrassment.

"I can't believe you're gonna do this to me."

"People have a right to know, Harper. You get crazy and a bit cocky when you win," informed Kiley.

"It was the wine!"

"Yeah, okay. We'll go with that." Kiley turned toward Emily, who was on the other end of the couch, waiting for the story to continue.

"Okay, so after about seven excruciating hours, the game was coming to an end. A dumb move on my part made me lose the rights to Park Place and in the end, Harper won. But she refused to leave it at that. She took a swig of wine and a celebratory bite of her pizza. Then she proceeded to do a little victory dance around the room singing 'I'm the best, I'm the best, it's written on my chest. Try to sneak a peek and I'll punch you like the rest.'" Kiley was demonstrating Harper's dance.

"It was a chant I remembered from grade school," interjected Harper, whose face was purple right about this time.

"She just kept repeating it over and over until she suddenly stopped and started coughing. And I started laughing. Then, the coughing stopped and she was silent. Then, she started pointing to her throat and I stopped laughing long enough to realize that she was actually choking. So I jumped up, gave her the Heimlich, and she managed to spit out a huge chunk of pizza. That stuck to the wall. It was probably the most disgusting, hilarious, memorable event I've ever experienced. And all because she had to do a little dance and sing a little ditty to rub it in my face that I lost." Kiley looked over at Harper. "Two words for you, hun: kar-ma."

Harper was bright red from embarrassment. "It was a chant I learned in the third grade! And I swear, to this day, I still maintain that was my sexiest moment ever. Don't be jealous."

Emily studied the interaction between the two of them with a sense of longing and curiosity. The longing stemmed from wanting to have a bond like that of her own with her sister. She was never quite able to compete with Kiley that way. The curiosity came from watching Harper's face whenever Kiley was around. It seemed as though there was a permanent smile tattooed on Harper's face. Emily had never seen her sister that happy, not even when Finn was around.

Emily continued to watch them and grinned. "Okay then. We'll nix the game and just do Chinese food and a movie."

"Probably a safe bet," assured Kiley. "All right, so I'll see you later Harper. Depending on how everything goes, I'll either call you by nine o'clock tonight or I'll call tomorrow morning."

Harper nodded solemnly as Kiley headed out the door.

"Kiley?"

"Yeah?"

Harper inhaled deeply for a moment. "Nothing. I'll see you later." She closed the door after Kiley walked out and stood there for a brief moment.

Emily observed every moment of what had just played out before her and decided to vocalize what she had been thinking for quite some time.

"Wow. So how long has THAT been going on?"

Harper turned around, still keeping one hand on the doorknob. "Huh?"

"How long has that been going on?"

Harper shot her sister a clueless look. "How long has what been going on?"

Emily gestured toward the door. "This thing with you and Kiley."

"What thing?" While Harper was trying to figure out exactly what Emily was getting at, her heart started beating rapidly.

Emily knew she was going to have to spell it out. "You obviously have a thing for Kiley."

Harper stood there awestruck. Her lower lip hung open, moving slightly to try to form a word, but to no avail. Her breathing had quickened and she suddenly felt all the blood drain from her face.

"What?!"

"Harper, it's okay. Really."

Harper finally loosened her death grip on the doorknob and started walking toward her room.

"I'm actually not that hungry. Just order whatever you want. I'm gonna go lie down for a bit."

Emily got up and tried to follow her sister, but stopped abruptly when Harper's door closed in her face. She tried knocking.

"Harper? It's really okay! I promise."

No response. She knocked again.

"I'm sorry, okay? I take it back." Then Emily mumbled to herself, "I shouldn't have said anything."

CHAPTER 18

Harper was horrified. She began to pace around her room. Unsure of exactly what to do, she took a seat on the floor and leaned against her bed. She brought her knees up to her chest and tried to drown out the sound of Emily knocking on the door. Harper was so upset that she couldn't fathom facing her sister at this moment. So many thoughts were swirling around in her head, it was hard to pin one down.

Where the hell did Emily get off suggesting such a thing? She abandoned Harper for two years, then all of a sudden reappears and automatically she's an expert on her life? She couldn't possibly know what goes on inside Harper's head. Then to state it as a fact, not even a question, showed an immense amount of audacity and disrespect. It simply wasn't true. It just wasn't. Harper had grown to deeply care about Kiley. Did she love her? Yes. It was a love built out of mutual respect and admiration. But to suggest that she was "in love" with Kiley was a preposterous notion and one that she would be sure to set straight with Emily.

Harper was beginning to feel restless, unable to get Emily's words out of her head. Once the knocking had stopped, she opened the door and, without her sister noticing, quickly slipped down the hall and through the door that leads to the garage.

If she couldn't wish these thoughts out of her head, maybe she could beat something until she forgot what was upsetting her. Once her gloves were secured, she hit the play button on her iPod and began attacking the bag. Since Queen wouldn't quite cut it this time, Guns 'n' Roses was blaring from the speakers. Axl's powerful voice didn't seem to distract Harper's thoughts, but she kept right on striking the bag.

There was no possible way Emily was right about this. There were times when Harper would perhaps allow a sideways glance in Kiley's direction to turn into a mild gaze or let a hug linger a little longer than it should have. Mainly lately since she lost her entire family and needed as much human physical interaction as possible. But that by no means meant she had a "thing" for Kiley. Theirs was a bond stronger than friendship. It was hard to explain, but from the moment they met, they just understood each other. Harper had never had that kind of connection with someone before, or that kind of intimacy or honesty. They had always been brutally honest with each other because they both knew that no matter how bad a confession was, there would be no judgment between them and their friendship would always forge on. Harper pondered this as she tried to control her breathing while attacking the punching bag. Nothing she had shared with Kiley so far had damaged their friendship, but that's not to say something wouldn't eventually harm them. Harper couldn't even imagine what would happen if Emily had been right. How would Kiley react? Well, that didn't matter anyway because it simply wasn't true. Emily was wrong. After a cross-hook-uppercut combo, Harper was beginning to question whether Emily was doing drugs again seeing as how you'd have to be really out of it to suggest such a thing. She absolutely did NOT have a thing for Kiley.

She continued throwing left and right punches, even adding in a few front and round kicks for good measure…anything to get her mind off of this. Her pace quickened rapidly as her punches grew stronger to the point where she pushed herself away from the bag.

Slow yourself, Foley. Breathe, she thought to herself.

She stepped back, entranced by the punching bag swaying side to side. She removed her gloves and sat down, almost unwilling to believe the notion that just entered her mind.

She continued to think to herself as she slowly began to calm down, *Okay. Okay Harper. It's okay*. She felt a jolt moving from her stomach, to her throat, all the way up to her eyes as she shuddered while releasing the first of several tears. *It's time*.

Really, who was she kidding? She could deny it to herself all she wanted. It didn't change the fact that Emily was indeed right. A sick feeling began to materialize in her stomach as she gradually allowed herself to come to terms with the emotions she had worked so hard to stave off. There she sat with her head in her hands, completely alone at this moment; this moment being the first time she ever admitted it to herself. Harper was in love with Kiley. It wasn't just "a thing" as Emily had said, but it was real, honest-to-God love. She had been from the moment they met when she walked through the door at Tyson's bar and spotted that five-foot-eight frame behind the bar. Her breath caught in her throat when she heard Kiley speak those first words "Why the two guitars?"

A Fine Mess

There was always something in the back of Harper's mind that kept nagging at her, suggesting that something was a little off. And yes, the idea of harboring same sex tendencies did creep up from time to time, which Harper immediately pushed back down to be thought or worried about some other day. She really could not fathom how the hell her sister figured it out. Especially since she always did her best to hide it due to the potentially serious ramifications it would bring about. The whole 'being raised Catholic' thing didn't help and only further conflicted her. What would her parents think? How would they react? It pained her to think about that, especially knowing that she'll never know the answer to that. And Finn. How would he feel about it? Everything she felt for Finn was real. Every emotion, every butterfly in her stomach, every kiss, every "I love you." She meant it all…up until the end when there was a greater power constantly looming over and haunting her. There was always something that kept her from giving one hundred percent of herself to Finn. She tried to ignore it, but eventually it got so big she started to crack under the pressure. The only way to slightly alleviate that weight was to break it off with him. It was the only reasonable option. With the split came immense relief, but it was only a mere cure for a symptom of a much bigger issue.

Harper had never actually said it out loud. Then, out of nowhere, Emily just spews it out like a Bible passage. Like it was something so universally known, it was stated with such little fanfare.

Harper's tears lead to sobbing. Her hands were shaking, trying to wipe the tears from her face. At this point, her Catholic guilt was the least of her worries, especially since her faith had been severely shaken long ago. She thought of Kiley and how devastated she would be if her friend ever found out about this and reacted badly. After all, Kiley was obviously very much straight. And Harper…well, she simply didn't know what to call herself. Yes, she had found other girls attractive in the past, but what did that mean? Surely it didn't mean she was gay, did it? How could it mean that when she's only had boyfriends in the past and she's only slept with men? Obviously there was some sort of untapped issue plaguing her, but gay? How is that possible? Apparently for Emily, it seemed very much possible.

This wasn't an easy thing to finally accept and admit. She had been holding this inside of her for so long. Almost too long.

***

Harper's eyes twitched a bit until they slowly opened to the sight of a DVD symbol flickering and changing color on the TV set. She let out a yawn and wondered what time it was. It had to be well past midnight by this point. She didn't realize how exhausted she was. But apparently she fell asleep halfway through the movie because the last thing she remembered was Alvy Singer going over to Annie's place to kill a bug for her just before their imminent reconciliation. She stretched a bit and realized she had fallen asleep in her clothes. Jeans weren't the most comfortable thing to sleep in due to the amount of chafing involved. She still had her makeup on as well.

She and Kiley had gone to a concert with some friends that night. Since Finn was visiting his parents for the weekend, Harper took this opportunity to hang out with the friends she hadn't seen in a while. She and Kiley had been friends for eight months at this point, so Kiley tagged along since she wasn't working that night and wanted to meet Harper's other friends. After the concert, everyone wanted to go out for drinks, but Harper and Kiley decided to call it an early night. Instead they hung out at Kiley's place to watch a movie. When they settled on Annie Hall, *they also settled on Kiley's room for the location seeing as how the DVD player in the living room was broken. Harper figured she'd stay for a bit and then head home since it was near the end of her last semester of college and finals were coming up. So much for that plan.*

Harper carefully rolled over and found that Kiley, too, had passed out. She was sound asleep and was also still wearing her concert clothes. With the help of the ubiquitous glare of the TV set, she couldn't help but smile upon seeing Kiley's eye makeup completely smudged, almost raccoon-like. She softly brushed a strand of hair out of Kiley's face. Knowing it was much too late to try and drive home, she then made every attempt to fall back to sleep. Yet no matter how tired she was, it just wasn't working. She lay there for another hour or so trying to will herself to sleep, but her mind was racing a mile a minute and she couldn't figure out why. Harper had always been a fairly sound sleeper who could fall asleep at the drop of a hat, so she couldn't understand the difficulty she was having trying to sleep tonight.

She turned back over to face Kiley, who was still deep in slumber. Harper just lay there unwittingly watching Kiley's chest methodically rise and fall, memorizing her breathing pattern, tracing her silhouette that the faint light the TV was creating. As bad of a friend as it made her sound, sometimes she found herself jealous of Kiley. In this moment she was jealous of the fact that, even in sleep, her friend was absolutely stunning. But was it really jealousy taking over her? Perhaps it was something else...a feeling of awe and wonderment. Because if it were jealousy, she wouldn't be feeling so content and at peace right now, regardless of not being able to sleep.

Harper immediately shook those thoughts from her brain. What the hell was she doing? She was almost embarrassed by acting like a stalker. She turned over on her back, being careful not to ruffle the sheets too much, closed her eyes and eventually fell asleep to the rhythm of Kiley's breathing.

***

Harper's tears were nearly dry as memories of that night came rushing back like it happened yesterday. She thought about her restlessness that night, how she was unable to sleep and was now suddenly able to pinpoint that night as when and where her insomnia first started. It all made sense to her now. She thought about that moment, Kiley's face, her body, her breath...that was the moment. It was the moment she knew. There was no avoiding it, no denying it. Harper was in love with Kiley.

She sat there on the garage floor, finally removing her head from her hands. She looked around and studied her surroundings, wishing there was a way to seal off the door and keep the rest of the world out of this sanctum. Unfortunately, that wasn't possible. She thought of Emily, how it was that she knew. How did she pick up on it so fast? Was it that obvious? She thought of Kiley. *Oh, God...Kiley.*

This was a revelation she never saw coming. And if she did see it coming, she did her best to prevent it from actually happening. But it was too late. It's out there. You can't take back such a considerable admission, even if it was just to yourself.

She rested her hands on the floor, leaned back and looked up at the ceiling.

"Fuck."

***

Once she regrouped, Harper rejoined society out in the living room and found Emily chowing down on a bowl of Fruit Loops. Harper could not grasp how her sister stayed so skinny while eating so much crap. Cereal was Emily's biggest vice when it came to food and she had a tendency to lean towards the ones made of pure sugar. Whereas Harper had to struggle to deprive herself of the food she loved and had to consistently exercise in order to maintain her flat stomach and her one hundred twenty-pound frame.

Emily looked up at her sister. "I'm sorry. I shouldn't have said anything. It was a stupid thing to say."

"I'm sorry I freaked out."

Emily held up the box of cereal. "You want some?"

"No thanks. I'm not hungry." Harper joined her sister at the kitchen table and perused the back of the cereal box, playing the word finder game and trying to occupy her brain for a moment until she was ready to talk.

"Em?"

"Yeah?"

"How did you know?"

Emily shrugged. "I just knew. When you're on the outside as a third party, it's a little easier to pick up on things. The way you look at her, the way your smile brightens when she's around…"

"Is it that obvious?" Her stomach, churning and weak, made her feel like she was going to vomit.

"To me, yes. But I don't think anyone else could tell."

Harper nodded. Emily was always much more adept and in tune to her surroundings than most people.

"The Kiley thing, I just noticed since I've been back, but something tells me it's been going on for a while."

Harper nodded in defeat. "Four years."

"Jesus! You've been holding that in for that long? How do you deal with that?"

"I don't let myself think about it." Harper was now reading the label on the cereal box, trying to figure out exactly what "pyridoxine hydrochloride" was. The thought of looking anywhere in the vicinity of her sister was unbearable. Her face was burning and her body felt like it was nearing the point of a hot flash.

"Doesn't it drive you crazy?" asked Emily.

"I've been able to handle it so far."

"Maybe you should just tell her."

Harper's face turned bright purple. She put down the box. "Oh no. No way. Are you kidding me? Not a chance. Never."

"Okay, okay. Just think about it for a bit. I know it might take some getting used to."

"I still can't believe you figured it out."

"I've known about your proclivity for other girls for a while."

Harper could swear Emily was able to hear her beating heart pounding out of her chest. Thank God for her trusty ribcage holding it in. "What?!"

"Oh please. I've known since I was ten. You were a sophomore in high school."

"I…how…how did you know?"

"I observe things. I may have been young, but I wasn't blind. Besides, it was pretty obvious when you wouldn't stop raving about Jessie What's-Her-Face. It wasn't exactly subtle."

Harper lowered her head. She knew exactly what Emily was talking about. Looking back, it was painfully obvious she had developed a crush on Jessie Stonem when she was fifteen. But she barely even knew her. And at the time, it seemed like she simply wanted to be her friend and nothing more. That whole ordeal was starting to make more sense now.

"How is it possible that you knew and I didn't?"

"Power of denial. Trust me, I know all about that. Besides, I wasn't about to tell you. You needed to figure it out on your own. I thought eventually you would, but then you met Finn and the next thing I knew, you were engaged. And then a part of me thought maybe I was wrong." She took a bite of her cereal. "Clearly I wasn't."

Harper started massaging her temple with her hand. "Fuck."

Emily reached out and put her hand on top of Harper's. It was the first physical contact they had shared in a while. In fact, this was the longest conversation they've had since Emily came back. Harper's first inclination was to jerk her hand away, but she knew her sister was being sincere at this moment. This was definitely something she didn't want to go through alone.

For Emily's part, she was just thankful for the minor breakthrough in their otherwise awkward and icy relationship. Feeling bold, she slowly pulled her hand away and finally decided to open up.

"I went to Chicago."

"What?"

"Right after I left, I stayed with a friend down in Orange County, scrounged up some money and bought a bus ticket to Chicago. I went to meet Damien."

"Damien?" Harper tried to discern why that name sounded so familiar.

"Yeah…you know…"

Suddenly, a light switched on. "Oh, Damien?! Your sleazy ex-boyfriend? The one that was way too old for you?"

"He wanted to get back together."

"Emily, I HATE that guy. Mom and dad hated him. We practically celebrated when you two broke up and he moved away."

"And I now understand why. But we started talking again right after mom and dad died. He said he missed me and I should come out there and be with him and he'd take care of me. He said he was making really good money out there."

"Doing what?"

"What do you think? Anyway, it sounded nice. In my warped mind, I thought it could work. So I met him there and moved in with him and, you know, worked for him."

"Selling drugs?"

Emily nodded.

"What did you sell?" Harper had no idea why she asked that. She really didn't want to know.

"Pot, cocaine, meth…whatever we could sell. He had some connection, and I didn't question it. I'm not proud of it. It was beyond stupid, I know."

Harper wanted to yell at her, scream at the top of her lungs, 'What were you thinking? Jesus! You could have been arrested! You could have been killed!' But she managed to stop herself from overreacting and just listened to her sister talk.

"Anyway, after about a year, I just couldn't do it anymore. I hated myself, but I couldn't bring myself to leave Damien because I loved him. And I thought I had nowhere else to go. But it got to the point where all we ever did was either *deal* drugs or *do* them."

Harper did *not* want to hear that.

"And I was miserable. I just wanted to be with him without all that other stuff, but then I came home one day and the apartment was empty. All his stuff, and most of my stuff was gone."

Harper clinched her fists. She knew from the day she met Damien, she should have decked him for even thinking he was good enough to be in Emily's life. Now she wished she had–a preemptive punch.

"He was just gone. I called him a few times. The last time, he answered and just said, 'Lose my number whore.' And some girl was laughing in the background. And that was it. It was over."

There were a million things Harper wanted to say to her sister at this moment, but she had to let it all sink in.

"I'm so sorry, Em."

"I'm glad it happened. Hell, I deserved it. Besides, he didn't know I had been hiding any extra money we made in one of our vents, so I took that and went on my way. I think I ended up in Iowa after that…or Ohio. It's kind of a blur. Then I went to New York for a bit and eventually made my way down south and ended up in Nashville. But I was never in one place for very long. Eventually, I ran out of money. And my drug issue didn't help that situation too much."

Harper squirmed in her seat. Her poor baby sister had been fighting a drug problem completely alone. This is where Harper's protective nature wanted to kick in. All she wanted to do was scoop her up and take her away from anything harmful this world had to offer. It would have been too little too late, though, knowing now some of what Emily had been through. Keeping her protective vibe in check, she let Emily finish the story while keeping herself restrained.

"How did you stop?"

"Sheer willpower. Thankfully it was more of a recreational thing for me, but that didn't make it any less difficult."

"So you're…clean now?"

Emily sighed. "Yeah."

They sat in silence for a moment, unsure of what else to say. Harper had a hundred more questions. What did she do in the other cities? Who did she meet? Where did she stay? Emily didn't seem to want to answer any.

"Okay, I think we've had enough confessing for the day. You've had enough emotional shit to deal with. Don't you have a gig tonight?"

"Yeah I did, but I'm not going. I'm not really feeling up for it."

"You should go. Seriously. It might help. Besides, I want to see you play again."

"You're underage."

"Oh please. Graham will let me in. I haven't even seen him yet. He'll be so thrilled I'm back, he won't even remember I'm only nineteen."

"Or he'll let you stand outside and put your ear to the door."

"Even better," Emily retorted.

Harper shook her head. "I don't think so. Not tonight. My voice isn't all that great right now. All that crying left a big lump in my throat."

"Okay, we'll go with that for an excuse and completely ignore the fact that Kiley is gonna be there."

"I just don't want to deal with it right now. Thanks for humoring me."

"Of course."

Harper looked pleadingly at her sister. "Look, I can trust you with this, right? I mean…" Harper sighed. "Please don't tell Kiley, okay? I don't think I can handle her knowing that—"

"Don't worry. I wouldn't dream of it."

***

"Why do you keep checking your watch?"

Erin took notice of Kiley's constant time-checking and it was beginning to make her nervous.

"It's almost ten."

"Yeah. But we don't get off until two. So the more you look at your watch, the longer it's going to seem before closing time." Erin put the finishing touches on the three lemon drop martinis ordered by the ladies at table five.

Kiley swiped a credit card and returned it to a customer at the bar. "Here you go. Thanks, have a great night." She took the receipt and put it in the register.

Erin walked past her with the tray of martinis. "Pace yourself. We've got all night."

Kiley was taking another order when Graham appeared from the back office. "Kiley, just so you know, we're running low on Heineken until our delivery on Tuesday, so we may run out tonight."

"So should I tell anyone who orders one to 'lay off my Heiny'?"

Graham rolled his eyes. "Tell them whatever you want. As long as you keep them happy and apologize for us running out."

"I make no apologies."

"Just keep the customers happy, will you?"

"Whatever you say, boss." Kiley checked her watch one more time.

"I'm sorry. Is your job keeping you from some important appointment?" asked Graham.

"Actually yes. I'm late for my life to start."

Graham smiled. "Well, you're not gonna get very far by standing behind this bar. But for tonight, I need you to. We're almost at capacity tonight."

"So I noticed. That's why I'm wondering where—"

Through the bustle of the crowd, they heard the office phone ringing and Graham ran off to answer it. "Sorry, Kiley. I gotta take this."

Erin came back with a tray of empty glasses. "Can you believe how packed it is tonight?"

"I know."

"Graham called in Simon to help out tonight. He should be here in a bit."

219

"Good. Hopefully Harper gets here soon. She's got a huge crowd to play for. She was supposed to be here by now."

"Oh, didn't Graham tell you?"

"Tell me what?"

"Harper called a while ago. She's not coming in. I guess she's sick, or something."

"Seriously?"

"Yeah."

Kiley pulled her cell phone from her pocket and checked for any missed calls. There were none. "Why didn't she call me?"

"I don't know. Hey, can you grab table nine?"

Distracted and dejected, Kiley slowly put her phone away. "Sure."

CHAPTER 19

Emily knew she would eventually have to come face to face with this. She enjoyed the half hour walk on the way over. The afternoon sun was warm on her back, but the breeze felt nice on her face. Walking gave her time to think and reflect and prepare herself for what she was about to walk into. When she reached the door of her destination, she took a deep breath and braced herself before opening it. It took a moment for her eyes to adjust to the dim light after being outside in the bright sun for so long. She looked around for any sign of life.

"Hello?"

Emily took a few more steps in as the door closed behind her.

"Hello? Graham?"

Graham peeked his head out of the back office of the bar. "Well, shit."

Emily smirked and gave him a half wave as Graham disappeared back into the room to finish what he was doing only to reappear thirty seconds later.

"Emily, is that really you?"

"It's really me."

"You've been back for over four months and you're just now coming to see me?"

"I know. I'm sorry. I just wasn't ready to see anyone yet."

"Well come here. Give me a hug." He gave her one of his infamous bear hugs, then stood back to look at her. "You look good. Taller. A bit on the skinny side, though. You need to eat more."

"So I've been told. Harper's been stuffing my face since I got back."

Graham came out from behind the bar and pulled out a chair at a table near Emily. "Have a seat. Can I get you something?"

"Ginger ale."

"You got it. Grenadine?"

"Nah. Just straight up."

Graham prepared her drink while watching Emily fiddle with her hands. He hadn't seen her in a couple years, but she still looked every bit like her parents. She had her mother's hair, her father's eyes, a mixture of both their complexions.

"You know, I'm just gonna come out and say it and get it out of the way. I'm not gonna let you get off that easy."

Emily nodded. "Bring it on."

"You hurt a lot of people when you left."

"I know. I'm sorry. All I can really do is apologize."

Graham came back around with the ginger ale and took a seat next to her. "You know, after you were born, I promised your parents I'd look after the two of you. I don't like breaking my promises."

Emily took a sip of her drink. The ginger ale's effervescence helped calm her nervous stomach.

"I know you don't." Emily's guilt was warranted. She knew Graham had lost two good friends when her parents passed away. He was her father's college buddy and best man at their wedding. He was there for Harper's birth and Emily's baptism. He would babysit them whenever their parents needed a night away from their two young children. And being a confirmed bachelor, Graham often spent Thanksgiving and Christmas with them if he had nowhere to go.

"Well, you're back now," said Graham. "And you're probably getting enough guilt from Harper, so I'll go easy on you. How are you two doing, by the way?"

"Me and Harper? Better than we were. Surprisingly well, actually. I think we're slowly getting there. I think she's starting to trust me again."

"So…where were you?"

"Lots of different places. I stayed with friends."

"What friends? You were born and raised here."

Emily slurped up the last of the ginger ale. "I kind of don't want to get into it if that's all right with you."

Graham nodded. "But you're okay?"

She used her straw to dig the cherry out of the glass. "Yeah. I am. Best I've been in a long time."

The dim room suddenly filled with natural sunlight as the front door opened to reveal two giggly girls in the midst of a conversation.

"Hey Graham," said Erin. "Kiley and I are here for our paychecks." Erin stopped when she realized Graham had company. "Oh, hi. You must be Harper's sister."

"How did you know?"

"You look like a younger version of her. Only more blonde."

Emily laughed. "I get that a lot." She looked over at Erin's accomplice. "Hey Kiley."

"Hey." Kiley hung back, waiting for Graham to grab their paychecks.

Graham took that as his cue. "I'll be right back."

"Actually, I should get going," said Emily. "I just wanted to stop by and say hi. But I'll come by again soon." She got up to give Graham a hug.

"You better. Ladies, just give me a minute. I'll be back with your easy-earned money."

As Graham disappeared, Emily rifled through her purse to make sure she had everything.

Erin took a seat on one of the bar stools. Sensing the tension between Emily and Kiley, she thought she'd try to lighten the mood. "So you actually took that guy home last night?"

"Yup," replied Kiley.

"Shocking," mumbled Emily.

Kiley heard the snide remark, but chose to ignore it.

"My God. Your bed sees more action in a week than mine has since I bought it five years ago," said Erin.

"It's just sex. It's not that big a deal."

"He wasn't even your type," declared Erin.

"You mean he didn't have a pulse?" asked Emily.

Kiley decided to react to that one. "What is your problem?"

"Who me?" asked Emily, innocently.

"Yes. You think I can't hear you?"

"I'm not trying to be subtle."

Feeling uncomfortable, Erin got up and headed to the back office. "I'm gonna go see what's keeping Graham."

Neither Kiley nor Emily paid any attention to Erin. They were locked down in a staring contest with each other, neither of them wanting to break first.

"You need to check yourself. Seriously. You have no right to talk to me like that," said Kiley. "My personal life is my business."

"Oh and you haven't been butting your nose in my business?"

"Um, no, I don't believe I have."

"Oh please, I know you've been dying to find out where I've been and what I've been doing."

"Okay, maybe I have, but I know it's none of my business. And at least I'm not acting like a spoiled little shit."

"What?"

"You bailed on Harper and then show up walking around like a wounded little puppy. You're a brat."

"A brat?"

"Yeah. Okay, I admit I sleep with a lot of guys, but at least I'm not being self-destructive. You don't see me running off and doing drugs. You had a perfect, normal life and started screwing up and hating everyone. Even yourself."

Emily slammed her hand down on the bar, venting her frustration. "I kind of went through a tragic event, Kiley."

"I know. But you started doing that shit before they even died, so I really don't think you can use that defense."

"Well what about you?" It was time for Emily to turn the tables.

Kiley scoffed. "What about me?"

"Look at you. You think you don't hate yourself? You're the most self-loathing person I know. You fuck every guy who pays you the least bit of attention. And you don't even care. You don't give a shit about what it can do to your psyche, and you obviously don't care about how much it obviously upsets Harper."

Whatever Kiley was preparing to say next screeched to a halt. "Wait, why would Harper care?"

Emily shook her head and started heading out the door. "Just forget about it."

Kiley grabbed her arm. "Seriously, why would Harper care?"

Emily jerked away from Kiley's grip. "She doesn't care. No one cares what you do, Kiley. Now if you'll excuse me, I have to go run off and do drugs."

Kiley watched Emily walk out. The room became bright and dull again as the door closed. Kiley was shaken by her encounter with Emily. She couldn't remember the last time she raised her voice like that, but she's pretty sure it took place in her car after being cut off three times in a row. She began to feel guilty about everything she said to Harper's sister and had no idea where it came from. She pulled out her phone, but instead of dialing Harper's number, she just stared at the keypad until the numbers became a jumbled mess.

***

Kiley lie on her back on Harper's bed pretending to peruse the wedding planning book Harper brought home from work. She was on the chapter of the maid of honor's responsibilities when her mind wandered. This was the third Ingrid Michaelson song in a row that Harper's iPod was blaring from the dock speakers and Kiley found herself humming along as she looked around. Harper's room was always a fun place to be because there was always something interesting to look at. Being awake most nights, Harper had to be visually stimulated at all times. There were framed posters of different movies from

All About Eve *to* Rebel Without a Cause. *There were music posters of Michael Jackson, The Beatles and a few bands that Kiley never would have heard of had it not been for Harper. Her desk was cluttered with guitar picks, tuners, strings, old copies of Spin magazine and even a few non-music related items like a giant bag of Reese's peanut butter cups and her laptop. Her bookshelf was full of all the classics:* Pride and Prejudice, Jane Eyre, Catcher in the Rye, The Great Gatsby, One Flew Over the Cuckoo's Nest *and some modern classics like* The Girl With the Dragon Tattoo, The Da Vinci Code *and* The Help. *Kiley always felt rather inferior to Harper when it came to her knowledge of books. Her attention span was more suitable for shorter reads like magazines or Dr. Seuss books.*

It had been a year and a half since Harper's parents died and Emily was long gone by this point. Harper was tired of putting off the planning. Last year after everything settled down a bit, she and Finn had finally set a date and now the wedding was just seven months away. Harper flipped through the pages of her bridal magazine. Frustrated, she finally closed it and moved on to the next one.

"I'm never gonna find the right kind of dress."

Harper's words brought Kiley back to the here and now. "Well, you said you wanted something simple. Long, white, spaghetti straps, right?"

"Yeah, but all of these are strapless. I can't do strapless. It's annoying."

"Don't worry. We'll find the perfect dress for you. Even if we have to hit every wedding shop in town. And trust me, there are a lot."

"It feels weird."

A Fine Mess

"What?"

"Planning all this. You know…without my parents. My mom was supposed to take me dress shopping and my dad was supposed to pretend to whine and moan about how much it was costing him until I batted my eyelashes at him and he gave in. And Emily should be here complaining every minute about how this is lame and how she's blowing off her friends for a stupid dress fitting."

Kiley rolled over on her stomach. She was starting to feel a bit remorseful about not whole-heartedly putting all of her effort into helping her friend plan this wedding. It was difficult, though. She didn't quite understand why. She chalked it up to fear of losing her best friend. "Well, you have me. And we're in this. I won't rest until we find you the perfect dress. And the perfect location. And the perfect color scheme. Or if you want, we can even postpone it for a while longer if you're not ready. Finn would understand."

"No. I've been putting this off for too long. I mean, we've been engaged for two years. It's time to move on. The sooner I start my new life, the sooner I can let go of my old one."

Kiley nodded solemnly, but didn't say anything as a Joshua Radin song filled her ears.

"I just have no idea what I'm doing," continued Harper.

"You don't have to know just yet. I think it's kind of a 'learn as you go' kind of deal. The only time you need to worry about knowing what to do is AFTER the wedding. You know… wink-wink, nudge-nudge."

"I think I've got that covered."

"Oh, and during the honeymoon. That's important. You'll probably be too exhausted on your wedding night to do anything, so save it all for the honeymoon."

"Oh don't worry. Lots of sex will be had," said Harper.

Kiley bit her lip to keep herself from saying something and decided a subject change was needed. "Well, you better not put me in a hideous maid of honor dress. I look awesome in blue, purple, or burgundy. Are you writing this down? This is important. I don't want a strapless dress, either. My average sized chest doesn't need to feel inferior to your ample bosom."

"You're a C, too," replied Harper.

"I'm a solid B and you know it," informed Kiley.

"Isn't this day supposed to be about me?"

"Uh, you're guaranteed to be going home with a guy at the end of the night. I need a guarantee, too."

"You're really going to spend my wedding day picking up a guy?"

"No, I'll be getting a guy to pick ME up."

The disappointed look on Harper's face said it all.

"But not before I see to it that all of your needs and demands are met throughout the day. I won't forget my duties. Don't worry," assured Kiley. "Let's just try to do this one step at a time. Where do you want the wedding to take place?"

"Well, Finn wants it in a church."

"Hmm."

"What?"

"Well, I just always pictured you having an outdoor wedding."

Harper smiled. "You know me too well. That's exactly what I want. In a vineyard."

229

"Ooh, a vineyard would be perfect! You could have the reception in a tasting room or a nearby barn or something. We can deck it out with lights and lanterns."

"Wow, this is the most animated I've seen you about this whole thing. That's exactly what I want, but Finn wants it in a hotel ballroom."

"That's a bit trite."

"I know. But I figure maybe I can at least negotiate full control over the music we have."

"Yeah, but what about the rest of it? What about what you want? Is he even taking that into consideration?"

"Well, my family's not around and his family is really traditional. I think he just wants to make his mom happy."

"I'm pretty sure his goal should be making YOU happy. Ugh, he's such a mama's boy. Are you sure you want to be doing this?"

Harper stared at the young woman modeling the white dress in the magazine in front of her. She heard Kiley's question, but was still trying to formulate an answer.

"Harper? It was a joke. A stupid joke. Of course you want to marry him."

Harper looked blankly at Kiley. "Yeah."

Kiley sat up, took the magazine from Harper and tossed it to the floor. "Okay, I think it's time for a break. You're on wedding-planning overload. Let's go grab a burger or something."

"But—"

"But nothing. I'm hungry. We can discuss the reception playlist on the way."

***

"Kiley?"

"Huh?"

"I've been saying your name for the last five minutes," informed Erin. "Here's your paycheck."

"Oh. Thanks."

"Are you okay?"

"Yeah. Emily just tends to get under my skin."

"So I noticed. What's her deal?"

Kiley shrugged. "She thinks she knows everything."

CHAPTER 20

Kiley had been putting off this day for as long as she could, but figured it was finally time to pay her parents a visit. She made the dreaded hour-and-a-half trek out to Ojai and sat in her car in front of her old house for a good ten minutes until she ultimately got out. Before opening the front door, she grabbed the mail that was bursting out of the mailbox and strewn onto the porch. With her hands full of envelopes, magazines and junk mail, she walked in to find her mom sitting at the kitchen table reading the newspaper. She could hear the TV in the living room playing the football game. Kiley put the mail down on the table and gave her mom a one-armed hug.

"Mom, you keep letting the mail get piled up. It'll attract burglars."

"Kiley! This is a nice surprise."

"I figured I owed you a visit."

"Well, sit down. Tim, Kiley's here!"

No answer from the living room. Kiley wasn't too surprised.

"So how is everything? How's your exciting life in LA?"

Kiley smirked at her mother's wide-eyed interest. "Oh, it's uber fun. Movie stars, personal trainers, streets paved with gold."

"Well aren't you Little Miss Sassy?"

"Sorry. Everything's pretty much the same. You know, just trying to find my way and all that fun stuff."

"You're still bartending?"

Kiley nodded.

"And how's that friend of yours, Harper? Wasn't she getting married?"

Kiley didn't realize exactly how long she had managed to avoid her parents, but apparently it was quite a long time.

"Uh…no, actually. She called off the wedding. Like six months ago. I thought I told you that."

"No. That's terrible. Poor girl."

Kiley shrugged. "She's better off. Trust me."

"Well, as long as you're there for her."

Kiley nodded and lowered her head.

"Something wrong? You guys are still friends, aren't you?"

"Yeah, it's just…complicated."

"It always is. Nothing worth having in this world is ever easy."

Kiley looked at her mother wondering if she was actually tuning in to her confusion or if she was just offering up a polite platitude. She actually found herself considering telling her about everything that's been going on and the uncertainty she's been feeling.

"I just wish things weren't so— "

Her mother's eyes lit up at something she was reading in the paper. "Oh, they're having a sale at Kohl's! We need to go shopping sometime."

With those words, Kiley got her answer: platitude. She faked a smile at her mother's half-hearted attempt to bond with her daughter. She could only recall one time they had gone shopping together and it was uncomfortably awkward to say the least. Kiley often wondered why her parents even had a kid or if they even wanted her in the first place. When she was younger, she constantly found herself speculating on whether or not she was a mistake. Kiley didn't dare ask her parents because she didn't want to know the truth. She sat at the kitchen table for a while, watching her mom and trying to think of something else to say to her.

"Well, if you need me, I'll be upstairs for a minute."

"Okay, sweetie."

Before going upstairs, she slowly walked past the living room to see if her dad would peel his attention away from the TV for just a moment to acknowledge his daughter. He didn't.

So she made her presence known by taking a seat next to him on the couch.

"Hey, Dad." Kiley hoped the commercial break would help in her quest for his attention.

"Oh hey, Kiley. When did you get here?" It worked.

"Just a few minutes ago."

"You staying for dinner?"

Kiley found herself wondering if they even ate dinner together anymore. "I don't know. Maybe."

Her father nodded and looked back at the TV.

"Starting to get cold again, isn't it?"

"Yeah, a little," replied Kiley.

Once the game was back on, she knew she had lost him.

"Who's winning?"

"The Patriots."

After watching a few plays in silence, Kiley excused herself. That was enough father/daughter bonding time for her.

Breanna Hughes

As she trudged up the stairs and made a right, her hand anxiously turned the doorknob to her old room. It was no different than when she had moved out eight years ago. Every time she would come home to visit, she expected to see some huge change to her room. She thought maybe her dad would finally get the pool table he always wanted and turn it into a game room, or that her mom would turn it into a fitness room of some sort. But it stayed exactly the same, untouched and unscathed. Kiley found it comforting, like maybe her parents actually cared about her enough to keep it that way. She closed the door behind her and examined the contents on her dresser. She used her hand to dust off some figurines different people had given to her over the years for her birthday or Christmas. She had no need for them, but never threw them out. She picked up a notebook of really bad, angst-ridden poetry she had written during her "dark teen years." She tossed the notebook down and picked up the college rejection letters from the only two places she applied just to appease her parents. She had no clue why she kept them. Maybe as a reminder that college wasn't meant for everybody.

On the floor next to her desk was a stack of books she was assigned to read in her high school English classes. The bindings were barely even cracked. Next to that, was a stack of CDs of her favorite artists from back then. On top of her desk was her old address book filled with numbers she hadn't dialed in years.

On the bed lay her favorite childhood stuffed teddy bear that she named Tommy. She could never officially part with it, so left him lying comfortably on the bed. She joined Tommy on the bed as she kicked off her shoes and hopped on backwards. A bit of dust rose up from the maroon duvet cover as she plopped down. It didn't take long before a sense of familiarity seeped in to her mind. She remembered lying in this very bed while listening to her parents argue every night. This is the bed where she cried herself to sleep some nights. It's where she lost her virginity after sneaking Zack Marshall into her room sophomore year of high school. The fighting between her parents was so loud, they didn't even notice Zack shimmying down the tree in their back yard at four in the morning. It's also where she would anxiously lie awake every Christmas Eve as a kid waiting for 6 a.m. to roll around. It's where she would say her nightly prayers until she realized it was a rather futile thing to do. It's where she decided she wanted to move to LA and leave behind this house and all the memories it held. She stared up at the blank ceiling that once held her *Titanic* poster and her thoughts shifted to Harper.

She had only brought Harper home once to meet her parents a few years ago and it was a fairly short visit. That was the only time Harper had seen where she grew up. Harper had a field day perusing through Kiley's old room. She particularly took a liking to the old high school yearbooks on the book shelf, mainly because Harper finally got to see Kiley in her "awkward" phase. Kiley was the butt of many a joke that day. She reached over to her bedside table, opened the drawer and pulled out a gray hooded sweatshirt. She felt the soft material in her hands and sighed. Harper had left it behind after her visit and Kiley never gave it back. She didn't know why. She just kept it in the drawer and took it out every time she came back to visit. There was something comforting about the simple article of clothing in a place where she felt nothing but indifference. She brought the sleeve up and caressed her face with it. She rolled over onto her side, clinging to the sweatshirt and inhaling the lingering scent it contained. And for the first time in years, Kiley cried. She allowed the sweatshirt to catch most of her tears while a few landed on the pillow case. After fifteen minutes of a good cry, she fell asleep holding onto the one reminder that everything would eventually be okay.

CHAPTER 21

At the bookstore, Harper was standing at the register with another coworker waiting for someone to come up and make a purchase. Since it was a rather slow day, the manager asked Harper to abandon her post at the register to scour the store for go-backs. She was grateful for the break from standing around and doing nothing. She grabbed a basket and started out on the first floor looking for any stray books that needed to be put back in their proper section.

She had begun to wonder why she was still here at a thankless job, barely making enough money to get by. Thankfully, she was able to cover the mortgage every month with the money her parents left them, but her wages barely covered the other monthly bills. While she enjoyed the peace and quiet that came with working in an environment such as this, she knew it was a far stretch from what she should really be doing with her life. However, now was not the time to get into this. She had plenty of other things to worry about and at least it was a steady, albeit pitiful, paycheck.

Kiley had called her three times since Saturday night when Harper failed to show for her gig. An interminable feeling of guilt plagued Harper for not calling her back, but what could she say? How was she supposed to act? It would take Katharine Hepburn's acting ability to be able to pull off appearing normal in front of Kiley now that Harper was fully aware of her emotions.

She picked up a copy of *1984* that for some reason was resting amongst the romance novels. The fourth Harry Potter book somehow found its way to the true crime section and Harper had no idea how *If You Give A Mouse A Cookie* ended up next to Nabokov.

"Excuse me. I seem to have mangled my copy of Paris Hilton's *Confessions of an Heiress.* I read it so much it fell apart. I'm simply lost without it."

Harper smiled upon hearing the familiar voice and turned around. "Actually, I think it's probably out of print. She hasn't really been relevant since 2007. But can I interest you in Miley Cyrus' autobiography?"

"Hmm…sounds riveting. But I'll pass."

"What, no coffee or donuts for me today?"

Kiley dug through her purse, pulled out a Payday candy bar and tossed it to Harper. "I never come empty handed."

"Is it your goal in life to fatten me up like a cow?"

"Hey, if it weren't for me, you would never eat junk food. Enjoy it. You're too skinny as it is."

"Well, thank you. On both counts."

Kiley picked up a copy of the works of Pablo Neruda and tossed it into the basket. "This goes in the poetry section, right?"

"Yeah."

Kiley continued to help her friend find and gather more abandoned books. "So, you know why I'm here, right?"

"If this is about Saturday night, I really wasn't feeling well. My voice just wasn't up to par."

"Okay. That's fine. I can accept that. But you didn't call me to let me know. And I know you don't have to, but you call me if you get a paper cut. Just to tell me and complain about it. And then you haven't been returning my calls. So I'm left to believe that…I don't know…are you mad at me or something?"

It was a genuine question layered with real, raw honesty. Harper could see the concern on Kiley's face.

"Of course not. Why would I be mad at you?"

"I don't know. I do bad things. Maybe one slipped by that I didn't catch."

"No. I'm not mad at you. I promise. It's just…I kind of spent the rest of the weekend holed up with Emily. We had a really good talk. She told me a little about where she was all this time and what she had been doing. At the moment, tending to her seemed to be more important than performing. And after what she told me, I really didn't feel well."

"Oh wow. Well, that makes perfect sense then. What did she tell you?"

"It's a long story, but basically she was in Chicago with her ex-boyfriend."

"What was she doing out there?"

"Unsavory things. I don't want to get into it. But the bottom line is: she stopped, he broke her heart, and she moved onto other places. That's pretty much all I got out of her." Harper decided to leave out the drug information. She didn't know how Emily would feel about her story being completely disclosed to Kiley.

"Well, it's good that you guys are talking. You're on the right track. It seems like she trusts you enough to tell you things."

"Yeah. Even things I don't want to hear."

The girls were heading upstairs to the nonfiction level of the bookstore. Harper found it surprisingly easy to pretend that nothing was wrong. Kiley always had a way of making her feel perfectly at ease.

"So, apparently Seth is having a party."

"He is?"

"Yeah. I guess he moved into a bigger place and wants to show it off," informed Kiley.

"Oh. How do you know?"

"He sent out a mass text message. I'm surprised he still had my number. I hadn't seen him since that night he came to the bar with Finn to celebrate his raise."

"You probably made an impression on him." She grabbed a gardening book from one of the benches. "Are you gonna go?"

"I was thinking about it. It's not for another two weeks, so maybe something else will come up. But I think you should go, too."

Harper laughed. "Right. THAT'LL happen."

"You really should. You need to get out and have some fun. When was the last time you went to a party?"

"I have a dance party in my room every night whenever Michael Jackson comes on my iPod."

"Harper—"

"I just don't think it's a good idea. First of all, I'm not invited."

"The text said the more the merrier. You can be my 'plus one.'"

"I broke his best friend's heart. I don't think I'm welcomed there."

"He'll be so drunk he either won't notice or won't care."

"And what about Finn?"

"What about him?"

"He's probably gonna be there. Won't that be kind of awkward?"

"Nonsense! It's time for you two to grow up and accept your past mistakes and be in the same room together without him pining for you and without you feeling bad for ending your relationship. It's time to evolve. You're going and that's that." Kiley tossed another book into the basket and put her hands together as though washing her hands of the task. "Well, my work here is finished. Now if you'll excuse me, now that I know you're not mad at me, I must attend to much more important things. Taco Bell is calling my name. So, Seth's party. Two weeks. We'll go shopping for something cute to wear."

"But what about Fi—"

"Don't worry about Finn! Silly girl. Just come to the party with me. Have some drinks, mingle a bit, and if you want to leave early, we'll leave early. Finn's a big boy. He can take care of himself."

***

Later that week, Finn found himself panting heavily as sweat was pouring down his brow. He peeked his head out from behind the wooden barrel he was stationed at and his anxiety led to full-on trepidation when he spotted his nefarious aggressor thirty yards away from him. He wanted to remove his mask and wipe away the burgeoning sweat, but he was told under no circumstances was he to remove his mask or helmet. He remained perfectly still and began to wonder why he agreed to this. He felt like calling it a day, truncating this overly stressful experience until he heard an ally whisper to him from behind a haystack.

"Psst. Hey, Finn."

Finn looked over to see Dr. Harris motion to him. He crawled his way over to her, holding his gun close to his side.

"These guys aren't giving up. The rest of my team is out, so we either have to surrender, or die trying."

"Can I vote for option A?"

"Of course you can, but as captain, I'm overruling you, so we're going with option B. On my count, jump out, start running, and shoot every one of them you can find. There are four of them left."

"Okay, but do you have any water left? I'm dying here."

"Water is for wimps. Let's do this. One..."

Finn was not ready for this. "Wait."

"Two…"

"Just give me a minute."

"Three!!!"

Without thinking, Finn jumped up and started running and shooting his paintball gun at any moving target on the course. He managed to take down one of the opposite team members right away. He spun around and saw Dr. Harris running in the other direction, taking aim at someone else. He only hesitated for one moment while watching her, but it was a moment too long. The second he turned back around he was greeted by two members of the other team who immediately fired at him. He was covered in yellow and red paint as he hit the ground. One of the guys bent over and reached out his hand.

"Nice job, man. Not bad for a first-timer, but you're out."

Finn walked off to the sidelines and tried to catch his breath. The rest of Dr. Harris' team greeted him with pats on the back.

"Way to stick it out, Finn."

"Looks like we're pretty much done. They have her cornered."

Finn turned to see the remaining three team members gang up on Dr. Harris, and before he could even take another breath, she fell to the ground, covered in paint.

"Aw man. That sucks," muttered one team member.

"Hey, it's only our third loss this season. We'll get 'em next week."

Once the applause died down, Finn removed his mask and headed over toward Dr. Harris.

She took off her mask and helmet and ran her fingers through her matted hair. She shrugged as Finn finally reached her. "We tried."

"Yes we did. I can't believe I lasted that long."

"I hope you don't say that to all the women."

"No, only the ones I'm not afraid to be honest with."

"So what did you think?"

"It was a lot of fun. I can't believe you do this every week."

"Yeah, it takes a lot out of you. You'll probably sleep pretty well tonight."

They walked back to the sidelines and changed out of their coveralls. Finn downed a bottle of water in about ten seconds flat. As everyone started clearing out, he and Dr. Harris started walking back to their cars.

"So Dr. Harris…"

"Susan."

"Sorry. Susan, what are you doing later today? Did you want to go get some dinner, or something?"

Susan smiled and shook her head. "You are gonna cause me nothing but trouble, aren't you?"

"What do you mean?"

"I can't believe I invited you to come today. I mean, I'm glad you came, but it's really not appropriate."

"Yeah, I know. You've been saying that all day. But you asked me, and I'm here. So now I'm asking you to go to dinner with me."

Susan hesitated. "I really shouldn't. I have to pick up my son."

"He can come with us."

Susan opened her trunk, taking her time putting the equipment back in so she could have a moment to process what Finn was proposing. She had never introduced Andrew to any of the men she had dated in the past. So what would it mean to do it now with a guy she isn't even dating? He's only a patient. What kind of confusion would that bring to Andrew?

"No, Finn. I don't think so. Thanks for the offer, but I don't think it's a good idea. But thanks for coming today. I'm glad you had fun."

Finn leaned against Susan's car. "So that's it?"

"Well, I'll see you on Thursday for our next session."

"Okay. Fair enough."

Susan closed the trunk and got into her car. Before she closed the door, Finn made one last effort to see her again outside the parameters of her office.

"Look, I know your answer is gonna be 'it wouldn't be appropriate,' but I'm going to just throw this out there. My friend Seth is having a party next Saturday. I'm going. And I'm inviting you to go."

Susan, while touched by the invitation, couldn't help but laugh at the preposterous idea. "I'm going to be twenty years older than everyone. I don't think I'd fit in very well."

"You'll fit in just fine. No one will care."

Susan thought for a moment. "And you're right. It wouldn't be appropriate."

"Susan, please."

"I'll think about it."

"That's all I ask."

"I'll let you know by Thursday, okay? But my answer is probably going to be 'no.'"

"That's fine. As long as you promise to think about it."

"I have to go. I don't want to keep Andrew waiting."

Finn closed the door for her and lingered for a moment. "I had a lot of fun today."

"Me too," said Susan, allowing Finn to hover over the open car window. Her breath suddenly caught in her throat. "I should go. I'll see you Thursday."

"And then again next Saturday." Finn couldn't resist egging her on.

"Bye, Finn." Susan drove away leaving Finn behind with a rather goofy grin on his face.

CHAPTER 22

The flickering light outside the Macy's dressing room set the perfect tone for where Harper's brain was at right now, flickering on and off with images of Kiley. Since her feelings for Kiley had been brought to the surface, nothing else has been on Harper's mind. She continually tried to make sure it wasn't written all over her face whenever Kiley was around, which was often.

The flashing images of Kiley soon turned into the real thing when she stepped out of the dressing room donning a blue and white spaghetti strap dress. Harper was rendered speechless the moment she looked up and saw the older girl in front of her. She was a vision, utterly stunning. Harper soon became conscious of her mouth hanging wide open and closed it immediately.

"What do you think?"

Harper excitedly and emphatically nodded her head. "Yeah. That's the one. Definitely get that."

"Good. I kind of love it." Kiley spun around to look at the dress from behind. Harper instantly felt her crimson cheeks get warmer as her eyes darted from Kiley to the floor. A tinge of excitement came alive inside of her, but she made it a point to not let it show.

"All right, enough stalling. Time for you to try those on." Kiley gestured to the dresses hanging up in the next dressing room.

"Fine, but no laughing at me if you see my chub sticking out."

"You have no chub! You're the fittest person I know. Stop being a woman and fishing for compliments."

Harper started trying on the dresses she picked out and heard Kiley trying on her last dress, just to make sure she wanted to go with the blue and white one.

Slouching in front of the mirror and feeling frumpy, Harper immediately took off the first dress. "This one just doesn't hang right."

"Yeah, I'm not a fan of this last one," replied Kiley through the divider. "So how are things with Emily? Still doing okay?"

"Yeah, I think we're a little more relaxed around each other. And she really likes her job. It seems to be helping her. She's even made a few friends there."

"You mean there are people out there who actually *like* her personality? Weird."

"Hey, that's my sister you're talking about. Watch it."

"Oh, I see. She can insult me all she wants and you let her, but when I say something about her, you scold me."

Harper tossed her next dress aside. It was too baggy on her. "I play favorites. You know that. Maybe you shouldn't have told her the Monopoly story. I'd be a little nicer to you."

"Touché."

Harper struggled to zip up her next dress, but once she did and looked in the mirror, she perked up. This was definitely the dress for her.

"Um…"

"What? Did you find one?" asked Kiley, as she finished getting dressed.

"I think so."

"Then get your ass out here. Let's see it."

Harper stepped out of the dressing room giving Kiley a coy smile as she revealed the dress.

Kiley froze, unsure of exactly what to say. Harper looked down and brushed the dress with her hands, trying to make it as smooth as possible.

"What's the verdict?" She looked back up at Kiley who couldn't take her eyes off of Harper.

"If you don't buy that dress, I'll buy it for you. You must own it." Kiley didn't know what else to say. She couldn't decide if the sexiest part was that it hugged the hips and accentuated Harper's curves, the short hemline stopping four inches above the knees, or the plunging neckline that made Harper's assets rather prominent.

"It's kinda hot, isn't it?" Harper was feeling rather pleased with her find.

"I'm thinking that might be the understatement of the century. Damn." Kiley couldn't stop gawking and Harper was secretly loving every second of it. "Turn around."

Harper obliged and slowly spun around so Kiley could get the full effect.

"You are so gonna get laid at this party."

"Oh gee. Just what I've been dreaming about. Hooking up in a skintight dress with some beer-guzzling guy fumbling for the zipper."

"Hey, don't knock it. Besides, the zipper won't be needed. That's the beauty of wearing a dress. Easy access."

"Wow, you are a class act, aren't you?"

"Just promise me you won't stand next to me in that dress. I'll disappear into the ether."

Silence fell upon them as the two girls stood there almost mesmerized with each other. Kiley couldn't believe how incredible Harper looked and couldn't tear her eyes away. Harper desperately searched Kiley's eyes for any sign of what she may be feeling or thinking at this moment.

Little did she know that Kiley wasn't really thinking anything. Her brain had somehow forgotten how to do the thing that makes it think. She was purely working on impulse right now and her impulse led her to take off the necklace she was wearing, turn Harper around to face the mirror and leisurely place it around her neck. The hair stood up on the back of Harper's neck as her friend's hands grazed her skin, leaving a trail of goose bumps. Once the clasp was secure, Harper played with the dangling necklace as Kiley remained fixated on the neck it was hanging from.

Harper watched in the mirror as Kiley started to close the gap between her lips and Harper's neck, both girls feeling the extreme heated energy that passed between them. Suddenly remembering how to breathe, Kiley anxiously exhaled, breathing warmth onto Harper's skin.

Kiley was now centimeters away from Harper's neck when her brain chose that exact moment to start working again. She was yanked back into reality in time to realize what she was doing, then suddenly pulled back. The movement jolted Harper, who turned around to face her friend.

Kiley backed up all the way to the wall, grabbed the dress she wanted to purchase and started to walk out of the dressing room.

"Um…I'm gonna go stand in line. I'll meet you out there." She turned around and gave Harper one final glance. "You should wear that necklace. It looks good with the dress."

All Harper could do was nod.

"I'll meet you at the register."

***

When Finn walked through the door into the lobby of Susan's office, there was an extra spring in his step.

"Good morning, Janine." He happily greeted Susan's secretary.

"Hello Mr. Lewis. Go ahead and take a seat. She's running a little behind."

Finn sat down and right away, he took notice of a young boy dividing his attention between playing with matchbox cars and Teenage Mutant Ninja Turtles action figures. His Angels baseball cap was a little too loose on his head, but he wore it with pride.

"You like the Angels?" asked Finn.

The boy didn't look up from his toys. "Yeah."

"I'm a Dodger fan, myself. But the Angels are a close second."

"Dodgers are okay."

Finn chuckled. He didn't know why he found this kid so endearing.

"Who's your favorite Ninja Turtle?"

The boy held up a turtle with the blue bandana.

"Leonardo, eh?" He reached over and picked up the turtle with the red bandana. "I've always been partial to Raphael. I didn't even know these guys were still around. I loved them as a kid."

"My mommy thinks they're silly."

"Oh yeah?"

"Yeah, but she likes to play cars with me."

Finn handed Raphael back to the boy. "Sounds like a cool mom."

"She's taking me for ice cream after this."

"Ice cream?"

Susan stealthily appeared in the doorway. "Yes, ice cream. If he behaves and obeys Janine."

"I have been," affirmed the boy.

Susan gave the young boy a kiss on the forehead. "Just a little bit longer, kiddo."

"Okay, Mommy."

Susan gestured to Finn. "Shall we?"

Finn was dumbfounded. It hadn't even occurred to him that the boy he was talking to was Susan's son. He assumed the kid belonged to a patient.

Susan closed the door behind them as Finn stayed standing, leaning up against the desk.

"So, that was your son?"

"Yup. That's Andrew. I forgot his school had a half-day today and I couldn't find a sitter in time."

"He's a nice kid. Very opinionated."

"Yeah. He gets that from me."

"He really dotes on you."

"Probably because I bribe him with ice cream." She leaned up against the desk next to Finn. "I wasn't expecting you to talk to him. Sorry if that was weird for you."

"It wasn't weird at all. I liked talking to him."

"I tried to warn him of the dangers of talking to strangers. I guess he's just a really trusting kid, which just gives me more reasons to worry about him."

"I guess I have a trusting face."

Finn could feel Susan's arm brush up against his. Her hand grazed against his hand and lingered there.

"Do you have an answer for me about Saturday?" he asked, trying to control his excitement.

Truth be told, Susan had given it a lot of thought and decided against going. However, after seeing the interaction between Finn and her son, she had a change of heart. "Well Finn, this is going against everything I believe in and everything I've been taught and it couldn't be more wrong, but…yeah. I'll go with you. As friends."

"As friends. Okay, I'll take it. You know, you're such a pushover." He leaned over and nudged her.

"I am not. I just need a fun night out." She nudged him back.

That physical contact pushed Finn over the edge and he couldn't resist the urge any longer. His hand caught her hand and their fingers intertwined.

Susan turned to face him. "Finn…"

"What?"

"I can't be doing this."

"Doing what?"

"This is really…"

"Inappropriate?"

Susan nodded. That was the last thing she remembered before her lips attached to his as she hungrily gave into every desire she had been fighting over the last few months. Finn wrapped his arms around her waist and pulled her in tighter. He had been fantasizing about this moment for quite some time, but didn't expect it to actually happen–at least not right now in the middle of her office. When they finally peeled their lips away from each other, Finn knew he had to say something to palliate the situation before Susan began to regret anything.

He gave her a half-smile. "That was, like, nineteen kinds of inappropriate."

***

Emily tugged at the collar of her dark blue uniform shirt. She was beginning to work up a sweat unloading the new shipment of field berries they just received at Gulcher's. She wasn't exactly used to manual labor, but welcomed this as a humbling experience. By this point she had been reminded ten times over of what a great life she had growing up and how easy she had it. Even after their parents died, Harper made it clear to Emily that she would never have to want for anything. But she was young and stupid and her restless ways led her to rule with her stubbornness instead of her heart.

As she moved on from the strawberries to the blueberries, Emily's thoughts led her to become even more contemptible of herself. She hated who she had become. Look at her, she was a walking statistic: drugs, alcohol, theft, a black sheep, a runaway. No one wants to be defined that way, least of all her.

"Hey Foley, do you need a ride home?" Emily's supervisor seemed to appear out of nowhere.

"Oh, that's okay. I usually walk."

"Well, it just started raining. You're off in an hour, right?"

"Yeah."

"Well, if it's still raining, I can give you a ride if you want."

"Okay, thanks." Emily peered out of the sliding glass doors of the entrance and watched the rain soak up the cement outside.

***

The bus stopped at a station just outside Santa Fe, New Mexico. This was as far as Emily could get with the money she had left, so it had to do for now. After asking a bus station attendant where the closest hostel was, she lugged her bag a mile and a half northwest. Halfway through her destination, the sky opened up and rain started violently pounding down upon her. The drops were the size of marbles and the torrential downpour soaked her from head to toe within sixty seconds. This is one thing she definitely missed about Los Angeles: there were no flash floods or sudden thunderstorms that started out of nowhere. The hood pulled over her head didn't do much to keep her dry.

It was nearly pitch black outside and after finally reaching her destination, she ran up the walkway leading to the hostel and tried to open the door, but it was locked. She knocked loudly on the door until someone answered.

"Sorry. This door sticks when it rains."

Emily looked pleadingly at the young man who answered the door. "I don't suppose you have any vacancies."

"I'm sorry, but we're all filled up."

"Seriously?" Emily was partly disappointed and partly relieved. With four dollars in her pocket, had there

been a vacancy, she wouldn't even have had the money to pay for one night.

"There's a motel about a mile down the street. They might have a room available. It's about fifty a night."

Emily stared at the young man, unsure of what to do or say. She started shivering violently and dreaded the thought of being stuck out in the deluge of rain. The young man at the door watched as her eyes began to well up.

"Look, we're completely full but maybe you can come in and just wait out the storm." He stepped to the side and allowed a profusely grateful Emily to walk in. "Our lobby is this way. It's not really a lobby. More of a fancy way of saying 'common area.'"

"Thank you. Thank you so much."

"No problem. I wish I could help you out with the sleeping situation. If you want to try to call the hotel down the street, there's a pay phone in the corner."

Emily made her way through the near-empty common area and grabbed the receiver of the pay phone. She put her last two quarters in to the slot and began to dial, her hands shaking from a mixture of nerves and the cold.

"Hello?"

It had been a while since she heard Harper's voice.
"Hello?"

Emily hung up the phone and backed away. There was fifty cents well wasted. With nowhere to go, no one to call and no money, she sat on the musty, stained couch in the middle of the room weighing her options. She hoped she wouldn't have to spend another night in a bus station.

The front door swung open letting in a brisk wind. Emily spotted the guy who walked in. He looked like he was in his early thirties and his closely shaved head contrasted his unshaven face. He took off his coat to reveal a tight muscle shirt tucked into his jeans. Her attention moved to the McDonald's bag he was holding and she suddenly realized how hungry she was. Emily caught the man's eye and he swaggered over to her grinning in a way he thought was charming, but in reality looked creepy.

"Hungry?" He sat down next to her.

"Starved."

"I always order too much. I'm Albert."

"Michelle." Emily did not feel comfortable enough to share her real name with this guy, so she opted for her middle name.

"You know they're all filled tonight, right?"

"Yeah. They're letting me wait out the rain." Emily sat with her hands in her lap, still shivering. Only now, it was a combination of the cold and the essence the guy next to her was giving off.

Albert leaned over toward her. "Well, I just happen to have a private room," he revealed in his eastern European accent that Emily couldn't quite place. "If you're hungry and need a place to stay, we might be able to arrange...something."

Emily avoided eye contact and tried to keep her distance. He wasn't exactly being subtle. His overpowering cologne was making her nauseated and his breath was exacerbating her aversion toward him.

Near tears at this point, Emily thought this through. Four months and seven states ago, she woke up in a seedy motel bed and swore to herself she would never, ever allow herself to do that again no matter how dire the situation was. Her stomach was nagging as she inhaled the aroma from the McDonalds bag. The rain outside was only getting louder and showed no signs of stopping anytime soon. Midnight was quickly approaching and she was exhausted. The thought of what she was potentially about to do made her sick, but the thought of spending another night trying to find shelter was way too daunting.

She tentatively reached out to take the McDonalds bag when Albert grabbed her wrist and took the bag with his other hand.

"Let's eat in my room. It's warmer up there."

He led her up two flights of stairs, then turned left down a dark hallway. They passed by several twenty-somethings smoking pot, playing card games, and socializing along the way. Albert opened the door to his room and walked in putting the greasy fast food bag on the dresser. He turned around, sat on the bed and started unbuttoning his pants as Emily entered the room, saw Albert sitting at the edge of the bed and looked down at his pants and boxers in a pile on the floor. She heaved an audible sigh, closed the door and locked it behind her.

***

"Emily, there's one more pallet in the back. Can you bring it in? Then you can go home for the day."

Emily looked at her supervisor. "Sure. And if your offer still stands, I'd love a ride home."

"No problem."

She solemnly walked through the store toward the back to get the other pallet of berries and mumbled to herself.

"I fucking hate the rain."

CHAPTER 23

It was difficult for Harper to believe that a guy like Seth would have a lot of friends. He often came across as pompous, conceited and–for lack of a better word– douchey. Maybe it was his overconfidence that made him so appealing to others, yet so unappealing to Harper. She seemed to lack it while he had it in droves. Judging by the nearly one hundred people crammed in Seth's new apartment, it was clear that he was pretty well-liked.

Arriving in style and donning their new dresses, Harper and Kiley had to surrender their "three feet of personal space" rule for the evening as they slid by complete strangers to try and find their way to the kitchen for some drinks. After preparing their vodka tonics with a splash of cranberry juice, they managed to find an open spot on the couch in the living room. With Jay-Z blasting from the speakers and the crowd loudly verbalizing their excitement for whatever subject was being discussed, Harper glanced around to see if she recognized anyone. The car ride over was a little awkward. Neither girl had said much to the other. Harper didn't know if the incident at Macy's had something to do with it, but it was probably a safe bet seeing as how it was all she could think about since it happened. Without even realizing it, she had downed the last of her drink.

"Whoa. You might want to pace yourself," warned Kiley.

"I guess I'm thirsty," replied Harper.

I'll get you another one. Just go a little easy on it."

"Amaretto sour if they have it."

When Kiley got up, Harper breathed her first sigh of relief of the night. Why was this so difficult? Even sitting next to her, Harper couldn't relax. What if she was too close? Not close enough? She adjusted her dress and fixed the chain of the necklace that Kiley had lent her. She crossed her legs and tried to calm herself down by doing a little people-watching. It didn't take long for her to notice the guy sitting on the arm of a chair across from her staring at her chest. Harper wanted to scoff, but she sort of had it coming by wearing a dress like this. It was supposed to garner attention and whether it was wanted or not, she was getting it.

Kiley returned with two fresh drinks and took her place next to Harper. Upon noticing the polo shirt-clad young man who was blatantly staring at Harper's chest, she handed Harper the Amaretto sour and snapped her fingers to get the guy's attention.

"Are you expecting them to do tricks?"

Huh?" The young man was perplexed after being so visibly entranced.

Take a picture. It'll last longer."

That last comment did the trick as he retreated back to his friends and did his best not to look back over in their direction.

"Thanks," said Harper.

"Of course. I really regret the 'picture' comment. How trite was that?"

You could have done better. But it was a valiant effort."

I do my best." She clinked her glass against Harper's. "Cheers."

"Slainte." Harper took a sip of her drink. "I don't see Finn anywhere."

"I'm sure he'll be here if he isn't already."

Three drinks in, the girls migrated from the couch to the hallway only to be greeted by Seth.

Ladies! Wow, you look gorgeous. Both of you." He looked both of them up and down. "Harper, I didn't think you'd be here."

"I invited her," informed Kiley.

"That's cool. It's good to see you." He gave Harper a one-armed hug. "I know I should treat you like a she-devil for what you did to my best friend, but I'll go easy on you."

Uh…thanks."

"So I'm just gonna move past the informalities and go straight into the inappropriate. Kiley, you just made my pants a little tighter. And Harper, did you always dress this hot for Finn? Because damn! No wonder he was so depressed."

"Seth! That's not cool." Finn appeared from around the corner. "Can't you ever be a gentleman?"

"What? I thought chicks like honesty."

"We do," replied Harper. "Just maybe in more subtle doses." She could feel her stomach turning over repeatedly at the sight of Finn in front of her. He appeared surprisingly calm, his eyes lined with kindness instead of bitterness.

"How have you been, Harper?" Finn greeted her with a hug.

"I'm okay."

"Yeah? You look really good."

"Thanks."

"Finn? Oh there you are, I thought I lost you."

Harper's focus was pulled from Finn and fell on an older, slender brunette woman who pulled up to Finn's side and took his hand.

"Oh, sorry. Susan, this is Harper, and this is her friend, Kiley."

Susan was slightly caught off guard but refused to show it. She extended her hand out with a timid uncertainty. She tried to ignore the fact that Finn had divulged to her a significant amount of information that Harper would probably not want anyone to know, especially her. "It's nice to meet you."

Harper took her hand, trying to piece everything together. Was this Finn's date? How old was she? Mid-thirties? Late thirties? "Nice to meet you, too."

"Finn, do you want to see if there's any more food?" asked Susan, who couldn't quite explain this tinge of jealousy she felt toward Harper.

"Sure. We'll talk later, guys."

As they walked away, Seth turned to the girls and answered the question that was on both their minds. "She's forty-three."

"Wow. Seriously?" asked Kiley.

"Yeah. She looks good, right? She has a kid, too."

"She has a kid?" asked an appalled Harper.

Seth nodded. "All right. Now that the awkwardness is out of the way, let me give you the tour. You saw the kitchen and living room with my fancy balcony. Down here we've got my roommate's bedroom. Tonight it's known as the 'pot room' if you guys are craving any…you know."

"I think we're good," assured Kiley. She leaned over and whispered to Harper, "You okay?"

"I don't know. I mean, who was that?"

Seth continued the tour. "Bathroom's here. And this is my room."

"Hey Seth, so what's the deal with Finn? Is he dating that girl?" Kiley wasn't a fan of beating around the bush.

"I don't know. I think there's a little something going on, but how serious can it be, right?" He peered back out into the living room and spotted Finn and Susan. "Oh."

"What?" Harper turned around to see her ex-fiancé kissing another woman right in front of her. She didn't know why she suddenly felt agitated and somewhat stupefied. She knew this day would eventually come and it had been over six months since they broke up, but it still felt like it was too soon.

"I need another drink," declared Harper.

Kiley whizzed past her before she even finished the sentence. "I'm on it."

Seth stepped up to Harper and smirked. "So…what's Kiley's story?"

He was met with a blank stare, then Harper turned and walked away.

***

The fresh air felt good on her skin and the noise from the party guests were significantly drowned out once the sliding glass door leading to the balcony was closed. Harper rested her elbows on the cold brick and looked out into the darkness in front of her.

The noise from the crowd grew louder, then faded out again as Kiley stepped out on to the balcony and closed the door. "There you are." She handed Harper another drink.

"I needed some air."

Kiley stood next to Harper and rested her drink on the ledge. "It's a nice night."

"I shouldn't have come tonight."

"Don't say that."

"I really shouldn't have. I don't feel welcomed. Seth hates me."

"No he doesn't."

"Finn hates me."

"Finn does not hate you," argued Kiley. "He seemed fine."

Feeling a lump build up in her throat, Harper took a drink. "This is good."

"Made it myself."

Harper took some time to calm down and breathe in this moment. This was not a time for her to break down. At this moment, she was thriving on the heat Kiley was giving off next to her. Suddenly, she became very aware of her surroundings and aware of everything her body was feeling. Their arms were lightly touching and it was all Harper could feel. Was Kiley aware that their arms were touching? Was she intentionally keeping it there? Was that the only thing Kiley was thinking about at this moment, too? Did she feel the charge in the air, like Harper?

Harper shook her thoughts away and brought herself back to the here and now. "I should go."

"Don't go. Aren't we having a good time? Despite the whole Finn thing?"

"I don't belong here. I'm beginning to think I don't belong anywhere."

Kiley sighed and looked up at the sky above her. "Now you know that's not true." She then locked eyes with Harper, her thumb slowly caressing the top Harper's hand.

"What about me?"

"What about you?"

Kiley finished the rest of her drink and turned to fully face Harper. Harper couldn't help but feel like something was about to happen. Something incredible. Her heart began beating out of her chest. She had to remind herself to breathe. She knew what was about to happen. She recognized that look in Kiley's eyes. It was the same look Harper herself had every time Kiley was near her. A look of longing and uncertainty. A look of fear and passion. A look of confusion and desire. Kiley leaned in and brushed her lips softly against Harper's lips, slightly hesitating to make sure Harper was okay with it. Harper graciously welcomed the kiss as their lips moved together in one fluid motion. She couldn't feel her legs. She never thought a kiss could turn her legs to jelly, but it happened. Her once fervently beating heart had now grown silent and still. Harper was overwhelmed. The inexplicable sensation shooting through her body was almost too much for her. As she gently pulled away, she kept her eyes locked on Kiley. She couldn't say a word. All she could do was stare.

After what felt like an eternity of mind-numbing silence, Kiley broke away from their staring match and backed away. "Um…I'm gonna go get another drink."

Harper didn't even have a chance to respond. Kiley was gone in a flash. After drinking the remainder of the alcohol in her glass, Harper gripped the ledge with her shaking hands and exhaled deeply.

Finn and Susan were next in line to challenge each other in Guitar Hero. Initially, he was a little nervous about bringing Susan to a twenty-something laden convivial gathering, but after just a few moments, Susan easily fit in.

"Do you even know how to play this?" asked Finn.

"Who me? Oh no. I'm afraid I'm not familiar with these newfangled video gaming thingies," retorted Susan.

"Are you being facetious?"

"I have an eight-year-old at home. What do you think? This is all he plays."

Finn placed his hand on the small of her back and leaned in. "We'll just set it on 'expert' then." He tightened his grip just barely enough for her to notice.

"By the way," she whispered. "I'm having a really great time."

"Good. I knew you would. So am I."

Amongst a sea of partiers, Finn was about to throw caution to the wind as he leaned down to kiss her. Before he could make contact, Susan's cell phone went off.

"Oh, sorry." She fumbled for the phone and looked to see who would dare call her at such an inopportune time. "It's my sitter. Sorry, I have to take this. Hello?…Uh huh… Oh, really?…Did you try giving him some Benadryl?…And nothing?…How bad is it?…Okay… No, that's fine. I'm glad you called me. I'll be there in twenty minutes."

She hung up the phone and gave Finn an apologetic look.

"You have to go?"

Susan nodded. "I'm so sorry."

"Don't worry about it," said Finn, trying to hide the disappointment in his voice.

"I hate to make you leave right now."

"You should go straight home to your son. I can get a ride home from someone else. Or I can just crash here tonight. It won't be a problem."

"Are you sure?"

"Yeah. It's a good thing you insisted on driving."

"What can I say? I'm a modern woman."

Finn walked Susan out to her car. "I hope everything's okay with Andrew."

"I'm sure it'll be fine. He gets allergies from time to time, but it usually turns out to be okay." She opened her car door, lingering for a moment.

Finn smiled. "I'm just gonna bypass the awkwardness and kiss you."

He tilted her chin up and kissed her gently. "Drive safe."

"You too...I mean...have a good night." Susan was letting her giddiness get in the way of her sanity.

"I'll call you tomorrow," said Finn.

***

After a half hour of agonizing over what had just transpired between them, Harper went back inside. Consuming all that alcohol probably wasn't the best idea seeing as how she was feeling nauseated and wanted to go home. Maybe at home, the room wouldn't spin as much as it did here. She was Kiley's ride, but wasn't in any shape to drive home. She had lost track of Kiley since the kiss, but maybe she was in much better shape to drive. She stumbled through the living room passing by people doing shots of every kind: body shots, Jell-o shots, blow job shots. It was a scene directly taken from a college frat party. The music seemed to be on an endless loop of Rihanna and Katy Perry, which really made Harper question Seth's taste in music. She turned the corner down the hall, but not before catching Finn's eye as he walked back in the front door. She made her way down the hall, hoping to find Kiley. After failing to find her in the line for the bathroom, she clamored for the door leading to Seth's room. She opened the door while simultaneously knocking, which probably wasn't the smartest idea. Harper felt like she had been punched in the gut and had the wind knocked out of her when she found two people under the covers caught in the midst of a very private moment in the bed. After hearing the noticeable moaning, Harper froze in place.

"Get the hell out!" yelled Seth.

"Sorry," was all Harper managed to choke out. Then a voice she would recognize even if she were deaf called out her name from the bed.

"Harper?" Kiley called from underneath Seth.

Instead of answering, Harper backed away growing even dizzier than she was before. She closed the door and in a daze found her way back to the living room. The party was slowly dying down, so there was room on the couch for her to sit and try to make her head stop spinning. All the while trying to drown out the image that was now permanently burned on her brain.

Finn watched Harper's every move from the moment she distraughtly sank into the couch. He realized something was definitely off. Carrying his beer, he sat down next to her. "Too much to drink?"

Harper massaged her temples, her body shuddering as little hiccups escaped her. It had nothing to do with the alcohol, but everything to do with the tears that were now flowing freely down her cheeks.

"Maybe," she answered. "Where's your date?"

"She had a mini-emergency and had to leave early."

Harper wiped a few tears away, tasting the saltiness left in their wake. "She seems nice."

"She is. Very nice." He could no longer pretend not to notice her crying. "Are you okay?"

"I'm an idiot."

Harper left herself wide open for a barrage of comments Finn could have made. Though her tears were leading him once again to be the nice guy and take the high road.

"Why do you say that?"

"Never mind. I don't want to talk about it." She looked at Finn through her swollen eyes and sniffled. "You look really good."

"I've lost some weight. Gained some muscle."

"What's your secret?"

Finn wanted so badly to respond with: 'Heartbreak and a new relationship.'

"Pilates."

"Really?"

"No. Not really."

Harper laughed through her tears. Finn started to feel really bad about seeing her in this state. He polished off the rest of his beer and put a comforting arm around her as she cried into his shoulder. She inhaled the scent from his shirt and recalled a time when that smell was the safest thing in the world for her. The memories of nights they would lie awake in bed together talking until sunrise infiltrated her thoughts. Even then, she had a feeling that maybe Finn wasn't the one for her. But she had pushed those ideas aside because how could she possibly question something this easy and this fun and this safe? After everything that's happened and after what she just witnessed, at this moment, Harper would have given anything to feel that safe again. Her mind was a mess and her heart was aching and she was beginning to question the validity of everything around her.

"Finn? Can you take me home? I don't think I should drive right now."

"Sure. Where are you parked?"

"Just across the street."

Finn got up and extended his hand out for Harper to take.

"All right. Let's get you home."

***

Not wanting to wake up Emily, the ex-lovers entered the house as quietly as they could. Harper's wobbly walking was the deciding factor for Finn to come in and help her to bed, even though part of him just wanted to go home and call Susan to see if Andrew was okay.

"Finn?"

"Yeah?"

"What's wrong with me?"

"Nothing. Nothing's wrong with you."

"Then why can't I just be happy?"

"It's the human condition to be perpetually unhappy. When they say ignorance is bliss, it's true. The problem is, you're too smart for your own good. So you're too smart to settle for less than what you want."

"What if it's too far out of my reach? Am I always gonna feel like this?"

"I don't know. Maybe." Finn couldn't bear seeing Harper so distraught. He used to think she could tell him anything, but lately she had been so cryptic, it made him begin to feel useless around her. He didn't like feeling useless, especially when it came to Harper. Finn wrapped her in a hug, his entire body enveloping her five-foot-three frame. They were in her room in the dark, halfway to her bed when they both allowed themselves to take in every moment of the embrace. Harper's head was in a fog and perhaps the alcohol didn't help with her decision-making abilities But at that moment she held on to the only thing she knew could be relied upon. Then, she took it a step further by guiding Finn's lips to hers. He hesitated for a moment, but after feeling those lips on his once again after so long without them, he forgot about all the progress he made in getting over her and kissed her back.

It was different, not as familiar as it used to be for Finn. Something had changed in the way she kissed him, but he ignored it because he had to. There was no way he could pull away now.

"That's a really pretty dress," he stated as he ran his fingers over the material.

Harper instinctively started unzipping his jeans as he hiked up the lower part of her dress, gripping her thighs and slowly taking off her underwear. Once his shirt was removed, Harper's hands made their way back down to his pants. She was slightly stunned upon discovering his erection because it made her realize that this was a real thing. It was actually happening and her mind was such a wreck, it had no power to stop her body.

The way he held her, the way he touched her, the way he tasted was exactly the same. It was as if no time had passed and nothing had changed. At the moment, she thought that was what she needed. Something constant and unwavering, anything to keep her from feeling any more pain. She wanted to need him, but she couldn't. She didn't ache for him the way she did for Kiley. But Harper needed a taste of the way it used to be. It hurt too much to think about Kiley and how badly she wanted her. She was simply an ancillary appendage in Kiley's life and it hurt too much to think about that. So she turned to the one person she could trust not to hurt her. Was it a selfish act? Absolutely. But once again, her Scarlet O'Hara complex kicked in and she decided to worry about it tomorrow.

There was really no method to Finn's madness, but it did seem to go like clockwork. Barely two minutes of foreplay and he was ready to go. It's not that he was selfish or uncaring, he just didn't know any better. Harper never revealed to him what she preferred in the love-making department.

He lowered her onto the bed and fervently kissed her. He was unable to remember the last time he wanted something so badly.

Harper tried to stay in the moment, but she couldn't help but think of Kiley. Then, she thought of Kiley and Seth and having to actually see them together. Is that what led her here? Is this some sort of revenge? Harper was brought back to the here and now when she heard the condom wrapper crinkle in Finn's hand, then thrown to the floor. Her dress was still half on as she felt the pressure when he entered her. She exhaled slowly with each movement he made. It was dark enough for her to hide her tears.

"I love you," whispered Finn. "I've missed you so much."

Harper caressed his back and before she could even think of anything to respond with, she felt him shudder on top of her and let out a moan. She felt a familiar, pulsating feeling inside her. Finn lay on top of her for a moment, trying to regain his composure. Harper laid perfectly still, feeling like the worst person alive for wondering when he would leave. Based on his position, it seemed like it would be a while.

CHAPTER 24

The sun seeping through the curtains was Harper's deliverance. She spent the entire night waiting for the sun to rise and morning to come so that the living proof of last night's drunken bad decision would finally leave and let her commence the process of denial. She could barely hear herself think over Finn's snoring. Had it been this bad when they were together? Or was it just the alcohol that produced the grating sound coming from his nasal passages? Either way, Harper didn't know how much longer she could stand it.

The moment Finn gripped her tight and fell asleep next to her, Harper immediately felt horrible about what had transpired between them. The flashes of Kiley with Seth didn't help the situation. For some reason, revenge sex just lost its luster in the harsh light of day. She felt disgusted with herself. Suddenly riddled with an anxiety attack, Harper knew she couldn't be here at this moment. She couldn't be in this bed, with this man, in this house. Her restlessness gave way to full blown panic.

"Finn?"

"Mmm…" Finn rolled over to his side, still in sleep mode.

"Finn. Get up," she tapped him on the shoulder. "Finn."

"Mmm…don't worry about it. Don't have to work today. Let's just sleep in." He rolled back over and put his arms around her. Harper was right back where she started.

Finn suddenly sat up. "Sorry. I forgot. You've probably been awake for a while, haven't you?"

Harper nodded, trying to scoot away from Finn, not wanting her naked body to touch his. It seemed like a moot point by now, but she didn't care.

"Pretty much all night," said Harper.

"Still? Even after everything we…"

"Yes." Harper did not want him to finish that sentence.

"Wow. I'm sorry."

"Don't be." Harper sulked, dreading what was about to come next. She shook her head. "Why are you so good to me?"

Finn smiled. "Because I love you. And you deserve to be happy. Especially after all you've been through." He began to stroke her matted down, champagne-colored hair.

"Don't," she flinched.

"What?"

"Just don't, okay?"

"Okay. Fine." Finn rested his head on his hand. "What's wrong?"

Harper kicked the covers off of her and reached for a nearby shirt on the ground. "You don't think we did anything wrong last night?"

"How could that be wrong? It was amazing," replied Finn.

She stared at Finn, unsure of what words she was trying to get out. Finn's facial expression changed significantly with each passing moment of silence.

"Wasn't it? I mean...you...you liked it, right?" asked Finn.

Harper rubbed her head. "Finn, we broke up."

"I know, but—"

"And you're with someone now."

Finn felt the blood drain from his face. The thought of Susan hadn't even entered his mind until now.

"Yeah, but...this is us. I mean, it's you and me. How could I have said no to this?"

Harper shook her head. "I'm sorry. This is all my fault."

"What is?"

"This." She gestured to the bed. "All this. I was drunk and sad. And stupid."

"Stupid? You think this was stupid?"

Harper could hear the controlled panic and rage in his voice.

"Isn't it?"

"Harper, I fucking love you! How is this stupid?"

She didn't know how to answer that.

"Oh. I see. It was stupid of YOU to do it."

"I just don't think we thought this through."

"Of course we didn't. We were drunk out of our minds, but I wanted it. And so did you. Right?"

Harper was silent.

"Do you even love me? Like at all?"

"Finn— "

Finn angrily got out of the bed. Harper felt stupid for averting her eyes from his naked body, but for some reason, she felt like she was being far too intrusive by looking at him.

"Answer me."

Harper remained silent. She could see Finn's shoulders shivering in desperation through her peripheral vision. Harper kept her focus on the unraveled thread on her comforter and wondered why she never asked her mother to teach her how to sew. It looked so easy when she watched her mother do it. Now instead of obsessing over a single thread, she could easily fix it with a needle. Although at this moment, it was important to remember that a skill like sewing wouldn't be able to get her out of this situation. She pulled at the snagged piece of thread, hoping it would be removed and disappear, but it only grew longer. No matter how much she pulled, it kept getting worse and worse until there was a noticeable crease in the bedspread. Why couldn't she have just left well enough alone?

It had been four and a half minutes since she spoke.

"Please don't be angry." Harper hugged the sheet to her naked body as she braced for the worst.

Finn stood there in disbelief. He finally reached for his clothes and without taking his piercing eyes off of Harper, began to dress himself. He kept waiting for her to say something more, but evidently that was it. Once he got his left shoe on, he'd had enough silence.

"Do you have any idea what I've given up for you? What the hell am I supposed to tell Susan? I screwed everything up with her. I'm in so much shit right now, you know that? She *trusted* me!"

Harper knew he was looking for some sign, some explanation of why she couldn't love him. Maybe if she told him, he'd find some kind of peace. Maybe he would have a better grasp of what kind of turmoil she was in. Maybe he would forgive her for being so cruel, but she simply couldn't bring herself to tell him the truth. She refused to speak and still couldn't look at him.

Finn took one long last look at the only girl to whom he'd ever fully given his heart. "You're a horrible human being, you know that? You just fuck with people's emotions and use them and you don't give a shit. So I'm done with you. I'm done."

Without another word, Finn walked out the door and slammed it shut. Harper sat there, unable to move for fear of falling over. Any sudden movement would cause her to break at any moment. Stillness was her only comfort, at least until her emotions caught up with her. She knew she would cry, but it was just a matter of when.

***

Emily had just grabbed her keys to head out to work when Finn came storming out of Harper's room and didn't even acknowledge her as he charged out the front door. As she pieced together what she had just witnessed, Emily's eyes moved from the front door to the hallway as she headed toward her sister's room and knocked on the door. She didn't bother waiting for a response before opening the door to find her sister in a somewhat catatonic state.

"Hey. Um…so I don't have much time because I'm late for work, so I'm just gonna fire away. Why did I just see Finn storm out of the house?"

Harper looked at her sister. "We had sex last night."

Emily lowered her head. "I had a feeling that was the case. I was hoping it was just the TV I was hearing through the wall. So, you told him about Kiley?"

"No. But…"

"He still loves you and you rejected him."

"Pretty much."

Emily nodded. "Have you talked to Kiley?"

"She fucked Seth last night."

"You're kidding me, right?"

"Nope. It was right after we kissed."

"Wait, you two KISSED last night?"

"Yup."

Emily dropped her bag and her keys on the ground. "Okay, I'm calling in sick. I can't leave now."

"No, don't worry about it. I'll be fine."

"Like hell you will. I'm calling in sick. Deal with it." Emily watched her sister agonize over what happened in the last twelve life-altering hours. "Harper?"

"Yeah?"

"You want me to make you some pancakes?"

Harper smiled and nodded.

"Come on. You jump in the shower and I'll make breakfast."

***

Unbeknownst to Harper, Kiley's night ended abruptly, right after she and Seth were interrupted. Upon seeing the look on Harper's face, Kiley tried to push Seth off of her. It took some force seeing as how he was too into it to stop, but she managed to knee him in the stomach. She wanted to run after her friend, but by the time she found the last of her clothing and was fully dressed, Harper was nowhere to be found. So she left the party.

Kiley headed back home and walked into her empty apartment. Her new roommate had become a ghost and was rarely home anymore ever since she met "Shane." Kiley liked to use air quotes when talking about "Shane" because she had never met him and wasn't entirely sure he actually existed. So here she stood, alone in the dark in her quiet apartment with nothing to do but reflect upon the undoubtedly severe damage she had inflicted upon her best friend. Why did she kiss her? What was that about? Why did she *want* to? And why did she want to again when it was over? What possessed her to have sex with Seth mere minutes after kissing her best friend? Why did everything that once made sense in her life now confuse and scare the hell out of her? The abundance of questions combined with the lack of answers was too much for Kiley. She made the decision right then and there that she had to make it right. She had to find Harper. She had to apologize for being so wretched. She had to do it now before she lost her nerve. But unfortunately, there was one thing she had to before she could do anything else. She ran to the bathroom and barely made it in time for the entire contents of her stomach to be thrown up. Apparently alcohol and undying guilt don't mix very well. All Kiley knew for a fact was that she was in no shape to go anywhere tonight.

She didn't quite remember how she fell asleep, but waking up was a painful process. Sometime in the middle of the night, karma had bitch-slapped her to the ground. She found herself in the middle of her living room floor still in her dress with one shoe on. She could only assume she crawled her way back from the bathroom, but had no idea why she didn't aim for the bedroom. Or maybe she tried and thought she ended up in the right place. Her head felt like it had split in two and apparently falling asleep on top of her purse wasn't the best thing in the world for her back. She could still smell the overpowering scent of Seth's cologne and could feel a little bit of dried vomit on the side of her face. If there was ever a time for an emergency shower, this was it.

So this is what rock bottom feels like, she thought as she pulled herself up and dejectedly headed toward the bathroom.

CHAPTER 25

With the exception of work, Harper managed to keep herself holed up at home for the next week while avoiding any and all phone calls from Kiley. She was also dreading any kind of confrontation with Finn, but it seemed he was serious when he said he was done with her. With Emily helping to pick up the pieces of her irreversibly screwed up personal life, Harper threw herself into her music. She emerged from the garage only for work, sustenance or a shower. By Saturday, she was well-rehearsed for her show at Tyson's Bar that night. She knew a reunion with Kiley was inevitable, but tried to push it out of her mind. She didn't know what to do or how to act. Was she supposed to be angry with Kiley for sleeping with Seth? Or was she supposed to feel guilty for sleeping with Finn? Either way, it appeared they both made a huge error in judgment.

Harper decided not to dwell on what would happen when she saw Kiley. For all she knew, her best friend probably didn't want to see her either. To add to Harper's nerves, this would mark the first time Emily would ever attend one of her shows. She arranged it with Graham beforehand. His job was to stay with Emily at all times and monitor her drinks making sure they consisted of only soda or water, and nothing else.

Harper was incredibly proud of the strides Emily had been taking and couldn't have asked for a better companion while going through this not-so-ideal situation. She never thought of Emily as being someone you'd want to have on your side, but apparently her sister had many surprises up her sleeve.

"You ready to go?" Emily excitedly burst through the door leading to the garage, startling Harper.

"Jesus. Yeah, just give me a minute. I'll meet you out at the car."

"Can I drive?"

"Sure. I plan on imbibing many spirits for this one."

"Just put Kiley out of your mind. Focus on the music."

"Lame."

"Be the guitar?"

"Even more lame," replied Harper.

"Just do it," offered Emily.

"Nike lame."

"Put your fingers on the stringy thingies with one hand and strum with the other without thinking about the mess you left in the wake of getting drunk and sleeping with your ex-fiancé when, in reality, you're in love with your best friend."

Harper paused for a moment. "Okay, that's an axiom I can get on board with."

***

Kiley couldn't put it off any longer. She stayed in her car in the parking lot for as long as she could during her work break before she would officially get into trouble for being more than an hour late coming back. She even watched as Harper and Emily went into the bar a half hour ago. Harper would no doubt be wondering where she was. When she got a text from Erin saying that Graham was looking for her, she finally talked herself into going back in. Upon walking in, she saw Harper setting up for her gig with Emily helping her. Usually that was *her* job, but in this instance she'd let it pass. She avoided looking directly at the stage and made her way behind the bar.

"Where were you?" asked Erin.

"I fell asleep in my car."

"Well, I covered as much as I can, but Graham is pissed."

"He'll get over it."

"What's going on with you and Harper? She didn't even ask where you were. And now you're not even talking to her?"

"It's a long story."

"I like long stories," replied Erin as Kiley walked away.

She grabbed a bottle of Stella and slowly made her way to the stage. Kiley anxiously approached Harper, hoping her peace offering would expiate the situation.

She cleared her throat. "I noticed you were beer-less. I can fix that."

Harper turned around and Emily quickly made herself scarce and headed back to the bar area. "Thanks," said Harper as she grabbed the bottle.

The two of them stood there deeply immersed in a standoff of O.K. Corral proportions. Neither of them wanted to budge until Kiley figured, since she wasn't the wronged party she should be the one to cave.

"Harper, I'm really sorr— "

"I slept with Finn." The words exploded from Harper's lips before she had a chance to stifle them. The ripping-the-Band-Aid idea was suddenly beginning to seem like a stupid plan after she saw the look of utter disappointment in Kiley's face.

"What?" This was the last thing Kiley expected to hear.

"I'm sorry," offered Harper.

Kiley didn't want to hear another word. She turned around and walked straight out the back door leading to the alley. Harper followed suit. Once the door slammed shut behind them, Harper immediately launched into panic mode, needing to explain herself.

"Kiley, I'm sorry, okay? I freaked out when I saw you with Seth and then I ran into Finn and I was really drunk and…I don't know what else to say."

Kiley wasn't ready to speak yet. She turned to face Harper, whose eyes were provocatively burning into hers. She drew closer and closer to Kiley, completely spellbound by her intense gaze. She was inches away from Kiley's face.

Kiley didn't know what to do or say. She just stood there in silence. Harper needed to be closer to her friend so she reached her hand out to touch hers and immediately felt the intense smoldering energy that passed between them. Harper was now centimeters away from Kiley's face as she whispered to her.

"Why can't I stop thinking about you?"

Kiley was frozen. She honestly believed at that moment her heart literally stopped. She could feel her breath growing shorter and shorter the closer Harper came. She could hear Harper's breath grow smaller and sharper as she gripped Kiley's hand tighter. Harper stayed there, so close to Kiley. Their lips were just barely grazing each other, but not enough for either girl to feel it. As Kiley tried to steady her breath, she attempted to gain the courage she needed to just meet Harper the rest of the way. She just needed the strength to lean forward ever so slightly. But somehow, Kiley was immobile. Perhaps it was the shock of this situation being all too real. Both girls stayed in this position until Kiley realized what was happening. She began to speak and as her lips moved, she could faintly feel them against Harper's lips.

"Harper, don't." Kiley backed away.

Harper felt as though she had been jolted out of a dream. "Why?"

Kiley's jaw tightened. "Because."

"You can't possibly be this mad at me. Not after what you did," said Harper.

If she wanted to elicit a reaction, she used the right line.

"What the hell did I do?" asked Kiley, defensively.

Harper stared blankly at her. "Are you kidding me? You slept with Seth!"

"So? That's what I do, Harper. I sleep with guys. Lots of them. It's nothing new."

Harper had no intention of bringing this up, but her anger and frustration was too much to handle at this point.

"You...you slept with him after you kissed me," she stated meekly, slowly stepping closer to her friend. Her head in a fog, she knew she wasn't thinking straight when her hand reached out to take Kiley's once more.

Kiley deflected Harper's advances. She knew there was no way around this conversation. She had braced herself for it over the past week and knew exactly how she would react to anything and everything Harper would say. But at this moment, face-to-face with her best friend, she knew they were heading into very dangerous and uncharted territory. And she was unsure of how their friendship would survive it. Kiley knew she wasn't ready to have this talk. With a heavy heart, she said the one thing she knew would send Harper running back inside.

"Yeah, we kissed. It was the alcohol. A momentary lapse in judgment. Right?"

Harper felt a tinge of pain in her chest the moment Kiley unleashed those words. She never really thought words could be so painful. She was more of an 'actions speak louder than words' believer, but now she knew how wrong she was. Harper slowly backed away.

"Right. I have to go. I was supposed to start five minutes ago."

Kiley's first reaction was to run after her, but once again, she ignored her instincts and let her walk away. Close to tears, she began to pace along the side of the building trying to get a grip on every emotion coursing through her in the past few weeks. Why was she so enraged? Why did this bother her so much? Why did she just lie to her best friend? When those thoughts proved to be too overwhelming, her mind raced as she moved past the previous two weeks and focused on the past few years. She never thought it would have to come to this. She could hear Harper singing through the back door. This would mark the first time Kiley had ever missed one of Harper's shows since they first met. She stopped pacing and allowed herself to listen to Harper's voice. She finally succumbed to her two biggest fears: facing the truth and feeling completely helpless about it.

***

A Fine Mess

Gathered around a crowded table at a sushi restaurant on Ventura Boulevard, Harper and a group of her friends were on their second round of sake bombs, cheering each other on when they all finished and slammed the glasses on the table. Harper had two main sets of friends: her high school friends and her college friends. This was the first time they had all gathered together. Harper called everyone up and invited them all for a girls' night out. She was surprised by how many of them showed up, although the groups were pretty much divided into their respective categories. This posed a problem for Kiley, who was sitting next to Harper. She didn't know these girls very well and, while she joined in the conversation as much as she could, there was still a small outcast factor surrounding her. She didn't go to school with any of them and having only known Harper less than a year, had the least amount of history with her than anyone else here. But she didn't let that faze her. She managed to be her charming self, making everyone laugh and being the envy of every girl at the table with her flawless looks and killer smile. She had the waiters bringing extra food on the house and free drinks. If she felt uncomfortable at all, she didn't show it.

"So, are you having fun?" asked Harper.

"Yeah. This is some of the best sushi I've ever had. I can't believe I've never been here before," said Kiley.

"Finn took me here last year. I love it."

"Speaking of Finn, where is he?" asked Diana, one of Harper's high school friends.

"Oh I wasn't about to invite him to ladies' night. Besides, he's probably home sleeping. He's been working double overtime since Christmas," replied Harper.

"Why's that?" asked Sarah, a fellow student in her English 305 class.

Harper shrugged. "Oh, I don't know. Probably to pay for..." Before she continued, Harper stood up and got everyone's attention. "Um...so, there is a reason I gathered everyone here tonight. I really wanted everyone together for this."

Kiley could feel her stomach drop before Harper said anything further. Something told her to look carefully at Harper's left hand and sure enough, a shimmering diamond attached to a ring reflected off of her ring finger. She could feel a lump rise up into her throat and took a sip of water to try to swallow it back down. She couldn't believe what was about to happen and couldn't explain why she was dreading hearing the next words that came out of Harper's mouth.

Harper held up her left hand for all to see. "Finn and I are engaged!"

Over the deafening shrillness of the collective screams, Kiley could feel her face fall, but picked it right back up again when Harper looked at her. She watched Harper's face. It was plastered with a smile, but there was something in Harper's face that didn't seem to fit. Her smile was wide and exceedingly bright, but there was a lack of excitement behind her eyes coupled with a look of uncertainty.

"When did this happen?" asked an excited Lizbeth, another high school friend.

"Christmas morning. He did it with my family there in our living room."

"Really," said Kiley, unwittingly out loud.
"What?"
"Huh? Oh, no nothing. Never mind."

"No, what did you mean by 'really'?" asked Harper.

Kiley knew for a fact Harper's idea of a perfect proposal was pretty much the exact opposite of how it happened. A private moment on any given day with very limited clichés, was more Harper's speed. Perhaps that's the reason for the uncertainty behind her eyes.

"I didn't mean anything by it. I was just surprised."
As the others talked amongst themselves Kiley smiled, stood up and hugged her friend. "Congratulations. That's so amazing. I'm really happy for you. Why didn't you tell me earlier?"

"I haven't really had a chance."

"We've talked on the phone like five times since Christmas."

"I know. I just..." Harper didn't know what to say. She knew she should have told Kiley before this and that it should have been done in a more personal manner. Kiley was her best friend and though she knew everyone else at this table much longer, she rarely even saw them anymore. Part of her just wasn't ready for Kiley to know and if she announced it in front of everyone, it might make everything a little easier.

"Well, let's not worry about that," offered Kiley. "We need another round here. It's time to celebrate." The entire table cheered at Kiley's suggestion. They sat back down and Kiley launched into the typical questions. "So, have you set a date? What do you want your dress to look like? Colors? Themes? Bridesmaids?"

"Whoa. Okay, slow down a bit. It JUST happened. Let me graduate college first and then we'll probably start thinking about setting a date."

"Fair enough," said Kiley.

After a round of toasts and more sake bombs, Kiley excused herself to the bathroom. She had just finished drying her hands, but wasn't ready to go back to the table yet. She leaned her head against the paper towel dispenser contemplating the news she had just learned.

"There you are. I thought you escaped out the window," said Harper as she came into the bathroom.

"No, just giving myself my daily pep talk in the mirror."

"So...truth."

"Truth?"

Harper nodded.

"I think it's so great that you and Finn are getting married." Kiley lied.

"But?"

"But nothing. I mean, I guess I just didn't realize you wanted to get married so young."

Harper walked over to the sink to wash her hands. "I didn't. I mean, I certainly didn't plan on it. But this is just how it's happening. Besides, it's not like we're gonna get married right away."

"Right. Of course." Kiley sported her trademark smile and took Harper's hand, bringing her closer to her. She reached out her other hand and fixed the fallen strand of hair falling over Harper's face. The two of them lingered there for a moment before an older lady came bursting through the door. They immediately pulled apart and Kiley, recovering from their interruption, reapplied her lip gloss in the mirror. "So, who's gonna be your maid of honor?"

***

A Fine Mess

When Harper announced last call and declared that this would be her last song of the night, Kiley finally caved and walked back in so she could see at least part of the show. Harper knew she had gained one more audience member. She could feel Kiley's presence before she spotted her silhouette standing in the shadows at the back of the bar. Focused solely on Kiley's form, Harper introduced her last song in the simplest terms she could think of.

"So, I just made a complete ass of myself earlier tonight," she said while taking a swig of beer. "I'm tired of being cryptic. It's not getting me anywhere. This song is called 'I'll Wait for You.'"

Harper had no intention of even singing this song tonight. It had been hidden deep within her repertoire, only to be heard by her own ears. It was a song she had written a few years ago that was never meant to see the light of day. But now, it was time. Her previous interaction with Kiley made her realize how badly she ached for her. As she began to sing, she bravely refused to take her eyes off of that figure in the back.

"When you look at me that way, I don't know what to say,
I just hope that you're not looking right through me.
And when you take my hand, I know you understand
I'm feeling everything you're feeling, too.
And I was so unsure of everything before
Until I heard your voice and I felt it in my soul..."

There was no turning back now. The song had already started and the audience was expecting a chorus, so she had to give it to them no matter what the cost. She braced herself for what was about to come.

"And in case you didn't know, I'm in love with you.
And if you're not ready to say you love me, too
That's all right, I'll wait for you."

There. It was done. She finally did it. It wasn't even remotely done in the way she thought it would happen. It wasn't a private moment with just the two of them. It wasn't after one of their deep, heartfelt conversations. It wasn't even blurted out when Harper was drunk, but consciously knew exactly what she was doing. It was at a bar, in front of a crowd of fifty people. She had just confessed her biggest secret for all to hear. Harper Foley was in love with Kiley Young. And based on what had just occurred between them, it was obvious Kiley did not feel the same way. But Harper steadfastly forged on with her song.

"When you pull away from me, I hope that you can see
It breaks my heart because all I want is you.
So I'll walk a step behind and if you ever need to cry
Just turn around and you'll always have my shoulder.
 And in case you didn't know, I'm in love with you.
And if you're not ready to say you love me too,
That's all right, I'll wait for you."

The words flowed through Kiley like a raging flood. Each line speaking the undeniable truth punctured her heart as they continued to escape from Harper's lips. She knew Harper was speaking directly to her. She knew she was hurting, but didn't realize how much until now. Even though every fiber in her being wanted to look away from Harper, she couldn't. Harper wouldn't let her. Kiley just sat there, feeling powerless over Harper's magnetism and control. Kiley felt the tears welling up in her eyes as Harper continued singing.

"But after all is said and done, you're always my best friend,
And if you decide that's all you want from me,
I'll still be happy in the end."

Harper gripped her guitar tighter with every passing strum. She had never before felt so naked on stage. She felt one hundred eyes gaping at her raw and exposed insides. And while they were clueless about the context of the song, one pair of eyes became much more visible as Kiley slowly stepped forward into the light, hanging on to every word Harper was singing. Harper's heart rate began to quicken as the light revealed Kiley's face. She hadn't run away, which is what Harper half-expected Kiley to do. She stayed there and made her presence known to Harper. She couldn't explain it. She didn't know why Kiley invaded her thoughts so much. But now, maybe with these words, she could get her point across. Kiley had to know what was in her heart, but at the same time she didn't want to lose their friendship. They had too strong of a bond to be ripped apart. Harper's heart began to shatter a little bit when she saw Kiley begin to cry. She wanted to cry too, but managed to fight back the tears in order to get through the rest of the song.

"And in case you didn't know, I'm in love with you,

And if you're not ready to say you love me, too
That's all right, I'll wait for you.
I'll wait for you."

The song was over and the crowd applauded. Harper could hear Emily's cheers and spotted her standing up amongst the crowd. Once she received her accolades and unplugged her guitar, she tentatively walked off the stage. Emily walked up and greeted her with a smile.

"That was incredible, Harper. I really had no idea how good you actually were. I mean, I knew you were good, but seeing you on stage like that…you were in complete control the entire time. Everyone loved you."

"Thanks," replied a beaming Harper. "That means a lot coming from you."

Emily hugged her sister. It was the first full embrace they've shared since Emily's homecoming.

"So…that last song…"

"Yeah…"

"You gonna go talk to her now?" asked Emily.

Harper nodded.

"Okay then. I'm gonna get a ride home from Graham."

"No, Em. You really don't have to. I can take you home."

"Come on, Harper. We have no idea how long you and Kiley are gonna talk. I'll be fine. Graham will make sure I get home okay. I'll see you at home."

Emily ran over to Graham as he was putting on his jacket.

"Great job, Harper," yelled Graham from across the room.

"Thanks!"

295

Graham grabbed his keys. "Kiley, Erin had to leave a few minutes ago. Since you pulled that disappearing act earlier, you get to lock up."

"Sure. No problem. Sorry about that, by the way."

Once they were out the door, there were only four patrons left. A group of girls were waiting for their friend to come out of the bathroom. Harper was putting her microphone stand away when she finally came out and the gaggle of girls left.

Once they were gone, it was just Harper and Kiley left in the empty bar. One girl was focusing on cleaning up the mess everyone had left behind. The other one was gathering the rest of her music equipment, trying not to focus on the awkwardness that seemed to constantly haunt her. Silence was a motif that somehow kept finding its way into their lives.

Kiley was halfway done stacking the stools and checked out of the corner of her eye to make sure Harper was still on the stage. She swallowed and approached Harper, standing behind her as she was putting away her p.a. system.

"So, why have I never heard that song before?"

Harper shrugged. "I had it in my back pocket."

"It was beautiful."

"Thank you."

Kiley picked up a cable and began to coil it. "Is it true?"

"What?"

"The lyrics. Are they true?"

"Does it matter?" asked Harper, still avoiding eye contact.

"Harper," Kiley grabbed her arm and turned her around.

"You're done here, right?" asked Harper. "I can lock up if you want to go meet up with Seth."

Kiley's grip tightened around Harper's arm. "That was low. Unnecessary."

"Oh, so no Seth? Is there some other guy you plan on mounting tonight?"

"That's enough! I already feel like shit as it is. And I know I shouldn't have said what I said earlier. But what about you? I made one mistake and you ran to Finn, who you have a history with. You were in love with him for the longest time and you were so quick to jump back into bed with him. How do you think that made me feel?"

"Why should I care about how you feel? You don't give a shit about anyone but yourself." Harper jerked away from Kiley and headed for the door. Kiley followed close behind her.

"You think I don't care? How could you say that?" Kiley headed off Harper before she reached the door. She was near tears by this point and grabbed Harper's shoulders.

"Let me go."

"No."

Harper struggled to break free, but Kiley's grasp only grew more intense. "Let me go!" Harper was now crying, unable to hold it in any longer.

"Not until you forgive me," replied Kiley, whose tears were freely falling, as well.

"Why? Why does it matter to you so much?" Harper tried once more to break away from Kiley, but her attempt proved futile. She didn't even have time to respond when Kiley pulled her in and pressed her lips to hers. The moment her lips came into contact with Kiley's, something happened within Harper. Nearly four years of utter anguish and yearning had been bottled up inside her and at this moment, it all came flowing out. Every emotion she had inside of her had suddenly been brought to the surface and for the first time since she could remember, she finally found a moment of peace and complete contentment. Even though she was angry with Kiley, Harper didn't fight the kiss. She couldn't remember a time when she wanted something so badly. Tears started streaming down her face uncontrollably as their tongues relentlessly devoured each other.

Harper threw her arms around Kiley's neck. As she was fervently being pulled into Harper, Kiley loosened her grip on Harper's shoulders and grasped her shirt as tightly as she could. She did her best not to hurt her in the process. But if such a travesty did occur, she couldn't help it. The passion raged through her entire body, shooting out through her fingertips. So she held on to Harper for dear life, just to make sure she was real and this wasn't a dream. They continued their impassioned kiss, bringing relief to their aching lips. Harper studied the feel and the smoothness of Kiley's mouth. Their emotions were running high as their tears mixed together leaving a salty taste in their mouths.

The bar was dark with the exception of a few dim lights and the neon signs glowing. The atmosphere wasn't the most ideal place to be doing what they've been longing to do for so long, but it would have to suffice because there was no slowing down. Kiley broke away from the kiss and slowly moved her tongue down Harper's neck memorizing the feel of her skin. She pushed Harper up against the bar and brought her lips back to meet hers, unable to satisfy the innate thirst she had within her.

Harper's back began to feel pain as it dug into the bar, but she didn't care. She ran her tongue along Kiley's lips, familiarizing herself with the taste of her mouth. Kiley lifted Harper up onto the bar knocking over some glasses she forgot to put away. Neither of them flinched after the glasses shattered into a million pieces on the ground. Harper's legs wrapped around Kiley's torso as they continued to move deeper and deeper into their kiss. Kiley's hands, which were strategically placed at the small of Harper's back, began to roam and explore. They moved up and down the side of Harper's torso and came around to graze across her toned stomach. Her breath caught in her throat with a tinge of apprehension as she grabbed at the hem of Harper's shirt and pulled it off over her head.

Harper did the same for Kiley and as her hands came back down, they took their time to explore every inch of Kiley's shoulders. Then her arms and then her back, sliding their way down to her lower back. Harper's breathing grew heavier as she recognized the longing behind Kiley's eyes; the same look that she had harbored for so many years. She knew what was about to happen and felt her body become just a little bit more rigid as Kiley reached up behind her, unhooked her bra and removed it in one fluid motion. Kiley's eyes grew wide as she discovered what had just been revealed to her. Among the dead silence, all that could be heard was the erratic breathing of the two girls.

Running solely on instinct now, Kiley slowly leaned Harper back and began to trace her tongue along her stomach. She gradually moved her way up toward her chest, tantalizing Harper. As her mouth finally reached its target, Harper let out a long sigh followed by a moan. She could feel her body stiffen with a mixture of fear and pleasure. Craving more Harper sat up and slid off the bar, standing face to face with Kiley. It was only a split second before Harper leaned in and kissed Kiley, pushing her back up against the wall. Kiley could feel the cold temperature of the wall on her bare skin. Harper's wandering hands made their way down to the zipper of Kiley's jeans. She slowly unbuttoned and unzipped them, pulling them down until they lay in a pile on the floor. Kiley was left there standing in nothing but her bra and underwear, feeling incredibly vulnerable being half naked in her place of employment, but she had no objections.

Knowing there was no going back now, Kiley took Harper's hand and led her toward the back room. In the room, there was a desk where Graham took care of the business aspects of the bar. There were some refrigerators to store alcohol and a single lamp bright enough to make the room visible, but dim enough to set the perfect mood. There was a twin-sized bed tucked away in the corner for when Graham or any of his employees were too tired to drive home. It was rarely used. Kiley looked over at Harper, as if asking her what they should do. Without missing a beat, Harper closed the door behind them and locked it.

She brought Kiley in for another kiss while driving forward, pushing the taller girl toward the bed. As Kiley sat down on the edge of the bed, Harper made a bold move by climbing on her lap and straddling her while eagerly kissing her once more. Their hands were intertwined as Harper began squeezing Kiley's hand harder with each heightening pleasure.

Kiley was nervous, but did her best not to show it. She didn't know why she was so nervous. It was just sex.

Sex was definitely not something she was new at, but this time it was different. Very different. This time, it was Harper. This was the first time she had ever really *wanted* to do this. Every other time was just a distraction…a means of blocking Harper out of her mind for one moment of peace. But now it was real and it was actually happening.

Harper slowly lowered her onto the soft, white sheets and hovered over Kiley as the kiss continued. She brought her hand down to Kiley's abdomen and placed her hand on her waist. Kiley caressed Harper's back, gazing longingly at the vision above her. The two held onto each other in a longing embrace, their lips quivering with each kiss. Harper couldn't seem to control her shaking. She didn't know if it was out of pure nerves and fear, or just excitement. Kiley feeling just as lost and unsure, took notice of her shaking and gave her a reassuring look.

"It's okay," she whispered. "We're okay."

Four years of pent up desire, pent up passion, pent up love was being unleashed and coming undone with each passing moment. Kiley peeled off Harper's jeans, along with her underwear, leaving Harper fully nude. She took a moment to study the honey blonde's form in the dim light, and then ardently kissed her.

Their tongues ignited sparks between them and they could not get enough of each other. They clung to each other tightly as Harper pressed her cheek up against Kiley's and tried to gather the courage to say to Kiley what she had been yearning to say to her for so long. It was terrifying. She had learned to keep it suppressed all this time. But they were walking a fine line between passion and lust and Harper desperately wanted to land on the side of passion. She softly whispered while trying to catch her breath.

"I love you." She watched Kiley's eyes for any kind of reaction. Kiley, overwhelmed with everything that was happening, simply nodded, finally understanding what Harper had been coping with for all this time.

Their bodies converged as each girl was discovering every new sensation. Harper followed her heart's rhythmic beat as she kissed Kiley, her soft lips moving with the same rhythm. She felt herself being carried away at the feeling of her legs moving with Kiley's, almost as if it were a perfectly choreographed dance. Harper, needing to feel the whole of Kiley's flesh against her body, languidly removed Kiley's underwear, then worked her way up to unhook the bra that was so strategically hugging her skin.

Kiley felt her breathing grow heavier as she began to feel a dull aching rise from deep inside of her. The feeling of Harper's body moving so rhythmically and effortlessly on top of her stirred up something deep inside of Kiley. She craved more of Harper, searching for any part of her skin she had yet to explore.

Harper inhaled and exhaled sharply as Kiley's hands decided to take an immediate liking to her breasts. She gripped onto Kiley as if she had nothing else to hold on to. Harper's body was awakening to something completely new and different that she had never felt before. She felt weak and yet completely euphoric and content at the same time. She could feel her entire body pulsating as little beads of sweat began to form on her brow due to a mix her rising body temperature and the lack of ventilation in the office. She ran her tongue along Kiley's neck to her jaw line to her ear, which gave Kiley chills. Her tongue lingered there a minute before it maneuvered its way back down. The anticipation was almost too much for her as her mouth encountered Kiley's smooth and perfect breasts, which immediately elicited a whimper from Kiley.

Kiley closed her eyes and panted heavily, unable to control the urges her body was craving. She felt like she would explode at any minute, so she decided to take control and rolled Harper onto her back. She lingered above Harper's body, absorbing the sight of her best friend lying naked beneath her, reeling in the surrealism of the situation. She shared a secret smile with Harper, then lowered herself onto her, grazing her breasts against Harper's. At this point, she'd had enough taunting and teasing. She moved her hand down Harper's body, stopping just between her thighs. Harper slightly opened her legs and the second Kiley reached her destination, Harper opened her mouth and let out an intoxicating moan. Her breathing became more rapid and she arched her back as Kiley moved her hand around, causing Harper to writhe in ecstasy, gratifying every impulse within her body.

Harper, nearly unable to control herself, began to touch Kiley simultaneously, evoking a faint, exhilarant murmur from the girl on top of her. The deep breathing turned into moaning echoing through the room, as the girls continued trying to desperately satiate each other. They had no other way to vocalize the intense charge between them seeing as how they were both rendered speechless.

It wasn't long before their clandestine moment gave way to an enraptured catharsis as they both began to move at a more frenzied pace. Harper was entranced by

Kiley's eyes, which were burning into hers, penetrating her entire being. She had never felt more wanted or desired in her entire life than she had in that moment. Between the thirst they had for each other, the taste of each other's skin, the teasing of their hands, and the friction of their bodies both girls climaxed, holding each other tight as their bodies quivered with pleasure. Shuddering and shivering, Harper began to tremble with goose bumps covering her entire body. Kiley rested her head on Harper's chest, enveloping her in her warmth.

Not another word was exchanged between them as Kiley listened to the pulsing of Harper's heartbeat and fell asleep in her arms. Harper soon followed as her critical need for slumber outweighed her need to analyze everything that had just occurred.

CHAPTER 26

Harper lay peacefully strewn across the bed, deep in slumber and still unclothed from the night before. The sheets clung to her in the more convenient places, almost as if it had been staged for a PG-13 movie. She barely stirred when the bed jiggled slightly as Kiley got up and quietly but quickly gathered her clothes and put them back on, doing her best not to disturb her friend. She pulled her long messy hair into a ponytail, trying to smooth it down as much as she could. Wiping the sleep from her eyes, she paused for a moment and watched Harper splayed out on her back. One arm under the pillow and the other resting on her stomach. Kiley was spellbound, unable to take her eyes off of the blonde. When the memories of what had happened just nine hours earlier came rushing back, Kiley had trouble fending off the smirk on her face.

What the hell happened? she thought to herself. The smirk gave way to Kiley biting her lip, as her eyes filled with panic. The panic then gave way to a look of terror. This was her best friend; the only person on this earth that meant more to Kiley than her own life. How could she have squandered such an incredible thing by doing the one thing she always does when she gets scared, fuck and run.

"Shit."

The walls began to close in on Kiley. She could feel herself begin to hyperventilate. In a daze, she slowly staggered to the door and walked out before giving anything, including Harper, a second thought.

***

Harper opened her eyes facing an unfamiliar concept in an unfamiliar room. For the first time in years she actually felt rested. It was as if the two-ton block of cement that had been resting on her shoulders was smashed into pieces with a sledgehammer and the shackles that once held her down had been loosened, freeing her of her seemingly unending burden. She squinted over at the clock on the wall. It was 11:45am.

"Jesus," mumbled Harper as she ran her fingers through her hair.

She glanced around and suddenly realized she was completely alone. Next to her in the bed was utter vastness where the flesh of another should be. Looking around, she found no trace of Kiley. No clothes, no keys or cell phone, no note, no sign that she was ever even here in the first place. Kiley had managed to make herself invisible. Harper rolled over onto her side with her body feeling the lasting effects of last night's transgression. Every part of her was sore, but in a good, rather satisfying way. Her head felt heavy with a sensation of vertigo. Every time she moved her head, the room would relentlessly spin with her. If this is what it felt like to sleep nine hours straight, then maybe it was overrated.

Despite her body feeling like it had just run a marathon and her head throbbing, those hindrances weren't exactly at the forefront of her thoughts. She

306

reached her left hand over to the right side of the bed, smoothing out the soft sheets along the way in the hopes that somehow, Kiley would magically reappear. Part of her was disappointed in waking up alone, but it just wouldn't be Kiley if she hadn't been thinking solely of herself. Her heart, which was so filled with contentment last night, now felt flaccid and void. There was no taking this back. It had been done. Kiley knew the truth, and now she was gone. Harper clung to the sheets and pulled them up over her head trying to block out reality, but it was a futile move. The cement block and the metal shackles she thought had disappeared were now once again fixated to her person. This was a whole new chapter in their lives that shouldn't have been written, because once it's been written and read, there's no taking it back.

***

Finn spent the week immersing himself in work and spent his evenings with friends, including Seth. After hearing about Seth hooking up with Kiley, he was actually surprised at how angry he got and began to feel protective over her. He knew it was time to let go of anything having to do with Harper, and that included Harper's friends. So he laughed it off and played the part of the high-fiving friend, congratulating Seth on landing such a hottie.

He considered himself lucky that Susan had been so consumed with work and taking care of Andrew, who had the stomach flu over the last week. They had spoken on the phone a few times, trying to fit in a time to see each other. But every time their schedules clashed, Finn would heave a sigh of relief. He knew the longer he waited to tell Susan about what happened with Harper, the worse it would be. He wasn't ready to confess his sins to her just yet. But today, it seemed the universe was ready for karma to take effect on Finn. Andrew was finally feeling better and Susan made it a point to not make any plans for the weekend in order to recuperate from her hectic week.

With a heavy heart, especially upon hearing how excited Susan was to see him, Finn had agreed to come over tonight. Susan managed to find a sitter for Andrew and she felt like getting out, not caring about where they went. Finn spent the entire day with a knotted stomach. He even downed a Xanax he managed to procure from a high-strung co-worker, but it didn't seem to help much. He spent the day planning out what to say to Susan. He knew that while it wasn't entirely her fault, blaming Harper was the easiest thing to do, so that would be his story. Harper seduced him, made him believe she wanted him back, made him feel needed, and used him. He was all prepared to deliver the speech victimizing himself and vilifying the evil witch that had spurned him once again.

The tension that had been building up all day was now about to implode as Finn approached Susan's door and rang the doorbell. As the door opened, his head lowered in order to make eye contact with the young man who opened the door.

"Hi!"

"Uh…hey." Finn was not expecting this.

"My mom said I could open the door and say hi to you."

"Did she?"

"Yeah. I wanted to show you this." Andrew gestured to the Dodgers hat sitting atop his head.

"Oh wow. Look at that. You've come around to be a Dodgers fan," replied Finn.

"Well, I still like the Angels more." Andrew smiled, revealing his two missing teeth. His prominent dimples weren't lost among the freckles on his cheeks.

"I suppose I can live with that. Is your mom here?"

"Yeah." Andrew turned around and ran off shouting, "Mom! He's here! He's here!"

Finn officially felt like the biggest asshole that ever walked the planet. What was once a difficult thing was now made nearly impossible thanks to the cutest eight-year-old kid he had ever met. He waited at the door, each passing moment feeling like an hour until Susan finally met him.

"Hey! You could have come in. Sorry. My son is still trying to learn manners."

"Oh that's okay."

"How are you?" Susan greeted him with a small kiss on the mouth.

"Um…I'm good. I'm good." He maneuvered his way backward to avoid any more lip contact for the time being. No matter how badly he wanted to kiss her, it just wouldn't be right.

"Andrew insisted on answering the door when I told him you were coming over."

"Really?"

"Yeah. But don't worry. The sitter's got him in her grasp now, so I think we're good to go."

"Excellent. How does Houston's sound?"

"Great! I'm starved."

A Fine Mess

***

After a bit of an awkward silence during dinner, Susan thought she'd offer a nice tidbit of information in order to lighten the mood.

"You know, you're the first guy I've dated that I've allowed Andrew to meet." Little did she know, it had the opposite effect on Finn.

Of course, thought Finn. He forced a smile and continued to eat the grilled artichoke in front of them. "That's really great. I hope you remember that."

"Why do you want me to remember that?" Susan took a sip of her iced tea.

Finn tensed up. All he could hear was the "rhubarb" and "watermelon" chatter from the restaurant patrons around them. He finished off the last of the artichoke and brought his eyes up to meet Susan's. Her hair was cascading down her back with long, loose curls hanging at her shoulders. Her eyes met his with a look of serene contentment and he felt horrible for having to be the one to disrupt such a genuine feeling of placidity.

"I have to tell you something," said Finn.

"You've been tightly wound since you picked me up. What's going on?"

Finn sighed and began tapping his fingertips on the table. "Well, you know I really like you, right? I mean, I think it's pretty obvious."

"I have an inkling."

"So I want to be one hundred percent honest with you."

"Okay."

"I screwed up."

The faint smile that once lay across Susan's face slowly faded.

"In what way?"

Finn lowered his eyes to the table. His plan fell apart. He knew Harper wasn't to blame. He wanted her that night. He wanted to cling to his past so badly. He needed to hold on to a time when his life made sense and had some direction. He made a mistake and now he had to own up and stop blaming Harper for his error.

"I slept with Harper."

Susan didn't say anything. She just leaned back against the booth, as if in need of some sort of physical support after the bombshell Finn just dropped.

"It was the night of Seth's party. After you left," Finn continued. "I know it's no excuse, but we were both really drunk. I honestly don't even know what I was thinking. It was one of those things where you see yourself doing it and you want to scream 'stop!' but for some reason, you can't. It's like trying to wake up from bad dream, you know?"

Finn was met with silence. He looked up to see Susan's eyes beginning to well up. She looked to the ground, half nodding and trying to make sense of the situation.

"She was crying. I felt really bad and for some stupid reason, I felt like I was obligated to make her feel better. And I was wrong. I see that now, and I know it now and I'm done with her. I'm never seeing her or speaking to her again. It was just a weak moment." Finn moved his head to try to catch her eye. "Susan?"

"Take me home."

"Just let me explain."

"Take me home."

"I'm so sorry."

"Take me home, now."

Finn nodded. "Let me settle the check."

***

The conversation on the car ride home was non-existent. Finn looked straight ahead while Susan watched the buildings go by out the passenger side window. He pulled up to her place and left the engine idle. Susan took off her seatbelt and hesitated for a moment. Finn braced himself for the worst.

"Due to these circumstances, it's probably best that you don't contact me anymore or come back as a patient. Though, you obviously still need help in sorting through your issues, so call my assistant on Monday and she'll give you a list of referrals. I'll send you to someone really good. I'll make sure they take care of you."

Finn traced his finger along the steering wheel. "I'm really sorry. I'm such an asshole."

"You're a good person, Finn. You really are. You're a good person who did a really stupid thing. It means you're human. You're allowed to fuck up. And the fact that you feel bad about it is a good thing. It means you're not a sociopath."

"Is this really over?" Finn was reliving flashbacks of the moment Harper broke off their engagement.

"I'm afraid so. Maybe it's for the best. This is the most unprofessional thing I've ever done. I guess it had to end sometime. Better sooner than later."

"I'm sorry, Susan."

"I know. You mentioned that. You take care. And make sure you keep seeking help, okay? It'll get better, eventually. I promise." Susan got out of the car.

The door slammed shut and she walked up to her door and disappeared inside her house. Finn sat there re-evaluating the situation, trying to pin down exactly what point his life started on this downward spiral. Harper flashed into his mind, but quickly disappeared. Flashes of work, therapy, college, high school and his childhood all flickered into his mind and he realized it wasn't just one catalyst. It was a little bit of everything.

CHAPTER 27

Emily was in the kitchen putting away the last of the groceries she had picked up when Harper walked through the front door. She looked terrible, as if she had been in a fist fight. Her golden hair was matted and a tangled mess. Her eye makeup was smudged as if she had been crying and then slept in it. Her shirt was wrinkled and a noticeable tear had formulated at the seam. She walked in and dropped her purse on the floor, then grabbed a carton of orange juice out of the fridge and proceeded to drink it without the use of a glass. She wiped her mouth, put it back, and headed for her room. Feeling Emily's eyes watching her, she cut her off before a word was said.

"I don't want to talk about it." At that, Harper closed the door to her room, leaving Emily to decipher what exactly went down last night.

But Emily being the stubborn Taurus that she was, wouldn't accept Harper's dismissal of what happened. She only knocked twice before she opened her sister's door.

"I said I don't want to talk about it." Harper was in the midst of changing her shirt.

"Jesus! What happened there?" Emily pointed to Harper's back, which had a very conspicuous bruise along the middle of it.

Harper twisted her head around to try to see what her sister was talking about. "Oh that. It's nothing."

"Harper."

"It's nothing, Em."

Emily sat on the bed slightly confused. "Kiley didn't do that, did she?"

Harper shrugged. "In a way, I guess."

"What do you mean?"

After a dragged out sigh, Harper acquiesced to her sister's incessant interrogation. "It wasn't exactly Kiley. It was more the bar that she pushed me up against."

"She pushed you up against the bar?" Emily was growing incensed.

Harper smiled coyly, despite her annoyance. "Not like that, Em. I mean…in a good way. She pushed me up against it in a… fun way."

"A good way…" Emily thought about that for a moment until she finally hit a brick wall. "Oh! Oh wow! Are you serious?"

"Yup." Harper adjusted the shirt she just put on and started brushing out her hair.

"Holy crap! Well, tell me what happened!" Emily excitedly sat Indian-style on her sister's bed in hopes of hearing a juicy story.

"Not really in the mood to discuss it."

"Why not?"

"Because when I woke up, she was gone."

"What?"

"And she hasn't even attempted to contact me yet."

"Have you tried calling her?"

"No, but she's the one who left."

Emily nodded in understanding. "Well maybe— "

"Emily! Just drop it, okay? Why do you even give a shit, anyway?"

The words stung Emily, and Harper knew they would, but she really didn't care at the moment.

"You've been gone all this time and now you're suddenly pretending to care about what happens in my life? You think I can't take care of myself? I've been doing a damn fine job of it. I've been on my own for a while. No mom, no dad, no you, no Finn. And now it looks like there will be no Kiley."

"Are you really saying this? You really think I don't care about you?"

"You haven't earned the right to care," replied Harper. "Caring means sticking around."

"Can't you see the changes I've made? I've been working my ass off to make things up to you! And I know it's gonna take time, but I'm trying."

Harper looked at her sister. Emily was right. She had been taking giant leaps toward redemption. She's not only matured mentally, but physically as well. Where there once sat a scrawny, pale little girl was now a young woman whose maturity and beauty were shining through. Yet every time Harper looked at her, all she could see was abandonment and resentment.

Emily stood up. "You need to stop feeling sorry for yourself, Harper. You tried. You showed her how you felt and unfortunately her true colors finally shone through to you. Kiley's a bitch. She always has been. I'm sorry this happened, but maybe now you'll get it through your head."

"She's not a bitch."

"Stop defending her!" yelled Emily.

"Stop cutting her down!" replied Harper. "I don't know what Kiley ever did to you, but I'm sick of you constantly berating her. She fucked up. She left. And it

316

sucks. And it hurts. And maybe I'm the one who screwed up by acting on my impulses. I just lost my best friend."

"Because she's a coward."

"Enough of this. Just leave me the hell alone." Harper stormed out of the house, leaving Emily reeling.

A sense of panic began to set in for Emily. Her sister wanted nothing to do with her. Running away obviously caused some irreparable damage to their relationship and no matter how hard she tried, nothing she did was good enough to make it better. She felt herself becoming unnerved. The anxiety was building up and her breathing suddenly became more rapid. She was alone. Completely alone. She had no friends and the only family she had was pushing her away. She felt a sense of darkness falling on her even though the sun was shining brightly outside. Emily often ran on the 'first thought, best thought' idea to get through life, which meant that she never really thought things through before acting on her first instinct. And her first instinct now was leading her directly to her bedroom and directly down a path she swore she'd never go down again. On her hands and knees, she felt around under her mattress for the little hole she cut into it years ago. She pulled out something she brought back with her just in case she needed it. Fully aware is was a moronic idea, she often contemplated throwing it out. But something inside her told her to hold onto it just a little bit longer. Grasping the clear plastic bag full of the white, powdery substance that she often equated to her escape, she got up, opened the bag and poured part of it out onto her dresser. Looking around for something to cut it with, she reached into her desk drawer and pulled out her dad's old Swiss army knife. She examined it for a moment thinking it was far too awkward and clunky to use for this kind of job, but for some reason she couldn't bring herself to put it down. Forgetting about the means of escape strewn out on her dresser waiting to be absorbed by her nose, she sat down on her bed and scrutinized the red and silver object in her hand, pulling out each individual accessory one at a time. She remembered stumbling upon it while going through their parents' things after the funeral.

Suddenly, a memory she had been avoiding crept up on her. Her heart dropped the moment she realized what day it was.

"Shit. Oh shit."

She placed the knife on her desk and went to her dresser to wipe off the Cocaine and residue it left behind. She made one stop to the bathroom to flush it and the remaining contents of the bag down the toilet before she ran out the door in the hopes of finding her sister.

***

The leaves rustled in the trees above. The sun shined down on Harper's face causing her to squint as the light breeze blew strands of hair over her face, tickling her nose. All this coupled with the robust green grass surrounding her equaled an atmosphere that didn't exactly match the location. She stood there in deep reflection face-to-face with something she hadn't seen in a year. She knelt down and traced her finger along the engraved wording on the granite headstone: "Paul Foley: 1960–2008 Beloved Father" and "Trisha O'Neal Foley: 1961–2008 Beloved Mother and Sister." The 'Sister' part always caught Harper's attention. She initially didn't want it because her mother didn't speak much of her sister and Harper and Emily rarely got to see their aunt Karen. But when they died, aunt Karen put up a huge fight over what would go on her sister's headstone. Harper added the 'Sister' on there to assuage her and was even convinced that maybe now she'd get to see more of her. Maybe her aunt would come in and check on them every once in a while. The fact is, they hadn't seen her since the funeral and only heard from her on Christmas. Harper felt a tinge of sadness thinking about her mother's strained relationship with her sister and began to equate it to her own situation. Her finger was outlining the T in Trisha when she suddenly felt a presence behind her. Without turning around or standing up, she acknowledged the new visitor.

"I was wondering when you would show up."

"I can't believe I almost forgot." Emily was out of breath when she approached Harper.

"It's a day burned on my brain."

"I'm sorry." Emily shuffled her feet as she stood next to Harper looking down at the top of her head.

Harper took Emily's hand and pulled her down to the same level. "Me too."

They knelt there for a while, silently observing the spot where their parents were laid to rest three years ago, until the pressure on their knees got to them and they both sat next to each other with their legs crossed.

"I haven't been here since the day we buried them," observed Emily.

"I come back every year. But that's really all I can handle. Otherwise it's just too hard."

"I guess we both have our ways of dealing with our grief. You fight it head on, while I choose to run."

Harper nodded.

"And I'm sorry," added Emily. "But I really am trying."

"I know."

Emily leaned back, her hands digging into the grass. "The thing is…" she hesitated. "The thing is, I almost screwed everything up again."

"What do you mean?"

"I mean this…us. We were doing so well, considering. Just now, when you took off, I—"

Harper didn't allow her sister to finish. "The stuff under your bed?"

Emily cocked her head to the side. "How did you—?"

"I searched your room. Sorry. I know I shouldn't have. But after everything that happened, I just wanted to know how honest you were being. But I left it there for you to handle. That's your deal."

"I threw it out. All of it."

"Good."

"I'm telling the truth. I really did."

Harper put her hand on Emily's knee. "I know. I believe you." After a few more moments of silence, Harper added, "Mom and dad would be proud."

Emily scoffed. "Oh please. You don't have to try to make me feel better."

"I'm serious. They'd be really proud of the strides you've taken. Whereas I on the other hand, have allowed my life to implode."

"Don't say that."

"It's true," exclaimed Harper. "They wouldn't even know who I am anymore. I'm no longer engaged to Finn. I'm working a thankless job at a bookstore to make ends meet. And I'm pining for my best friend, who happens to be a girl and I have no idea what the fuck is going on anymore. Why do I constantly feel like I'm letting them down? Even now that they're gone."

"Parents are made to make their kids feel guilty. Remember that time I peeled that inch of wallpaper off the wall in their room? Dad would never let me live that down. And it got worse every time he brought it up. 'Remember the time Emily ripped that square foot of wallpaper off? Remember when Emily ripped half the wall of wallpaper? Remember when we used to have wallpaper before Emily ripped the whole thing off?' I was four! I mean, I know it was a running joke, but I still felt bad about it. You just have to come to terms with the fact that the only person who matters in your life is you and how you view yourself. Everyone else is just there to help guide you."

Harper began to look at her sister in a whole new light. "Em, when the hell did you get so insightful?"

"I've always been insightful. I've just never vocalized it before."

Harper drew a deep breath and exhaled slowly as she leaned her head on Emily's shoulder. "Kiley and I had sex last night. And it was really, *really* good. Like, incredible. And for a brief moment, I felt everything else just kind of lift away. And it was just me and her and at that moment, that was all I needed. And I cried. And she cried. And it was this great big beautiful mess. And I slept. I fell asleep in her arms and for nine full hours, I just slept. When I woke up, she was gone."

Emily could hear Harper's voice cracking and quivering. She took her sister's hand, trying to comfort her any way she could.

Harper sniffled, and wiped away a stray tear. "I love her, Em. I've tried so hard not to, but I can't help it. I love her. I knew almost immediately after I met her and I've tried so hard to just push it down so it would never see the light of day. Even when I was with Finn, I still felt it. And now I don't know how she's feeling about any of this and I just feel sick."

"I'm sure she'll come around eventually. She's just trying to take this all in, like you."

Harper shook her head. "How would they feel about this? How would they react?" She gestured to the plot in front of them.

"They loved us despite all our flaws. I'm sure they would have been fine with it," assured Emily. "Hell, *I'm* fine with it, and I hate that girl."

Harper let out a small chuckle. "And how would Finn react?"

"It doesn't matter. He's not a part of your life anymore. And maybe he'll finally be able to move on and understand why you broke up with him."

"God, this is so humiliating."

"Don't be embarrassed. Everyone's allowed to be a fuck up at one point or another. And really, Kiley's the fuck up in this situation, so the blame lies solely with her. I can't believe she just left you like that."

"Well, that's Kiley."

"Well, that's bullshit." Emily didn't know why, but she felt herself craving a cigarette at that moment, but willed the craving away as best she could. "I miss them. A lot."

"Yeah. Me too."

"The thing is, if I let myself think about it too much, it makes me crazy. And I feel like if I start crying, I won't be able to stop, you know?"

Harper nodded.

"But this isn't so bad, being here with you. I think it makes it easier."

Harper stared out at the vast acres of land that surrounded them. Almost every inch was covered in headstones and she couldn't help but think about death and how natural and unnatural it was at the same time. Sure it's a part of life. But does it have to be such a horrific, wretched affair where people are just ripped out of your life without warning? Millions of people have lost loved ones, but have any of them really, truly felt as much pain as Harper felt when her parents died? If so, then how did they get through it? And does it ever get easier?

Before Harper could delve too much into her philosophical wonderment, Emily interrupted her train of thought with a sigh. "I should get going. I have to be at work in an hour. Did I tell you they promoted me to Supervisor?"

"Already?" asked Harper.

"Yeah. Apparently I'm good at this job. Who knew?"

Emily got up and helped up her sister. "I'll have to come by and see you in action," said Harper, as they started their trek back home.

***

After they left the cemetery, not ten minutes passed before Kiley showed up bearing flowers, cradling them in her right arm. Her heart was pounding thinking there might be a small chance she'd run into Harper, but clearly she was nowhere to be found. Part of her was relieved, but part of her was rather disappointed. She figured this would be much less painful than having to actually call her up on the phone and suffer through a conversation full of awkward silences. Having behaved so badly, the only thing she could hope for was a convenient random run-in where Harper would be forced to talk to her. Hindsight being what it is, Kiley wholeheartedly regretted sneaking out on Harper this morning. How could she possibly expect Harper to talk to her after that? Last night was the culmination of everything they both had been feeling over the past years and how did she react? She just blew it off like it was nothing.

The thing about Kiley is that denial had always been her greatest talent. To this day, she still believed that her childhood dog Roxie, really was sent to live on a ranch in Wyoming when she was six. Even though deep down she knew the truth, she refused to accept it. She still firmly believed that Lauren, her best friend in high school, wasn't the one who spread those anorexic rumors about her. Even though Kiley heard Lauren telling people just that in the bathroom as she was hiding in one of the stalls. And she still has herself convinced that her parents are still happily married despite the incessant fighting and obvious affairs her father was having. And so it went her entire life. Ignorance is bliss. Denial is just easier, so it was a natural reaction to deny any alleged feelings she had for Harper. But denial can only last so long before the truth begins to find its way out.

***

*"Okay, left leg in first. And now the right,"
instructed Kiley. Once both of Harper's legs were in,
Kiley pulled the sweats up to her waist and laid her down
onto the bed. Then she sat on the side of the bed and
adjusted the pillow.*

*Through the bedroom door, Kiley could hear the
murmurs of the guests still milling about in the living
room. She was hoping they wouldn't stay too much
longer. She had two emotionally exhausted girls to worry
about, a mess to clean up, and a well-meaning, but
clueless fiancé of her best friend to tend to. But she
drowned all that out and kept her attention on Harper,
whom she had just tucked in after long day of enduring
her parents' funeral and the somber gathering afterward.
Kiley remained hovered over Harper as her friend looked
up at her.*

*"Thank you, Kiley. Thank you for everything. You're
the most amazing person I've ever known."*

*Kiley grinned. "Funny. I always say that you about
you." She lingered a bit longer, watching Harper's eyes
slowly close. Kiley studied the contours of her face,
wondering how it was possible for her to be so brave and
put up such a strong front in the past four days. She was
in complete awe of her friend. And right now all she
wanted more than anything at the moment was to take
away any sort of pain she was feeling. The sad fact was,
she didn't know how. She started to get up, but Harper
grabbed her arm and pulled her back without even
opening her eyes.*

*"Can you stay with me a little bit? Just until I fall
asleep?" She slid her hand down Kiley's arm and rested
it in her hand. Kiley just held on, not knowing what else*

to do. From the moment Harper called her from the hospital letting her know what happened, Kiley felt like the wind had been knocked out of her. She had never heard Harper sob as much as she had that day and though she wanted to cry with her friend, Kiley knew the best way to help her was to just be there and be strong. But at this moment, the weakness was way too overpowering for her and she was slowly giving into it. She fought back her tears, just like she had been for past few days. She gently grasped Harper's soft hand.

"Of course I'll stay with you."

Those words were the last thing Harper heard that day. She was asleep within minutes with Kiley right there by her side. Kiley couldn't quite explain why, but she couldn't bring herself to leave. Even though Harper's slow and steady breathing was a sure sign that she was deep in slumber. She kept her hand clasped to Harper's, watching her thumb run over the other girl's index finger, admiring the freckles that adorned Harper's fingers. She was always jealous of her friend's freckles and thought it was adorable that they were literally everywhere. They weren't overpowering on her skin or too prominent, but made their presence known even on her kneecaps. Kiley brought Harper's hand up to her lips and gently kissed her fingers. She had no idea why, but felt that it might somehow help to ease her friend's pain just a little bit. Kiley let go of her hand and began to run her fingernails through Harper's hair along the right temple. It was a move Kiley's mom used when she was younger. It never failed to help her fall asleep.

Kiley could feel her body temperature rise as the back of her neck began to sweat. She wanted to tie her hair back, but was afraid it would wake up Harper. As *carefully as she could, she took off her black cardigan and tossed it on the floor. It helped a bit, but she couldn't get rid of the flushed feeling in her face.*

Harper abruptly began to shift and let out a soft moan.

"Shhh..." Kiley returned to her temple, trying to keep her asleep. The heat from her breath was hitting Harper's cheek as she moved in even closer to the younger girl. Suddenly, a spark. An explosion in the pit of her stomach as her lips were on Harper's, moving softly, drinking in the warmth emanating from Harper's mouth. Kiley had no idea how she got to this point. Lingering above the young blonde, the smooth skin on their lips still igniting sparks. She slowly pulled away, her heart about to beat out of her chest, terrified that Harper might wake up. She didn't. She just lay there peacefully unaware of the kiss they had just shared. Kiley got up, grabbed her sweater from off the floor and tip-toed out the door, closing it quietly behind her.

Before she could even recover from what just happened, she ran into Finn. Literally. Her head was down, so she had no way of knowing that Finn was right in front of her until her head hit his shoulder.

"Oh! Sorry. Sorry." Kiley was flustered. This was the last thing she needed at this moment.

"No, I'm sorry. You okay?" asked Finn.

"Yeah. Yeah, I'm fine," replied Kiley, slowly regaining her composure.

"Are you sure? You're looking a little flushed."

"Oh, probably the embarrassment of bumping into you. I thought Harper was the klutz. Apparently it's rubbing off on me." Kiley brought her hand up to her face, trying to hide the palpable guilt.

"Well, I was just gonna go check on her," said Finn.

"Oh, she's okay. She's fast asleep."

"Really? Wow. Well, good then."

"Yeah." A brief moment of silence passed between them as Kiley kept awkwardly nodding her head. "Well, I'm gonna go check on Emily. And then, start cleaning up. Is everyone pretty much gone?"

"Yeah. Harper's aunt just left. She was the last one."

"Excellent. Well, I'm actually gonna go outside for a bit. Get some air. I'll be back in a few." Without another word, Kiley walked through the kitchen and out the back door. She hoped the outside air would somehow cleanse her and help make more sense of things because she had no idea what the hell had just happened.

***

Kiley bent over and placed the flowers on the grave. She bowed her head and reflected for a moment, recalling the time she first met Harper's parents. They took an immediate liking to her and insisted she stayed for dinner. Both even offered her their couch to sleep on if she was too tired to drive home. Kiley had never met anyone so warm and obliging. She could see where Harper got it from. They were the polar opposite of her parents and it was a devastating shock when they passed away.

Kiley sighed deeply. "I'm not really used to talking to headstones, or anything. But I just wanted to say that I miss you guys. Harper and Emily really miss you, too." She paused for a moment and rolled her eyes, feeling stupid for saying something so obvious and average. She decided to start again. "I'm sorry. The thing is, I think I really screwed things up with your daughter. I didn't mean to hurt her. I didn't mean to fall in love with her either, but it happened. It couldn't be helped. I can't believe I just said that out loud." She looked around to make sure no one was in earshot. "The thing is, I can't lose her. She's pretty much all I've got, you know? I inevitably tend to just mess everything up. Anything that's good in my life, I somehow let it slip away. And I don't want to do that with Harper."

Again Kiley looked around to see if anyone was watching her. She never really understood why people talk to headstones at the cemetery. What was the point? Could they even hear her?

"Anyway, sorry for venting. I just wanted to pay my respects." She stood there for a few more minutes, hoping that perhaps Harper would make an appearance. When it became clear that she wasn't coming any time soon, Kiley thought maybe she had already missed her. So she acknowledged the Foleys one more time, then turned and headed back to her car.

CHAPTER 28

The passage of fifteen days didn't really bring much relief to Harper's heartache. It was bad enough being rejected by Kiley, but the fact that she hadn't spoken to her best friend in over two weeks was devastating to her. In the past, if she ever needed to talk to someone, Kiley was always the first person she would call. Even if they were annoyed with each other, it wouldn't matter. They'd forget all about what they were fighting over and discuss the problem at hand. There was nothing they couldn't power their way through. That is until the truth came out. Harper thought it would be a relief to finally admit her feelings. But this unrelenting love continued to be an albatross around her neck, slowly dragging her down. She cried a few times but the tears proved to be futile. Harper had cried so much in the past three years with her parents' death, her broken engagement, her M.I.A. sister and the deepest secret she ever harbored suddenly surfacing. She was tired of her face being constantly soaked by tears, so she replaced them with a general sense of malaise. The deep funk Harper was in made the days seem to all run together for her and she was back to her old habits running on maybe forty-five minutes of sleep every night. She tried to immerse herself in work, but being employed at a quiet bookstore only gave her more time to be alone with her thoughts. She sought comfort any way she could, with her guitar, her morning jogs, her late-night Krav Maga sessions, and even her newfound ability to bake. That was a talent Emily very much approved of seeing as how it satisfied her daily sugar rush cravings.

Harper opened the oven, encountering a blast of overwhelming heat as she pulled out her cinnamon streusel cake.

"Smells good," said Emily as she washed her cereal bowl in the sink.

"Well that's good, because you're taking it to work with you."

"Hey, no arguments here. They love it when I bring stuff in. I'm like their hero. And I hope you don't mind, but I usually take the credit for making it."

"Glad I can help make you popular."

"Oh, I do that all on my own. This is just icing on the cake…no pun intended," replied Emily.

Harper wrapped the baking dish in aluminum foil and handed it to Emily. "Enjoy."

"Thanks."

"What time are you off tonight?"

"Around nine. But some of my co-workers invited me out to karaoke after work, so I'm thinking I might go if that's cool with you."

Harper shrugged. "Why would I have a problem with it?"

"I just wanna make sure you're okay…you know…if you're by yourself tonight."

Harper stifled a chuckle. True, she and Emily had spent pretty much every night hanging out together over the last two weeks. But that didn't mean Harper needed a babysitter. She could do just fine on her own.

"It's okay, really. I'll be fine."

"You wanna come? It's karaoke, which means you'll pretty much blow everyone away."

"Haha…it's karaoke in Los Angeles, which means everyone who can sing worth a damn will be there showing off their mad skills. It's like *American Idol* for those who were either too lazy to try out or didn't make the cut."

"I'm assuming that's a no?"

"That would be a no. Sorry. But have fun. Where is it?"

"Some pizza place in Santa Monica."

"Well maybe bring home a slice for me."

***

Emily's turn as a supervisor at Gulcher's specialty grocery chain was far surpassing any expectations she had for herself. She had a knack for leadership and it was becoming increasingly clear to her that she could easily start her way down a management path. She was well-liked by her co-workers and seemed to find a comfortable niche working there. It wasn't as dreadful as she thought it would be to actually work and make an honest living. It wasn't exactly her goal to be a lifer here, but it certainly was a rather enjoyable place to work. Compared to where she was a year ago, this was without a doubt a much more desirable situation. Emily was beginning to really come into her own. She could feel the change in her and often found herself cringing at the thought of who she used to be compared to who she is now. Sure, venturing off the beaten path certainly had its advantages that befitted Emily's personality. She never knew what was coming next. It was the excitement and fear of the unknown that enlivened her. It was an adventure.

And now she was punching in a timecard day in and day out, knowing full well what her day would entail. Emily never thought she would be okay with such a mundane day-to-day, but this life of routine simplicity was a welcomed change. As fun as it was to not know what the future held, it also meant not knowing where she was sleeping that night or when her next meal would be. The stress and pain it caused outweighed the excitement. The novelty shortly wore off. So here she was, plugging away at a monotonous routine. Half of her secretly loved it while the other half longed for something with a bit more panache. Well, maybe it was more like sixty/forty. The only real drawback was the uniform she had to wear. Emily was never really a 't-shirt and khaki pants' type of girl.

She made her way along the back aisle with the cereal boxes, taking stock of everything there when her stupor was interrupted by all-too-familiar voice.

"Nice Martha Stewart pants," remarked Kiley, whose basket was half full of random items.

"They make me look like I have a pancake ass."

Kiley cocked her head to the side and turned her focus to Emily's backside. "Hmm…yeah, not a good look for you."

Emily went back to her clipboard, trying to ignore Kiley's obvious attempt at pushing her buttons. "What do you want?"

"I was just picking up some stuff and I saw you over here and thought I'd say 'hi.'"

"Okay. Hi. Are we done now?"

Kiley ignored the question. "How are things?"

"You mean how is my sister?"

"I just said 'things.'"

Emily took notice of everything that was in Kiley's basket. "So you're buying cat food, cooking spray, soy milk and…what is that? A six-pack of protein shakes?"

"I'm becoming more health conscious."

"That's not gonna help you."

"What's your point, anyway?" asked Kiley.

"Well, you don't have a cat, you don't cook, you hate soy milk and…well I've never once seen you with a protein shake. Just throwing random stuff into a basket as an excuse to talk to me seems a little pathetic, even for you. If you want to know how Harper is, just ask me."

Kiley put down her basket in defeat. "How is Harper?"

"Why should I tell you?"

Kiley rolled her eyes. "Come on, Emily. How is she?"

Emily's patience was wearing thin with this girl. "How do you think she is? You know you're breaking her heart, right?"

Kiley took a step back. Emily's words were powerful enough to elicit a physical reaction. Looking somewhat ashamed, Kiley warily conceded. "I know." Her voice cracked with just those two syllables.

"You know?"

Kiley nodded.

"Then why are you doing this to her? Why won't you call her?"

"You don't understand. That girl is my life. As sad as it may sound, she's the most stable relationship I've ever had, and I can't jeopardize that. I think I really fucked it up by giving in. The problem was, I didn't bother trying to envision what the next morning would be like. All I could see at the moment was what I wanted right in front of me, and I didn't think about the consequences it might bring. And then the next day came and I just…" Kiley trailed off, trying to search for a better explanation. For some reason, this sounded better in her head, but the moment she heard it, she couldn't find any logic to it. "I haven't had a relationship last longer than the one I had in seventh grade with Todd Curry. It lasted three months. That's it. I just can't commit. I suck at relationships, and I can't do that to her. I don't trust myself to not freak out and run. I can't ruin our relationship. It would kill me."

"Why would you run from her?" asked Emily, looking around to make sure her manager wasn't watching her socializing.

"It's what I do. Kind of like you, I guess. Only, I run from people, not life." Kiley shuffled her feet apprehensively.

"Can we not make this about me?"

"Fine. It's just that, I don't know what this is. I don't know what it means. I don't know why I've fallen for her. I don't know how it is that after 25 years on this planet and an endless line of suitors, I'm now faced with the overwhelming confusion of falling in love with a girl. A girl who happens to be my best friend. I mean, what's that about?"

"So you're afraid of being labeled as a lesbian?"

"No! That has nothing to do with it. Gay, straight…it doesn't matter. No, I just…I don't know what it means. That's all. And until I know, I don't want to fuck with Harper's emotions any more than I already have."

Emily finally put her clipboard down and pulled Kiley by the arm to the back corner. "Do you love her?"

Kiley was silent for a moment until she slowly nodded. "Yeah, I love her. Probably from the moment I met her."

"Then why can't you just admit it to her? She was terrified to tell you, but she put it all on the line because she felt you deserved to know."

Kiley shook her head. "I can't. I'm sorry, I can't. Nothing can come of it. I'm not risking losing her."

Emily let out an exacerbated laugh. "You're losing her by not talking to her. Did that ever occur to you?"

"Well, what am I supposed to say? I don't know if I'm ready to face her yet. What if she hates me?" She felt her hair falling over her face and tried to tuck it back behind her ear.

Emily grew tired of this exchange and started to walk way. "You know, over the years I've called you many not-so-nice names and thought some pretty shitty things about you. Conceited, unreliable, erratic, way too pretty for your own good. But the one thing I never saw you as was a coward. Thanks for proving me wrong."

Kiley was near tears by this point. "Why do you have to be so spiteful? Can't you see I'm hurting just as bad? I'm just as torn as she is."

"Oh, you poor baby."

"Why do you hate me so much?"

Emily stopped and turned around. "You really don't know?"

Kiley shook her head. "What did I do?"

"You and Harper, you guys just clicked from the moment you met. Suddenly, you were attached at the hip. She was always bringing you around and you guys would just talk and laugh and do your silly little dances and stupid voice impersonations. It got annoying after a while. Even Finn told me that it was starting to get annoying because all you guys would do was giggle. Harper would have a smile on her face every single day after seeing you. She would never look like that after hanging out with Finn. And she certainly didn't with me." Emily lowered her head. "I tried so hard to get close to her, but there was always a wall there. You were the only one that was able to tear it down. You had a relationship with Harper that I was never going to have. She was so real with you. She was herself. Do you know how hard it was to watch an outsider come in and break down her wall within days of knowing her? I'm her sister. I've known her my whole life and I was never able to do that. You have a bond with her that I could never compete with."

"But you guys have a built-in relationship," protested Kiley. "Sisterhood trumps friendship."

"No it doesn't. And it certainly doesn't trump love. Not in Harper's case. You know how passionate she can be. Jesus, she'd step right off a cliff into icy cold water if there were any chance you were there at the bottom. I love my sister, but she is hopelessly flawed. And her biggest imperfection is being loyal to a fault. Especially to you. And you just take it all for granted. You're the most selfish person I've ever met. Even more selfish than I am. And that's saying something."

Kiley was left defenseless from Emily's venomous words. "That's not—"

"We're done here. If you wanna know how Harper's doing, call her. If not, then I suggest you stop fucking with her emotions." Emily walked away and headed straight for the break room, emphasizing the slamming of the break room door so Kiley would know there was no chance of following her.

CHAPTER 29

The following week, Harper was entering the third hour of yet another sleepless night. She stared up into the darkness which had now turned into a thousand little red and yellow dots and speckles from her eyes being open for so long. Not even the melatonin she took earlier that night was helping. Over the years, she had tried many different tactics to assuage her insomnia. She tried reading everything from the dictionary to the Bible, watching TV at a low volume, every over-the-counter sleep aid she could find, listing all the states and their capitals, and one night even resorted to trying a glass of warm milk. That one didn't go over too well and she felt nauseous the rest of the night. Her mind had always been too busy to simply shut off. Every minute there were new thoughts, new lyrics, new problems entering her brain and it was all too easy to fall into the pattern of dwelling on each and every one of them. She had nothing but time on her hands. Before Kiley, finding sleep had never been an issue for Harper. She had even slept through several big earthquakes when she was a kid and even bragged about sleeping right through the Northridge quake of 1994. But now, being a grown up in a grown up world with grown up problems, sleep was something she would look back on with fond memories. She never knew it was something that could be taken for granted. Now the only time she could find any peace at night was when Kiley would call her knowing she would be wide awake and they would talk until the sun came up.

Harper spent the better part of the last month feeling sorry for herself. The self-pity soon turned to simple heartache, then anger, then all-out rage, then feeling stupid and embarrassed having been so honest with Kiley. Finally, she was back to good old-fashioned self-pity. It was the emotion that seemed to best suit her and thanks to that, she was in no short supply of lyrics. Having been through so much in her life, Harper found herself asking when enough was enough. Would there ever come a time when she could be truly happy? Or is happiness just a myth that keeps you striving for something better than what you've got?

Her head was beginning to hurt trying to contemplate too many difficult questions. She was tired of the silence, tired of the loneliness, and tired of the foolish pride and stubbornness that plagued her relationship with Kiley. She got out of bed, threw on her clothes and started dialing a number on her phone. Finally, after a month of only dialing half of the numbers, she completed the full phone number and waited anxiously for someone to pick up.

***

Shots at the bar while she was on the clock was never a good idea. Kiley knew this. She had learned this lesson years ago, but tonight she would have to learn it all over again. Now that she was sobering up, she was beginning to remember why it was such a bad idea. Her bedroom was dark and she's pretty sure they may have left the front door open in their haste of getting to the bed. But Kiley was more preoccupied with the stench of stale whisky on the breath of the guy who came home with her. Elliot? Evan? She couldn't exactly remember his name at the moment, but thinking was the last thing she wanted to do right now. Regardless of his name, he was doing a good enough job of keeping her mind off of the debacle she created with Harper. Still fully clothed and not exactly one hundred percent into their little tryst, Kiley lay on her bed as he sloppily pulled his shirt and pants off while aggressively kissing her neck, grunting with each suctioning sound he made. Kiley winced in pain, trying to guide his lips up toward her face. Seeing as how she hadn't been in high school for quite some time, she wasn't exactly keen on the idea of having to cover up any hickeys the next day. She thought those days were over.

"You're so hot," he said as he started to take her shirt off.

Kiley held her arms close to her body, trying to keep her shirt on a little longer. Her plan had been foiled as her thoughts immediately went to Harper.

He tried harder to remove her shirt as she tried harder to fight off his advances.

"Are you okay?"

Kiley nodded, then shrugged.

He took that as a sign to continue with what he was doing. Before he got much further, the ringtone on Kiley's cell phone gave her an excuse to pause what they were doing. When Kiley saw the name of the person calling flashing on her phone she froze for a moment, then braced herself for what was about to come next.

"Hello?"

"Taco Bell run. You in?"

Kiley gave a half smile. "Your place or mine?"

"Yours. I can be there in ten," replied Harper.

"Okay. Sounds good." She hung up the phone and stared at it for a moment. Then she turned to the nearly naked guy next to her. "Get out."

"What?"

"Go home, Eli."

"Eric."

"Whatever. I need you to leave." She grabbed his pants and threw them at him.

He hurriedly put them on and fastened his belt. "What the fuck?"

"Don't forget your shirt," said Kiley.

Eric grabbed his shirt and turned to leave. "Bitch."

"Okay, bye." Kiley didn't have time to worry about what some guy she met at the bar thought of her. She needed to prepare. Harper was coming and things needed to be said and she needed to shower and her place needed to be tidied as much as possible.

Roughly ten minutes later, Kiley buzzed Harper into her apartment building, which was a rare occurrence seeing as how Harper had a key and always walked in freely. Obviously, this time it was very different circumstances. The chain hung off the front door, swaying side to side as Kiley watched the door in eager anticipation. Upon hearing Harper's footsteps, she positioned herself on the couch to try to appear more casual and comfortable, but her insides were writhing.

"Come in," yelled Kiley after Harper uncharacteristically knocked. "It's open."

"Hey." Harper tentatively peeked her head through the door, then finally entered Kiley's humble abode (humble being an understatement). With her hands full of taco bell bags, she padded over to the coffee table and splayed out the food. Almost in an obsessive-compulsive way, organizing everything by category. Anything to avoid being the first to speak. Once she was done, they stared down at the array of food: three taco supremes, a chicken soft taco, two twice-grilled burritos, a bean and cheese burrito, nachos and two sodas.

Neither of them ate. They just sat there and stared at the food that was getting colder by the minute. Harper took off her sweater, placed it on the arm of the sofa and looked around at the familiar walls. Kiley hadn't done much with the place since the last time she was here. Her new roommate, who was often M.I.A., thankfully had a nice new couch to dress up the otherwise dreary living room. The dark blue upholstery matched well with the gray carpets. The television was still the same tube TV Kiley had bought five years ago during a clearance sale at Best Buy. Kiley wasn't much for watching television too often anyway. It was more for decoration and to have some background noise from time to time. The sole picture hanging in the living room was a framed lithograph of Picasso's "Blue Nude" painting. Kiley had always said that particular painting spoke to her. She could relate to exactly what the girl was feeling and often found herself curling up into that exact same position with her back to the entire world, trying to shut out everything around her. She wasn't a huge art connoisseur, but she knew what she liked. They found the print at an early-morning swap meet. Harper insisted on buying it for her because Kiley kept going back to it and trying to haggle the price lower. Harper was touched that the only real decoration in Kiley's living room was a gift from her. Not to mention the fact that the only photo in her apartment was a framed one of them at a Christmas party that sat on her dresser. Kiley never really saw her apartment as a home, just a place to rest her head when she felt like sleeping.

Harper studied the Picasso for a bit, then took a sip of her soda. And then she caved. "I didn't know what you wanted, so I got a little bit of everything."

"It looks good. Thanks."

Harper began to absentmindedly crack her knuckles, a habit she sorely wished she hadn't picked up. Each crack grew louder and somehow seemed to be echoing through the room. She stopped and cleared her throat. It had been four weeks since the two of them had any contact with each other and now Harper suddenly felt weird and regretted coming over. Sitting in such close proximity of Kiley, she was reminded not only of what they shared together, but also what she had missed.

"I guess I'm not as hungry as I thought," said Kiley.

"Is this irreparable?" asked Harper.

"Well, I think it'll be fine if we just re-heat it."

"No. Us. Are we just damaged beyond all repair?"

Kiley sighed and shook her head. "No. No, not at all. It's just a little glitch in the matrix."

"I still haven't seen that movie."

"I know, I'm so humiliated for you. You really need to break down and see it already."

"It's on my list, Miss I-Haven't-Seen-Lord of the Rings-Yet."

"It's long and boring and there are three of them. I have no desire to invest ten hours of my life to a place called Middle Earth."

Harper smiled. "So we can fix this."

"I don't even really think it's broken. Just needs a little tune up."

Harper put her hands on her knees and looked down. "I missed you."

Kiley, choosing a different approach, scooted closer to Harper. She brought her feet up and sat cross-legged, her knee just an inch away from Harper's.

"I missed you too! You have no idea. My life has never been so quiet as it has been in the last month. I hate it."

Harper smiled to herself, relieved that Kiley missed her too. But disappointment soon found her. It was becoming increasingly clear that Kiley had no interest in re-exploring any sort of romantic relationship. Harper pretty much knew this all along. Kiley was almost otherworldly, in a sense. She was simply too beautiful, too vivacious, too alluring and far too charismatic to really belong to anyone. There were scores of paramours lined up for just a chance at Kiley. How could Harper ever compete with that? She pretty much resigned herself to the fact that all she could really cling to now was that night they spent together. It was perfect and painful at the same time, but as was always the case with Kiley, it was rare to get sweet without the bitter.

"You look like you've lost some weight. That can't be good," observed Kiley.

"I've been eating. But I've also been working out three times a day."

"Me too."

"Really?"

"No, but I've THOUGHT about exercising three times a day. And that alone wears me out." Kiley playfully nudged Harper.

"Well, it's the thought that counts," offered Harper.

"Have you been sleeping?"

Harper shook her head. "Why do you think I have so much time to work out?"

"You really haven't slept at all?"

"I did sleep for nine hours straight one night." Harper immediately regretted saying this. She knew exactly where it would lead and it was a subject they were both purposefully avoiding.

"When?"

"The night you and I…you know. I woke up in the afternoon and it felt like I'd slept for days."

Kiley was silent. She had no idea how to react to that. She wanted to apologize, but it almost seemed pointless after so long. She watched the skin on Harper's arms gradually become covered with goose bumps. Harper rubbed her hand against her arm, trying to warm it up. Kiley allowed her fingers to stray over to Harper's hand and graze the skin on her fingers as they passed by. The blonde stopped moving her hand and looked over at Kiley.

Kiley's mind was racing, but she willed it to slow down and just focus on what was in front of her at that moment. Harper's eyes were locked with hers. What was in them that made them so magnetic? Loyalty? Lust? Love? Whatever it was gripped onto Kiley and made it impossible to look away. Things were finally starting to get back to normal, so why was she being pulled back into this beautiful mess? Why was Harper's hair suddenly tangled in her fingers? Why was she leaning in closer when she knew it was best to pull away? Why were Emily's words tattooed on her brain at this moment? Coward. She was a coward. It's true. She refused to let anyone but herself control her emotions. But in this moment, she was slipping. She felt herself allowing Harper to manipulate the strings. Her initial instinct is usually to run. Instead, she finally allowed herself to do the bravest thing she had ever done in her life. She let go of her fear.

The kiss started slowly, each girl absorbing the other's lips, surrendering to the one thing they both tried to evade. Harper started to pull away, but Kiley wouldn't let her. She shook her head while trying to keep her lips on Harper's.

"No." Kiley pleaded with Harper to stop pulling away and found her lips once more. Each girl began to pant heavier, breathing life into each other as their lips grappled with a force neither of them expected. Moving deeper into the kiss, Harper moved herself on top of Kiley, slowly leaning the older girl back on the couch. She sat astride Kiley, then lowered her body to lie fully on top of her.

Kiley closed her eyes and breathed deeply, trying to control every urge in her body. Stroking Harper's face as the kiss grew more intense, she spoke with every breath she took. "All I could do was think about you. I couldn't stop. Why can't I stop?" Harper didn't answer. She was too enthralled with feeling Kiley's breath on her face as their kiss continued.

The loud knock on the door caused a visceral reaction as both girls suddenly bolted up as if they had been caught doing something wrong. Kiley's heart pounded as they both started laughing at how ridiculous they were being. Two grown girls acting like teenagers.

"Maybe they'll go away," said Kiley.

The knocking grew louder and more forceful the second time around. "Or not. I'll get it." Harper opened the door and Eric walked in uninvited.

Kiley could feel her entire face go white. She wanted to jump up and push him out the door before he said a word, but she was paralyzed with fear.

"Can I help you," asked Harper, assuming he was looking for Kiley's roommate. "I left my phone here," replied Eric.

Kiley's fear took hold of her voice. She searched for something to say. Anything at all. *SAY SOMETHING!* Her brain screamed from inside her head, but nothing came out. "Um…okay. Where did you leave it?" asked Harper.

Eric looked at Kiley. "I think it's on your nightstand. You didn't give me a chance to grab it before you kicked me out of your bed." He went into Kiley's bedroom to fetch his phone.

Harper stared at Kiley aghast, waiting for an answer to a question she didn't even have to ask. Kiley's stunned silence was her answer.

Eric came back out, phone in hand and opened the front door. "Got it. Thanks for nothing."

"Wait," said Harper. "When did you leave that here?"

"About an hour ago. Bitch just told me to leave. Out of nowhere, she—" Harper slammed the door in his face. She didn't care about anything else he had to say. She stood next to the door, her hand still on the knob. "So you kicked him out when you found out I was coming over." Kiley nodded. There was no point in lying or trying to hide this. Harper clung to the words Kiley had said to her just moments ago.

"All you could do was think about me, huh? What a load of bull shit."

"Harper." Kiley stood up, carefully watching Harper's hand to see if it showed any signs of turning the doorknob.

"Stop. Just don't say anything. I'm tired of believing your words."

"But I was telling the truth. I thought about you every minute of every day."

"Except when you were with him."

Kiley took this opportunity to take Harper's hand and guide her to the middle of the living room, leaving as much distance as possible between her and the door. "We didn't do anything. I promise nothing happened. I mean, I stopped it before anything could."

"After I called you."

"I didn't want anything to happen. I would have stopped it anyway." She gripped Harper's hand tighter. "I screwed up. Again. I know. He was the only one I brought home since…since that night. It just got too hard missing you."

Harper turned her focus on the coffee table where her keys were resting. Kiley knew exactly what she was thinking.

"Don't do this, Harper. Please stay. Please."

Harper slid her hand out from Kiley's, grabbed her keys and walked out the door without saying a word. Kiley was left alone in the middle of her sparsely decorated living room wondering how it was possible that she had managed to foul things up even more than she previously had.

CHAPTER 30

Emily sucked down the last of her sprite as the waitress came and placed the check on the table. Without even hesitating, Emily grabbed the check before her cohorts even registered that it was there. Since working at Gulcher's, she had made quite a few friends. Most of them were considered "work friends" but the two girls at the table with her had recently moved into full-fledged friend status. She almost forgot what it was like to have friends, so she wanted to assure them how cool she was by footing the bill for their lunch. Maria was twenty-two and finishing up her senior year at Cal State Los Angeles. Between work and school she rarely had time to hang out, but the trio made it a goal to have lunch together every Thursday. Sian was Emily's age and a bit of a free spirit. Not quite as far gone as Emily used to be, but definitely not nearly as reserved as Maria. It was her week to choose where to have lunch and Sian wanted to do some shopping, so she thought Third Street Promenade near the beach was the perfect choice, even though it was a half hour drive for them.

Emily liked both of her new friends equally. They seemed to be the perfect balance for what she needed in her life to stay grounded. They weren't exactly close enough for her to divulge her past to, but she hoped their friendship would evolve enough so she could eventually tell them.

"What do you think you're doing," asked Sian.

"I'm getting the check," replied Emily.

"Oh, hell no. You got it the last two times," protested Sian.

"So? Need I remind you I'm being groomed for a management position? Soon, I'll be making enough money for you to resent me and then you'll be expecting me to pay for all your lunches."

"Right, but until that day comes, you have to let us pay for some of them. It's only fair," said Maria.

Emily reluctantly handed over the check. "Fine. But I don't want to hear you complaining when I boss you around and make you get your hands dirty."

"Yes, we know, we know. No special treatment." Sian grabbed the check and handed it to the waitress along with her credit card.

"So have you heard anything new about the promotion," asked Maria.

"Not yet, but they said it might be a couple months. They want to make sure they're not moving me up too quickly."

"Well, they're jackasses if they screw you over," offered Sian. The waitress brought the receipt back and Sian signed it and left a tip. "Shall we?"

They walked outside and were immediately greeted with sunshine and fresh ocean air.

"I need some new shoes. You guys wanna come with me?" asked Sian.

"Actually, I have to get back. I've got a mid-term on Monday that I haven't started studying for," said Maria. "Emily, do you need a ride?"

"That's okay. I'll hang around a bit longer."

"Drinks tomorrow night, ladies? My place?" suggested Sian.

Maria hesitated. "Maybe. We'll see how far I come with my studying tonight."

"Emily?"

Emily paused for a moment to pet a beagle that was walking by on a leash. She knelt down and patted his smooth head. "Well hello there, puppy. Aren't you adorable?"

She got up and brushed her hands together to try and get the excess fur off of them. "I don't think I can make it. Sorry."

"You never do margarita night with us," complained Sian. "What's up with that?"

Emily didn't feel like delving too much into her reasons. All she knew for sure was that the less temptation she allowed herself, the better chances she had of not doing anything stupid.

"I'm only nineteen," replied Emily.

"So am I," responded Sian. "Doesn't stop me."

Emily vacillated for a moment, wondering what the harm would be in just telling them about her troubled past. She decided against it, seeing as how Maria was in a hurry to get home and this wasn't just something you casually drop into a conversation. A subject change would be best at this juncture.

"I'll think about it. Didn't you want to get some shoes?"

"Ah yes. Thanks for reminding me. Maria, I'll call you later." Sian blew her an air kiss and then grabbed Emily's hand, leading her to the closest shoe store across the way.

Emily stopped before going in. She looked to her right at the sign for Broadway Street and suddenly remembered she was only blocks away from an old acquaintance. When Sian realized she was minus one shopping buddy, she came back out to look for Emily.

"Hey. You okay?"

"Yeah. Actually, I should go. I just remembered there's something I need to do."

"Are you sure?"

"Yeah."

"Well, do you need a ride? I can come with you," offered Sian.

"I'll be fine. Thanks, though. I'm just gonna go say hi to an old friend. He works a few blocks from here. I can catch the bus back home."

"To the valley?" Sian was appalled at the thought of a friend of hers using public transportation to get from the west side all the way home.

"I'll figure it out. Don't worry. I'll talk to you tomorrow, though, okay?"

"Call me tonight, actually. Just so I know you got back safe."

"Okay. Deal. Good luck with the shoes." Emily felt a little guilty about leaving her friend alone, but her curiosity got the best of her. So she walked the three quarters of a mile it took to get to Finn's office building.

***

Finn was both dreading and looking forward to this day for the past two weeks. He just didn't realize it would get here so fast. He coughed a little as the dust from his desk rose up while he unplugged his computer speakers.

He rolled up his sleeves as he blew the dust away from under the speakers. He placed the speakers in the box by his desk, then looked up at the framed poster on his wall. It was a cheesy inspirational poster he found at a garage sale and couldn't resist buying. "THE *FUTURE* IS YOUR SPECIAL *PRESENT* TO YOUR *PAST* SELF." Finn chuckled to himself. There was no way he was taking this with him. He would just have to leave it up for the next person to scoff at.

"What's going on here?"

Finn was startled. "Jesus!" He turned around to find a young blonde in his doorway. "Emily. Hey. This is a surprise."

"I was in the area. Thought I'd say hi." She looked around. "Doing some spring cleaning?"

"No. Today's my last day."

"They fired you?"

"No. Of course not. I quit."

"Why? I thought you liked it here."

"I did. Not so much anymore." He sat down in his leather desk chair. "I got this great job offer from an ad agency in Seattle. I couldn't pass it up. Plus, I think it's time for a change. A fresh start."

"An ad agency? Do you know anything about working in advertising?"

"Of course. I studied it in business school. But thanks so much for the vote of confidence. Means a lot."

Emily stared at him. "I can't believe you're leaving LA."

"I never fit in too well here, anyway." He opened his bottom drawer and started throwing some things into the box while other items were being tossed into the trashcan.

Emily walked over to the trash and pulled out a photo of Finn and Harper. She held it up and looked at him questioningly.

"Oh yeah, that. I figured a new start would be a little difficult with elements of my past hanging around. You want it?"

"Sure. Something I can remember you by." She wiped a smudge off of the frame. "It's a good picture of both of you."

Finn shrugged as he continued cleaning out his desk.

Emily sat down in the chair facing the desk, lamenting over the past year as she studied the photograph.

"Can I ask you a favor, Finn?"

"Sure."

"Please don't blame Harper for everything that happened."

Finn stopped what he was doing and looked at Emily skeptically.

"It's kind of a messed up situation," continued Emily.

"I know."

"She's just a different person now. Tragedy changes you, but so does time. Things were just…beyond her control." She wanted to tell him about Kiley. Maybe if he knew the truth, the he wouldn't feel so bad about what happened, but she knew it wasn't her place to tell him.

"I know." Finn put his foot on the drawer and leaned back in his chair, hoping Emily would get to her point in a less roundabout way.

"She was just really confused, you know? For a long time. And now she finally seems to know what she wants."

Finn leaned forward in his chair and sighed. "I know. I think I've known for a while. I just didn't want to admit it, so I tried to hold on to her as tightly as I could."

"Wait, what do you know?" asked Emily.

Finn smirked and shook his head. "I was no match for Kiley. I don't think anyone could match her in Harper's eyes."

Emily sat there, aghast. "You knew?"

"It took me a while to figure it out, but eventually…yeah. Once I fully accepted it, I was finally able to start getting over her." He stood up and leaned against his desk. "You know I often wonder what my life would have been like if Kiley had never come into the picture. I'd be married. Maybe with a kid on the way. I'd be happy, I think. I guess you can never really tell. But I'd still be at this job, which…well, just thinking about that depresses me." He leaned and whispered to Emily. "Because this job is *really* boring."

"I can't believe you knew."

"I only realized it recently. After Seth's party. The thing is…sometimes I question. Was it me? Was I not man enough to keep her?"

"You know that's not true. That's such a guy thing to say. Besides, don't be so self-involved. Not everything is about you, you know. Harper had serious issues and feelings she had been wrestling with for years. Had she gone through with it and married you, she may have ended up resenting you. I think she did you a favor, really."

"She was using me because I was the safe choice."

"And you were using her because she was a perfect fit for your all-American dream. A wife, a house, two kids and a mortgage," retorted Emily.

Finn turned away, feeling slightly guilty. "I did love her, though."

"And she loved you."

"But she loved Kiley more."

Emily nodded. "That's something I'll never really understand, but yes. It's overwhelmingly tangible. You can feel it whenever they're in a room together. It's almost surreal."

Finn looked at the ground and unconsciously began to chew on the inside of his cheek. He suddenly felt very uneasy discussing his ex's affinity for her best friend.

"So, what's new in your life, Emily?"

Emily accepted the change of subject. "Oh the usual. Drugs, alcohol, debauchery, no regard for other people's feelings or emotions. Same old stuff." Emily gave a cute half smile. "Actually, things are good. I'm getting my GED next month. Thinking of applying to a junior college of some sort. Maybe LA Valley College or Pasadena City College."

"Good. That's good to hear."

"I'm getting promoted to assistant manager."

"That's awesome! Congratulations." Finn took a moment to regard the young woman in front of him. He could hardly believe this blonde haired, blue-eyed girl was the same one he found on his doorstep eight months ago. "I'm proud of you. You done good, kid. Sounds like you're gonna be okay."

Emily nodded. "Are *you* gonna be okay?"

"I think so. I mean, there's a lot of stuff I have to do before I leave, but I'm really excited. I think this will be good for me."

"When do you leave?"

"Next month."

Emily stood up and walked over to give him a hug. "Well, good luck. And call or email me once in a while. Let me know what's going on with you, okay?"

"I will."

Emily grabbed the photo he gave her. But before she could leave, Seth came bounding in, grabbed Finn and put him in a headlock.

"Last day, asshole. That means drinks are on me tonight!" He proceeded to give his friend an ever-so-mature noogie. "Half the office is coming. And lots of girls, so we're gonna get you laid tonight." He glanced over at Emily and immediately let go of his death grip on Finn. "Well hello."

"Hi?" responded Emily, cautiously.

Seth walked over looking her up and down, giving her the "elevator eyes."

"And you are?"

"Emily."

He reached out to take her hand and kissed it, trying to give off the façade of a gentleman. "It's a pleasure to meet you, Emily."

After straightening out his hair, Finn thought it was time to intervene. "Seth! Don't even think about it."

"But—"

Finn shook his head. "No."

"Yeah, but she's hot."

"Seth? I said no."

Seth rolled his eyes and backed away from Emily. "All right. Fine. Come find me when you're off. Shooters and hooters!" At that, he ran out the door, but not before giving Emily one more harmless glance.

"Wow. I see why you won't miss this place," said Emily.

Finn smiled. "Take care of yourself."

Emily nodded and walked out the door.

"And your sister," mumbled Finn when she was out of earshot.

Finn sat down and began to massage his temples. Seeing Emily again certainly wasn't expected, but now it brought up all sorts of memories he thought he'd gotten rid of. He briefly considered calling Susan, but knew that was obviously a bad idea. He never went to see the doctor she had referred him to. He hadn't had time with the new job offer and the arduous task of moving and constant apartment hunting on the internet. He opened his top drawer to grab a pen and a notepad and started scribbling down some words. He frantically wrote, hoping he would be able to capture on paper each thought that passed through his mind before it was lost into the ether. After about twenty minutes, he stopped and read back what he wrote.

"Wow. That sucked," said Finn as he ripped the paper off and crumbled it up. He leaned his chair back and looked up at the ceiling. A task like this was going to take a lot more time and effort than he had just given.

***

Emily hopped on the bus as it pulled up to the curb. She sat in the middle, wishing she had brought an iPod for the long trek back to Studio City. She wasn't sure if she was going to tell Harper about seeing Finn. On one hand, she should know that he's leaving. But on the other hand, Harper had enough to deal with right now. She shouldn't have to worry about Finn, but ultimately, Emily knew her sister's bleeding heart would try to reach out to him and take on his burdens. She found herself reflecting on his words. He said he was proud of her and that it sounded like she was going to be okay. She wondered if he was right. Sure, she had come a long way from where she was eight months ago, but would it stay this way? Her biggest fear was returning to what and where she was a year ago, and even worse, having Harper witness it.

***

She could feel the sudden jolt in her head during the moment of impact. Her nose burned and her eyes watered as the line of powder on the table disappeared. Emily sniffled and grabbed her nose. She hated this process more than anything and couldn't figure out why she still did it. It was painful, caused a number of nosebleeds and while she felt the incredible high for half an hour, every time she came down, she ended up loathing herself. She knew it was wrong and certainly unhealthy and often asked herself why she continued to do it. When she turned around and saw Damien on the bed having sex with some girl he brought home, she suddenly remembered. He was presumptuous to think that she would allow him to fulfill his threesome fantasy when she repeatedly told him it was never going to happen.

I shouldn't have refused, *she told herself. If she hadn't said no, maybe he wouldn't be punishing her like this. She really thought that she was enough for him, that he loved her more than anything. Now Emily was beginning to believe that she did, in fact, live up to the nickname Damien had given her: Stupid Girl. It was now her mantra. Whenever he made her feel guilty over something, he would find a way to hurt her and she would think, 'Stupid girl.'*

She didn't even know the name of the girl in bed with her boyfriend. But she was beginning to grow weary of her relentless screaming that was supposedly from pleasure. Emily knew there was no way any girl would enjoy herself that much with Damien. He was as selfish in bed as he was in his daily life.

The scene in front of her was grim. They had been living in this rundown apartment for a few months and nothing was changing. He told her that once they made enough money, they'd be living in a much nicer place with a pool. They could lay out in the sun all day and make love all night and life would be perfect. But the longer they stayed in this place, the more her expectations were dwindling. And now she was faced with watching the man who promised her all these things screwing some girl he picked up in a bar.

The woman's shrieks grew louder and Emily needed some way to drown out the sound. She leaned over and snorted one more line, grabbing her nose as the burning sensation moved all the way up through her head and down her throat. She leaned her head back and then allowed herself to fall onto the carpet. She lay on her back, watching the ceiling fan violently move around and around.

She thought about how she ended up here. She thought about Harper and what her sister might be doing at this exact moment. Was she happy? Was she in the final stages of planning her wedding? Was she thinking about her at all? She thought of her parents and how it would be so easy to blame them for her situation. If they weren't dead, then maybe she wouldn't be here. Maybe

361

she would have straightened out her act and be an upstanding citizen. Well, maybe not, but she'd at least have a family. Emily didn't want to think anymore. She had the urge to call Harper, but couldn't move. Suddenly the ceiling fan turned into five ceiling fans that were dancing their way across the ceiling. Emily moved her head around to try and get her bearings straight. Somewhere between the whirring of the fan and the sex sounds from the bed, she passed out, finally able to get some silence.

***

When she alighted from the bus and walked into her house, she was greeted by Harper, who was sitting on the couch waiting for her to come home.

"Hey."

"Hi. I was hoping you'd be back sooner."

"Sorry. I got caught up. Everything okay?"

"Yeah," replied Harper. "Yeah, everything's fine. Sit down for a minute."

Emily did as her sister asked. "You're kind of scaring me. You've got that manic look in your eyes."

"That's because I thought about what you said the other day. And–here's the kicker–I think you're right."

"You do?"

"Yeah. You made some really valid points, so I thought about it and you're right. I think it's time."

Emily put her bag down and tried to wrap her head around what her sister was agreeing to. "Are you sure?"

"Yeah. I'm sure."

"It's probably gonna hurt. A lot."

362

"Well," said Harper. "That's why I'm glad you're here with me."

Emily shared a genuine smile with her sister. She was grateful that her sister was finally beginning to see how serious she was about sticking around. "I'm not going anywhere. We're in this together. I just want you to be one hundred percent sure this is what you want. I mean, it's a pretty big decision."

"I know. It'll be really hard, but it's for the best. And I know you think so, too," said Harper.

Emily nodded. She had only briefly brought up the idea with Harper as a means of distracting her from the Kiley situation. And she certainly didn't think Harper would agree to it so quickly. It turns out for the first time in long time, Harper actually considered taking Emily's advice.

CHAPTER 31

Finn put his car in park and shut off the engine after pulling alongside the curb next to Susan's house. He gripped the steering wheel and inhaled deeply. He was relieved to find that her car wasn't in the driveway. His body still tensed up as he unfastened his seatbelt and opened the car door. He treaded upon the walkway leading up to her door, gripping the envelope in his right hand. The walkway was only thirty feet long, but Finn felt as though he were walking from one end zone to the other on a football field. When he reached the mailbox, he loosened the grip on the envelope and placed the contents inside the mailbox. He closed the lid and walked away, leaving behind five full pages of words that had taken him three days to write. He knew this was the right thing to do. After what he did to her he had no right to attempt to talk to her and say goodbye face-to-face.

His 2003 Honda Accord was packed from top to bottom with all his earthly possessions. After two flights to and from Seattle, he finally found a place suitable enough for him to start his new life out there. He had visited his new place of employment and gotten to know a few people there. He was ready. He had three full days until his new job started and he was looking forward to driving up there while exploring the coast along the way.

After driving away from Susan's place, he headed toward the beach and enjoyed his very last LA sunset. He had one more stop to make along the way before his journey officially began. He pointed his car east and headed out to Harper's place. Once he got there he was met with an overwhelming sense of confusion, which led him to make one more unexpected stop.

The sun was now fully swallowed by the sky. Finn pulled into the parking lot of Tyson's Bar and walked in, half expecting to see Harper performing on stage. The stage however, was empty. He regarded the vacant area where he used to watch Harper perform so many times and wondered if he would ever see her play again. Then he remembered that it no longer mattered. She was soon to be a distant memory.

***

Finn descended the cement steps comparing his ticket to the rows he was passing until he finally found his seat. It was a crisp November night coupled with a rather uncommon wind chill that made him wish he had brought more than just his USC hooded sweatshirt to wear. He finally found the row corresponding to his ticket and took his seat along the seventy-yard line. He looked around to see if any of his friends had shown up yet. He knew they were more than likely still tail-gating in the parking lot and getting as drunk as they could before stumbling in sometime during the second quarter. Seeing as how it was his senior year and that this would likely be the last USC game he would be attending as a student, Finn wanted to make the most of it and remain as sober as possible for the occasion. He shuddered and put his hood up over his head to keep his ears warm as he watched the teams on the field call the coin toss.

A Fine Mess

It didn't take long for Finn's attention to turn to the girl in the row in front of him, one seat over to his right. Her blonde hair was covered by a purple beanie and the freckles on her face were made more prominent from the goose bumps on her skin, no doubt brought on by the cold. She seemed to be quite vested in the conversation she was having with her friend. But the moment she laughed, something happened to Finn. It was a rather minimal reaction, but something inside him had changed. Suddenly, he felt warm and even a little bit bold. He pulled the hood off his head and grinned as he noticed her matching purple gloves make an appearance. They had been hidden by the cloak of the UCLA blanket she was huddled under. Finn knew he should have been focused on the game, but he couldn't stop his eyes from casually wandering over to the blonde. What could he possibly say to break the ice? Without thinking, he tapped her on the shoulder and decided to go with the first thing that came out of his mouth.

The blonde girl turned around to see who was rudely interrupting the conversation with her friend.

"Hi. Um...can I buy you a beer?" He immediately cringed. A misfire. Definitely not his best line.

She looked at him quizzically. "They don't serve beer here."

"I mean after the game."

"I'm nineteen."

He was flailing, but figured he had nothing to lose. So before she turned back around, he let his instincts take over once again.

"Don't tell me you're a Bruin," he said, gesturing to the blanket over her lap.

"Would that be a problem," she asked.

"Well that would make us rivals. Never a good way to start off a relationship."

She opened her mouth to respond just as the crowd jumped up and screamed when USC scored a touchdown.

"That's rather presumptuous," she yelled.

"Is it?"

"Besides, I'm not big on the whole rivalry thing."

"Good. Less pettiness between us," replied Finn.

"What are you talking about? There is no 'us'."

"Not yet." Finn couldn't believe what an ass he was sounding like, but the words just kept coming out of him so naturally.

The young woman scoffed and shook her head, then went back to talking to her friend.

It wasn't too long before Finn's friends finally met up with him. After the game was over, Finn spotted the young blonde walking out to her car. He bid his buddies adieu and ran over to her. This time, he made it a point to act more like himself and not some college boy caricature.

"Hey!"

"Um...hi."

"I just realized I didn't get your name." Finn was walking backwards as she and her friend trudged on, trying to find her car.

"It's Harper. And this is my friend, Sarah."

"Hi Sarah. Nice to meet you."

"Hi." Sarah laughed. She was enjoying this way too much. "Uh, Harper? I'm gonna go look for the car. I'll text you when I find it. Stay. Talk. Have fun."

Finn watched Sarah leave and turned back to Harper. "So, Harper, would you like to go out with me?"

Harper stopped walking. "Seriously?"

Finn stopped as well. "Yeah. Like on a date."

Harper shook her head. "I don't think so."

"Why not? You have a boyfriend?"

"No."

"Girlfriend?"

"No!"

"Scary father?"

"Only when the Dolphins lose, so yes."

"Well, he'll love me. I guarantee it. So will you."

"Oh really?"

Finn nodded. "I'm harmless."

"How do I know that?"

"I'm from the Midwest. We all have that hometown boyish charm."

Harper gave a slight side smile. "Well that remains to be seen from you."

Finn knew he was wearing her down. "Come on. One date."

"Why do you want this so badly?"

Finn took a breath and prepared himself for the most genuine thing he had said all night. "Honestly? Because the moment I saw you, my heart and my stomach simultaneously dropped. I kind of liked the feeling. And I'd like to feel it again."

Harper's half smile turned into a full-fledged grin, which soon led to some intense blushing. She dug through her bag and grabbed a pen and an old receipt from the Cheesecake Factory and began to write down a series of numbers she rarely made public.

"Here's my number," she said while handing him the receipt. "If you call, I just might answer."

Finn took the piece of paper and watched as Harper ran off to join Sarah in their hunt for the car. He took out his cell phone and immediately began to input the numbers. To him, there was really no sense in waiting three days to call this one. Not when she had such a tight grip around his heart upon their first encounter. She would simply have to learn to live with his tenacity.

***

"I don't care if he's rich, he's still a douchebag," yelled Kiley as she came in from the storage room with Erin close behind her.

"I know, but he told me he really cares about me," replied Erin.

"Before or after he went home to his wife?"

Erin lowered her head. "Before."

Kiley could see Erin wasn't in the mood to talk about yet another soon-to-be-defunct relationship. "Just be careful, okay? We can't have another incident where I have to come pick you up in Venice at 2am filled with tears and missing your shoes."

"That won't happen again. I promise."

Kiley was about to say something, but a familiar face at the bar made her forget what her next snarky comment was going to be. "Um…do you mind grabbing table eleven? I have to go take care of something."

Erin looked over at Finn. "Sure."

"Hey stranger." Kiley gave Finn a half-hearted hug.

"Hey."

"What brings you here?"

"Actually, I was looking for Harper. Have you seen her?"

Kiley held her tongue for a moment. "No. I haven't."

"Well, she's not answering her phone and I really wanted to talk to her."

"Did you try her house?"

"Yeah, but obviously that was a bust."

"Why?"

"Well…because it's empty."

"What do you mean it's empty," asked Kiley.

Finn cocked his head to the side. "When was the last time you talked to Harper?"

Kiley shrugged. She didn't want to tell him it had been over a month since they had spoken.

"Well, I guess I didn't expect her to tell me she was moving," said Finn.

Kiley had a hard time controlling her visceral reaction to Finn's matter-of-fact statement. She felt as though someone was choking her and she was fighting for air.

"Oh yeah. That."

"You DID know she moved, right? I mean, her whole house is empty."

Kiley's heart rapidly beating faster. She was too taken aback to answer Finn.

"Anyway, can you do me a favor and give this to her?" He handed her an envelope similar to the one he dropped in Susan's mailbox. "It's a letter. Don't, like, read it or anything."

Kiley shook her head. She was still in shock, but was lucid enough to realize how rude she was being. "Did you want a drink? It's on the house."

"No thanks. Actually, I should get going. I have a long drive ahead of me."

"Long drive? Where are you going?"

"Wow, I figured Emily would have told Harper this. I'm surprised she didn't tell you. I'm going to Seattle."

"For how long?"

"Indefinitely. I got a job out there."

"You're moving? Why am I always the last to know things?"

"I'm leaving tonight."

"Oh, my God. Well, come here!" She pulled him in for another hug. This one had more warmth and meaning behind it. "You're really gonna leave without seeing Harper?"

"I was hoping to talk to her in person, but I'm already behind schedule."

"And this is your goodbye letter to her?"

Finn shrugged. "Yeah, I guess you could call it that."

Kiley gripped the envelope. As selfish as it sounded, she was thrilled that she now had an excuse to call Harper.

Finn watched Kiley's troubled face, unsure of what exactly she was thinking about. He reached into his pocket, grabbed his keys and nervously twirled them around his finger. He couldn't quite look Kiley in the eye. "So, take care of her, okay?"

"Harper? Of course. Always." *Just as soon as she starts speaking to me again*, thought Kiley.

"I mean it," stated Finn. "She deserves to be happy, after all this. Even if I can't be the one to do it. So, make her happy, Kiley. Okay?"

It took a moment, but Kiley finally began to realize exactly what he was referring to. She supposed it didn't take a genius to figure it out. Finn had managed to solve the mystery. Which obviously meant that she and Harper hadn't been too successful in masking their emotions all these years.

Kiley stared at Finn with her mouth agape. "I…" She closed her eyes and nodded. It was all she could do. Words evidently were not her friend at the moment.

"Take care of yourself, Kiley."

Kiley nodded again and barely managed string together two words. "Good luck."

As Finn walked out the door, Kiley carefully studied the envelope in her trembling hand.

***

Finn's view from his rearview mirror was slightly obstructed from all his belongings packed in the backseat of his car. He managed to catch a glimpse of the city lights as he headed north on the 5 freeway. His heart began to sink, but he took pleasure in not knowing what was ahead of him. A contented smile crept across his face as he left behind the town he called home for the last eight years.

CHAPTER 32

Kiley hadn't moved from her spot since Finn left. Her hand was beginning to get sweaty from gripping the envelope so tightly. Little did she know that Graham had been watching her for the past few minutes.

"You know, it would be nice if, just for one day, you would do more than five minutes of work during your shift. Is that really too much to ask?"

Kiley looked at Graham, her face devoid of any emotion. Obviously something was wrong. He had never seen her face so vacant. "Are you okay?"

Kiley looked down at the envelope.

"Was that Finn? What did he say to you? What's going on?" Graham took a seat at one of the bar stools as he studied her devastated look.

Kiley's hand began to shake. Soon, her whole body was shaking. Graham took notice of this and reached out to take the envelope from her hand.

"It's for Harper," said Kiley. "Finn's leaving. Tonight. He wanted me to…" Her voice trailed off. Suddenly she felt sick; never before had she felt so physically ill. Harper had moved. She moved without telling her best friend, which led Kiley to believe that maybe it really was over. Maybe Harper had finally had enough of Kiley's fickle heart. Just the thought of Harper not being in her life was enough to make her want to fall to her knees, and she would have if the bar weren't holding her up. She looked at Graham with an innocent, almost pleading gaze.

"Did you know?"

"Did I know what?"

"That she moved."

Graham put the envelope down on the bar and began to tap his fingertips on the mahogany. "She mentioned it."

"Why didn't you tell me?"

"I didn't know she was serious. She said it was a possibility, but I never thought she'd actually go through with it."

"Well, Finn said she did. And she hasn't returned my phone calls, so it's not like I've been in the know."

Graham sat quietly, not knowing exactly what to say. He had been watching this train wreck play out for months now. Even years. But he always stayed out of it. It was none of his business what went on between those two, but there was obviously something there.

Kiley's gaze turned into a thousand-yard stare. Everything she had been feeling since that kiss at Seth's party had been culminating. Leading up to this very moment where she felt like if one more emotion took hold of her, she would implode—her raw nerves vulnerable and exposed.

"What am I so afraid of, Graham?"

Graham shook his head and placed his hand on Kiley's. "I don't know. But if you need to, take the rest of the night off. Clear your head."

"Are you sure?"

Graham nodded. Clearly, she was in no shape to work right now.

Kiley looked over at Erin, who had tuned into the last half of their conversation.

Erin nodded. "Go. I'll take care of things here."

Kiley grabbed the envelope and headed toward the door. She had no idea how she would find her, but she had to at least try.

Before she walked out, Graham offered up one helpful piece of information. "She's performing at The Fortress tonight. 11pm. I have a friend over there. Helped her book the gig a couple weeks ago."

Kiley gave Graham a little side smile, ran over to him and gave him a hug.

"You really are a great guy, Graham."

***

Harper showed up to her gig at The Fortress a bit early, but she wanted to be prepared and familiarize herself with the venue. At least, that's what she told herself. She also just wanted a break from everything that was happening and surround herself with some good music. Her life had been in complete upheaval in the last two months. This was the first sense of normalcy she'd had in a while and she was glad to get back to doing what she loves best. It was a new place with a new crowd and, thanks to tonight being an all ages night, her sister was by her side. They settled into a booth near the back and watched the opening acts. Harper had no idea Emily was crushing on the guy singing on stage at the moment and Emily had no idea that Harper was using every ounce of strength she had to not call Kiley and at least extend an invitation to the show.

A Fine Mess

***

The tires on Kiley's car screeched to a halt along the curb. She barely put her car in park before she leapt out and ran up the walkway. She stopped halfway when the streetlight revealed the "Sold" sign ominously displayed on the lawn. Kiley dismally meandered up to the front door. She stood on her toes and tried to peek into the glass window on the door. It wasn't the most ideal vantage point so, like some sort of night prowler, she made her way over to the window to her left. The blinds were pulled up and she put her hands on either side of her face to look through the window into what used to be Harper's living room. The couch and TV were gone and only two chairs remained, but they were covered by a tarp. The lights in the house were off, but the streetlights coupled with the moon helped to illuminate the scene in front of her. Her heart suddenly felt as empty as this big house. Unfortunately, the light revealed a little too much for her liking. She would have given anything for a blackout at the moment or the dark cloak of a moonless sky, anything to prevent her from seeing what she was seeing right now. She was hoping it wasn't actually true. Kiley had it in her mind that maybe Finn was wrong and maybe Graham was lying. She had clung onto a sliver of hope that her best friend hadn't up and moved without even telling her. That hope was now completely obliterated.

Kiley backed away from the window onto the grass. She fell to her knees right there on Harper's front lawn, then sat down facing the street and brought her knees up to her chin. It didn't make any sense. How could she move just like that? Harper loved this house and everything it stood for. Kiley weighed the possible reasons for Harper's decision. Maybe it got too hard having to live with the constant memory of her parents. Maybe now that Emily's back, Harper feels she can finally let go and move on. Maybe by moving, Harper wanted to start over, without Kiley in her life. Before Kiley's imagination ran rampant, the headlights of a car in the distance caught her attention. As the sound of the engine grew closer, she perked up, holding on to the slim chance that it might be Harper. It wasn't. She knew it wasn't. The car drove by without even tapping on the brakes. Kiley sighed and fell back to lie down on the grass. With the tall green blades tickling her neck, she looked up and watched the night sky come alive with stars, each one shining their faint light down upon her. Her tranquility was short-lived, however, when she remembered that Harper was somewhere out there and not here with her right now. Kiley grew increasingly nervous. Thanks to Graham, she knew exactly where to find her, but her body couldn't seem to move from the grass. She was torn between that ever-present struggle between passion and fear. She sat up and looked back at the empty house. Kiley hated fear, especially the kind that was strong enough to paralyze someone. She did not want to be paralyzed. Not when she had something worth running to.

***

When it was her turn to set up on stage, Harper plugged in her guitar and placed it on the stand to the right of the microphone. The guitar reverberated with a

377

fuzzy sound escaping from it. Harper cleared her throat and checked the levels on the microphone. She stared out into the sea of people, their faces barely lit by the ambient light. It was in this moment Harper's thoughts once again turned to Kiley, as they often did. She wondered what she was doing right now and wondered if she'd be proud of her for taking a giant leap of faith by performing at a club that was considered an impressive up-and-coming music venue. She wondered if Kiley would even care. Then her thoughts turned to instant regret for not telling her about this and for basically shutting her out completely. She knew it was for the best, though. Her vulnerable heart couldn't take another thrashing. After extensive analysis and a little bit of quasi-therapy from her little sister, Harper decided that Kiley's wavering heart had no place in her life. She only half-believed it, but made every effort to adhere to the decision, at least for the time being.

Though at this very moment, Harper wanted to renege on her decision. She began to feel overwhelmed as her debut at The Fortress was quickly approaching. She now had five minutes to nut up and get herself together. She grabbed her set list from the guitar case and laid it on the floor next to the guitar stand using her bottled water as a paperweight. When she stood up she looked over at Emily, who was staring rather dumbfounded at someone who just walked in. She followed Emily's line of vision and her eyes rested on a ghost. An apparition. A specter of some sort. That was the only explanation because there was no way that Kiley Young was actually standing twenty feet away sheepishly glancing from Harper to the floor. She watched as Kiley walked up to the stage.

"Hi."

So it's true, thought Harper. *It really is her.* "Hi," replied Harper, unable to give Kiley full eye contact.

"I need to talk to you." Kiley's voice was tentative, but firm.

"I'm about to go on."

"Just give me a few minutes." Kiley reached out and took Harper's hand. "Please." She needed to do this now before she lost whatever courage she was able to muster.

Harper conceded and allowed Kiley to lead her outside. She waited while Kiley gathered her thoughts.

"Look, I just…I wanted…" Kiley was struggling to get her words out. She wasn't exactly a paragon of proper verbiage while under pressure and due to the time it was rather difficult to say everything she wanted to say in just five minutes. She reached into her back pocket and grabbed the one thing that could possibly save this conversation. "Finn wanted me to give this to you."

Harper took the envelope while carefully studying Kiley's face. "Okay."

"Apparently he got a job in Seattle and he's moving there. Today, actually."

Harper nodded. "I know. Emily told me a couple days ago."

"Oh." Kiley was beginning to feel foolish knowing she was always the last to find out anything. "Well, he couldn't find you. So he came by the bar and asked me to deliver it to you."

"Well, thanks."

They remained standing just outside the front entrance to the club, each of them waiting for the other to say something. Kiley's time was running out. And her once-thriving valor had quickly faded.

"Well, good luck. I know you'll do great," offered Kiley, bringing chickening out to a whole new level.

"Oh," replied Harper. "Okay. Thanks." Harper turned around and walked back into the bar. Kiley remained behind debating on whether to go in or to leave. She didn't have too long to debate the issue because Harper came charging back out from the club.

"That's it? That's all you've got for me?"

"What?" Kiley was taken aback by Harper's intensity.

"You came all the way out here, sought me out after two months. Made me late for my set, and all you do is wish me luck?"

"That's not— "

"Fuck you, Kiley! Fuck you."

Kiley was shaken by Harper's words. It took a moment to find her footing. "Fuck you right back." Not the cleverest comeback, but it would have to suffice.

"Excuse me?"

"You heard me. You moved out of your house without even telling me?"

"Last I checked, you weren't exactly talking to me either," rebutted Harper.

"You stormed out of my apartment."

"You let me."

"So I'm just supposed to run after you?"

"If you really wanted me, you would have."

Kiley couldn't help but think what a female thing that was for Harper to say. She had to remember, she was dealing with a female here, one that she had hurt beyond forgiveness.

"I wanted to. Everything just happened so fast."

"Yeah, and that guy you screwed came back looking for seconds and…"

"That's not what happened and I didn't have sex with him!" Kiley was having difficulty controlling the level of her voice.

Harper threw her hands up. "Oh please, Kiley. That's all you do. You fuck guys. And then you fuck some more. And you keep doing it, and you wear your promiscuity on your sleeve for everyone, mainly me, to see."

Kiley took a step back. Now they were finally getting somewhere. The lines of communication had finally opened up.

"Yeah," conceded Kiley, "I've been with a lot of guys. I have. And I could never figure out why I was so addicted to it until recently. They gave me solace for one brief moment. But you have to realize, every single one of them reminded me of how badly I wanted you. And how I couldn't have you because you were with Finn. I would never have dreamt of coming between you two. And then you broke up, but I had trained myself so well to just push everything I felt for you way down. I got used to suppressing it. It just seemed easier. It was stupid, I know. I screwed up."

Harper was about to interject, but Kiley wouldn't let her. Not while the words that had been rolling around in her head for the past few years were finally coming out of her mouth. "But you screwed up too. You wanted me too and you never told me."

Harper felt her throat dry up as she tried to swallow. "How do you know I wanted you?"

Kiley took a step closer to the younger girl. "I may not have always known; I've been a bit dense. But I see it now. I've seen it ever since that night we…" Kiley paused. What was the right way to put it? Had sex? Made love? Hooked up? What was the protocol here?

"That night," repeated Harper, coolly. "That fucking night. Do you have any idea how much I thought about that night since it happened? Every single night, I lie awake and I relive it over and over. Your hair, your face, the way your hands felt on my skin, the way you fell asleep on my shoulder, the shape and the weight of your body as it rested on mine. Every little nuance, every detail I remember." Harper shook her head in disgust. "And I hate myself for it because you probably don't even think about it. To you, it was a mistake. A lapse in judgment because you're too afraid. You're afraid of what people will think. You're afraid of actually feeling something real in your life. You're afraid of ruining our friendship, which is pretty much in shambles, anyway. So excuse me if thinking that 'good luck' isn't the most appropriate thing for you to say right now."

"Harper— "

"I have to go. They're gonna give my spot away."

"Wait," pleaded Kiley.

Harper stopped and turned around. "What?"

Kiley was screaming at herself internally. 'Stop her from going in! Take her hand! Kiss her! Do something! Anything to keep her from walking away! This is your moment. This is it! Make something happen!' Kiley's subconscious was no match for the terror and trepidation inside of her. Harper was right. She was terrified of all those things and wasn't sure if she was ready to take them all on at once.

Harper lowered her eyes and turned to walk back in. "That's what I thought."

***

Once Harper was back inside and back on stage, Kiley was able to move. Her fists were clenched as tightly as her jaw as she punched the door. "Shit!" Why couldn't she have just said something? She opened the door and ran inside just in time to watch Harper perform her first song.

Harper didn't know Kiley had just walked in. She refused to let herself even think about what Kiley was doing at this moment. Right now, she needed to focus on her songs and nothing more. With her guitar strap around her neck and a pick in her hand, she started playing the first song that came to her mind. No introduction was given. She hoped it wasn't needed and allowed the words to simply say it all.

"She sends me a smile and I believe
It's meant for only me.
She offers her heart on her sleeve
I do my best to keep it pristine.
She tells me about her bad day
I just want to make everything okay.
She grabs my neck and kisses me so
I don't ever want to let go."

With the first verse out in the open and the words floating around in the air for everyone to hear, Harper knew there was no going back after she sang the first word, "she." It was a song she had written a couple days after that night with Kiley. It was never meant to be heard by anyone, but tonight, she was feeling brave. She was

383

tired of hiding, tired of denying and tired of her heart being hurled to the floor yet again. So she exposed herself the best way she knew how.

"She makes me smile
She makes me weak
She knows the hold she's got on me
For her I'd do anything
Just to keep her by my side
And I think it's gonna be alright."

Kiley couldn't take her eyes off of Harper. She let every word of the song sink in. She knew it was about her. There was no doubt in her mind. She tried to fight the urge to cry, but she couldn't. Those damn tears would not stop forming as she continued to watch Harper sing.

"She lays her body across my bed
And I forget the thoughts in my head
She hides away in her secret place
While I'm wrapped up in her embrace
We talk about our fears and doubts
And how we won't let each other down
I send her a song meant only for her
She is the melody and the words."

Everyone would know now. Everyone would know what lay in the depths of Harper's soul. The one thing she had tried to hide for so long was now out in the open. She gripped her guitar as tightly as she could while laying her soul bare in front of a hundred strangers.

"She makes me smile

She makes me weak,
She knows the hold she's got on me
For her I'd do anything
Just to keep her by my side
And I think we're gonna be alright."

Kiley remained captivated by every word. She had never been so moved in her entire life. Here she was worrying about the high cost of her undeniable to attraction to Harper. Wanting to reject every natural instinct her body and mind had simply because she was a coward. She never allowed herself to feel anything more than the slightest affinity for someone because she knew the kind of irredeemable damage it could cause. She never wanted to feel that pain. And now she realized just how selfish she was being by inflicting that same pain upon Harper. Harper was the brave one. She was the one on stage letting everyone in on her deepest secret. She invited complete strangers to listen to the tale of how much she loves Kiley. And Kiley couldn't even do it in the most intimate of settings.

"If she could only see
What she does to me
With one look, she brings me to my knees."

As her strumming reached a fever pitch, Harper belted out the last chorus with everything she had inside of her.

"She makes me smile
She makes me weak
She knows the hold she's got on me

A Fine Mess

For her I'd do anything
Just to keep her by my side
And I know we're gonna be alright."

The song ended and the entire audience roared with cheers and applause. Harper had a rather self-satisfied smile on her face as the cheers continued. Before she could even look down at her set list to see what song would be next on the agenda, Harper felt a presence next to her on stage. She turned to see Kiley step up onto the stage and before she had any time to react, Kiley's lips collided with hers. It didn't matter that they were on stage, obviously putting on a much different show than the crowd expected. She couldn't control herself anymore. Four years of unadulterated desire had been bottled up inside her and it was time to ease all the pain she had been feeling. The moment her lips came into contact with Harper's, she knew nothing would ever be the same again, but she didn't care. Unable to quench her thirst, Kiley pushed their lips harder together.

Harper didn't fight it. At this moment, this was all she wanted. She didn't care about the audience who, so far, had remained surprisingly quiet with the exception of a few collective gasps. The guitar was separating their bodies. Harper held onto it for dear life. But if any reason was good enough to put it down for a moment, this was it. She pried their lips apart long enough to put her guitar down. Then her lips rested upon Kiley's mouth once more as she affectionately tasted the soft flesh that was offered to her. She slowly pulled away, allowing her teeth to gently catch Kiley's bottom lip as they detached. Their eyes remained fixated on each other.

386

They were only separated briefly before Kiley realized that the small amount of contact they just had simply wasn't enough. She gripped Harper tighter as she felt their embrace begin to turn into a more sensual, carnal desire between the two of them. Her tongue slowly trailed down Harper's neck, just underneath her jaw line, making its way up to her swollen lips once more. Kiley gracefully maneuvered her lips against Harper's, making it impossible to resist her advances. Kiley wanted more. She craved more. But she knew this wasn't the time or the place. She slowly pulled herself way from Harper and smiled at her. It was only when the crowd started whistling and applauding when they realized they weren't alone. They turned to the audience, both blushing to their ears. Kiley turned to Harper.

"So…I'll let you finish this and…I'll just be over there."

Harper turned back to the audience, unsure of exactly what to say. She looked over at Kiley once more and smiled. She then stepped up to the microphone and said, "Well, that's all for me. I really hope you enjoyed the set."

She grabbed her guitar and ran off stage toward Kiley. Harper knew the repercussions of being so unprofessional, but didn't really care about that at the moment. There were more important things to focus on. Her future had walked off the stage to her left, and she had no intention of letting it get away from her this time, so she followed her heart and it led her straight to Kiley.

EPILOGUE

"You made me miss the mushroom!" said Harper with more intensity than she had initially planned.

"What? I did no such thing," replied Kiley.

"Yes you did. You made me miss the mushroom and now Luigi is gonna stay small forever."

"Well that's a bit overdramatic, don't you think?" asked Kiley as she took a drink of her soda, waiting patiently for little Luigi to perish so she could have her turn. She watched, enthralled with Harper as she maneuvered the controller as if her life depended on it. Kiley couldn't resist. She leaned over and placed a sweet kiss behind Harper's ear. Immediately following that display of affection, Kiley heard the familiar sound of a certain video game cartoon falling to his death.

Harper looked over at Kiley. "You made me fall off a wall."

"Wow. You really take your Super Nintendo very seriously."

Harper shrugged. "Gotta be passionate about something. For me, it's old school gaming systems with hideous graphics." She crawled over, popped Super Mario World out of the system, and looked back at Kiley. "Mario Kart?"

Kiley couldn't help but chuckle at Harper's appearance. They had already been up for an hour, but Harper's hair was tangled and tousled. She was still in her pajamas, which really only consisted of some plaid boxers and a tank top, and she still had remnants of last night's makeup on her face. Still, Kiley found her to be striking and flat-out adorable. She took a look around the room and noticed the path of destruction they left in their haste last night. Clothes were strewn about, Kiley's purse somehow ended up half-emptied in the middle of the floor. The lamp that was next to the couch was now somehow *on top* of the couch. Kiley remembered that once they got through the door, nothing else seemed to matter except finding their way to the bedroom. Kiley got up and grabbed her sweater from the floor.

"It's getting late. I should go."

"But..." Harper looked around while trying to find any reason at all for Kiley to stay. "But...you haven't finished your soda."

Kiley picked up her drink and gulped it down until the glass was empty. She looked at Harper victoriously.

Harper buckled. "But...but....you haven't seen the rest of my place yet."

Kiley looked around Harper's one-bedroom apartment. "Bathroom, closet, you introduced me to the bedroom last night...and I believe we're standing in the kitchen/dining room/living room area. I think that about covers it, right?"

"But you didn't see the best part." Harper took Kiley's hand and led her toward the sliding window out onto the balcony. "Look at the view. Isn't it incredible?"

Kiley looked out at the sky and agreed that it was quite a view. It was almost worth Harper living in this dump just for this view. "Not bad for a fifth floor one-bedroom in Silver Lake with no elevator."

"Just don't look down," warned Harper.

Kiley ignored that request and looked down to find an ally rife with graffiti along every wall and garage door, accented with countless broken glass bottles and cigarette butts strewn along the ground. "Meh...it gives the place some character." Kiley continued staring out at the view of the Hollywood Hills. "I still can't believe you moved. I mean, I'm proud of you. It was a healthy decision. But I just can't believe we're never gonna hang out there again. Seems so strange."

Harper leaned against the balcony railing. "Well, it's not like we'll *never* hang out there again."

"What do you mean?"

"I didn't want to say anything until it was official. I worked out a deal with the new owners. I lowered the asking price by $50,000 and in exchange, they're giving me unlimited use of the garage."

"What would you need the garage for?"

"I always said with the acoustics, that garage would make the perfect recording studio. So I put in my two-week notice at Between the Lines and with the money Emily and I are getting from the house, I'm using some of it to buy some recording equipment and open a studio. A small one, obviously, but it's a start."

Kiley smiled. "Well it's about time you put that ambition to good use. That's awesome!" Initially she was worried about what giving up the house would mean to Harper after living there her whole life. But this way she could still have a piece of the home that her parents bought and built their life around while molding a life of her own.

"I probably won't be making too much money with the studio just yet. It'll just be a place where local musicians can lay down tracks and hopefully word of mouth will travel."

"Hey, it's music and it's what you love. Who cares about money?" replied Kiley.

"By the way, they asked me back to perform at The Fortress."

"Seriously?"

"I got a call early this morning while you were still passed out. Apparently they liked what they saw…music-wise, of course."

"So they asked you back after hearing just one song?"

"Yeah. Crazy, right? They asked for an hour-long set this time. And they asked that I kindly remain on stage, by myself for the full set or I won't get paid."

"Paid?"

Harper smiled and nodded. "So no running off the stage for me."

Kiley was ecstatic. As Harper's biggest fan, she could hardly contain herself. She took a step toward her. They smiled at each other as they came closer together and slowly melted into a much-needed embrace. The hug was lingering with a gentle hint of longing behind it. It was saturated with desire, yet still held a sense of innocence. It was the first genuine hug they shared since the start of their physical relationship and it felt incredible for both of them. Neither of them considered bringing up the idea of a romantic relationship. They were both too terrified and there was still a bit of awkwardness between them after everything that had played out last night and the previous months, but this embrace spoke every word they couldn't speak.

As Kiley pulled away, she placed a soft, sweet kiss on the corner of Harper's mouth and headed back inside.

"So how's Emily doing? I didn't get to talk to her last night."

"She's great. She's all moved in."

"You said something about a townhouse in Sherman Oaks?"

"Yeah."

"How can she afford that?"

"She moved in with some friends of hers from work. Besides, she's making decent money now."

"So, she's all grown up and ready to take on actually paying rent and working hard for her money?"

Harper beamed with pride. "Looks like it."

"Damn. Talk about a complete 180."

"Well, we worked out some stipulations. She promised me she'd start going to some N.A. meetings and we have to have lunch together at least twice a week. I'm needy. What can I say?"

"Well, that's understandable. But she seems pretty dead set on staying around."

"It's so weird," said Harper as she closed the sliding door. "So much of my time was spent wondering and waiting and worrying about her and now that she's here and she's okay, I kind of don't know what to do with myself."

"Well, you can start living your life, for one."

"Hey, I've taken a huge step in that direction." Harper demurely looked up at Kiley. "And just for the record, I'm really glad you and I are talking."

"We're doing a bit more than talking, don't you think," asked Kiley as she flirtatiously raised her eyebrows.

"You know what I mean."

"Yeah, I know. I knew we'd get through it. We can get through anything. We're Harper and Kiley.

We're…Harley."

"No."

"No?"

"No. No celebrity names for us."

"Kiper?"

"That's worse than Harley." Harper leaned against the armrest of her couch. "Do you really have to go?"

"Afraid so. It's inventory day. Graham's expecting me." Kiley found it hard to break that news to Harper, especially when she looked as cute as she did with her chic just-woke-up-after-a-night-of-passionate-sex look. Kiley found herself smiling out of pure contentedness and soon, her insides matched her facial expression. Something inside of her had come alive last night and the feeling had stayed with her. She was surprised with herself and pleasantly satisfied with the way things turned out. She finally got what she had wanted, and evidently, so did Harper. It was exciting and new and scary as hell, but it ignited a fire within her that continued to blaze.

"Stay. Please stay." Harper almost couldn't believe the words that just escaped her mouth. What would have taken years to say, now took merely five seconds. After last night, solidifying what she already knew from their first sexual experience, Harper was no longer afraid to go for what she wanted. She refused to chance it by remaining silent. Kiley was here, finally. And so of Harper's pining had not been fruitless because Kiley wanted her, too. She was tired of verbally circumventing what she wanted; she was tired of dropping hints. It was time to just be real. She wanted Kiley to stay and she was finally in a place where she could ask for it.

Kiley walked over to Harper and kissed her on the forehead. "I can't. I'm sorry. But I'll be back tonight. As soon as we're done with inventory, I promise."

Before another word could be exchanged, Kiley was out the door, leaving Harper to turn her body and fall back onto the couch with her legs hanging over the armrest. It was silent. Unusually silent. There were no car engines revving in the alley, no screaming baby from apartment 5C down the hall, not even the whirring of her refrigerator, which seems to have fixed itself. The most prevalent silence she heard, however, was the lack of footsteps in the hall and the lack of knocking on her front door. Kiley had left in such a hurry, it began to cross Harper's mind that maybe she wouldn't be coming back. She pushed that thought out of her mind and decided to have faith in the most unpredictable girl in the world. If the past few months had shown her anything, it was that Kiley, capricious as she may be, always comes around in the end. So Harper just lay there, reflecting on everything, particularly dwelling on how in tune she had become with her body. Kiley had awoken something inside her and she giggled to herself as she felt her body turn to jelly at the thought of Kiley's touch. She could feel herself blushing, but figured it was okay since nobody was around to see it.

With her head still reeling from everything that had transpired, she almost thought it was a dream when someone frantically knocked on her door.

She opened the door and before Harper could say anything, Kiley charged in and pushed her back into the apartment. She kicked the door shut with her foot, spun

Harper around, thrust her up against the door and kissed her without thinking twice. Kiley continued to hold her against the door while vigorously attacking her lips. Harper had no complaints. At first, Kiley's actions threw her off. But once she realized what was happening, she fully accepted everything Kiley was giving her. Kiley brought her hands up to Harper's face, finding her lips utterly irresistible.

"I thought you had to work," said Harper, as she planted kisses along Kiley's neck.

Kiley tilted her head back against the wall, closed her eyes and exhaled heavily, taking pleasure in every move Harper made. "It wasn't that important. Just work. Graham will have to deal with it." She took Harper's hands in her own. "Besides, I forgot to tell you something. You know, I witnessed a miracle last night."

"A miracle?"

"It may not be along the lines of a Jesus sighting in the bark of a tree or a doctor reviving a dying patient or a baby being born, but it was a miracle, nonetheless. And it only took a matter of seconds. I saw it all play out."

Harper was intrigued. "Do tell."

Kiley leaned in and whispered. "Well, you closed your eyes and then, by the grace of God, you fell asleep. And you stayed asleep. For ten full hours."

"Well, that makes sense. You were with me."

"So does that mean your insomnia is cured," asked Kiley.

"Only if you're with me every single night when I fall asleep."

Kiley leaned in and softly kissed Harper. "I think that can be arranged."

ABOUT THE AUTHOR

Breanna Hughes' passion for writing began in high school. She went on to graduate with a BFA in Theatre Performance from Chapman University where she took screenwriting, fiction writing and play-writing classes.

She is also a singer/songwriter who has performed everywhere from Los Angeles to New York to Nashville, and has been working in the entertainment industry for over ten years in several different aspects of television, music and public relations.

She was born and raised in Fullerton, California and currently resides in Los Angeles with her fiancée and their two dogs, Dublin and Solo.

Other Titles Available From Triplicity Publishing

Never Quit by Graysen Morgen. Two years after stepping away from the action as a Coast Guard Rescue Swimmer to become an instructor, Finley finds herself in charge of the most difficult class of cadets she's ever faced, while also juggling the taxing demands of having a home life with her partner Nicole, and their fifteen year old daughter. Jordy Ross gave up everything, dropping out of college, and leaving her family behind, to join the Coast Guard and become a rescue swimmer cadet. The extreme training tests her fitness level, pushing her mentally and physically further than she's ever been in her life, but it's the aggressive competition between her and another female cadet that proves to be the most challenging.

For a Moment's Indiscretion by KA Moll. With ten years of marriage under their belt, Zane and Jaina are coasting. The little things they used to do for one another have fallen by the wayside. They've gotten busy with life. They've forgotten to nurture their love and relationship. Even soul mates can stumble on hard times and have marital difficulties. Enter Amelia, a new faculty member in Jaina's building. She's new in town, young, and very pretty. When an argument with Zane causes Jaina to storm out angry, she reaches out to Amelia. Of course, she seizes the opportunity. And for a moment of indiscretion, Jaina could lose everything.

Never Let Go by Graysen Morgen. For Coast Guard Rescue Swimmer, Finley Morris, life is good. She loves her job, is well respected by her peers, and has been given an opportunity to take her career to the next level. The only thing missing is the love of her life, who walked out, taking their daughter with her, seven years earlier. When Finley gets a call from her ex, saying their teenage daughter is coming to spend the summer with her, she's floored. While spending more time with her daughter, whom she doesn't get to see often, and learning to be a full-time parent, Finley quickly realizes she has not, and will never, let go of what is important.

Pursuit by Joan L. Anderson. Claire is a workaholic attorney who flies to Paris to lick her wounds after being dumped by her girlfriend of seventeen years. On the plane she chats with the young woman sitting next to her, and when they land the woman is inexplicably detained in Customs. Claire is surprised when she later runs into the woman in the city. They agree to meet for breakfast the next morning, but when the woman doesn't show up Claire goes to her hotel and makes a horrifying discovery. She soon finds herself ensnared in a web of intrigue and international terrorism, becoming the target of a high stakes game of cat and mouse through the streets of Paris.

Wrecked by Sydney Canyon. To most people, the *Duchess* is a myth formed by old pirates tales, but to Reid Cavanaugh, a Caribbean island bum and one of the best divers and treasure hunters in the world, it's a real, seventeenth century pirate ship—the holy grail of underwater treasure hunting. Reid uses the same cunning tactics she always has before setting out to find the lost ship. However, she is forced to bring her business partner's daughter along as collateral this time because he doesn't trust her. Neither woman is thrilled, but being cooped up on a small dive boat for days, forces them to get know each other quickly.

Arson by Austen Thorne. Madison Drake is a detective for the Stetson Beach Police Department. The last thing she wants to do is show a new detective the ropes, especially when a fire investigation becomes arson to cover up a murder. Madison butts heads with Tara, her trainee, deals with sarcasm from Nic, her ex-girlfriend who is a patrol officer, and finds calm in the chaos of police work with Jamie, her best friend who is the county medical examiner. Arson is the first of many in a series of novella episodes surrounding the fictional Stetson Beach Police Department and Detective Madison Drake.

Change of Heart by KA Moll. Courtney Holloman is a woman at the top of her game. She's successful, wealthy, and a highly sought after Washington lobbyist. She has money, her job, booze, and nothing else. In quiet moments, against her will, her mind drifts back to her days in high school and to all that she gave up. Jack Camdon is a complex woman, and yet not at all. She is also a woman who has never moved beyond the sudden and unexplained departure of her high school sweetheart, her lover, and her soul mate. When circumstances bring Courtney back to town two decades later, their paths will cross. Will it be too late?

Mommies (Bridal Series book 3) by Graysen Morgen. Britton and her wife Daphne have been married for a year and a half and are happy with their life, until

Britton's mother hounds her to find out why her sister Bridget hasn't decided to have children yet. This prompts Daphne to bring up the big subject of having kids of their own with Britton. Britton hadn't really thought much about having kids, but her love for Daphne makes her see life and their future together in a whole new way when they decide to become mommies.

Haunting Love by K.A. Moll. Anna Crestwood was raised in the strict beliefs of a religious sect nestled in the foothills of the Smoky Mountains. She's a lesbian with a ton of baggage—fearful, guilty, and alone. Very few things would compel her to leave the familiar. The job offer of a lifetime is one of them. Gabe Garst is a police officer. She's also a powerful medium. Her work with juvenile delinquents and ghosts is all that keeps her going. Inside she's dead, certain that her capacity to love is buried six feet under. Anna and Gabe's paths cross. Their attraction is immediate, but they hold back until all hope seems lost.

Rapture & Rogue by Sydney Canyon. Taren Rauley is happy and in a good relationship, until the one person she thought she'd never see again comes back into her life. She struggles to keep the past from colliding with the present as old feelings she thought were dead and gone, begin to haunt her. In college, Gianna Revisi was a mastermind, ring-leading, crime boss. Now, she has a great life and spends her time running Rapture and Rogue, the two establishments she built from the ground up. The last person she ever expects to see walk into one of them, is the girl who walked out on her, breaking her heart five years ago.

Second Chance by Sydney Canyon. After an attack on her convoy, Marine Corps Staff Sergeant, Darien Hollister, must learn to live without her sight. When an experimental procedure allows her to see again, Darien is torn, knowing someone had to die in order for this to happen.
She embarks on a journey to personally thank the donor's family, but is too stunned to tell them the truth. Mixed emotions stir inside of her as she slowly gets to the know the people that feel like so much more than strangers to her. When the truth finally comes out, Darien walks away, taking the second chance that she's been given to go back to the only life she's ever known, but she's not the only one with a second chance at life.

Meant to Be by Graysen Morgen. Brandt is about to walk down the aisle with her girlfriend, when an unexpected chain of events turns her world upside down, causing her to question the last three years of her life. A chance encounter sparks a mix of rage and excitement that she has never felt before. Summer is living life and following her dreams, all the while, harboring a huge secret that could ruin her career. She believes that some things are better kept in the dark, until she has her third run-in with a woman she had hoped to never see again, and gives into temptation. Brandt and Summer start believing everything happens for a reason as they learn the true meaning of meant to be.

Coming Home by Graysen Morgen. After tragedy derails TJ Abernathy's life, she packs up her three year old son and heads back to Pennsylvania to live with her grandmother on the family farm. TJ picks back up where she left off eight years earlier, tending to the fruit and nut tree orchard, while learning her grandmother's secret trade. Soon, TJ's high school sweetheart and the same girl who broke her heart, comes back into her life, threatening to steal it away once again. As the weeks turn into months and tragedy strikes again, TJ realizes coming home was the best thing she could've ever done.

Special Assignment by Austen Thorne. Secret Service Agent Parker Meeks has her hands full when she gets her new assignment, protecting a Congressman's teenage daughter, who has had threats made on her life and been whisked away to a Christian boarding school under an alias to finish out her senior year. Parker is fine with the assignment, until she finds out she has to go undercover as a Canon Priest. The last thing Parker expects to find is a beautiful, art history teacher, who is intrigued by her in more ways than one.

Miracle at Christmas by Sydney Canyon. A Modern Twist on the Classic Scrooge Story. Dylan is a power-hungry lawyer who pushed away everything good in her life to become the best defense attorney in the, often winning the worst cases and keeping anyone with enough money out of jail. She's visited on Christmas Eve by her deceased law partner, who threatens her with a life in hell like his own, if she doesn't change her path. During the course of the night, she is taken on a journey through her past, present, and future with three very different spirits.

Bella Vita by Sydney Canyon. Brady is the First Officer of the crew on the Bella Vita, a luxury charter yacht in the Caribbean. She enjoys the laidback island lifestyle, and is accustomed to high profile guests, but when a U.S. Senator charters the yacht as a gift to his beautiful twin daughters who have just graduated from college and a few of their friends, she literally has her hands full.

Brides (Bridal Series book 2) by Graysen Morgen. Britton Prescott is dating the love of her life, Daphne Attwood, after a few tumultuous events that happened to unravel at her sister's wedding reception, seven months earlier. She's happy with the way things are, but immense pressure from her family and friends to take the next step, nearly sends her back to the single life. The idea of a long engagement and simple wedding are thrown out the window, as both families take over, rushing Britton and Daphne to the altar in a matter of weeks.

Cypress Lake by Graysen Morgen. The small town of Cypress Lake is rocked when one murder after another happens. Dani Ricketts, the Chief Deputy for the Cypress Lake Sheriff's Office, realizes the murders are linked. She's surprised when the girl that broke her heart in high school has not only returned home, but she's also Dani's only suspect. Kristen Malone has come back to Cypress Lake to put the past behind her so that she can move on with her life. Seeing Dani Ricketts again throws her off-guard, nearly derailing her plans to finally rid herself and her family of Cypress Lake.

Crashing Waves by Graysen Morgen. After a tragic accident, Pro Surfer, Rory Eden, spends her days hiding in the surf and snowboard manufacturing company that she built from the ground up, while living her life as a shell of the person that she once was. Rory's world is turned upside when a young surfer pursues her, asking for the one thing she can't do. Adler Troy and Dr. Cason Macauley from Graysen Morgen's bestselling novel: *Falling Snow*, make an appearance in this romantic adventure about life, love, and letting go.

Bridesmaid of Honor (Bridal Series book 1) by Graysen Morgen. Britton Prescott's best friend is getting married and she's the maid of honor. As if that isn't enough to deal with, Britton's sister announces she's getting married in the same month and her maid of honor is her best friend Daphne, the same woman who has tormented Britton for years. Britton has to suck it up and play nice, instead of scratching her eyes out, because she and Daphne are in both weddings. Everyone is counting on them to behave like adults.

Falling Snow by Graysen Morgen. Dr. Cason Macauley, a high-speed trauma surgeon from Denver meets Adler Troy, a professional snowboarder and sparks fly. The last thing Cason wants is a relationship and Adler doesn't realize what's right in front of her until it's gone, but will it be too late?

Fate vs. Destiny by Graysen Morgen. Logan Greer devotes her life to investigating plane crashes for the National Transportation Safety Board. Brooke McCabe is an investigator with the Federal Aviation

Association who literally flies by the seat of her pants. When Logan gets tangled in head games with both women will she choose fate or destiny?

Just Me by Graysen Morgen. Wild child Ian Wiley has to grow up and take the reins of the hundred year old family business when tragedy strikes. Cassidy Harland is a little surprised that she came within an inch of picking up a gorgeous stranger in a bar and is shocked to find out that stranger is the new head of her company.

Love Loss Revenge by Graysen Morgen. Rian Casey is an FBI Agent working the biggest case of her career and madly in love with her girlfriend. Her world is turned upside when tragedy strikes. Heartbroken, she tries to rebuild her life. When she discovers the truth behind what really happened that awful night she decides justice isn't good enough, and vows revenge on everyone involved.

Natural Instinct by Graysen Morgen. Chandler Scott is a Marine Biologist who keeps her private life private. Corey Joslen is intrigued by Chandler from the moment she meets her. Chandler is forced to finally open her life up to Corey. It backfires in Corey's face and sends her running. Will either woman learn to trust her natural instinct?

Secluded Heart by Graysen Morgen. Chase Leery is an overworked cardiac surgeon with a group of best friends that have an opinion and a reason for everything. When she meets a new artist named Remy Sheridan at her best friend's art gallery she is captivated by the reclusive woman. When Chase finds out why Remy is so sheltered will she put her career on the line to help her or is it too difficult to love someone with a secluded heart?

In Love, at War by Graysen Morgen. Charley Hayes is in the Army Air Force and stationed at Ford Island in Pearl Harbor. She is the commanding officer of her own female-only service squadron and doing the one thing she loves most, repairing airplanes. Life is good for Charley, until the day she finds herself falling in love while fighting for her life as her country is thrown haphazardly into World War II. Can she survive being in love and at war?

Fast Pitch by Graysen Morgen. Graham Cahill is a senior in college and the catcher and captain of the softball team. Despite being an all-star pitcher, Bailey Michaels is young and arrogant. Graham and Bailey are forced to get to know each other off the field in order to learn to work together on the field. Will the extra time pay off or will it drive a nail through the team?

Submerged by Graysen Morgen. Assistant District Attorney Layne Carmichael had no idea that the sexy woman she took home from a local bar for a one night stand would turn out to be someone she would be prosecuting months later. Scooter is a Naval Officer on a submarine who changes women like she changes uniforms. When she is accused of a heinous crime she is shocked to see her latest conquest sitting across from her as the prosecuting attorney.

Vow of Solitude by Austen Thorne. Detective Jordan Denali is in a fight for her life against the ghosts from her past and a Serial Killer taunting her with his every move. She lives a life of solitude and plans to keep it that way. When Callie Marceau, a curious Medical Examiner, decides she wants in on the biggest case of her career, as well as, Jordan's life, Jordan is powerless to stop her.

Igniting Temptation by Sydney Canyon. Mackenzie Trotter is the Head of Pediatrics at the local hospital. Her life takes a rather unexpected turn when she meets a flirtatious, beautiful fire fighter. Both women soon discover it doesn't take much to ignite temptation.

One Night by Sydney Canyon. While on a business trip, Caylen Jarrett spends an amazing night with a beautiful stripper. Months later, she is shocked and confused when that same woman re-enters her life. The fact that this stranger could destroy her career doesn't bother her. C.J. is more terrified of the feelings this woman stirs in her. Could she have fallen in love in one night and not even known it?

Fine by Sydney Canyon. Collin Anderson hides behind a façade, pretending everything is fine. Her workaholic wife and best friend are both oblivious as she goes on an emotional journey, battling a potentially hereditary disease that her mother has been diagnosed with. The only person who knows what is really going on, is Collin's doctor. The same doctor, who is an acquaintance that she's always been attracted to, and who has a partner of her own.

Shadow's Eyes by Sydney Canyon. Tyler McCain is the owner of a large ranch that breeds and sells different types of horses. She isn't exactly thrilled when a Hollywood movie producer shows up wanting to film his latest movie on her property. Reegan Delsol is an up and coming actress who has everything going for her when she lands the lead role in a new film, but there one small problem that could blow the entire picture.

Light Reading: A Collection of Novellas by Sydney Canyon. Four of Sydney Canyon's novellas together in one book, including the bestsellers Shadow's Eyes and One Night.

Visit us at www.tri-pub.com